SIMPLE TALES OF POWER

A HIDDEN WORLD SHORT STORY COLLECTION

T. M. ELZY

SEVENTH WORLD PUBLISHING

For Dr. Carolyne Fuqua
A Clear and Perfect Channel,
The Prism that provided the Focus
For the Stories I was unable to tell the world
Before now
Yes...and Thank You

CONTENTS

FOREWORD

The task of assimilating ancient knowledge into modern day wisdom is not one to be taken lightly. Stillness is required...a willingness to listen, and to be guided in that listening, until your steps are directed.

It's pretty easy to see the difference if what is inside of you is guiding you to contemplation, or to some outer display of self-glory... traits to which the world of effects will eagerly give its approval.

If you are willing to be an instrument, you have the potential to experience something rather remarkable.

The potential to be a clear and perfect channel for That which is longing to express Itself...a creative force beyond imagination and unlimited in focus.

Therefore, it is clear to me that TanyaMarie Elzy, one of my most talented and gifted students has been willing to be and do what was necessary to allow this creative endeavor to channel through...an offering of ancient wisdom beautifully illustrated in modern times.

Brava.

Dr. Carolyne Fuqua

PROLOGUE

"They have cradled you in custom. They have primed you with their teaching. They have soaked you with convention through and through. They have put you in a showcase. You're a credit to their teaching. But don't you hear the truth? It's calling you."
Robert William Service

WHAT IS **the premise behind Simple Tales of Power?**

Most people on this planet have a dream; either a waking or a sleeping dream, we all have one. Usually in these dreams, the dreamer is the hero who saves the world. Using innate talents and gifts or following the culture of the current day, the dreamer possesses unique powers or abilities that enable them to change the world or uplift mankind to greater heights.

My waking dream is a little different.

In my dream, I'm not the only hero. In fact, in my dream everyone is the hero and everyone changes and uplifts the world for the better.

I realize that we've all been taught something a little opposite of this growing up; that the world is too complex and our resources too finite for one person to impact. That the idea of everyone having the same abilities is impossible. If everyone, all eight billion of us had the same ability to influence the world, there would be chaos.

So we should be told what to do.

Our limits should be explained to us, often and early on in life, so we don't question it or wonder why.

Well, today I'm going to share a secret with you.

I've found a world where everyone has the same access to unlimited power; the only restraint is their own ability to accept the truth.

Something worth considering, right?

I wrote a book about it; nine books in fact.

It's a world running parallel to this one because it's waiting for you to notice it and move to where it is. All that's needed is for you to accept the following:

That you are innately powerful.

That you can wield this power for the good of all.

That you're actually doing it right now.

That everyone is using this power.

And that, my friend, makes everyone a hero.

So one day I decided: Why not just compile a few stories from each book leading up to the conclusion of my dream? This dream quickly spread from one book to a trilogy; then six companion books full of stories of people from every corner of the globe. Stories of people who lived millions of years ago and freely offered mankind the light and knowledge of the truth; that nothing can stop them except their own belief system. Using universal storytelling elements, I released them into the current world, and because time is not linear, once they leaped from the keyboard and onto my screen, they showed me what unstoppable looked like.

There's an excerpt from the Trilogy that goes like this:

"Millions of years ago, in Earth's ancient past, there lived groups of humans all over the planet called channels and co-creators. They were responsible for the sciences, monuments and teachings of the current era. One day, like the dinosaurs, they disappeared.

This is the story of what happened…"

· · ·

IN ALL FAIRNESS, however, I must warn you:

Should you allow these stories to convince you of the universes inside you just waiting to be utilized and harnessed for good, it will be too late to try and shrink back into your previous life.

So...there's only one question left to ask.

Are you ready to remember?

PREFACE

This is the World of Science Fiction Possible.

For those of you who may not be familiar with the term Speculative Fiction, (Which is an exploration of science that may yet be possible and not pure fantasy) Speculative Fiction is a sub-genre of Science Fiction and is different from the sub-genre of Science Fiction Fantasy by a few key elements.

Science Fiction Fantasy contains for example mythical creatures that require no explanation, like dragons for example, that are huge reptiles that speak human words and breathe fire from their bodies, and magicians that have mysterious, unexplainable powers; chanting a combination of words called spells and wielding light that seems to come from nowhere. Horses called Unicorns with horns growing out of their foreheads and sometimes wings that can lift them into flight; that have unexplainable abilities and magical powers. These are elements of fantasy that are never questioned; because they have been a part of our mythology for so long; part of tales told to children at bedtime.

The stories within these pages have dinosaurs, whose bones have been found in the earth millions of years ago and therefore once existed. The part where speculation comes into play is the theory that communication between the species of humans and dinosaurs was possible through a form of mental projection; where the dinosaurs have the ability to transmit images into the minds of humans that were then translated into the human mind as words through sound and vibration, which is all that words actually are. The sounds emanating from human speech is then translated by the dinosaur into images that form basic communication so that the two species can understand each other.

Those identified as magicians are humans who, through training and the study of science, learn how to wield radiation, using the cells of the human body to distill and maintain it, much like how humans today use solar radiation from our sun to grow and develop. The speculation is that some adept humans are able to harness massive amounts of radiation; and similar to the studies done on how humans possess a measurable field of energy around their bodies, these men and women can not only store this radiation, they can dispel measurable amounts into the atmosphere around them and focus the radiation like a laser to strike and disrupt the cells of humans, with a range of results; causing injury, pain, slow cancers, or killing them instantly. The other speculative theory is that these humans are also able to transfer their abilities to some degree to others, who, if they survive the process, become magicians as well.

Then you have the humans who have been identified as channels or co-creators. These humans look normal on the surface and if you studied their DNA you would find no difference between them and any other human. No mutation or strange features, although some are able to display vast amounts of light from their bodies, a light which is usually visible on a spectrum that normal eyesight cannot detect. They are called channels because unlike magicians they do not store radiation in their cells and molecules. Most of them through a training process over many years learn how to channel the light of which all things are comprised of; to allow it to flow through on levels that are only limited by their ability to believe themselves capable of it.

In this world, time is not linear, so even millions of years ago, skilled teachers had access to the knowledge of all ages, including the so-called future, where Astronomy, then called Star Science, the Quantum Field, the Periodic Table, Earth Science and DNA were commonly known. Dinosaurs roamed in the same timeframe as humans and the cosmic radiation and energy of stars developed consciousness and humanoid form; they called themselves Star Children. Humans were give the power of choice; to align with magic and illusion or conscious creation; to become magicians wielding deadly radiation or creators and channels capable of harnessing all the limitless power of creation itself.

Those who chose creation could manifest without effort; they could move from place to place by use of thought alone. Without microscopes they could see the spaces between molecules and direct their movements; bend time and space like the illusion it truly is.

The attributes of magic resulted in separation and sterility; an inability to bring forth life and an increasing power to manipulate and destroy the elements by unnatural means.

A channel or co-creator had access to unlimited light, vibration, heat, sound, and power. They were completely unstoppable...until and unless they forgot their true inheritance and the power behind their name.

Blinded by doubt and disbelief, they lost the ability to control the elements and the movements of the earth and planets.

This yielded a future where millions of years later, the planet is now inhabited by over eight billion blind creators; the world you live in now.

This is a short story collection of excerpts from seven books; nine of which comprise the entire story of the Hidden World, a previous Earth that once existed and then was lost in battle with the First Brother who is now referred to as The Magician.

Millions of years ago the creators of the day fought The Magician to restore to humans the power of choice; the only thing capable of unleashing the full potential of all humans on earth.

The war raged for thousands of years and finally it seemed the co-creators and channels won freedom for every man, woman, and child.

But today we still live in a world of magic; where everyone believes in everything except their own innate greatness; where we have given our lives to the pursuit of everything except the power to create universes and bring peace to our planet. Where we believe that we need things outside of us to invoke change within. Those who want us to remain blind offer magic to sustain us and tools to entertain us and dull our senses to what would truly free us.

We now believe we need pieces of glass to see planets; cars and planes to cross distances and phones to speak to each other. We've forgotten how to manipulate the elements naturally and harness the quantum field; we now believe that to do so is impossible without tools; we've forgotten that we created these tools from an unlimited source; our own minds.

The biggest lie we've been taught is that we are not inherently creative; we've been trained to believe that creativity is gifted to a few when in fact, it is more a part of us than anything else:

Creation is as common as breathing.

If you don't believe this, you are very easy to control.

You can be told what to do, where to go, what to think, and how to react.

I'll give you an example:

Only thousands of years ago, not even twenty thousand years ago, no one was paying rent and working for others to sustain themselves; everyone was a contributing member of whatever community they were a part of.

So-called civilization brought lack and limitation with it; scarcity and crime; distrust of your neighbor and an unwillingness to support and help each other.

The word 'stranger' didn't exist.

Now all we wish to do is survive to the next day; worrying constantly how to feed our families and care for those we love.

Who has time to create universes if you're hungry?

Yet, this too, shall pass.

There is a prophecy that one day another creator will arise fully aware and ready to reawaken mankind. The question is:

Are you ready to remember?

INTRODUCTION

"Although it is true that every single thing that occurs is a result of a thought, most people are not aware of their subliminal beliefs and the thoughts that they generate; and they are the ones that wreak the most havoc."

    Dr. Carolyne Fuqua

Some important things for you to know as you read this book:

You hold in your hands nearly twenty short stories from the lives of the people who inhabit the Hidden World. Kings, Queens, Princes, Princesses, Regents, soldiers, tradesmen, common folk, healers, magicians, hunters, lords, ladies, and Star Children. All engaged in a raging battle for the Heart and Mind of Mankind:

Rasdeter, a prince who loses his inheritance and nearly destroys the known world in an attempt to regain it.

Paza, a being born in a nearby star who makes a fatal choice she cannot undo.

The Rook, a man who was meant to save the Earth loses his freedom to the very one he was born to defeat.

Saramis, a Woman of the Woods, leaves her home for a civilization she swore to avoid.

Addias, a scientist who only has faith in a physical world, cannot explain his long life, superhuman abilities or remember his origins.

Regent Ghent, a young father dedicated to the law is ensnared by unspeakable evil.

Hesta, a young noblewoman who chooses the life of a soldier over a life of privilege and ease.

Emmia, sold by her husband to the life of a concubine, learns her true inheritance from a group of nomads.

And finally, the child of prophecy, S'ateegra, whose life is the catalyst for every thread woven by every other person in these stories. She is the last chance this world has to reclaim its Heart and the one whose True Name can never be said aloud.

Yet all is not as it seems.

Magic comes from Science; Science comes from Creation and true power comes from knowing who you are above all things.

If you believe this, then like the channels and co-creators of these tales you are unstoppable.

If you don't...

You're just another blind creator among eight billion others; controlled and used by those who are just aware enough to see what you are without knowing or caring why.

Creators are born every single day.

Only a handful is necessary to take back this planet and only one of them has to be willing to wake the others up.

Only one...

A Taste of the Beginning of the End

"You failed me, Scientist..."

The voice of the man who stood before him in silhouette was full of condemnation. Both man and voice were from memory; the one recalling it struggled instinctively against his bindings, wrapped from feet to crown in thick linen straps that were glued to his body with resin, tight cords and burial spices. He relaxed again as his inner mind heard the voice of a woman speaking softly with a trace of amusement.

"You are the one who founded the Southern Arc?"

He felt his gut tighten as she caught her breath in pleased disbelief.

"Why, you look almost a boy…"

"The Southern Arc predates all nations, including this one," added her husband the king. "You should be thousands of years old," he speculated as he stared at him. "Perhaps you are a god."

"There are no gods, my lord," replied the man. "Some say this because of the hue of my skin, but I can assure you that there are many men of all colorings who have lived thousands of years…"

The king interrupted him.

"Is it true what they say; that you believe in neither creation nor magic?"

"I am a scientist, my lord," stated the man firmly. "I only believe in what I can prove with the five senses of the body."

"Yet, long life is a process of creation, Founder," surmised the queen gently, "How does one account for such prolonged longevity, if we are to believe your words?"

The Scientist was having a difficult time not staring at her. Though his people encompassed all eye colors and shadings, the startling mixture of deep brown in her right eye and the other a lighter hue threatened to stammer his speech. He felt the eyes of the king looking through him to his hammering heart.

He sighed deeply.

"The tale of it is a long one, I fear," he finally replied as he wisely turned back to the king.

"Then you must linger, Scientist, and tell us more…" he heard the queen offer as he watched the king's gaze shadow.

The coolness of the stone slab beneath him brought him back to the present moment. The darkness surrounding him was as complete and total as his grief. The scientist in him tried to accept his fate but his body betrayed him as it wretched in terror against his bonds. The queen was silent next to him; having left her body days ago. Her final words pulled him again to the relentless past.

"Why do you tarry, my foolish scientist," she rasped, "Do you not know he only waits for my last breath?"

"My feet will not carry me away from you," he choked, "I cannot leave while you can still see me..."

"Go, I beg you, and live," she whispered as her strength began to fade. "It will be the only victory I will ever know..."

But he could not move. The Scientist watched until the cells of her beautiful deep eyes began to dim. He faintly heard the king enter the room of her death and speak to the healers standing helplessly by.

"Is she gone?" At the solemn nod from his Chief Healer, the king spoke the words that The Scientist knew would seal his doom:

"You've failed me, Scientist," said the king flatly as his guards surrounded him. "Perhaps you two will rule together in the afterlife..."

RADIANT: THE HUNTER'S PROMISE

"Anyone who is following his heart and doing what he loves is living
an auspicious life, no matter how little money or few things he has."
Dr. Carolyne Fuqua

Although the building men referred to as the Temple predated the planet it stood on, the people who guarded it knew that one day, it would fall. The guardians of the building were called Hunters and trained from birth to protect it. Movements of the heavens were studied for centuries to predict the coming of the Star Children who would destroy it, but the wiser ones knew that it was better to not know when than to know. The Hunters had decreed long ago that should the temple fall, one of their number who knew the old ways would be given the most difficult task, that of survival. Forced to watch the destruction of all things, that Hunter would live to pass on what little would be left. But peace had ruled the planet for so long and The Great Day had cycled and returned numerous times; few still believed the predictions would ever come to pass.

In those days, the Hunters were accompanied by great cats; massive and strong beyond any species of felines currently on our globe. These cats formed symbiotic bonds with the Hunters, usually within weeks of birth and when the Hunter, male or female reached seven years of age. Like the great lizards, these cats communicated mentally with their human companions, sending images that translated to speech.

Tyant was hunting in the plains years ago with his father when they came upon a mother cat with cubs. Tyant's father swiftly placed his son behind him; the response of a nursing cat was unpredictable. Yet, as the mother growled a warning, Tyant's eyes met those of one of her cubs, who made a coughing sound; a particular cough only made during a bonding process. The mother snorted, and the cub came charging across the plains towards Tyant, who stepped in front of his stunned father as the two hundred pound cub playfully plowed into Tyant, bringing him to the ground.

The cub, Wajit, a female, had Tyant's scent and visited him frequently until she was weaned from her mother. She only left Tyant to have cubs of her own and always returned to him. Tyant became his people's strongest and most skilled Hunter. He felt his life was fulfilled when his lifemate Una, an accomplished wise woman and warrior joined him and gave him a family of his own.

Years later, word came swiftly of an attack on the buildings on the other side of the globe. This did not distress Tyant or any of his people initially; the buildings had been attacked before but never successfully. However, days later while Tyant and Wajit patrolled the perimeter of the great temple, he was approached by sentries who directed him to return to the main fields and plains.

"What has happened, brother?" asked Tyant, as he stroked Wajit's ears to keep her calm and distracted.

"Three temples have fallen, brother," responded the sentry who was visibly shaken by the news, "The elders have asked for all the Hunters to convene on the plains."

Blood roared in Tyant's ears as he quickly turned and began to run, Wajit easily keeping pace with his strides. He heard her thoughts.

Are the tales of the Star Children true, Hunter Brother? Asked Wajit.

"The tales are true, Cat Sister," answered Tyant grimly, "I only hope this is another threat, one we can repulse."

Yet when Tyant and Wajit reached the people, the expression on the faces of the elders caused him to sharply inhale his breath. The Hunters were all gathered and looking to Tyant for guidance as their strongest and most capable. He spoke sharply.

"Bring the reeds and stones."

As the elders began the ritual selection of who would stay and who would fight, Tyant's mind clustered around his children and Una, his wife. As the strongest, Tyant felt certain that his lot would cast for his sacrifice to save the others. His chest tightened as he realized that his family must also go and die with him. Wajit felt his dismay and brushed her shoulder against his.

It was the gaze of the elders that brought Tyant's mind back to the present. All lots had been cast and he looked down at his feet, mentally preparing himself to see the stones and reeds of his selection.

But Tyant saw nothing.

Blood pounded in his temples; there must be some mistake.

"Cast them again," he commanded, and raised his hand at the elder's subtle protest.

His fellow Hunters shook their heads to disagree but Tyant would hear none of it. He pointed to the ground.

"Cast them I said!"

"There can be no exceptions, Tyant," said one of his brothers, "You must stay. Another will lead us..."

"No..." he whispered.

"There is no shame in survival, Tyant," offered one of the elders, "You are our greatest warrior, you will live to pass this gift on, and your family..."

"Annar's wife has just given birth," Tyant heard himself say in despair, "My children are older..."

The elder's eyes shone with compassion.

"Someone must stay, Tyant, and the lot has fallen to you."

But as the gathering began to disburse, Tyant felt himself march over to Annar and strike the reeds and stones from his hands. Wajit began to softly growl. Tyant then knelt to remove the lots from the ground as the Hunters collectively gasped.

"Is this done?" asked a brother and looked in astonishment as the elders began to nod.

"It is his right," answered the elder, "As the one selected to remain. For this sacrifice, both families will stay."

"No, brother," said Annar, who began to weep.

Tyant came to his feet and embraced Annar, pushing him away as Annar tried to reclaim the stones.

"I will lead you," declared Tyant firmly, his chest heaving as his people began to roar.

UNA WAS WAITING FOR TYANT; she had heard that Tyant had drawn the lots to stay, but that was all she knew. Her feelings were mixed; as the wife of the people's most skilled warrior, she fully expected to die with him and all of their children, five in number, from twelve years to nearly eight. Their children had been prepared from the beginning of what should happen should the temples fall during their lifetime. Now they milled about aimlessly, unsure of what to do now that they knew that all of them would live.

The wife of Tyant had prepared parchments against this day, a way to pass on her knowledge to the family selected to remain. It would not be the same as her direct teachings, but it would have to do. Una looked to the door as she heard the dogs barking, they always heralded the approach of Wajit. She straightened quickly from her task however as she noticed the demeanor of her husband and the set of his jaw.

"What have you done, Tyant?" Una asked calmly, she knew right away that something had changed. Her husband tried to speak but couldn't; she watched the workings of his face in concern, and suddenly her own cleared.

"You rejected the lots," she whispered.

THE CHILDREN STOPPED their aimless movements and focused on their father, who moved towards a seat and sat down heavily. When Tyant still did not speak, Una took a deep breath and began to direct their children.

"Get your things together. Find your weapons, and any dried goods you will need; you must be ready to do battle..."

Tyant shook his head.

"They're not going," he said finally, "None of you are going..."

"What...what means this," Una stammered, "Did you accept the lots or not?"

Silence came to the house as Una waited for her husband's response. His eldest son came to embrace Tyant, and the rest of his children followed this movement; still the Hunter of the temple could not continue. Wajit turned away from the doorway to play with the dogs, who pounced on her legs and nipped at her tail.

Una's mind raced; she could not fathom what would delay Tyant's reply until she thought of all the people who would most be affected by Tyant's selection to remain.

"ANNAR..." she said in wonder, "You traded our family for his? Speak to me, Tyant, why do you grieve?"

"I must lead our people, Una," Tyant replied sadly, "I alone..."

A heartbeat, perhaps two before his lifemate reacted.

"I'm coming with you," she declared breathlessly, "Annar will raise our offspring; you have given them to him...!" She pointed at her husband, "You will not leave me behind, Tyant, you will not!"

The Hunter gazed upwards at the woman he loved.

"You cannot go, Una," Tyant protested, "You are the last of the true wise ones, you know you must stay..."

"You had no right to decide this without me, Tyant! You had no right!"

· · ·

IN HER DISTRESS Una looked wildly about her as though she sought a weapon to batter her husband with, then passionately flailed on him with her fists. Tyant raised his arms to protect his head from her blows, then came to his feet and embraced Una, pinning her arms as she vented her grief. He pressed his face to her hair as she tried to break free.

"I love you, Una..." he said against her hair.

"No...no!" she cried, "You will not leave me, Tyant, I won't stay...!"

HE BELIEVED HER.

Suddenly Tyant squeezed his lifemate hard and fast, taking her breath away. She slumped in his arms as their children gasped. Then Tyant bound his unconscious wife to their bed and gently covered her ears, eyes, and mouth. He spoke sharply to his offspring.

"Do not release her before the battle ends, no matter what she threatens or promises..."

"Yes, father..." they chimed in chorus.

Tyant opened his arms and his children rushed to him; he kissed them fiercely.

"Remember me..." he asked, and they rendered tearful vows to do so.

THE HUNTER SPOKE to his cat companion as he strode through the high grasses.

"You don't have to follow me to this certain doom, Wajit," said Tyant, "You have many years left in you, and cubs to nurture..."

The huge cat scoffed in Tyant's mind.

I've suckled enough cubs for this lifetime, Hunter Brother, said Wajit, and my claws ache to defend our people. What is left before me but to grow old and die? Let the Star Children run, I stand to the last with you.

Tyant's eldest followed him through the forest leading to the open plains; Tyant could see the people gathering, thousands of them, many were weaponless. Even from this lowered elevation, Tyant could see the brave Initiate on the steps; he knew then that the end had finally come. He knelt to speak to his eldest child eye to eye.

"YOU FIVE ARE ALL she will have left of me," Tyant said soberly, "So it is important that you listen and follow all that I tell you."

"Let it be as you say, father," replied his son.

"You will hear sounds, horrible cries and shouts, my son, but you will stay hidden and not approach the fields for any reason, lest you die. Listen until you hear a great silence; you will know it. Then flee back to the house and make sure all your siblings are with you. Cover your ears then and your eyes, as you have heard the elders tell of, or you will be deaf and blinded for life. Have your brothers and sisters do the same. Do you hear me, son?"

"I will do it, father, you can trust me."

Tyant held his son one final time and strode away. Before he was out of earshot, Tyant heard his son's voice.

"Don't despair, father," said his son, "Mother will forgive you…"

Tyant shook his head slightly to hold back his tears.

"No, son," he said quietly, "No, she won't…"

Tyant vanished into the forest, faithful Wajit beside him.

THE STAR CHILDREN appeared at the end of the road leading away from the temple. The dwellers and custodians of the temple had begged in vain for the people not to defend the building; their pleas fell on covered ears. Though miles away she could see their faces clearly; two of them, male and female against a multitude. She lifted her chin in a bleak attempt to hold back her tears. Her gaze hardened when she realized they too, could see her; the huge man smiled at her as though to say:

Soon…

The two stepped forward and the massacre began.

THE HUNTER KNOWN as Tyant increased his steps to a run; he saw thousands of people gathering on the paved road leading to the temple where stood the Initiate and all that was left of their world. Tyant saw two beings who looked like a man and a woman standing placidly on the road where a multitude from all the lands raised whatever weapons they had to bar the couple's way. The pair watched calmly as the number of people grew beyond what could be counted, from thousands to tens of thousands to a million or more.

Tyant took a ragged breath as he beheld the radiation rolling off the beings who stood on the road in human form; he realized that even a million people, were they all warriors would not be enough. His Cat Sister Wajit gave a low growl and Tyant reached out to stroke her fur and feel its warmth and softness; he was certain they only had moments left to live.

He heard her voice in his mind.

They are worthy of my best efforts, Hunter-Brother; let us be about it...

"I'm moving to the front, Cat-Sister Wajit; I must be among the first to fight them," stated Tyant firmly as he signaled to his tribe who waited for him at the edge of the forest.

"What shall we do, brother?

"The Hunters must be first to face the Star Children, brothers," answered Tyant resolutely, "Follow me, I will lead the way." Tyant grimly hefted his axe as he led his men, the archers came behind them, ready to darken the skies with arrows at Tyant's command.

AS TYANT GRIMLY stepped before the gathered people, the female Starchild turned her gaze on him. She surprised Tyant by speaking to him directly.

"Do you lead this pitiful defense, Hunter?" she asked as she indicated the multitude of humans blocking the road. "We are Izar, born of a twin star so far away you cannot even conceive of the distance. Our power can stagger this entire planet; you have no one capable of either wielding or repulsing radiation in this entire group; including yourself, I can sense it."

"Still we will stand against you, Starchild," Tyant responded as he gripped his axe tightly, "We have all sworn to defend the temple."

"A defense that is not required of you, Hunter Tyant," the woman said as his eyes widened that she knew his name, "We know this from the eleven other temples we have already destroyed; a massive loss of life that was unnecessary."

"Go home and live," agreed the huge man beside her, "Leave the temple dwellers to us; share this tale with your children and all who might follow them. Why die for nothing?"

The Starchild watched as Tyant's chest heaved with emotion; thoughts of his children and his wife hammered at him; but he answered them bravely.

"Your coming has been foretold since the beginning of time, Starchild," said Tyant as the pair now looked at him in amazement, "Followed by a time of great darkness. Shame on us all if it should ever be written that one temple bowed down to you while all others fell."

"You humans knew we were coming?" asked the woman incredulously, "You know you have no power to withstand us and yet still you defy us?"

"Even if every single one of us on this road dies today, "Tyant continued tensely, "You, Izar, still will fail; that too has been foretold."

Tyant watched as the female's gaze narrowed as she moved closer to him.

"You have indeed led these people to their doom, Hunter; and to show you my resolve, I'm going to save you and your cat for last. Now," she warned him, "Fire your arrows and begin your ridiculous assault; see what pain a Starchild can render an enemy."

Tyant stepped back and roared.

"Fire!"

Arrows rained down on the unmoving Starchild and her mate; in seconds, the road could no longer be seen, it was so covered with feathered missiles. Moments later, the pair stepped through the arrows unharmed; their skin too dense to be pierced, and Tyant felt fear thick in his throat.

Then he raised his axe and charged; his fellow Hunters shouting beside him as they ran.

Wajit was quicker; her roar was cut short by the huge man who struck her and sent her sprawling; her claws did nothing to him. There was the sound of a sickening crack as a flailing Wajit crashed against a huge tree, her massive body breaking it in half. She lay unmoving and Tyant cried out.

"Wajit!"

The female almost smiled as his axe failed to cut her, though Tyant swung with all his might. Tyant gasped in agony as she struck a glancing blow to his shoulder; it felt like the crush of a boulder; he struggled to keep his footing. A huge male cat sped past him and attacked; Izar kept her gaze calm on Tyant as the teeth and claws of the cat did not so much as scratch her; then the female Starchild wrapped her arms around the cat and snapped its neck like a twig; she flung the cat's huge carcass to the earth at her feet.

"Is this your defense, Hunter-Brother?" Izar said sarcastically as she mimicked the mental bond between Tyant and Wajit, "Animals, axes and arrows?"

FOR THE HUNTERS, it was like fighting stone, or an unmoving mountain; nothing they did affected the Star children; the pair shrugged Tyant off and focused on his tribe and those he loved; he grappled with them helplessly as the pair ruthlessly killed the adult hunters. Tyant roared mindlessly as each brother and sister fell; crushed by the punishing blows of the invincible Star beings.

As the huge man began to slay the brave children of the hunters, Tyant tried to crush his own body against theirs and the female turned and easily caught him. She held him in the air as he thrashed in an attempt to batter himself against her stone like arms.

"You should have listened to me and gone home to her, Tyant," the female said grimly. "Once we're finished with the temple I'm going to find Una and your children; yes, I see their names and images clearly in your mind. I make a promise to you, Tyant; you will still be alive when I slay them all in front of you."

TYANT GAVE a man's cry of agony as Izar systematically broke his right arm and his right hip; she tossed him on the ground and then as though she thought better of it; she propped his broken body up in a sitting position and hemmed Tyant in with gigantic rocks pressed painfully against his ribs so that he could not move. She leaned down to look at the hunter while her mate continued to slaughter thousands of people in the background. Tears flowed down his cheeks as he gritted his teeth against his pain of both body and spirit.

"Watch, Hunter," she said softly, "As we render all your prophecies and fore telling's as useless; this temple will fall as did all the others. Izar will find what it seeks, and you will be the last, as I promised you."

She kissed him then, as he groaned and turned his face away from her. Then she came to her feet and joined her mate; Tyant began to weep as the blood of thousands of innocents flowed and soaked the ground beneath him.

Then he heard a voice in his mind.

Hunter-Brother...

"Wajit," Tyant whispered, "Cat-Sister, you live?"

Tyant turned his head painfully in her direction; her eyes glinted in the sunlight; after a moment, Wajit slowly blinked. With great effort, the great cat lifted herself enough to crawl closer to Tyant; he tightened his lips as he witnessed her strain to reach him; her hind legs dragging behind her; overextended claws digging into the dirt beneath her. Finally, she was near enough for Tyant to reach her with his good arm; his fingers trembled with weakness as he stroked the softness behind her ears for the last time.

This is a good day to return to the nothingness, my bond brother, Wajit said as her hold on life began to fade.

"Don't leave me, Wajit," Tyant pleaded, "This cannot be how our journey ends."

The hunter heard a familiar snort come from Wajit's nostrils, but the voice in his mind began to seem farther and farther away.

Do you understand nothing, Hunter-Brother? I only die to be reborn again with you; whatever shape or form you take, Wajit will be there, to bond again...

TYANT GASPED as he felt the bond between himself and Wajit fade with her lifeforce. In despair he turned his eyes to the temple in the distance and he saw the Initiate again on the steps. His eyes widened as he saw the Star beings begin the ascent to where she stood; the blood of all his kin draining down the robes of the pair, staining the steps beneath their boots.

Tyant's body tensed slightly as he heard a voice in his mind; not the warm throaty sound of Wajit, but the mental voice of a woman; the Initiate reaching out to him.

Fear not, Tyant of the Hunters, the end is before us...

"She promised me," he began brokenly but the voice in his mind interrupted him.

You have another Promise, Hunter of the Plains, one that supersedes all others...

The hunter swallowed hard through his pain and responded.

"The Promise," he whispered, "that Light will return at the end of the age."

At the end of every age, Tyant the Hunter, answered the Initiate, the darkness never lasts forever. So now you have two promises, which one will you place your faith in?

"The One I have given my life to defend, Initiate," Tyant said strongly, "I stand with you to the last..."

.   .   .

SHE HAD HELD HER PLACE; even when the numbers in her head began counting backwards; even the children rushed forward to embrace the dark as their parents and older family members fell; they would defend the truth with their lives.

So would she.

Her fellow dwellers prepared for the end; once they beheld the fate of all others of their kind, they had no illusions regarding their chances. The young assisted the elders in destroying all the written records; parchments and books were heaved into a roaring fire set in the final Inner Room. The sacred things no longer mattered; the young ones struck the images on the walls and broke the statues until the elders bid them stop; there was nothing left to understand or discern. The elders soothed the weeping young ones; the images were only symbols of something else; something only a person who cherished all life could possibly see. The only image left that was still visible was that of a huge knot that appeared to be floating in the Infinite; they all gathered beneath it and held hands.

THE ONLY THING of importance was that the truth remain unknown to the ignorant and self-serving; the two attackers were the epitome of that. Their needs were simple; how to multiply their kind and subdue the earth. The key to this aim was knowledge; the information held in these temples pre-dated the pair's existence and they felt the destruction of each building brought them a step closer to the final goal. They were trying to translate one sentence from the only language they could not understand; all the rivers of blood they swam had only yielded two words:

"THE TEMPLE..."

And for this, untold millions had died.

. . .

YET THE INITIATE knew the names of each one; she gave a blessing to each soul as the body that housed it perished. Some hunters were among the last to fall; the great cats who always aided them fought to the ceasing of breath; the female snapped the neck of both the remaining hunter and the cat who defended him. Finally, the pair stepped over the mounds of bodies and began to ascend the steps leading up to her; their hair and clothing blackened by the shed blood of the innocent. It rolled from them until they stood before her, seemingly clean; yet they smelled of iron and rotting wood.

AS THEY REACHED the last step of the wide porch of the temple, the Initiate heard singing coming deep from the walls of the Inner Room; she barely lifted a corner of her mouth.

They were ready.

The huge man spoke.

"Greetings, Initiate."

He nodded at her widened gaze.

"Yes," he continued, "we know what you are."

The female beside him arrogantly smoothed back her beautiful dark hair.

"That information," she added smugly, "only cost you five temples."

The huge man waved his hand at the carnage behind him.

"We have already offered sacrifice; that is the way of you humans, is it not?"

The Initiate said nothing, but her eyes spoke volumes of her rage and distain. The woman patted at her mate's arm as though to quiet him; the Initiate's lips tightened at her attempt to placate her.

"Forbear, my love," she said with iron sweetness, "you know humans do not condone human sacrifice; we do."

The female placed her hand on her hip as she assessed the Initiate.

"We have not been introduced, Initiate," she said coyly, "We are Izar, better known as The Twins."

The beautiful woman smiled wider at the Initiate's reaction.

"Yes," she continued, "we come from and are made of that same star far away in the heavens. But you know this; just as you know you will not prevail against us."

"She will not speak..." noted the huge man as he attempted to stride past her; he struck a wall of energetic force and stepped back. "...Nor allow our passage."

"This is the last of your temples, Initiate," offered the woman dryly, "you have surely seen what we have done to all others; why die for information that is only of value to us? Allow our passage and we will grant you the millennium you will need to build your foolish temples again—"

"We have already learned half of what we needed to sustain these physical bodies," said the huge man, "That the physical body here renews itself every seven years, cell by cell; all we need is but to focus on it and it will last forever."

The Initiate shook her head in disbelief; how did they lean this?

"That," added the woman smugly, "we learned at the Temple of the Eastern Sky," she continued at the pain in the Initiate's eyes. "He was your lover, was he not? Had he been willing to tell us the rest, you could finish your petty lives out together. Now?"

The female's eyes darkened.

"Give us the key to reproduce in this form and we will allow you to bury him; otherwise, I will set your bones on fire myself."

For answer, the Initiate pulled elements from the air and formed a rod of pure radiation; it hummed as the Twins mutually gasped and stepped back; the man's eyes narrowed.

"She is the most powerful, my love," he said in anger, "we should have started here!"

The singing in the temple rose in the Initiate's ears; the sound of it filled her as she moved like water and music, her beam of light forcing the pair back down the steps. The Twins responded with lightspeed and she easily countered it; they could neither pass or touch her; and if her rod struck, they fell back miles away. The battle raged for hours; she never tired. The Twins pulled on the star that bore them; the atmosphere of the skies peeled like curtains and the universe was visible; yet she fought on, even as she realized the tide was turning against her. The Twins could and would fight her for millions of years if necessary, and she could not leave the temple unprotected if they chose to take out their rage and frustration on the remainder of the helpless populace.

At that moment she realized that she didn't need to fight them forever; her purpose was already fulfilled, and the truth would be safe.

AT FIRST, the female part of the Twins thought the singing in the temple was a distraction; there came a time where she now began to listen to it and her eyes widened as she began to discern the notes. In the same moment, it seemed the Initiate knew her thoughts; in slow motion, the woman noticed the Initiate just looking at her; the huge man saw this as opportunity and pulled the rod of radiation from her hands without resistance; the Initiate braced herself for the blow.

The words came back to the woman:

"The Temple..."

"Stop, my love," she screamed, "the temple is not the buildings!"

But in his bloodlust, the man had already run the Initiate through with her own rod.

"It is *Her*...!"

Made by spirit, not by hands, the Initiate thought as her life bled from her.

YET EVEN IN HER AGONY, the Initiate did not cry out; she held on to the instrument of her coming death with both hands. As she went to her knees, she heard the voice of the leader in the temple; the one who had pressed her shoulder in sympathy of her lifemate's death:

"Well done—"

THE HUGE MAN bent down to twist the rod in her chest.

"Worthless human," he said close to her face. She reached up to grasp his cloak with determination; the woman began running towards him, but it would prove too late; the Initiate would give him the power behind the word he had no respect for. The woman's hands flew to her ears and she beheld her mate double over as the Initiate's mental thoughts blasted through their minds:

YOU WILL LEARN respect for the power behind the word that describes us...

Her lips parted and the Initiate barely whispered:

"Hu—"

THE TEMPLE, its inhabitants, the Initiate, and the huge man all vanished in the vortex of power released by the sound of creation. The female part of The Twins was blasted backwards and smashed into an outcropping of rock half a continent away; the rock disintegrated and dissolved into the seas below.

The female part of the Twins learned that day what everyone in the temple already knew; that it was the burden of the Initiate to remain silent; she housed the power of the whole of creation on her tongue. The dwellers all knew the information, but the application of the force of sound and vibration could only be given to one who could control it in the face of annihilation. She was chosen to be the one who would protect the truth in the last days; it was The Twins who stepped up the timetable to reset creation on the planet. Yet the end of one age is merely the beginning of another. The Initiate knew one day the power and truth would come to one from whom it could not be stolen or forced. As the energy of creation roared through her, she knew it would only bring the Initiate to the arms of her beloved who waited for her at the veil between this life and the other side.

Finally free of her burden, the Initiate sang her own song as the atoms and molecules holding her physical form together spun away.

TYANT WAS the only one left alive on the plains. Unable to move, he watched the horrific battle between the Initiate and the Star beings known as Izar. He had never seen anything so beautiful and terrifying; the skies peeled back, and the hunter saw solar systems and things undreamed of. He felt himself grow more and more calm as the battle raged and his vision cleared; somehow he knew that the prophecy would protect his remaining tribe and loved ones.

Then the moment of silence came as foretold: Tyant could see the Initiate on the steps; he saw the huge man press his only advantage and when the power and Light blazed from the Initiate, Tyant felt himself smiling in joy as his pain ended and the Light took him home.

YET THE FEMALE Twin did not die when she struck the wall of earth and stone and sank beneath the flowing waters. There she lay inert for a millennia or more until the drifting seabed rolled her above sea level where she was discovered by the mage who would be one day known as Enith. He brought her and the strange shapeless mass that was growing beside her to his home. The creature shared her secrets in exchange for his help to restore her mate. The Twins who had come to conquer a planet now learned to fear the ancestors of those who would one day be known as creators.

The Beauty of Aris

The lands, plains and gardens of Aris were a marvel on the planet; many held the opinion that this natural beauty existed before mankind and other forms of life on Earth. People gravitated towards the area like a magnetic force and created dwellings that surrounded it for miles, but no one built anything inside the deeper parts of it. Like an unspoken agreement no one wished to add or take away from the magnificence of Aris. It was not unheard of to find men and women wandering its loveliness at all hours, and to rest on the ground at night and watch the heavens reveal the stars and galaxies kept Aris teeming with human life.

The passing of days did not have the significance that it carries now. Seasons for planting and harvesting were unheard of, since food was abundant and people took it upon themselves to gather food to share with others. A servant was not considered lower in stature than the ones they served, in fact, because of the nature of the word, 'to serve', these people chose it as a profession and were prized for their natural ability to be kind and consider the welfare of others. The stories they shared of their travels and experiences were among the greatest gifts these people could bring. Their residence with families could be days, weeks, months and even years. They roamed where they wished and were welcome on any doorstep, and when they departed they never took more than they could carry; there would be plenty of anything they wished on the way.

On this particular day one family that was heading to Aris blended in with another for company, and the servants greeted each other excitedly, eager to learn what the other's travels had yielded. One young woman reached for her servant's hand and held it tightly.

"You must promise me that you won't allow yourself to be swept away by their stories," cried the young woman, "I've grown so attached to you these past years; it would grieve me if you left."

But her servant only smiled and returned the gentle squeeze of her hand.

"Fear not, young one," she replied, "I've also grown to love you so much that I must stay at least until you are bonded with a lifemate; soon you will long only for his company."

The young woman flushed with the easy embarrassment of youth; she held on to her servant's hand.

"Yet I cannot imagine life without you; I shall ask father to build us a house where we will all dwell together."

The older woman laughed; she knew that life could ordain things differently; but she would not dash her young lady's hopes for the future.

"Let it be as you say, my lady, I serve at your will."

With this promise given, the young woman finally released her hand and the servant moved to embrace her fellow travelers; their joyful cries ringing through the high grasses.

Her parents moved closer to distract her; in the distance her father pointed at a gathering of people on the hills; even miles away they could see the light pouring from them.

"Look, daughter, do you see them?"

The girl gave a gasp of amazement as her mother took her arm.

"Such light and beauty, father," she said in wonder, "what is the cause of it?"

"They're called co-creators, daughter," her father answered, "a rare sight; I'm told they used to be everywhere. Our neighbors claim they still have halls of learning where you can be taught to harness the energy of creation itself."

"I've heard they can bring the stars in the heavens close enough to touch," declared her mother.

The father scoffed.

"Those who do this are not creators, ny wife; they use illusions to make you think the stars are closer. Stars are light bearing bodies with gravitational pulls that would destroy us if brought that close."

"Well, I've also heard that creators can stir the seeds in the ground and make the earth more bountiful," her mother persisted and watched as her husband nodded.

"That would be something worth seeing," he agreed.

"Can we get closer, father?" Whispered the girl, "will they welcome us?"

Her father paused a moment as though considering it; then smiled.

"Let us see, my daughter, I've also heard that they are as kind as servants; surely they will not turn us away."

The blended families surged towards the greater plains of Aris; waving, and greeting all the people on the way. Mankind in general had no fear of strangers then; in fact, the word for someone separate and unknown was not in their language. Every person was a future friend or family member.

Soon they were close enough to discern the faces of the people standing on the hills; a man and a woman were standing a little ways below the group above them; the man immediately began to descend the hill as though he knew the small family were coming to greet him. Behind him were a woman with two men; the young woman above smiled and waved as the men offered a raised hand to the families.

The young woman with her parents looked around and searched for the face of her servant, who grinned at her and waved her on; she was holding the hand of a young man who could be her son, and the girl wondered if he would be staying with them for a while; he seemed as kind as she.

Suddenly, the man approaching them stopped and stared past them towards another hill in the distance; they followed his gaze and paused in astonishment as the very air itself began to groan and warble in pain. The young girl marveled; was this the illusion her father spoke of; it seemed the night sky was visible in the daylight in a small hole in the air.

She heard the man shouting; the woman next to him instantly vanished as the girl's mouth gaped.

Then they all saw it; a man in dark robes standing in the middle of the air as though it were solid ground. Lightning flashed from his body and the girl felt a pain deep inside of her, as though her very insides were on fire. She looked to her father as he roared:

"RUN!"

The people on the plains began to scatter as fire came rushing forth from the man in the air towards the man on the ground, who quickly raised himself up to intercept the blaze. Even as she ran, the young girl could not help herself from trying to see what was happening; she felt her parents grab both her arms and propel her forward.

"Don't look back!" Her mother cried, "Head for the trees!"

Thunder and lightning darkened the skies above them and the girl heard a loud roar followed by screaming, then she coughed as her lungs filled with acrid air; the plains of Aris were on fire. Animals came crashing through the bush in terror; the girl screamed as her beloved servant was struck down; her son tried to lift her and was hit from behind by people who could not see them; her father grimly pulled her away.

"Father," the girl sobbed breathlessly, "we must help them!"

"Hold on to your mother," he growled, "We'll look for them later; I must see to you first!"

They made it to the sheltering trees, her father forced his child to stand behind the trees with her mother between; he pressed his body against them and tucked their arms with his to secure them as people and animals mindlessly ran past them, crushing and trampling each other in mortal fear. The young woman wept as her parents clung to her; scraping her cheek against the bark of the tree. She had never experienced fear in her whole life; now it seemed then world itself was coming apart as the vast beauty of Aris disintegrated under the relentless bombardment of radiation and fire.

The quiet that followed was as loud as the battle; her father hesitated before silently commanding his wife and child to be still as he cautiously ventured out from the shelter of the trees to see if the destruction was over. Soon the girl heard her father cry out; she and her mother moved as one to find him. He was standing with his back to them; smoke and fog a thick curtain before him and when they looked at him, his face was streaked with tears. Then mother and daughter gazed past him as the smoke drifted and froze:

Everything was gone; the inner and outer plains, the vast gardens, all the trees, the rivers of water, the pools and oasis no longer existed. Everywhere you looked was a burnt wasteland; sand and steaming dirt and mounds of charred flesh that used to be humans and animals greeted their unbelieving eyes. The trio stood weeping unrestrained at their unfathomable loss.

Where was Aris?

A few people were yet stumbling through the wreckage; the young girl was first to respond as she faintly recognized a pair of people she treasured; though their clothing and hair were burned in places.

"No!" She cried as she ran to her servant and her son, who was still holding her up; her right leg dragged at an awkward angle as she tried to walk upright. Her son was openly sobbing as they neared them.

"I don't know what happened," he said over and over, "I don't know what happened...!"

The young woman cradled her servant's face and gasped:

The woman was blind.

She reached out and gripped the girl's arms with strong fingers, but her eyes were sightless.

"There was a woman," the servant whispered, "the woman on the hill who waved at us; she was screaming—"

"By the Great One," the girl heard her mother say as she covered her mouth in grief.

"There was a bright light," the servant continued, "I saw it as I came to my feet; then I saw nothing..." her voice trailed off in pain; her son covered his face with his other hand, unable to restrain his tears. The girl felt her father move between her and the woman and help the boy to raise his mother more steady on her feet.

"You will live out your life with us," he said firmly, "Now we will serve you."

As they made their way back they found other families, most of them weeping and crying out for family members they could not find. The girl felt a touch on her shoulder and shrieked in joy as a group of her friends embraced her. Eventually, they were separated as other missing members joined them. The young girl focused on her servant, her mind already making the mental adjustments to her rooms that would accommodate her servant sleeping with her so she could see to her needs. The boy bravely nodded as the young girl held his hand.

"She has been like a mother to me," she assured the boy, "I will now be a daughter to her."

The sad group was almost in sight of her father's lands when they noticed another man in dark robes on the cleared path before them. On a different day, the family would have approached him without fear. The girl stopped as her father instinctively stepped in front of her.

"Greetings, my lord," said her father in a calm manner, "our home is on the way; may we offer you food and drink?"

The man's eyes glittered.

"My master's word binds me from dealing you harm this day," the man replied tensely, "Else I would render you as he has rendered Aris. I have need of only one of you; and he was quite clear on which of you it should be..."

The robed man raised his hand and pointed at the girl, who stepped back in shock. She felt her father's hand on her arm as the boy bravely charged the man in her defense. The touch of her mother's fingers pressing against her waist faded as light surrounded her and she heard her father's final cry:

"No! Not my child!"

And just like her servant, the young woman saw nothing else.

An Eagle and a Sparrow

The dark haired beauty known as Landa continued her new life under The Rook's protection in the manse he had built for her. As the years passed, the memory that was strongest for Landa was the moment her mysterious protector pressed her into his arms in grief. All her thoughts of confusion concerning why he both helped her and kept her at a distance vanished as Landa tried to comfort him. The warmth of his skin and robes engulfed her and Landa restrained her own emotions as The Rook vented his remorse.

HER WORLD HAD LITERALLY BEGAN with his face; how could he understand what he meant to her?

She stroked his long dark hair as he pressed his face against her cheek; but he could no longer look at Landa. She caught her breath as The Rook touched his lips to her forehead and then he was gone. The breezes on her patios were sudden and cold to her; Landa wrapped her arms around herself as though he were still there.

"Come back, my lord," Landa whispered, "Please."

BUT THE ROOK did not return. Dejected, Landa stood staring at the space no longer occupied by the man she owed her life to. She could not explain to herself what it was about him that made her long for his presence. Soon her maid offered a cloak for her shoulders and pleaded with her to return to the shelter of her home. Finally, the devastated young woman obeyed her servant, entering a building teeming with people and feeling completely alone.

Her letters to The Rook resumed; again unanswered.

LANDA TRIED to remember her life before she stood before him in the Landa Gardens where he found her but little that could be called a memory returned to her. She clearly recalled the look of horror on his face when she called him Michael; but he did not tell her what to call him, so in her letters she referred to him as Lord Rook as her servants did and he did not correct her.

But in her heart she called him Michael; she did not know then that he could read her thoughts. In her innocence, she could not guess that she was a part of the trap The Magician had set for his servant; Landa knew nothing but the house she lived in and the servants and staff The Rook granted her.

For his own part, The Rook still battled with the madness within him. Knowing Landa was a pawn in the chess game between himself and his master, he stayed away from her.

He'd been alone for eons and for the most part content with his memories of Sha-el. Unable to help himself, the powerful sorcerer traveled the past every day, pouring his might in vain against the amber wall between him and the cave where he relived over and over the moment he lost his connection to creation and consequently the woman he loved above all things.

Other times, he visited himself before that day, when he was known as Michael and it seemed that all power on earth belonged to him. The Rook followed this past self, the man he once was; blissfully ignorant of what lay ahead; watching Sha-el from a distance, an abyss now between them that he could never cross. Torturing himself with the vision of his innocence before his fall; how happy he was with Sha-el for thousands upon thousands of years. Once he had believed they would be together until the star that warmed Earth began its decay and the solar system itself would perish.

Or that one day they would both agree to return to Source; Michael would hold Sha-el's hand and they would sit in a quiet place watching a sunrise or sunset. He would kiss her hand one final time before they faded away into fine white ash, gazing into the other's eyes as he had seen so many other creators do.

The only time The Rook could enter the cave where Sha-el died was after she was gone and Maldoc had perished at his hands, only one of many murders he had committed on that first day. The blood of the innocent prevented him from changing that moment, and Landa's blood was among them. The Rook restored the cave and the mountain, that he could do. He brought together stones and fashioned two tables such as one might make for a resting place for the dead. And one thing more:

Sha-el's family had placed her and her brothers Rion and Lior in a similar cave. They grieved for a time and left, knowing that soon their children would turn to fine ash. Yet, as soon as they departed the resting place, The Rook took Sha-el's body, causing it to look as though it faded like her brothers. In truth, he brought it back to the cave where she died and used his power to keep her cells intact. He laid her on one table and kept her bathed in light; to one who did not know what had happened, Sha-el looked as though she were sleeping.

And there, The Rook swore, she would remain until the one who caused her death lay beside her.

Thus he had believed himself content to remain alone until his planned revenge on both his uncle and The Magician was completed. Yet Landa tested his resolve in more ways than he was comfortable with. If he broke his word to himself and destroyed her, The Rook felt he would be lost forever; but if his master were successful in whatever plans he had to use Landa against him—

He couldn't complete these thoughts; so the inner war continued. Her letters both comforted and tortured The Rook.

She cannot see me clearly, he thought, how can one love a monster?

BUT THE LIGHT within her pulled at him. One year later, Landa gazed from her balcony and beheld her benefactor standing in the fields below, staring up at her; his cloak billowing without wind. Her heart was thundering in her chest as she forced herself to walk through her house and down the stairs to greet him. Landa waited for him on the wide porch leading inside; the light wind felt different on her face as she clasped her hands together in front of her robes. Soon she realized The Rook would not leave the fields and Landa bravely strode out to meet with him. He watched as she moved towards him, her dark hair floating about her shoulders her nervous fingers clutching at her outer robes. Her eyes were as he remembered them, a deep warm brown that held no secrets; she began and ended with him.

"My lord," Landa said softly as she stood before him, "Will you not honor me and enter my home?"

"What do you want from me, Landa?" The Rook replied and watched as she lowered her eyes in embarrassment at his directness. "I am no longer a man of fine words and manners; in fact, I cannot recall how I was in those days; I am nearly as old as the Earth itself. Speak plainly to me—"

"Why haven't you responded to my letters, my lord?" Landa asked boldly, "A common courtesy, I would think for so many years unrewarded."

A rare smile teased the corner of his mouth as he listened; she adjusted quickly. He liked the way her eyes flashed as she gently took him to task. He stepped closer to her and reached for her hand; a movement that halted her words in surprise.

"I remember nothing of courtesy, my beauty," he said slowly as he tried to recall how to be civil; Landa blinked rapidly at his awkward endearment. He stared at her hand as his fingers caressed hers; Landa's olive skin flushed at his familiarity.

"You are exceptionally beautiful, Landa," The Rook said finally, "No doubt you are a woman of quality, one any man should be thankful for..." his voice trailed off as he began to choose his words.

"But The Rook is not a man," he continued, "The Rook is a monster; a creature of evil; made in his master's image---"

"I want to know you," Landa said breathlessly as she interrupted him, "You asked what I want of you; that is what I want. I'd like for you to dine with me, converse with me; if you've lived for millions of years as you say it, surely you can spare a moment of time?"

The Rook raised her hand to his lips and Landa could no longer speak; her blood pounded recklessly in her ears as she tried to focus on what he was saying.

"I will not come in, Landa," he answered gently, "You do not know what you are asking or who you are asking it of; it would be wiser for me to take my leave now."

"Have I offended you, my lord?" Landa said in agony and watched as his slow smile broadened.

"No, Landa, you have not," The Rook replied, "Thank you for the letters."

She stepped forward helplessly as he faded away.

"I don't understand," she whispered to the empty fields, "I don't understand."

Landa restrained her emotions as she gathered up her outer robes and headed back to her house, hoping dearly that it would not be another year before she saw him again.

The Rook, who was actually still there but invisible to her eyes, drew his breath in sharply as she unconsciously stood close to him; The Rook leaned in slightly to take in the fragrance of her hair. Yet she knew nothing; he watched Landa tilt her head in pain before turning to walk away from him; he watched this with narrowed gaze.

I cannot tell right from wrong or good from evil, Landa, he thought, the very air I breath must taint you.

The Rook became a terror in those days of uncertainty; both men and mages fled at the very sight of him. His master The Magician began to restrain his bound servant's power when The Rook came to his court; the body count was finally too high. But his master would not discipline or upbraid The Rook for his actions; he would not even mention it; and his servant knew that some dread task was ahead.

Only months later The Rook found the release he sought:

The Magician was expanding his plan to spread the use of magic in the kingdoms of men and to demonstrate the need for it, he sometimes used his mages to cause dissent in man's government. When the resolution turned to war, The Magician would pit one kingdom with mages among its regents against another that had either little magicians or none. Such was the case with two minor kingdoms who met on the battlefield of Lorith, a place very similar to the plains of Aris during Landa's original lifetime. The age and beauty of its trees were legendary, and many came to marvel at the huge trunks and branches that threatened to catch the clouds above in their leaves.

Despite the presence of greater magic on the side of the Kingdom of Sarkoth, the men of the Kingdom of Lorith were winning; a victory that The Magician was determined to prevent.

"Be careful to obey my words, my Rusch," said The Magician slowly, "Do not allow whatever has disturbed you to blind you to my promise regarding your uncle."

Chastised beforehand, The Rook nodded and waited for instructions.

"I want the Kingdom of Lorith to survive your handiwork, my Rook; it will do me little good if there is no one left to tell the tale. Bolster the forces of Sarkoth; march before them so there is little doubt whom you have come to aid. Bring the armies of Lorith to their knees; do not slay King Leith, his High General or High Regent. Allow the men of Sarkoth to sack and plunder; they will need gold and livestock to both pay and feed their armies."

"How many may I slay?" asked The Rook quietly.

The Magician sighed.

"Leave the calvary and archers intact for the most part; and the middle generals; slay half their infantry; that should be more than enough to give the Sarkoths the edge they need. The Kingdom of Lorith must have someone left to defend their boundaries."

"Their mages?"

"I leave that to you. Consider the impact, however if one or two survive to convince the king to change his mind about his magical defenses."

The Rook did not respond to this, he merely waited as his master searched his mind for ideas to further his agenda. Silence ruled the hall; everyone who loved his life fled as soon as The Rook appeared; The Magician's protection could not be predicted. Finally, the creature was satisfied that he had mentally covered all contingencies.

"Go," he said softly, and The Rook vanished.

.   .   .

THE KING of Lorith stood confidently atop a faraway hill overlooking the valley where his men fought and died to protect their kingdom. Though the attack by the Kingdom of Sarkoth appeared unprovoked, the king had acquired information through his spies that the men of Sarkoth were deliberately attempting conquest of Lorith using magic.

But the king was not afraid of the mages used by the Sarkoths. He had observed over the years how magic is wielded and developed his own defense, which was proving quite effective. King Leith was not a supporter of magic as wholesale protection for kingdoms; he felt men should rely on their own strength of mind and strategy to rule. He felt correctly that magic was somehow a shortcut to an end, and that if a man or woman applied themselves diligently they should be able to overcome any obstacles. So the king studied how the radiation wielded by magicians was used and applied; his main observation was that mages had varying levels of skills similar to how men studied war itself. Distraction, confusion, and disruption were his primary methods to shake off a mage's application of his craft, and during a battle there were plenty of opportunities to overcome any advantage held by magic.

"Can you determine for me how many mages King Arnoth has, my regent?" King Leith asked his mage; his mind imagined that his regent could serve as a scout might during a war to report back the number of men, archers, calvary and infantry an army may have to face.

King Leith's High Regent breathed deeply; from miles away he could see the nimbus of dark radiation surging from small pockets of light among the blanket of men marching across the land; the High Regent of Sarkoth flared the brightest; it was a bold warning to King Leith's meager defense. The High Regent chanced a glance to his fellow brothers; if the defense of their king did not prevail, they were all dead men.

"I see them easily, my lord," the High Regent replied quietly, "What is your will?"

.　.　.

THE SARKOTHS HAD five mages of great skill and three of lesser; these regents appeared on the field ahead of the infantry in order to intimidate the men of Lorith. King Leith hid catapults, archers, and men skilled with spears along the hilly terrain that was native to his country; huge trees provided shelter the mages could not anticipate. It was a stroke of luck that the Sarkoth High Regent fell first to King Leith's clever attack; it cost him a quarter regiment to take down the next two. Shaken by failure at the beginning of his campaign, the King of Sarkoth was forced to retreat and lick his wounds. By the third day, King Arnoth had lost all but his last skilled mage; his men and generals were in a state of agitation and fear. His High General reported in the morning that his archers had slain more than fifty deserters the night before; the campaign was not going well.

KING ARNOTH'S newly promoted High Regent set his jaw as the horizon began to lighten; it would not be well for him to report back to his own brothers in magic that the conquest of Lorith had utterly failed. That is, if he lived to report it. The loss of the previous High Regent had frightened him; he knew the mages of Lorith were no match for him; at least, that was what he was told. Sweat broke out on his brow as he contemplated the inconceivable; that the men of Lorith had a Master Sorcerer for protection; if so, he would not enjoy his promotion for long. A master could easily cloak his energies from Enroth, who was not nearly as powerful as the High Regent who died on the first day of the conflict. The mages remaining to him were barely above the rank of novice; Enroth had brought them to give them firsthand instruction on how to wage war on soldiers; now it appeared their first lesson would be how to die in service of their king. The voice of King Arnoth interrupted his dismal thoughts:

"WHAT NOW, HIGH REGENT?" the king asked tensely as he pushed away a pile of useless battle reports, "Shall we set out for home with our tails between our legs, or can this war be salvaged?"

The mage sighed deeply to control his shaking; he knew there was only one thing he could do. He turned away from the coming brightness on the horizon and gazed on King Arnoth.

"Remain behind the calvary, my lord," said the mage in resignation, "keep my two mages beside you at all times and use them to flee if your forces are routed. You must not risk using horses to place distance between you and the men of Lorith should I fall."

The king's eyes widened.

"What are you saying, Enroth?" he asked incredulously, "After all that has happened, you plan to lead an open charge on their infantry?"

The king looked helplessly to his High General; King Arnoth thought for certain that his High Regent had a plan of subterfuge; some way of stealth as opposed to direct confrontation that had already failed. His High General's next words mirrored this train of thought.

"Enroth," said the general, "Surely you speak of madness or suicide, to try again a strategy that will win us nothing!"

The mage swallowed hard before speaking again.

"I must," he answered hoarsely, "If King Leith has a Master Sorcerer in their employ and I do not show myself to distract him, he or she may materialize in this very tent and slay you both."

Enroth nodded as his king's face drained of blood.

"There can be no other explanation for how they have bested us," Enroth nearly whispered, "I fear I am not strong enough to protect you, my king; my life is the least I can offer."

Before King Arnoth could respond, High Regent Enroth strode purposely past his stunned High General and emerged from the king's tent. Enroth could not hear the orders the generals were shouting to the men who were already standing in formation; he walked through the lines and towards the front, mentally preparing himself for destruction. His two students looked wordlessly after him in grief; they knew their only function now was the protection of the King of Sarkoth. Enroth heard their mental cry:

May the Great One guide your steps, teacher, and bring you peace...

AS HIGH REGENT SIRK OF LORITH watched the very tip of the sun peak over the mountaintop, he took a deep breath and braced himself; he could see the energy that heralded the approach of Enroth. Sirk knew that if Enroth made a move of desperation and launched himself above the soldiers and into King Leith's tent, that Sirk could do nothing to stop him from burning the king to ash. His fellow mages moved to flank the king; they would only have a chance against Enroth if they banded their energies together. Sirk hoped desperately that Enroth would march the front line again, but he doubted that Enroth would actually do something that foolish.

From the corner of his eye, Sirk saw his king signal to his High General, who in turn motioned his middle generals. From this the lower generals knew to deploy the infantry, who would charge the mage and hopefully distract him enough for the archers and lances to come again into play. The mages of Lorith flared with dark energy as King Leith lowered his arm and the archers hidden in the trees took aim against the lone mage marching towards the head of the footmen of Sarkoth. Wooden wheels grinded and groaned as their burden of catapults and lancers moved from their cover to draw Enroth's attention and hopefully, his fire. But as Enroth's right foot stepped into direct alignment with the first line of the infantry, the mage glanced his eyes sideways at the bright burst of flame and darkness on his right and The Rook came into view.

MARCHING SWIFTLY past the startled Enroth, The Rook released a blaze of radiation that vaporized everything in front of him for a quarter of a mile; thousands of soldiers disappeared in a flash of light, the hidden archers of Lorith rendered to ash on the branches of trees and their spent arrows redirected at the remaining front line of men. Soldier fell like wheat as The Rook grimly made his way across the plains at an unnatural speed; his arms slightly raised, and fingers splayed as he became a tunnel of light, death, and massive destruction. The fruit of the catapults and lancers returned to their owners who screamed and died from the flaming balls of heavy linens, thick branches, oils, and wax released in a deadly rain.

King Leith froze in astonishment; what manner of mage was this on the battlefield? He had never seen anything like it; he faintly heard his High General roaring at his middle generals to bolster their defense. The king turned to gaze at Sirk whose warm brown skin lightened several shades as he struggled to reason who and what was annihilating their armies.

"What is it?" the regent heard King Leith shouting over the din.

"I don't know, my king," gasped High Regent Sirk, "His levels of power are beyond comprehension. Perhaps he is a creature of legend; we call them Ancients; I never dreamed they were real!"

The men of Lorith rallied and charged The Rook, who now paused and calmly waited for them. Regiments flanked him from east and west as the main bulk of the infantry shook the ground with their advance. The Rook took a deep breath as he reminded himself of his lord's wishes; how dearly he wanted to blacken the earth from the front of King Leith's army to the back of it. But as the brave men neared him, his robes suddenly lifted without wind; The Rook raised his right foot and stomped once upon the ground.

The earth split in a wide crack that yawned and shuddered for miles east and west; the planet rent itself open and downward towards darkness and inner fire; almost half of Lorith's army fell screaming into the abyss. The men charging forward could not stop their advance. Obedient to The Magician, his bound servant lifted his arms and using a field of energy, pushed back the wall of remaining soldiers from the edge, many of them crushed by the surging infantrymen behind them. The Rook then closed up the earth with a devastating rumble.

Wordlessly, he looked behind him at the stunned soldiers of Sarkoth; then lifted his arm and pointed. Without hesitation, King Arnoth's High General roared:

"Advance!"

The Rook watched as waves of soldiers and calvary charged past him, wading into the shattered forces of Lorith flinging death and destruction everywhere. The mage known as Enroth was terrified as the gaze of The Rook fell on him. He bowed deeply, expecting to be vaporized for even drawing his attention. He was startled at the sound of his name coming from the creature's lips.

"Enroth," said The Rook, "Come forth."

Instantly the mage appeared before the powerful being and bowed again, keeping his eyes lowered in profound respect.

"My lord," Enroth said carefully, and The Rook took his measure.

"Do you know who I am?" asked The Rook and watched as the man before him trembled.

"Forgive me, my lord," Enroth replied breathlessly, "To have knowledge of such a man as yourself is beyond my station, or any mage I know, may it please you for my saying it."

"It is my master's will--" began The Rook and smiled slightly as Enroth brought his head up in astonishment and fear at the implication that another existed more powerful than the one in front of him. "It is his will," The Rook continued, "That you become an advocate for magic among the kingdoms. In return for this victory against the Lorithans, you will expand your school for magicians with the intent of sending them out to other nations. You will be rewarded in direct accordance with how well you carry these instructions out."

"Your word is my will, my lord," responded Enroth sincerely, "Whom shall I say has sent me?"

"The Rook," the man before him answered simply, and watched again as Enroth's eyes widened in recognition and fear. So the legends were true; it took everything the mage had not to fall to his knees in terror of his life.

"How should I address my king, my lord," asked Enroth breathlessly.

"Tell King Arnoth The Rook offers greetings and that his actions have found favor. He will build a Hall of Mages at once and promote the cause of magic at the next King's Summit and any that follow.

Most importantly," and here The Rook paused, "He will not press his advantage over the Lorithans on this day and completely destroy them but will allow them to recover."

"As you say it, my lord, it shall be done," affirmed Enroth, and The Rook turned again towards the men of Lorith, fading away as he did so.

The High General of the Kingdom of Lorith bellowed at his men once he saw the powerful magician on the fields below turn again towards his army. He pointed at the king.

"Use your magic to take him away from here, Sirk!" cried the general, "Surely this creature's aim is now the king's life!"

But the High Regent and the mages surrounding the king looked at the High General in horror.

"We cannot move," gasped Sirk, and the general drew his sword as The Rook materialized in the king's tent. The king's guards moved forward and died without a sound, falling to the ground at the feet of King Leith, who drew his own sword instinctively.

"Greetings, King Leith of the Kingdom of Lorith," said The Rook calmly, "It has come to my master's attention that you have no respect for magic, is this true?"

"Who are you?" demanded the king, "Why have you interfered in our war?"

But The Rook did not answer this question directly.

"He has asked me to spare your life, King Leith," said The Rook darkly, "But there are many levels between where you are right now and what might be described as 'life', so do address your tone to me accordingly."

The bound servant of The Magician gazed at the mages in the king's tent.

"Which one of you is the High Regent?"

"I am," responded Sirk boldly, who then cried out as The Rook instantly vaporized every other mage in the tent.

"No!"

"I will pose my question again, King Leith," said The Rook, "Is it true that you have no respect for magic?"

"Once I had little regard for it, this is true," answered the king honestly, "But then I have never encountered anyone like yourself. You must tell me; is this why you are here?"

"It is," replied The Rook simply, whose gaze now fell on the High General, who also could not move; sweat poured from his efforts to break free.

"What is your will, my lord?" asked the king in a more measured tone and watched as The Rook acknowledged this sign of respect.

"You will change your mind, King Leith regarding magic and embrace it as fully as you once turned against it, else you will see me again. I trust I need not outline for you what will happen if you do."

After these words, The Rook faded from view.

He did not go far, however. The bound servant of The Magician stayed to watch the complete rout of King Leith's armies; the debacle lasted well into the night and next morning. The Rook stood on a hill overlooking the roads as the soldiers of Sarkoth, loaded down with the bounty of Lorith, headed back to their own lands. Fire lit up the night sky and grey smoke and ash greeted the morning sun.

In the stunned silence following the departure of the massively powerful Rook, High Regent Sirk, King Leith and his High General had trouble moving, even though the energy of The Magician's bound servant had released them. Soldiers streamed into the tent in response to the dread quiet and stopped in shock at the pile of bodies that once comprised the king's personal guard dead at their feet. At a nod from the High General, his men began the process of removal; Sirk felt the king's eyes on him but he shook his head at the king's unspoken permission to leave. Despite The Rook's promise of no further harm, Sirk felt he could not leave the king until he knew for certain no threat remained. His eyes returned to the piles of grey ash scattered around the king's tent, all that was left of the mages who died for their loyalty to the throne.

High Regent Sirk and the High General protected the position of King Leith; they watched in wonder as the men of Sarkoth overran the army and the outer city but stopped short of pillaging the palace even though the men of Lorith could not prevent it.

"What manner of being is this mage," asked the king, "who aids our enemies and still protects us from utter destruction at their hands?"

"One we should heed, my lord," answered Sirk grimly, "surely he wants us to know that the outcome might have been far more devastating."

The king turned to his High Regent.

"Go, Sirk," said the king firmly, "we've already received word that the royal family and all the palace is safe; secure your house; I know you fear for them."

With a glance of profound gratitude, Sirk disappeared.

As High Regent, Sirk's residence was within the inner gates of the kingdom and not far from the king. Yet, still he feared; it was possible that with barely a thought, the master sorcerer known as The Rook could slay every mage in the kingdom and probably had done so. He didn't bother with doors as he materialized within his home and directly into his inner suites; a woman turned at the sound of his atoms pushing the air around him aside.

"Sirk!"

His throat tight, the regent could barely breathe as he pulled his wife swiftly into his arms; the precious cries of his daughters ringing in his ears. His wife was a novice in the magic arts, and his eldest daughter had sworn to follow in his footsteps. His first thought as The Rook vaporized his brethren was of his family, fledglings in magic and vulnerable to nearly anyone of greater skill.

It wasn't possible a man of such power had overlooked them and his eldest confirmed his fears.

"Tennon," his daughter began, then dissolved into greater tears as Sirk felt his wife nod against his chest.

Tennon was a student Sirk had left behind to protect his family and take them to safety if he fell. Sirk's limbs were numb as his family led him to the place where Tennon had fallen silent to the ground and shortly after, faded into a pile of dark grey ash.

The tang of fear returned to his mouth as Sirk gazed down at Tennon's remains.

A warning indeed, he thought as his family clung to him.

"We couldn't move," his wife stammered in terror, "we couldn't even flee the house."

"Fear nothing," he finally said just above a whisper, "if he wanted you dead, you would be. This was a message for me and the king, to employ mages capable of repelling radiation at high levels. This time he has granted us is a mercy—"

Sirk kissed their faces fiercely as he held them; he swore in his mind that he would obey The Rook and find others who studied and hopefully mastered the magic arts. If he found one strong enough, he reasoned, Sirk would renounce his own position as High Regent to ensure the safety of the king and his own family.

"Come," he said sadly as he released them, "let us prepare a proper burial for our friend before I return to the king."

The Cost of War

His anger and frustration spent; The Rook sighed in remorse at the results of his wrath. The men of Lorith began the horrid task of piling bodies of the slain into trenches for burial, the skies now full of carrion birds and the tree trunks lit by the shining eyes of four-footed scavengers, waiting for the weary men to leave the guard of their dead. The Rook's thoughts turned to Landa, the innocent who longed to hold him in her arms.

He scoffed as he looked down at his hands.

I doubt your gaze would be so sweet on the horrors I've wroth; the least of which whatever dark plans for you lie ahead in the mind of my master.

He stayed until every single person on the fields of blood were gone; the last of the animals who feast on the dead were satiated; the deep puddles of gore absorbed into the earth and the sharp smell of iron dissipated. Then he returned to the battlefield and using his might, he cracked the earth open wide again; so deep he could see heat coming from it; a molten path to the planet's core. The Rook gazed down into the abyss and contemplated:

He knew he could survive if he dropped himself into it; he'd done it before. But—he wondered; What if he didn't wish to survive the planetary center; what if he just fell in and let go? He would be free then. But he would leave so much undone and promises unfulfilled. Could he bear to see Sha-el again in the shaded lands if he failed his quest; could he tell her he had left The Magician unscathed?

"You would forgive me, I know," he whispered, "You've always forgiven me..."

Landa could live out her life if he were dead, he thought, The Magician would have no interest in her except to torture him---

HE STEPPED over the edge and fell, plummeting downwards towards the heat and darkness he was made of. He closed his eyes and flung out his arms, focused on but one thought.

Sha-el...

It was a moment before The Rook realized he was no longer falling. Hung between the heat of the lower regions and the relatively cooler air above him, he opened his eyes in despair as he heard a voice:

My Rusch...

He felt the invisible chains tightening around his body and The Rook roared helplessly as his master drew him out from the earth and back into his presence.

RISE OF THE SOUTHERN ARC: THE END OF THE AGE

"Everything is energy, and all energy has a specific vibratory frequency."

Dr. Carolyne Fuqua

The Teacher of Mankind crossed his arms in resignation as he watched the slow but steady gathering of men from every known part of the globe. Addias had observed this gradual change before; how men would embrace the leadership of women; the collaborative and cooperative way of relating to each other and the planet for a mere thousand years. Then, eventually, the male need to dominate and delegate hierarchies of control over others would render them unable to listen any longer to matriarchal philosophies; the warriors became chieftains with more authority than the women; soon the wise women would be asked to remain silent while the men discussed what was truly important; boundaries of land and controlled access to rivers and streams. It would take twenty-five thousand years of strife before the men were in enough pain to hear again the feminine call to peace.

Addias sighed; this time he had only himself to blame. He thought the invention of the wheel innocent; a more expedient way of moving food and tents from place to place. Then the chieftains no longer wished to barter goods and services; they wanted a way to mark wheels and conveyances as their own, a way to distinguish one from another. Ownership of the domestic animals Addias had explained how to breed; they did not wish to share resources anymore.

The idea of commerce was initially a temporary measure The Scientist thought at the time; imprinting stones and carved metals with the symbols of the chieftains would appease their restless spirits; Addias was appalled when he learned that warriors were slaying one another over some perceived value of one metal over another. Addias remembered staring at the elemental compounds of gold, silver, and bronze in puzzlement; how were these things worth a human life?

His brother had warned Addias that men would not understand the underlying process that he was offering; they would appear to be agreeing with him, while their minds searched for a way to use his gifts to control each other. Once they did, his brother warned, they would turn from Addias and create laws to bind each other with.

"They do not search for a way to benefit all of mankind, as you do, Addias," he said patiently, "Once they control women and name their children, they will only think of things and methods to benefit individual families, not the whole family of man."

At the time, Addias had scoffed at his brother's words. But not that he saw the men gathering with colors and symbols to distinguish each tribe from the other, and how some of them eyed the others with suspicion and not openness, Addias began to fear his brother was correct.

They will not heed my words now, Addias mourned, I will sound to them as a theory that is no longer relevant.

And what were these new words the chieftains were using; First Ruler, First Warrior, First Lawmaker? Addias felt his gaze narrow; he detected the influence of the one he called the Outsider, the being from off-planet.

What did the creature seek to gain from increasing mankind's fear of each other?

His sharp eyes scanned the gathering for the presence of the creature known to men as the First Brother and soon to be called The Magician but Addias could not find him.

It had taken the eternally innocent Addias centuries to realize that the creature who constantly came to Addias for his ideas and sciences was using his wisdom to dupe and control gullible men and women.

This gathering called the Council of the Four Worlds was no doubt his doing, thought Addias, and mused that The First Brother was wise enough not to attend where Addias would surely confront and confound his objectives.

He could not know in this moment that The Magician had removed himself from the sight of all men after his victory over the channels and co-creators. Most men now doubted the creature even existed, which made it easier for the First Brother to exert his aims over mankind.

Addias noticed Lord Master Theron and his protégé Lord Brayten, though he did not approach them. He felt Brayten's eyes on him, but when Addias turned to meet his gaze, Brayten turned away.

The Scientist tried and failed to mask his displeasure when his own group of people, whom he thought still embraced the wisdom of the feminine stood up to address the multitude.

"May it please the assembly," began Chieftain Enke of the Southern Tribes, "After much discussion among the male warriors of the assembled tribes of the Earth, we have decided to form nations with hierarchies of government led by men, not women, who will designate boundaries for these nations that will include rights to water and vegetation. We will develop laws to guide us in our disputes and dealings with each other, with the final say in any such decisions to be handed down by a designated male ruler, which shall be known as a king, and his descendants to rule over us---"

"Nations? Rulers? Kings?" sputtered Addias as he interrupted,

"Who taught you these things, Enke? Where have you learned such words and assigned the meaning to them?"

"It is not important where we learned such things, Addias the Teacher," responded Enke graciously, "But that we did learn them and find them acceptable in replacement of the inefficient leadership of women. It is no longer feasible for men to be unaware of the lineage of the children we sire---"

"And you, Enke?" challenged Addias, "Are you unaware of who fathered your lineage?"

"No, Great Teacher," replied Enke calmly, "But I am only one of a few men who are certain; therefore as a committee of men we have decided to give our children 'surnames', which is literally a second name to indicate the male who sire them. These names will be decided by the man, that may indicate his profession or an area of land he owns or even an element that is associated with his household."

Enke paused to acknowledge the positive murmuring of the males who turned to gaze at each other and nod their agreement; then he continued.

"In this manner we may determine and assign land to children born to us from one woman, who shall be given a title such as "wife" to show others that she is bound to one man. The man in his turn shall be called "husband" which shall mean he is the male band, or 'house-band' surrounding and protecting his home and possessions. Women who honor this agreement shall from that day of bonding refrain from siring children with any other males, that the husband shall know for certain the heritage of the child inheriting his possessions."

"This is an affront to the old ways!" shouted one of the wise women, who was next astonished to be instantly surrounded by warriors.

Enke continued speaking.

"Only men have a voice in this assembly, wise woman," Enke stated arrogantly, "If there is a male in your group who is able to speak for you, we will listen to him."

"I will not be silent!" responded the wise woman, "We have never barred the men from speaking in the council; what you are saying makes no sense!"

"Remove her," said Enke, and the gathered wise women gasped as the warriors laid hands on the wise woman, whose own warriors came forth to defend her.

"Forbear!" cried Addias in a loud voice, "You will not shed blood in a peaceful assembly. What madness is this?!?"

At his protest, the warriors surrounding the wise woman felt a hint of shame, though they did not move from their place, having been instructed to uphold the will of the males leading the council.

"Brother against brother," said the wise woman in a broken tone, "There can be no doubt of it, my people, we have entered the End of the Age."

"The day is coming," said another wise one, "When the enslaved will not remember how sweet the air was or how fresh the waters; the brightness of the trees—"

"And the children will ask the elders, 'What do you remember of it, in the days when you were free?'"

"Let it be a sign between us, when we find ourselves enslaved..."

"To ask and remember..." said the last.

She then turned sadly away with her people, who followed her from the gathering as the mostly male crowd parted in a final gesture of respect for the end of the old ways.

Once that tribe departed, Chieftain Enke again spoke to a silent assembly.

"I should like to suggest in addition to naming our new nation the Southern Arc, in honor of its Founder, that we should also appoint you, Addias, as our first king," he finished proudly to the accompanying approval of his people.

Addias was shocked by this proclamation.

"Enke, you know how strongly I feel that all men are equal," answered Addias. "That none is greater than another; I will not be what you call this leadership, this government; I will not be a king!"

But the people would not listen to Addias; they drowned out his protests by shouting his name over and over:

"Give us Addias, Addias the king, Father of us all, Addias the king!"

"Please, father," asked Enke under the chanting of the people, "All the nations will be formed thus, we have already decided, and if you will take this position the people will listen more closely to your theories of brotherhood. Don't you see, they will not accept any longer this burden of women counseling us; we long to guide ourselves, and we are better suited for it."

Enke's friend and brother warrior Riar also urged Addias.

"We will form them after the positive attributes you've taught us, Addias," Riar offered, "The teachings of the Four Directions and the Five Pointed Star."

"You have no understanding of these things," protested Addias, "Or you would not feel compelled to separate from one another!"

"Only bear with it a short time, father," said Enke smoothly, "If the idea is ill-formed, surely it will not last, and the men of the Earth will become restless again and return to the old ways."

This line of reasoning seemed to mollify Addias; it would not be the first or last time the scientist in him trusted the motives of those around him. Addias could not see how his son and offspring Enke longed to rule over men or the lengths to which Enke would go to accomplish his dreams. Enke knew that sooner than later his father Addias would tire of government; his long lifespan assured it, and as next of kin and Addias's recognized heir, Enke would be selected to rule in his father's place.

As Addias turned away, Enke and Riar shared a glance of triumph; soon Enke would be king of the newly formed Southern Arc, the model of which all other nations would follow. Riar would be Enke's chief warrior. The Magician had already given this position a name: High General.

More Precious than Rubies

The main kingdom of the Southern Arc held many smaller estates, for the number of royal princes varied from generation to generation. Prince Andron's estate, as the youngest son, was only a little larger than Amara's, and hers greater still than her younger sister, the baby. Many estates were given to regents and generals, some were set aside to be used for whatever occasion suited the king.

On the day the Southern Arc fell, Prince Andron and his wife were separated; she remained at his manse while Andron sought his parents to attempt again to make amends for his legal but acrimonious disobedience. To soothe his father's ire, Andron did not often bring his wife before the court, and he hoped this day to mollify his parents discontent.

But this final discussion never took place.

King Bokmal never relied on mages to do his dirty work for him, but he was persuaded by High King N'Goth's High Regent Sathdan to allow his armies to be cloaked for the most damaging effect. It was a strategy that both kings knew could only be played once, and N'Goth was mostly doubtful that it would succeed. However, the results were so devastating and profound that the High King later cursed himself that he had not considered such a move against the Kingdom of the Circle of the Earth.

By the time Andron arrived at the main palace, it was charred and smoking; overrun by red-haired soldiers and cavalry. The armies of the Southern Arc were besieged in their barracks; men were fighting and dying partially armored; for most it was a slaughter. Wracked by dread, the prince and his men bravely joined the battle; Andron determined to find his parents and siblings. He was met at the palace entrance by the kingdom's High General, whose eyes lit with relief and horror at the sight of the prince.

"Surround him, now!" the general bellowed at his nearest lieutenant, "Get him away from here, to the agreed place, hurry!"

"No!" cried Andron, "We must see to the king and queen, they're all that matters!"

The general gazed at the prince in compassion.

"*You* are the king, my lord," he said quietly, "And you must obey me now, that you may live to rule…"

The former prince's beautiful dark skin drained of blood at this statement; he shook his head in disbelief. His whole family, father, mother, and older brothers, gone in an instant of time? Grief consumed him as the faces of his parents, heavy with disappointment in him, hovered before Andron's memory; the opportunity to mend and bind his emotional wounds with them had now passed forever.

"What of my younger sisters? Please, general," begged the prince, "Say that they live…!"

"I have men looking for them, that's all that I know, my lord," answered the general heavily, "But now we must see to you, and your wife, is she safe with you?"

Andron could not speak for the terror that gripped him as his mind turned to the woman he loved.

"She's yet at my house, on my estates, with my child…!"

"Take over the defense of what remains," the High General barked at his middle command, "The rest of you, follow me, and protect the king with your lives!"

THE ESTATES of Prince Andron were protected of course, by soldiers and his own personal guards. Had there been any warning of attack, the royal family would no doubt be moved together to a place of safety until the threat was repelled. There would have been regiments and more assigned to their survival.

Princess Chayil turned in confusion at the sounds of men and steel on the lands surrounding her manse. Instinctively she ran towards the nearest window, only to stop in horror as one of her servants, who reached the balcony first was impaled by a flaming arrow. Princess screamed as soldiers and archers burst into her rooms to answer this attack; her daughter's wet nurse brought her child to her side and then fell on top of them to shield their bodies.

General gazed dispassionately at the upper level as he watched the archers of the Southern Arc fire back at his men. He surmised that something of value must be in that room; he commanded his own archers to stand down and directed his footmen to storm the upper levels.

"Do not slay any women or children you find unless I give the order," and his lieutenants nodded obedience. The prize was a great one; soldiers of the Broken Meridian flowed without ceasing through the shattered doors of the manse. He waited calmly until the sounds of strife mostly subsided, and he heard the groans of men dying; then the general grimly entered the building.

The princess had never seen bloodshed; she hid Arachon's face against her bosom and kissed her cheek to calm her. Her daughter, who had never felt fear in her short life, clung to her mother in confusion. She didn't understand why the people around her were striking each other and falling to the ground without moving again. Princess closed her eyes in pain as the guards she knew and thought fondly of fought to the death to protect her and Arachon. Despite her pleas to flee for their lives, they would not leave her to her fate. After selling his soul dearly the last one fell, and a man stepped through the door who the princess knew by his clothing must be a general. The moment his foot touched the threshold, his soldiers stepped back immediately in formation, there was no sound except for the breathing of their deadly exertion. Their eyes met, and the princess knew instinctively that she must show no fear. The thought of her child brought steel to her gaze, and the general felt admiration for her composure in the midst of such battle.

The general summed up the devastation before him; nearly every man of the Southern Arc that was on the estate had died on the upper level; that they had ascended the steps to defend this lone woman and her child was clear. While he looked around, the princess studied him: he appeared to be a man in his late thirties or early forties, his hair was still a deep red and thick on his shoulders. He was muscled, scarred and powerfully built, the princess had no doubt that he could fight and slay his way out of almost any battle. Her thoughts went to her slightly built, scholarly spouse and she tried to control her breath; surely if this man crossed Andron's path, he would render her husband a memory.

As though to agree with this thought, the general's eyes as he turned back to her were cold. The princess could not know in this moment that the only reason she was still breathing was because of her and Arachon's bright red hair. The general was of the opinion that the woman before him might be of the Broken Meridian, but he wasn't completely sure. The noble women of his nation were beautiful as this one was, but not soft or weak; his curiosity bought her time she didn't know she had.

From the side of his eye, the general noticed the gaze of one of his men, who then looked pointedly at Arachon's wet nurse, who was still trying to be brave as she stood in front of her lady and offspring. The nod from the general was slight but perceptible, the soldier brutally struck the woman across the face with his mailed fist and then dragged her unconscious body to the bed of the princess, who tried not to blink as she heard fabric ripping.

But as the general stepped closer to the princess to stare at her like an insect under glass, a strange thing happened:

Arachon turned in her mother's arms and impulsively struck the general across the face as hard as she could with her tiny fist. She saw him correctly as the author of this strange event with blood and bodies everywhere and she lashed out at him, this man so unlike her father.

Princess locked her jaw and returned the general's stare defiantly; if this were their last moments on earth, she was proud of her daughter's actions and would offer no apology for it.

Yet these two events had an unexpected effect on the general, whose eyes held the barest hint of both admiration and amusement at Arachon's display of force. He would expect a woman of the Broken Meridian to spit death in the face and dare a response. In an instant, he made up his mind.

"You will come with me..." he commanded quietly, "...and control her, if you wish for her to remain alive..."

The general turned and marched out silently, knowing with that threat, the woman would follow him. He heard her footsteps behind him as he walked; his men except for the one he'd given leave to, surrounded them in expert formation, their boots clicking on the tiles. He smiled inwardly as his mind went to the child he did not know was named Arachon; he would never harm her. He'd lost his wife to illness years ago; this highborn woman would make a good replacement, and the girl would make a fine soldier one day, if her temperament was any indication.

THE FORMER PRINCE beheld his estates smoking and burning; he could not urge his horse any faster without slaying it. Though his High General bid him wait as his men searched, to spare him horror, Andron could not listen; the face of his wife and child hovered before him, condemning him for abandonment at a moment when they surely needed his help. His feet grew wings as he flew up the stairs, stumbling over fallen soldiers from both sides of the battle; calling out her name without ceasing; stillness greeted him.

A mound of bodies met Andron's eyes as he tore into his private rooms, every person who served his household stared at him with vacant half-lidded eyes.

"No..." he choked as their names floated in his mind, "Oh, no..."

But his wife and child Arachon could not be found among the dead.

"Search everywhere, damn you," cried the High General to his men, "They must be somewhere hidden...!"

The former prince was overcome as he whirled around in his once place of peace; now transformed into a house of death. In hours he had lost everything, parents, siblings, his nation in ruins and now this? Was nothing left to him, nothing at all?

Andron fell to his knees with a roar:

"My wife! My wife! Oh, my daughter, my little one! Arachon! Arachon!"

The Mis-Step of High Regent Valgus

Young Prince Sienne came abruptly from his rest; the sounds of steel and struggle crashing outside and below his balcony in the Eastern Crest. King Bokmal commanded his High General to use catapults to encourage confusion and disarray among the startled troops and people of the Eastern Crest. Sienne cried out as a huge chunk of masonry struck the walls of the building next to his; the screams and cries of women and children assaulted his ears. He dressed hastily and strapping his short sword, and longer sword in place, Sienne grabbed a spear as he ran to defend his home. As a prince too far away from the throne to aspire to it, his lands were far from the main palace, as was the custom. Sienne's immediate fear was for his family; did an enemy attack from the outer borders, did they have time to respond and repel, where were his parents and siblings?

His thoughts sped to Yasir, his regent, servant, and fast friend. Although his kingdom frowned on magic for the most part, Yasir was not considered a threat, he had proved that on more than one occasion. As the prince ran the torchlit halls, he was shocked to find bodies of both soldiers and servants alike littering the halls; he tried not to lose his footing on the blood slicked tiles.

"Yasir!" the prince shouted and was relieved to hear his friend's instant response.

"My prince!" cried Yasir in joy as he materialized in the halls, "You're alive!"

The friends paused in their reunion as the building rocked from the resounding boom of the catapult meeting its target.

"What has happened?" asked the prince while his manse rocked and groaned; Yasir reached out and grasped Sienne firmly.

"Forgive me, my lord, but I must keep you safe!" Yasir exclaimed as the pair vanished. The sensation of his cells stretching expanding and collapsing felt strange to Sienne, as did the feeling of the process abruptly halting as both Yasir and Sienne were roughly snatched from the ether and hurled to the ground within the main palace.

"No!" cried Yasir; he had intended to take Prince Sienne far away from the conflict, but he was interrupted by a practitioner of magic far more skilled than he, High Regent Valgus.

Prince Sienne was disorientated; he gazed around him in a daze; when his eyes focused he saw his parents, the king and queen of the Eastern Crest, spread out unmoving over the steps leading up to the throne. The High Regent and High General lay dead atop the bodies of his siblings, in a last bid to save the bloodline of the kingdom.

The prince did not know he was roaring in agony as he ran to their still forms, crawling over the mounds of soldiers dead and dying from the horrific struggle. Mindlessly, Sienne shook parents, then siblings, as though this was all that was needed to bring them back from the shaded lands.

He faintly heard the voice of Lord Valgus in the background of his grief.

"My thanks...Regent Yasir, is it? For bringing the last of the royal line to me, I was unable to find him before now..."

"Please..." Yasir did not know what else to say; he had no level of force to match that of the High Regent; he watched in despair the power emanating from the man before him. The mage smirked as he raised his eyebrow.

"Please?" he echoed snidely, "Is that the best you can offer your king in this moment? *Please*?"

The word 'king' brought the former prince in shock to the present moment, hammering home the fact that despite his pleas the truth remained, he was the only one left.

Regent Yasir gathered himself, pulling all of his strength together for a final attempt to save his new king. He pictured again a safe haven and hurled his power towards the hapless Sienne who now came to his feet in horror.

"Yasir...No!" cried the former prince, who vanished in a wave of light as a now irritated Valgus lashed out, vaporizing Yasir, who spent his last gaze on Sienne.

The sacrifice of Regent Yasir was partially successful; the new king materialized in the forests far away from his home, on a path frequented by tribes of Wanderers. Sienne fell again to his knees, undone by the last hour of his life. He watched the fires raging in the distance, his people screaming in terror as the dreaded Broken Meridian ended their lives.

For him.

Sienne came to his feet, resolute. Should he cower in fear, while his people died for him? Would it not be far more honorable to die with them, to the last man?

"If the Eastern Crest ends today," he vowed aloud, "Then I end with it…"

Yet as the heartbroken young king moved forward, High Regent Valgus appeared before him, smoking with power and radiation.

"This time," the regent said grimly, "I've found you myself…"

He smiled slightly at the former prince, who drew his sword and came at him with a roar.

The High Regent simply transported them both back to the palace, where he intended to slay the young king on his home ground. As they faded from sight, a small group of Wanderers stepped from the shadows, four children, two elders, and a contingent of warriors behind them. The smallest one spoke to an elder as the distant flames danced in his eyes.

"Now, Mother?" he asked calmly, but the elder shook her head before speaking.

"We do not yet have permission, if any will be given…"

Sienne came to himself in the throne room of the Eastern Crest, his family in a pile at his feet. The faces of his High Regent and High General fell under his gaze, faithful to the end. Only a pile of ash marked the spot where Regent Yasir stood.

He knew he would not have time to mourn them.

He lifted his eyes to High Regent Valgus, who stood across and below him on the tiles of the vast hall where the last of the royalty of the Eastern Crest stood ready to die. It was the only time in his life that Sienne was glad Amara was not his wife.

"Tell me why you have done this, whoever you are," asked Sienne tightly as he prepared himself to vault the space between them, "Why you have destroyed in a day a nation, a family!"

The regent dared to bow to the man he was about to slay.

"I am Valgus, High Regent to The Magician, whom you know nothing of, my lord," replied the regent calmly, "...and I indulge you with this information for you will not live to repeat it. Also," he added with a flourish, "The Broken Meridian and I have destroyed *two* kingdoms, the Southern Arc has fallen beside you, all the monarchy is dead..."

The mage watched in grim amusement as Sienne's face contorted in shock and grief. All the monarchy...slain? His brother Andron's face hovered before him and the one who he most wished to be safe, the one whose life made his coming death easier to bear...*Amara*?

"Amara!!!"

Sienne howled his pain at the smirking Valgus, who watched as the young king gripped his sword and launched across the space between them, desperate to reach the one who tormented and mocked his last moments. Valgus, having achieved his objective of causing the young king the most pain he could inflict before slaying him, calmly gathered his power, ready to bring down Sienne as soon as he neared him.

In slow motion, Sienne beheld a blinding light come between him and Valgus; assuming the mage now attacked him, the young king strained to close the space between him and Valgus before his death, to pierce the mage as he'd just been pierced.

Neither blow fell.

Sienne crashed to the tiles beneath him as he spied a man appear in front of him, bearing the full brunt of the blast of radiation from the High Regent. His confusion shifted as Sienne noticed how the regent backed away in fear from the heat and darkness coming from the stranger.

"Greetings, High Regent Valgus," said the man tightly as the former prince scrambled to his feet and away from the pulse of radiation and power that dwarfed the might of his once tormentor.

"The Rook..." Valgus gasped, "What are you doing here? Does the master have need of me in this moment?"

Flames shone in The Rook's eyes as he answered his prey.

"It seems you've forgotten both promise and warning, regent," answered The Rook fiercely, "Thousands of years ago I warned you that The Magician eventually forgets all things except the coming battle at the end of the ages, and that his protection and his memory fade together...!

"No..." Valgus cried out, "No!"

The Rook's hands began to glow with power and Valgus raised his arms helplessly.

"...And I promised you what I would do the instant he forgot...!"

The young king covered his eyes as The Rook rendered his once irritant a memory; the screams of High Regent Valtus were short; a pile of dark grey ash gathered on the tiles at The Rook's feet.

The bound servant of The Magician breathed deeply, savoring the fulfillment of his dark vow. Then he looked about him in curiosity, scanning the death and devastation without emotion. When his gaze fell on Sienne, The Rook looked startled for a moment, then his face cleared as he seemed to find a secret joke amusing, one obviously leveled at himself. The young king crouched in a defensive position as the powerful sorcerer faced him, after all, The Rook was still a magician.

"King Sienne..." The Rook drawled his name as he studied him, "I almost have no words for this turn of events; did I just save you from death at the hands of Valgus?"

The mage chuckled to himself.

"Have no doubt from this day forward, Fallen Noble and future king, the mantle of destiny rides high on your shoulders. Had The Magician forgotten Valgus one minute later, you would now be dust, and perhaps my own fate changed..."

"I do not understand your words, sorcerer," Sienne choked as his thoughts turned to the love he lost, "My kingdom is crushed...I have nothing worth living for...!"

The Rook's eyes narrowed as he scanned the former prince.

"Valgus lied to you," he said flatly, "To torture your final moments. The Southern Arc has indeed fallen, but both Andron and Amara remain alive..."

The gasp of disbelief and happiness from a surprised Sienne rubbed a raw nerve with the eternally unhappy Rook; with preternatural speed he closed the space between them, his hand painfully on Sienne's neck as he crashed the once prince into the wall behind them.

Sienne clawed at the fingers tight on his throat, trying to breathe.

"Even now I feel his power drawing me back to his side," growled The Rook as his thoughts turned to his master, "The only reason I do not end you now is because I do not know how such an event may affect my plans; the things I want to happen must happen, and the things I do not..."

The Rook dropped the choking Sienne who gasped and rasped for air, his skin burning from the radiation in the master mage's hands.

"Let us just say that perhaps you too, as with Valgus, may make a mis-step..."

The powerful sorcerer began to walk away from Sienne, fading as he did so, but his final words did not.

"A most promising path to Amara lies with King Roe, Fallen Noble," offered The Rook with an edge to his voice, "But no doubt like Valgus, you will not remember my words..."

Young Sienne passed out from the agony, and the throne room was silent but for the final death rattles of the slain.

SIMULTANEOUSLY, scouts and regents poured into the neighboring kingdoms of the Western Hills, the Northern Walls, and The Far Isles with news of the dual attack on the Southern Arc and the Eastern Crest. King Roe, King Garrin and King Sumter all came to their respective feet in astonishment. The kings did not yet know that mages had muffled the sounds of battle in order to discourage assistance.

"Both kingdoms?" Demanded King Roe of the Western Hills, "In a day?!?" he finished incredulously as he read the reports. "Assemble the troops!" he shouted to High General Baynes, who nearly ran as he relayed orders to his middle generals.

"To arms," cried King Garrin of the Northern Walls as his servants scurried, "We must repel them and salvage what we can!"

King Sumter of The Far Isles, who at eighteen, had just finished grieving the loss of a loved one, spoke urgently to his High Regent Polymus.

"Summon High General Marcus at once," he growled, "If the Broken Meridian is bold enough to strike thus, we may be next!"

THE WANDERERS yet stood on the hills after the mage and Sienne's departure, waiting patiently while the twilight deepened. The Second Elder finally stirred.

"We have permission..." she said quietly; the children and other elders around her vanished, only the warriors remained behind her. One of them chanced to speak.

"How long will men bear the burdens of civilization, Great Mistress?" he asked in quiet dismay.

The Second Elder sighed.

"Until it no longer makes sense to them..."

THE WANDERERS SPLIT THEIR FORCES, two children and one elder apiece in each kingdom. A child appeared in the beleaguered throne room of the Southern Arc, a blaze of light coming from his small body as he pushed back the whole army of men within the palace, forcing them outside. A mage tried to repulse the young creator with disastrous results, he burned brightly as his own might returned to him to the third power; in seconds he was dust, blown away by the rushing feet of the retreating soldiers he came to defend. The elder and the second child moved in from the outskirts of the Southern Arc, pressing both the soldiers of the Broken Meridian and the mages who had previously cloaked them inward to where the recovering warriors of the Southern Arc could rally and defend themselves. Any mages foolish enough to attack the Wanderers suffered the same fate of the first mage, annihilation.

The rout continued: In the Eastern Crest, Sienne opened his eyes as a child kneeled beside him, having placed her hand on his chest. The warmth from her fingers chased away his physical pain and healed his cells of harmful radiation. He raised himself up to look at her more closely and saw a woman behind her, dressed in the clothing of the Plains. She waited for a nod from the child affirming that Sienne was well, then she vanished from his sight. The young king covered his eyes as the child began to glow with light; she walked to the balcony and descended it, scattering the forces of the Broken Meridian, and pushing them back from the wounded soldiers of the Eastern Crest. Mages came into view to frighten her; she calmly pushed them back as well, and when they attacked her... well...you might imagine the result.

The little one on the borders of the kingdom was having a more difficult time; an ancient sorcerer materialized on the battlefield and her concentration wavered. She tried to rally as he hammered her; this restored the confidence of the other mages who boldly joined the ancient until the child went to her knees.

A flash of light heralded the entrance of the elder behind her, who pulsed her light once, and all not wise enough to flee her died by their own fire.

"Forgive me, Second Elder," said the little one in despair, but the elder embraced her and shushed her fears.

"Only remember your Source, and not your own strength and nothing can harm you," reminded the elder gently. "Now come, let us shine light over all they have hidden..."

With renewed determination, the small one glowed like the sun; the elder smiled as the darkness fell before her. They pushed the Broken Meridian back until the enemy armies in both the Southern Arc and the Eastern Crest found themselves surrounded by the marching armies of three kingdoms, the rising dawn behind them glancing off their gleaming armor.

THE CHILDREN OF GHENT: ARAZON,
THE FIRST ANCIENT

"In relativity, movement is continuous, causally determinate and well defined, while in quantum mechanics it is discontinuous, not causally determinate and not well defined."

David Bohm

After the coming of the Brothers, creation soon began to feel the effects of magic on the planet. The First Brother endlessly roamed the earth, intoxicated by physical manifestation. His arrogance in determining that he was separate from creation and in control of all of it soon rendered him unable to stamp his will upon it. He could not admit the truth to himself, that everything he touched was affected by time. The First Brother could not do anything without it; and when he finally remembered that his brother was yet a part of an unending creation, he could no longer find him. The curious humans that followed him were as innocence in their ignorance as he was, and when he first tried to transfer his power, they died from his touch.

He did not understand death when he introduced it to physical form, and it was Paza, a Star Child, who began to discern what had happened to humans who were learning how to die. She, too, was innocent when she followed the First Brother into time; a place where all physical things begin and end. It was Paza who showed the First Brother how to give his magic to humans without permanently disrupting their now fragile mortal coil.

Mankind was designed to live forever; his cells renewing completely across all physical systems and structures every seven years. But as the body follows the belief system of the mind, man began to believe himself only capable of sustaining human existence for centuries instead of thousands of years. Soon, it came to pass that only those who practiced magic or followed creation could live pass two or three hundred years and those who attained a thousand years, or more were called Ancients or Immortals. Because creation required diligence and study if you were not born with the ability and magic only required a transference of energy from the First Brother, many who craved power flocked to the creature, following him all over the planet and bending themselves eagerly to his will.

The first Ancient was called Arazon. He was the first to harness power from the First Brother without harm to himself or others and the first to use it destructively. Arazon marveled when he attained the age of five hundred years, yet it was a time marked by bitter sweetness, for all those who could celebration this milestone with him were already gone. He buried them all, and when the last of his tribe breathed their last at a mere three hundred and forty years, Arazon felt a heavy sorrow. He began to roam the planet aimlessly, unaware that he was already considered a myth; a bedtime story for children. Now and again Arazon settled among men, the burden of his life a secret. He fathered children with women who frequently lived out their lives without ever seeing him again. Some he clung to, unable to leave until they, too, passed away while Arazon remained unchanging with time or season. Madness followed Arazon slowly, creeping behind him as he tried to outrun his loneliness through the centuries, then ages of time. When men learned who he was they came to him, asking his help and might against this chieftain or that one and he began to see a pattern to it; one with little variation. As soon as one so called enemy arose and fell and enough men died, another would be born to one day take the last one's place. Arazon lost interest in intrigue and battles; the tides of scheming men who approached him were often turned away.

The last woman he remembered truly loving, one called Milca, watched with concern as Arazon moved more and more slowly around their shaded lands, pausing to stare at nothing. He spoke to people who weren't there, some who if she pressed him about, Arazon admitted they were long gone, lost in a stream of time that he was becoming increasingly fascinated with. Milca came home one day to find her husband standing in an open place staring at the sun, which could not blind him.

He did not respond to her before the sunrise of the next day. Arazon looked down at Milca unseeing, then finally a glint of recognition came into his eyes and Milca knew without knowing that Arazon was nearly incapable of responding to human life.

"Milca?" he asked hesitantly as she stroked his face.

"I know you are going..." she said quietly, "and you will not return..." Milca caught her breath before continuing, "...if you ever think of me again, and do not recall my name, remember that this face...loved yours..."

Arazon embraced her then, trying to hold on to a feeling of attachment to her, to the home and family they had nurtured together, but he couldn't. Arazon was strong and his power almost unmeasurable, but he could no longer feel anything. Something nameless was pulling him; distancing the sorcerer from all those around him and for all his might, Arazon had no remedy, no answer for this ailment.

So, he surrendered to it.

Milca watched Arazon wander away from her, knowing full well that now she was a part of the time stream he would speak to centuries from now, as though she still walked with him. Their last offspring together, a son and daughter, would care for Milca until she died, still grieving him and their illusion of life together.

Arazon roamed the planet again for a few more centuries, finally stopping along a grassy plateau that overlooked a thriving young populace. He sat down on a comfortable knoll, overrun with flowering bushes and mossy stones. A movement caught his eye and Arazon focused on it; his thoughts distracted and wandering. After a while, the mage found himself entranced by the beauty of life unfolding; from the leaves of the trees to the animals and humans far below him striving to tame the fields and feed a swarming multitude.

He watched it all, the sun moon and stars the seasons and the tremors of the earth. Trees grew up around him and died decades later, and he turned his focus from the tiny insects on the decaying bark to the lands before him again. His thoughts ceased as rivers flowed over him and receded, birds would rest on his shoulders undisturbed. Arazon now saw nothing but still he looked, ensnared by atoms and butterflies alike.

ONE OF HIS SONS, six hundred years old and now a powerful sorcerer like his sire, found him one day; it would be another thirty years before Arazon shifted his gaze to look at him. This son cleared the area and built a shrine around his father. People came from miles away to gaze on the ancient in wonder. If Arazon felt the final kiss from his son on his brow he gave no sign of it; his child would become an ancient himself and die half a world away in battle with a young creator named Rior.

TWICE IN UNRECORDED time events on the planet were of sufficient disruption that Arazon unconsciously left his place of suspended animation: the death of the Initiate and the destruction of the twelve temples by Izar, and again during the great battle between the channels and The Magician.

Though stirred by the significance of these events, Arazon stood as mute witness to their unfoldment. He could not affect the outcome of either battle or rouse himself enough to intercede for either side.

A millennium later, Milca's daughter, also an ancient sorcerer, found Arazon through what would one day be called the bloodlines of mages. She had spent most of her life in conflict, fighting one battle after another, unconscious that her unending war was against the unhealed pain in her heart. Finally, her warlike ways caught up with her and her enemies dealt her a blow she felt was unrecoverable. As they built up their destructive radiation in sufficient amounts to annihilate her physical form, she focused her final glance on the horizon and the hills beyond. One ray of light seemed to distinguish itself from all others; a ray of pure green against a piercing blue sky. A feeling of longing infused her, and she determined that she would die there, where the ray of light ended. As she materialized at the source of the green radiance, she stumbled and fell at Arazon's feet. She would never know that a miracle occurred as she looked up in wonder at her father, whom she had not seen in millions of years, shifted his gaze and met her eyes. His throat stirred in unaccustomed vibration as he stammered to speak.

"Milca?" Arazon asked softly as his daughter's eyes began to mist.

"Father," she whispered, "father...is it truly you?"

Arazon saw his own blood coursing through the body of the woman before him and even in his madness; the deadness of his separated mind, he recognized her. The ray of light connected the pair from heart to heart, and the Ancient blinked; the first time in ages.

The horizon darkened as her enemies blazed into view, ready to deliver the death blow. But his daughter was no longer afraid; the thing she blindly sought for her entire life was before her, a final glimpse of the man who once loved her mother.

"Father..." she said again, as all conflict fled her presence.

She closed her eyes, her heart at peace as unbearable light surrounded her and a complete absence of sound.

Time, it seemed had ended and she could no longer feel her body. Still...after a moment, the sorcerer opened her eyes to notice her cheek against the ground and the grass waving gently. A tiny beetle scurried past her on some unfathomable errand. In confusion, she painfully rose up on her elbows and looked behind her, expecting to see her enemies halting for a moment to gloat before they destroyed her.

But she saw nothing.

She sat up then and looking around saw but the beauty of the mountainside, spread in glory, slightly marred in places by piles of dark grey ash. She turned to her father in alarm, expecting to find him dead or damaged by battle, yet he looked as undisturbed as she first found him, his gaze again vacant and unreachable. The ones who planned her destruction had preceded her in death. Despite their great might, in seconds, Arazon had rendered them, thousands of powerful mages to dust.

As weariness overcame her, she lay back down at her father's feet to rest and heal from her wounds.

Over time, the sorcerer would return again and again to her father, as her brother had before her. She brought children to see him, generations without number, but Arazon never again responded as the first time. She took comfort in the occasional glance at this descendant or that, it could not be predicted. One day she joined her father as her own unshakable lethargy grew past the point she could resist it; and she only longed again to rest near him. She pressed her back to his knees and rested her head against his thigh as a child would, an arm under her cheek for comfort. Instinctively she locked her glance as he did, on nothing, and it became her focus, as his was. The pair became a legend of curiosity as the years progressed and people came from everywhere to view the spectacle of the man and woman frozen in time.

Little ones brought flowers and seeds to plant that grew and died around them. Mages paid their respects from a distance; the story of how thousands of sorcerers perished for approaching Arazon's daughter was not easily forgotten. As the centuries turned, she remembered once how he rested a hand on her shoulder and left it there. It was then she closed her eyes on life for the final time.

Arazon was not consciously aware of his daughter's death; he simply kept her form from dissolving for untold ages. His protection of her remained of mindless resolve; sorcerers hoping to awaken

Arazon for future schemes died with their plans unspoken. Many soon learned not to approach the ancient unless his bloodline could be detected. One day, as all things, Arazon simply forgot her body was there and it dissolved in peace, sinking into the ground around his feet.

The Ancient had few visitors who could approach unscathed; among them were Paza, the ancient Starchild, who came to say farewell to Arazon before she fled the presence of the First Brother, who was now known as The Magician. Lord Enith, who was under the protection of Izar, who was first to learn from Arazon the fearful price of separation. It was Arazon who would show and prove to Enith that once an ancient turns away from life, it was rare if ever a magician would turn back again. His last visitor was Lord Master Theron, who brought his young protégé Lord Brayten.

The Cost of Conquest

"Fate is that which you cannot change. Destiny is that which you are meant to do." ~~~Anonymous

Over sixteen centuries before the birth of King Valtus of the Far Isles, the Ancient known as Enith brought low the Kingdom of the Sky Vault through treason and war. King Izhar was the first king in untold ages to push back against the advance of magic, and the then High King of the Unnamed Lands cared little for the intrigues of sorcerers. Yet when asked by Enith not to interfere, the High King agreed, and the Ancient filled his coffers with blood money, gold, and contracts for valuable land.

KING IZHAR of the Sky Vault died on the battlefield after a campaign that spanned five years. The usurper was Mitracedes, the son of King Izhar's father and a concubine. The king who fought to keep his lands free of dark magic was brought low by it; the entranced

Mitracedes did not slay his half-brother by his own might. A treacherous blow came between the brothers as they fought and Izhar felt his life's blood ebb from his body. Mitracedes lowered Izhar to the ground as the defeated king held his armor tightly.

"Mitracedes..." gasped Izhar, "By all you hold holy, spare my wife; spare my..."

Mitracedes removed Izhar's helmet and his head rolled awkwardly as his mouth gaped; the King of the Sky Vault was gone.

Overcome, Mitracedes held the brother he never knew next to his chest and wept.

THE NEW KING returned to the lands he was driven away from with his own army, bolstered by the forces of the Kingdom of the Rim of the Sea, whose king was also promised the spoils of war.

The people of the Sky Vault were silent as the conquering troops entered their now wide open gates, uncertain of what was to follow until they saw the Ancient sorcerer Enith stride through before the king's horsemen, his gait unnaturally swift and his robes billowing with power. Then the people fled the streets in terror; tales of Enith's ability to slay with a glance preceded him. The frightened populace now watched behind closed doors and windows. Although new King Mitracedes kept his face a mask to those who viewed him, inside his guts churned as he gazed about his birth home.

HIS MOTHER WAS his father King Zadok's First Concubine and as such her seed with him was guarded carefully, meaning, her offspring were either strangled or suffocated shortly after birth. The reason for this was centered around the acquisition of a queen. At the time of her appointment as First Concubine, her king was unmarried. A First Concubine could also become a First Consort, and possible queen, a dream Mitracedes mother cherished while she bore fruit for the man she belonged to.

Yet once the selection of a queen for his nation occurred, King

Zadok would have several options. Should his queen be found barren, the First Concubine's children would become the queen's and raised as her own, seeing that Zadok's blood was intact. But if the queen was not barren, the children of the First Concubine became an automatic threat to the throne for that same reason and must be dealt with accordingly. Mitracedes first siblings were allowed to remain with his mother while her lord and master sought his queen.

Yet in her heart she held secrets against the day her dreams came to nothing.

Mitracedes was her third child; the first two were female and she knew two things; that the king longed for a son and that with two female births, her midwives would be expecting a third. She bound her son as a girl child and presented the newborn as such and because there was yet no queen, the midwives moved on to the birth of another of the king's concubines. Mitracedes was given to a servant his mother trusted who later reported to the staff that the child had died during the night and was buried immediately as was the custom.

It was her hope of her son's survival that helped the First Concubine endure the horror of watching her daughters slain when the king married and his queen gave birth to Izhar, the crown prince. Though female, the blood of a king was in their veins; she pleaded with the man who owned her for a swift and mostly painless end for them, poison over strangulation or beheading. King Zadok, who felt compassion for her plight, granted her wish, and she held her children in her arms as they drifted to sleep, to awaken no more.

Even though this sad history was reason enough for the once general to slay and overthrow his father, King Zadok, Mitracedes did not wish to slay the younger half-brother who sat his throne. King Izhar knew nothing of how his father had treated his concubines; and fell in love with his future queen before an introduction to the horrid practice of concubines could take place for him.

It appeared only happenstance that brought the half-brothers together at the King's Summit, where Mitracedes was a general in the armies of the Rim of the Sea, unaware of his heritage. A scheming Lord Enith, who for many years had kept a close eye on the Kingdom of the Sky Vault, brought Mitracedes and his king to a secret meeting where the stunned warrior learned of his roots.

Yet the future king was a man of decency. When the general balked at the idea of slaying a man who had personally done him no wrong, Enith persuaded the unsuspecting High Regent Roane to use magic against Mitracedes and thus Roane found himself ensnared as well.

Lord Roane had refused to watch the consolidation of Mitracedes new rule. Roane used his forced magic to whisk himself away from his distracted master Enith and to the edge of a waiting sea.

But the new king could not flee as his new High Regent had. Mitracedes found himself in his new hall facing the regents, soldiers, guards, and staff of King Izhar. A recurring image of Izhar's eyes as the life faded from them returned to haunt the victorious king as he tried not to imagine the innocent blood on his hands.

Enith turned in subdued pleasure at the appearance of his once student and now ally in intrigue, Iroh, who nodded in respect for his former master.

At a glance from Enith, High General Eknath stepped forward and addressed the people.

"I am Eknath, High General of the Rim of the Sea. This..." and now the general pointed at Mitracedes, "...is your new king, Mitracedes, King Izhar's half-brother."

A soft gasp came from the assembled people, followed by quiet weeping. The general continued.

"You have heard the reports and now you know it is true; King Izhar died on the battlefields of Koa, and his brother has come to take possession and rule these lands."

General Eknath paused a moment to allow these last shocking words to sink in; then he issued a command.

"Step forward if you are loyal to King Izhar."

This statement was at first greeted with confusion; to name yourself loyal to the dead king automatically placed one in danger of an accusation of treason. After a moment, a woman boldly moved forward to stand in front of the High General. She held her chin up proudly and Mitracedes blinked rapidly as she calmly met his eyes. Several men and even soldiers walked over and stood beside her. A number of servants wiped their faces and joined her; one smiled tearfully as the woman took her hand. Soon regents and a variety of personnel gathered behind the woman; they clasped hands together and bowed their heads, waiting silently for the new king's condemnation.

Before the former general turned king could say anything, Enith crossed his arms and spoke.

"Archers..."

The people standing behind the ones who stepped forward screamed and began to scatter but the troops of the new king hemmed them in and forced them to stand in place. The soldiers grimly wielded long spears to contain the people and keep themselves from harm's way. Some of the more determined to flee the High General's arrows found themselves impaled and gouged on sharp blades.

The regents, soldiers and people standing next to the woman did not lift their heads; they already knew their fate should their king fall in battle. Though the servant holding the woman's hand pressed her face against her arm to contain her trembling, she kept her place.

The woman breathed deeply and stepped even closer to her waiting death.

The archers armed their bows and swiftly drew them back; at a word from General Eknath they released their arrows.

Mitracedes shouted.

"Stop!"

Lord Enith turned slightly in mild surprise as the deadly missiles halted in mid-air. All the people in the room except for Enith, Iroh and King Mitracedes were frozen in place.

"Iroh?" asked the Ancient, and his former student shrugged acknowledgment that he was the author of this display of power.

Then Iroh answered his mentor.

"Indeed, my lord, there are two people in this crowd whom

Mitracedes might wish to survive, if he knew of them, yet he does not, so he will have to answer for himself."

Enith turned to his pawn.

"Speak, King Elect, and tell me why I should not annihilate every one of these souls in front of me."

But the new king struggled to keep his emotions in check; he couldn't look at the frozen arrows inches from their targets; his face worked as Mitracedes tried to find his words.

Finally he whispered.

"Not her..." he choked.

Lord Enith's brow furrowed.

"Who?" the Ancient asked aloud, then his face cleared as he turned back to the woman in front, an arrow less than an inch from her frozen bosom.

The Ancient pointed at the woman.

"You mean her?" Enith affirmed, "Izhar's *queen*?"

Enith was honestly puzzled as he gazed at Iroh while still directing his words to Mitracedes.

"But you could have any female you wanted, Mitracedes; a pick of an endless number of princesses to raise to the Queen's throne..." Enith stated to Iroh's silent agreement.

"Not...*her!*" repeated the new king stubbornly as Mitracedes glared at the man who controlled him.

Then the Master Sorcerer's eyes lit.

"He's in love with her..." said Iroh in quiet wonder.

The Ancient scoffed.

"Your half-brother's *wife*, Mitracedes?" asked Enith incredulously, "Why, you barely know her..."

This statement from the Ancient hurled the new ruler back in time to a memory of the King's Summit. When Mitracedes first laid eyes on Queen Thora she was not with her husband. The new young queen was accompanied by her retinue of servants and guards as Thora roamed the halls searching for her parents, whom she knew had also attended the Summit. The general and future king had stood mute as Thora passed, unaware of his presence. Thunderstruck, Mitracedes dared to hope this unknown noble beauty might be within reach. Several days passed before he learned how truly hopeless his cause.

An honorable man, the general resolved to put the queen from both mind and heart.

Imagine the general's dismay even later when his king and a mysterious mage introduced as Lord Enith approached Mitracedes with devastating revelations of his birth.

Despite these miserable disclosures, the general remained resolute.

"Even if these events came to pass as you have stated it, my lord," Mitracedes responded at the time, "The king who fathered me is dead. The man who now sits his throne is a stranger to me, though my half-brother, and has done me no harm. I have no desire for things that were never mine, and these are not the actions of a man of honor."

He felt the matter finished as his king and the mage with him merely nodded and changed the topic. Mitracedes believed the discussion merely a test of his character and not a true offer. But a moment unrecalled returned to him, a moment when his king and the mysterious mage shared a mutual glance; a glance that the general now knew had sealed his fate.

Months after the King's Summit ended, the general was called to the palace for a mundane task, to oversee the transfer of a prisoner. It was then a regent in Lord Enith's employ named Roane approached Mitracedes and swiftly stabbed him through the heart with an enchanted blade.

The following five years became a cloud of blood and blurred memory for Mitracedes, that was only shaken by the sight of his half-brother dead at his feet and the jolt of recollection when his eyes met those of the woman who yet held his heart.

The once general knew then he could not watch Thora die while his arms yearned for her still.

Iroh speaking in the present moment brought the new king back to his senses with a jolt.

"Allow this, my lord," interjected Iroh calmly, "A queen is great currency, well above the worth of a princess. Mitracedes desire for Queen Thora is completely understandable."

"She will hate him, Iroh," countered Enith with crossed arms, "Izhar is her first love…"

The Master Sorcerer pondered this for a spell and then sighed.

"I can do something temporary to dispel such an outcome, Enith," replied Iroh, "At least long enough for Mitracedes adoration to take hold."

The Ancient conceded with a wave of dismissal, and Izhar's wife appeared by the new king's side as the arrows completed their flight and struck home. Mitracedes could barely restrain himself from stroking Thora's upturned face and sightless eyes as her people died screaming. But the queen could hear or see nothing, her gaze focused on Mitracedes, who now looked to Thora like Izhar, her lost love restored to her forever.

THE DAY FOLLOWING the execution of hundreds of people loyal to Izhar, Mitracedes came to his first morning court as king. His time with his new queen was full of mixed emotions; it was clear that Queen Thora did not know who Mitracedes was. When she said his name the sound of it was garbled; it sounded like Thora called him 'Izhar', but Mitracedes couldn't tell for sure.

Yet Thora did not treat him like a stranger. When Mitracedes reached for his new queen, her response took his breath away and the king discerned Thora was entranced. Yet his love for her burned his heart and Mitracedes knew he would accept whatever had happened if it meant Thora would not leave his side.

The new king was lost in such thoughts when his High Regent Roane returned and began the establishment of his court, overseeing the government and presenting his new cabinet, men who were eager to win the king's favor.

Mitracedes raised his head from a stack of parchment to behold Master Iroh entering the court with two children flanking him. Iroh paused before Mitracedes with his hands on the shoulders of a young girl and small boy, who looked up at the king fearfully.

"Who are they, Master Iroh?" asked Mitracedes kindly, "Are they children without a father?"

"They are, my lord," responded Iroh, "Although it is true that they have a brother who is the most powerful man in these lands."

The king paused as the words of the sorcerer sank in, then Mitracedes came to his feet, scattering the parchments beneath his hands.

"I have siblings?" the king said in amazement, "How is this possible?"

Later in his private rooms the Master Sorcerer would explain to Mitracedes how his mother had formed a bond over time with other women who shared her captivity. One of them suffered a period of time where her children died stillborn. On two occasions this coincided with the birth of two of the First Concubine's children and the women swiftly swapped their offspring while the midwifes handled multiple births. The other concubines children were marked as slaves and sold, but such chances could not be taken with the offspring of a First Concubine, and the women bonded over shared pain. The lower concubines were allowed to nurse children and raise them for a time until they were old enough to train and sell.

That Mitracedes's mother had managed to save more than one child was something that Iroh was unaware of ahead of time. The day of Mitracedes victory Iroh had impulsively scanned the crowd gathered for mass execution with Queen Thora and noticed the DNA of Mitracedes in the two children cowering against the wall waiting for death.

Enith found himself smirking at his former pupil's actions and remarked on it.

"You begin to grow a fondness for intrigue as I, Iroh," Lord Enith said with a smile, "No doubt the survival of Mitracedes siblings will provide much entertainment in the centuries to come."

But Iroh only smiled slightly at this comment; his future plans for the Kingdom of the Sky Vault did not include the king's siblings at all.

.   .   .

IN THE PRESENT moment Mitracedes quickly came down the steps from his throne and impulsively embraced his lost siblings, who endured his arms stiffly, uncertain how to respond, knowing it was death to touch a king.

The girl, he thought in wonder as he stared down at her, she looks just like me...

"Is their mother living?" Mitracedes whispered as he returned his eyes to Iroh.

Iroh gazed in compassion on the new king.

"Delay your morning court, my lord," said Iroh sincerely, "and come with me post haste."

The once general felt his legs were no longer steady as he swiftly followed the mage through unfamiliar passages in his own palace. The Hall of Women stood in front of the Hall that lead to the king's hidden treasure, as the people referred to it, where a king keeps his captive women. While Izhar ruled it remained empty, save for the women his father kept. King Izhar could not bring himself to have them slain or sold, as was the custom of some kingdoms, and the ones who did not wish to be married off to regents, soldiers or generals were allowed to live out their lives there.

The First Concubine of the Sky Vault chose to remain; not because she did not seek an honorable alliance, but because her heart still held secret hope that she would hear news of her son before she died. It was a slim hope, but she clung to it, even as her body began to weaken.

The staff and guards fell back respectfully as their king entered the shaded and curtained chambers, his heart beating erratically as he followed the sorcerer to the rooms of the woman who gave birth to him.

Out of respect for her station in life King Izhar left Mitracedes's mother with all the comforts she was accustomed to. Her bed was lined with silks and linens; servants cared for her and brought her food. Healers were summoned but none could help her; a life of constant despair and subtle cruelty had taken its toll.

Mitracedes had spent most of his life imaging this moment during childhood; as he became a man he gave up hope of ever learning his origins. The child in him sprang forth as he laid eyes on his birth mother.

She was still beautiful, her mature glory radiant even as the final blush slips from the fading flower. Lovely streaks of silver ran riot through her deep dark tresses and her son noticed how the more pronounced veins on the back of her hands resembled the fainter patterns of his own. The nose with an awkward slight bend near the brows and full lips with a barely discernible crook in her pained smile made the king draw his breath in acknowledgment; he had never seen a face so like his own.

"Mitracedes," she whispered as he neared her, and the king went to his knees.

"You named me?" he asked in agony while she touched his face and stroked his beard. "This is truly the name you wanted for me?"

"Yes," She affirmed tearfully, "I never dreamed you would be allowed to keep it."

He pressed his lips to her hand then, holding her fingers as though he could not release them; her other hand she used to caress his arms and neck.

"I can die now," she said with a sigh, "I have been blessed beyond deserving."

But her long lost son shook his head.

"Mother," he choked, "Mother, I've slain my brother..." and the new king bent down with silent racking sobs over her bed; she rubbed and patted his back.

"I know," she whispered, "I know, my son, and I grieve for you, for you both..."

His mission completed, Iroh turned at these words of sorrow and departed. The sounds of the weeping king intensified, now that Mitracedes had gained what he wished for at the cost of his soul.

.   .   .

THE FIRST CONCUBINE of the Kingdom of the Sky Vault died less than a month after her son's triumphant return to his birthplace. King Mitracedes visited his found mother every day until she passed away in her sleep, then gave her a queen's burial and a national week of mourning.

Both blinded by love, the bonds of the king and queen grew ever more passionate and soon Queen Thora was discovered to be with child. With a king sympathetic to magic on the throne again, the Ancient known as Enith moved on to more pressing campaigns than monitoring a sovereign's bloodline and finally Roane was allowed to appoint another High Regent, a skilled mage named Zayn and return to his home, the Kingdom of Everet.

Yet Roane was not deceived, he knew the one who controlled him would soon have need of him again. With the encouraging words of the stranger in his mind, Roane began to plan his freedom from Lord Enith.

One Dream's End

Some years later, the mage Iroh came again to visit King Mitracedes of the Sky Vault. As the sorcerer awaited his audience with the king, Iroh wandered the halls admiring the workings of glass goblets and vases on the long tables beneath the windows. The artisan was of passing skill and Iroh lifted one such goblet to the light; watching it catch fire from the afternoon sun.

He was thus engaged when the mage heard a voice behind him. "Why?"

Iroh set the goblet on the table and clasped his hands behind his back before turning to meet the eyes of the nation's queen.

"My lady..." offered the mage politely.

"Why, sorcerer?" Thora insisted.

But the mage did not ask the queen for the topic of her query, instead he began to muse aloud.

"There's almost a disturbing beauty in the simplicity of the word 'why', my lady," mused the mage, "an elegance in how it can be applied to the beginning of hundreds of sentences, even thousands, each one requiring but a single response."

Iroh paused at the pain in the eyes of the woman before him then posed to her a question of his own to answer her first.

"When did you begin to notice that the man you are now in love with was not your first husband?" asked Iroh gently, and the queen covered her mouth and tried to hold back further agony.

An entrancement such as Iroh's was powerful and sublime in application: Thora was persuaded that what she prayed for had come to pass; that Izhar returned victorious from the war and that her near death experience was but a dream. The illusion ensnared them both as Mitracedes heard his own name coming from the lips of the woman he loved.

But the people were not deceived. The nobles, regents, servants and soldiers looked askance at one another when they heard their queen call her new husband 'Izhar', and knew a dread sorcery had taken place, one they should not disturb, lest the author of it return and wreak havoc.

As the years passed Queen Thora noticed a gradual change in her husband as the features of Izhar slowly changed: his golden hair began to darken, and his form and features slipped away by inches into the features of Mitracedes. Yet the intensity of love in her husband's eyes never faltered, even as the eyes themselves changed color.

By the birth of her third child Thora knew for certain that her prayers had failed her.

IN THE PRESENT MOMENT, the deceived queen finally controlled herself.

"You entranced me..." She whispered, and to this the mage nodded.

"I did," He simply responded.

"Why?" Thora asked again in despair and the Master Sorcerer shrugged.

"I suppose the simplest answer would be because Mitracedes loved you and did not want you to die, but you already know this my lady."

The queen took a shaky breath.

"Izhar..." Thora paused to catch her breath again and continued, "Izhar was my life, and you gave me to the man who killed him."

"Yes." Iroh responded again.

"Why?!?"

And to this, the mage lifted a corner of his mouth then walked closer to the queen. When he reached her, Iroh leaned over her shoulder and whispered.

"Because you wanted to live."

Iroh smiled at her shocked reaction, then continued.

"I am aware that you did not know Mitracedes, my queen," Iroh said graciously, "and I know you meant that bold display before all others when you sought your death. Yet I also know something that no one else knows, including the man who was forced by sorcery to slay your husband Izhar, his half-brother."

The master sorcerer leaned in again to whisper in the queen's ear.

"Your first child was not fathered by Mitracedes."

And now the sorcerer watched as Thora's eyes widened in horror and her face drained of color. Iroh moved away from the young queen to resume his study of the fine glassworks on the nearby table.

"Do you know what your first husband's last words were, my lady?" offered the mage quietly. "I'm almost certain your king did not tell you..."

And the mage brought a display before the anguished queen's eyes of the battlefield that her beloved died on, and Thora saw Izhar grasp the breastplate of Mitracedes.

"Mitracedes," the king gasped, "By all you hold holy, spare my wife, spare my..."

The horrid scene faded as the devastated queen watched Mitracedes begin to weep.

"Your husband thought Izhar was repeating himself, yet I think you and I know better, do we not?"

Helplessly, Thora turned away, shaken to the core by the sight of her beloved first husband's final moments.

"So yes, I entranced you, my lady," Iroh continued, "But now we see that you were not so willing to die if your last treasure from Izhar could be saved."

The queen looked up at the sorcerer with a heart destroyed.

At first Thora had thought herself mad. Had the man she loved ever existed? Then Queen Thora recalled what she once believed a dream; that she stood before the general, resigned to die. When her eyes proudly met those of the usurper Mitracedes, she recalled a strange look in his eyes as the new king stared at her that Thora now knew was desire and when she glanced at the sorcerer Iroh, his gaze narrowed, then everything stopped and faded away.

Thora could not deny that without her husband's great love for her, both she and her child with Izhar would be dead. But an even deeper guilt grazed her soul. The truth was, Thora hated herself for loving Mitracedes, a love that, despite all that had happened, was still strong in her heart.

"He must not know, my lord," Thora choked out, "He must not know..."

"And he will not, my lady," replied Iroh calmly, "Mitracedes loves his firstborn son like his own life. But...when the time comes, you will give Izhar's son to me, and your second born, conceived by Mitracedes, and his true heir, will ascend his father's throne."

Queen Thora nodded numbly; her eyes shadowed by a pain unfathomable.

"Allow me to be clear," continued Iroh, "Once I have possession of the prince, you will never see your son again in this life, Queen of the Sky Vault. Yet know that one day, centuries from now, Izhar's seed will once again sit his throne."

At the sound of boots clicking on the tiles Iroh respectfully stood back from the queen, and the pages entered the hall to escort the mage to his audience with the king.

But as the sorcerer turned away and neared the doorway leading to the outer halls, Iroh heard again the voice of the queen.

"Sorcerer..."

Iroh wordlessly paused to await the queen's next words.

"Give me back my illusions, I pray you," Thora asked softly in anguish, "Allow me now to be willingly blind and happy."

Iroh lifted his gaze to the pages, who wisely fled; then he closed the space between himself and the Queen of the Sky Vault.

"You were always willingly blind, my lady," responded the mage in equally soft tones, "No matter how deep an illusion goes, there is always a part of you that will know the truth."

The Master Sorcerer sighed in compassion as the young queen covered her face.

"Despite the evil behind it, Queen Thora," stated Iroh kindly, "It was love that saved you, and saved your child. Accept it and thrive. Remember, it was also Izhar that wanted you both to live, no matter the cost."

With these words, the mage left the presence of the grieving queen.

KING MITRACEDES PREPARED for bed with a heavy heart. An audience with the Master Sorcerer filled him with dread, however innocuous the reason might be. Lord Iroh had requested a Hall of Mages be built near the palace and Mitracedes solemnly agreed to it. The king's scar on his chest throbbed while the mage spoke, a reminder of how determined a magician can be to ensure his will be done.

Unlike many kings of his station, Mitracedes often bathed and dressed alone. It was not only because he was raised as a man of little stature or even because he became a general. Many generals who rise to a certain rank can expect a higher level of creature comforts that men of noble birth receive.

It was due to the fact that a scar such as the king received was normally viewed on a corpse as opposed to a living man that Mitracedes did not easily disrobe before his servants. He was viewed as a usurper and conqueror; the former general did not wish to be seen as an abomination as well. Few nights passed that the king did not consider his life's path and the wide demarcation line between what he thought was the anguish of not knowing his parents and where he came from and the devastating reality of his new life.

Mitracedes remembered being proud that he had literally fought his way up the ranks to the position of general. He was a self-made man of principle who looked forward to serving his king and country; he dared to hope that the path of the High General might lay before him. To learn that his father was a king and that his mother had lived a life of such degradation and despair secretly mortified Mitracedes; he felt certain all his life that his parents were likely farmers or craftsmen who simply could not afford another mouth to feed.

He was lost in such thoughts as Mitracedes rose from his bath and robed himself, taking extra care as always to ensure his inner robe covered the wound over his heart before donning his outer evening robe. He looked up to see his queen enter his rooms, unbinding her hair as was her custom. It comforted him to watch her move about their chambers; Thora would never know how her presence gave Mitracedes the will to live on. Her entrancement was but another thing the king felt he must suffer for loving her; the price he must pay for wanting a life that he believed was out of his reach.

Yet he noticed a change in his wife these past few months, how she seemed to stop and stare at things that once before could not gain her attention; how certain objects she passed for years appeared new to her; he had watched as she paused to study them, a look of puzzlement on her face. The king wasn't certain why he felt these things, he only felt sure that the woman he loved was connecting somehow the past to the present and as she turned to him now, her eyes looked different. The queen drew close to her husband, holding his gaze as she placed her hand inside his inner robe, her fingers caressing the raised scar over his heart as that same organ skipped its beat.

He could barely speak.

"You see me..." he choked and drew his breath in pained surprise as she nodded. The silence lengthened in their chambers as Mitracedes experienced a moment he doubted he would live to see;

when his wife would know who her husband truly was. It took him a moment more to continue.

"Do you hate me?" he asked in a voice just above a whisper.

He watched as her eyes reddened slightly and she tilted her head as the queen mouthed the word 'no'.

"Your children with me?" Mitracedes breathed and saw a corner of her mouth lift at his question, the heartfelt foolishness of a man.

"If a woman loves her children at all, my lord," she whispered, "she loves them, whatever pain she bears their sire."

He tried to turn from her then in agony but the slight pressure of her light fingers against his wound bound the king to the floor beneath him like molten iron.

"Mitracedes," the queen said softly, and the king gasped at the sound of his name on her lips; he had always known in his wounded heart that before this moment she had only referred to him as 'Izhar'.

Every shred of illusion between them was now gone yet still the king feared to meet the gaze of his queen, to view her condemnation. He dared to place his hand over hers, to feel this last softness before she left him forever. He shut his eyes tightly as her other hand stroked his long dark hair.

"Lord Iroh showed me the last moments of Izhar, my king," said the queen as her husband could no longer hold his place; he strode away from her and to the window, grasping the curtains as he bowed his head in despair. Thora followed him and as she gently placed her palm against his back Mitracedes voiced his fear.

"How can you possibly forgive me?" he rasped.

"Forgive?" Thora echoed, "What should I forgive, Mitracedes; that it was love and not lust or politics that spared me once I was resolved to die? Should I forgive you for extended years and children I would never know or bear? Izhar asked for my life, a request you had no obligation to answer or honor."

Her soft fingers turned his strong frame back towards her and the queen held her king's face in her hands.

"Tell me the truth, Mitracedes," asked the queen, "Did you know me before the arrows from the general sought my life?"

He could not yet meet her eyes; he pressed his cheek against her palm.

"Yes," he admitted finally.

Her eyes brimmed as she asked one more question.

"Did you love me then, Mitracedes, once of the Rim of the Sea? Was it love or lust that made you ask for my life?"

Now the king met her eyes boldly as the moment the young queen passed him at the King's Summit flashed before his vision.

"It was love, my queen," Mitracedes replied fiercely, "A love I despaired of ever feeling, ever knowing, long before I learned who you were. I was but a general, less than nothing to you!"

Thora held her husband's face with one hand as her other slid back to the scarred wound on his chest, causing his eyes to close again in pain.

"Then am I bound to a man of honor," Thora said softly, "This wound you bear attests to resistance, an unwillingness to bring down a man that you knew also loved me, enough to beg with his last breath for a continuation of my own."

Unable to hold his emotions back any longer, Mitracedes pressed his wife to his chest, his arms enfolding the reason for sanity and existence as he buried his face in her hair.

"Will you stay with me, Queen of the Sky Vault?" asked the king, "Will you stay with a man who does not deserve you?"

The young queen's eyes shadowed as she gave answer.

"You deserve me, Mitracedes," Thora whispered as she now kissed his scarred flesh, "as I deserve you. I am bound to you by more than one oath, one I willingly honor, for I love you, as I was not able to love the one who bound me to you."

Thora reached up to stroke again his face.

"Comfort me now, my husband, as the man you truly are, and the woman I now am."

Wordlessly Mitracedes lifted Thora and moved deeper into their shared rooms.

. . .

SEVEN YEARS LATER, on the Crown Prince's sixteenth summer, young Prince Kalos fell deathly ill. The prince was running the hounds with his friends and fellow nobles when he experienced a great weakness; he slumped over his mount and his closest friend barely seized his robe and sleeve before the boy tumbled from his horse to the ground. A nearby cart from a farmer was pressed into service for him and his distressed friends brought him home, accompanied by terrified pages and servants. When the king's soldiers saw the banners of the prince they surrounded him at once, sending one of the pages ahead to warn the king and queen.

Mitracedes ordered a covered carriage for his son to be borne into the inner gates and rode beside it himself, almost unable to breath at the sight of his child pale and still in his robes.

Thora stood at the entrance to the palace; her summoned healers flowed around her and down the steps to the fallen prince. The queen's heart hammered in her chest as soldiers lifted her son and brought Kalos to his private rooms while healers rubbed herbs and salves on his arms and face. Unconsciously her hand drifted to her mid-section where once she had carried him; a woman's silent cry of remembrance.

The healers were able to bring down the prince's fever but were unable to rouse Kalos; he lingered for days between life and death.

On the third day his eyes opened, and the prince saw first his mother; a sight which calmed his fevered breath. When he spoke, his voice was raspy and cracked.

"Am I alright, mother?" the boy asked and felt relief when his mother nodded, unable to say anything aloud. The prince focused on her face and then she saw a spot of fear in his gaze.

"Where is father?" the prince asked with quickened breath and then turned his head at the deep sound on his left.

"I'm here, son, I'm here," his father said quietly and watched as his Kalos's eyes filled with tears.

"It hurts, father," said the prince, and felt his father's warm hand cover his, "I'm trying to be brave like you, but it hurts..." Mitracedes locked his jaw as his other hand cupped his son's face and rubbed his thumb along his firstborn's cheek.

"A man feels pain, my son," the king said hoarsely, "You're not less to admit it, you're a strong man if you do."

The prince trembled as he kept his eyes focused on his father, the strongest man Prince Kalos knew. He barely noticed as his mother rose from his right side and joined his father so he could see them both. Mitracedes felt his son's fingers tighten on his.

"I love you, mother; I love you, father," Kalos said weakly.

"Give him something for the pain!" his father roared without taking his eyes away from the prince. The healers whispered behind the king in great fear.

"We've given him everything, my lord, we have nothing stronger..."

The boy locked his eyes on the king.

"Father," the prince whispered, "I cannot see anything..." his voice trailed away in a rasping sigh.

Mitracedes pulled his son's limp body to him and sobbed on his unmoving chest.

Queen Thora did all she could, but she could not prevent her husband the king having the healers put to death for failing to save their son. She was only able to smuggle out her favorite while her king was occupied searching for and rounding up every servant and page who had accompanied the prince on his run with the hounds. She sent letters warning the nobles to stay away from the palace; Mitracedes jailed everyone else. The servants and pages faced archers and the axe while he worked out his grief over his heir's sudden death.

"He was counting on me," Mitracedes repeated with great pain while they were alone, "Do you not see it, Thora; he thought I could save him!"

"You're the king, Mitracedes," replied Thora in despair, "Not the

Creator of All Things; there's only so much you can do; that anyone can do!"

Thora covered her face as the man she loved roared out his agony and helplessness.

Soon enough, Crown Prince Kalos was interred in a stone house, as was the custom; his name and title carved on the outside and murals of his brief life. Thora knew she had to be strong for her husband and remaining children; because of the king's maddened grief she advised against the usual rituals and pageantry. There were alliances to be upheld that would become fragile indeed if the king executed nobles or regents in his rage.

Yet even while Queen Thora mourned in the private rooms she shared with her husband, her heart could not be quiet, and on the third night of the prince's burial, Thora cloaked herself and visited her firstborn's grave.

She had her servants and personal guard wait for her as she entered the huge stone gates and passed the outer walls of his rest. Thora only paused a moment when she beheld a soft pale light coming from the inner room, then she boldly stepped inside.

Master Iroh was quietly waiting for her, his hands clasped behind him as he stood over the marble slab where lay the prince's body.

Queen Thora took a ragged breath.

"It was you."

The Master Sorcerer slightly inclined his head towards the queen in a gesture of profound respect.

"Yes," he said simply.

Thora bravely closed the space between her and the true end of her happiness; she gazed down in grief on the child she loved.

"Is he truly dead then?" she asked softly.

"Only to you and your family, my lady," Iroh replied as soft, and watched calmly as Thora placed her hand on her son's arm and released a sound of dismay as she experienced the warmth of the prince's skin. Then the Queen of the Sky Vault began to quietly weep.

"I promised you…" began the sorcerer, but the queen interrupted his words.

"I know," she said after a moment, "It was simply a matter of learning if I mourned a physical death or a spiritual one, and in this moment, I cannot be sure which is the greater suffering."

"He will not remember you," said Iroh quietly as Thora lifted her head to stare at the sorcerer in stunned misery, "Kalos will not remember Mitracedes or his former life at all. It will be necessary for my purposes; I cannot allow him to seek you out, and this will be the best way to ensure that does not happen."

"Oh, my baby," whispered Thora brokenly, "What life have I given you, to deprive you of it with me?"

Lord Iroh allowed the queen to continue her grief for a time and finally he spoke.

"You have something for him; I will allow it."

The queen fumbled in the semi-darkness for a moment and brought it forth from a pouch she carried; a necklace of gold. Iroh smiled slightly as Thora adorned her son with it; she stroked the face of the prince and kissed his hair.

"Would that I had something of worth to barter for him," she mused sadly.

"Never deal with darkness, my lady," responded the sorcerer with a strange light in his eyes, "It rarely turns out well."

Queen Thora nodded a numb agreement; then took a deep breath and turned to go.

At the entrance, the voice of the sorcerer halted Thora's steps.

"My lady, you know this was the only way to keep Prince Kalos alive."

The queen was in such agony of spirit that she could barely look back over her shoulder at Lord Iroh; her fingers trembled on the cold stone threshold.

"And this, sorcerer;" she whispered, "Did I know this was my choice when I faced the general's arrows; do you believe I chose this as well?"

The mage was quiet for so long a time that the queen felt she would go unanswered; but as she looked away from Iroh, he did.

"Yes."

．　．　．

Twenty years after the death of Crown Prince Kalos of the Sky Vault, Queen Thora took to her bed, never to rise again. King Mitracedes, now in his early sixties, stayed by her side through the long days and nights of her passage to the shaded realms, his love for her unfading. Cullen, their second born, now the new Crown Prince, was the only offspring left to them, all the others married off in bonds of alliance to other nations. At the beginning of his rule, Mitracedes had kept his siblings nearby and trained them for positions in government or trades. But finally he sent them to other countries and outposts; he began to fear for intrigue against his son's future rule.

The king would never know that his fear of conspiracy would infect his Crown Prince. Once Cullen ascended the throne he would invite his aunt and uncle back to their former home under pretense of exalted positions then have them jailed, tried and slain.

But this was yet to come; now the king sat in his rooms with his beloved to comfort her and mourn their coming separation. On what would be their last day together, the queen asked her husband to send all the servants and healers away so she could speak the words of her heart to him.

"What will you do, my husband," asked Thora, "You who have given so much for love; once I am gone?"

The king scoffed lightly as he pressed her fingers to his lips.

"If you will not tarry and remain with me, my queen," Mitracedes mused sadly, "Then I must follow; and will our son Kalos not ask for me? I cannot live without you both."

Thora reached out and placed her palm against her husband's cheek; he watched in wonder as her eyes brimmed.

"Oh, my love, do not force me to seek my rest with this unspoken between us."

"Speak your heart to me, my only love," Mitracedes declared kindly, "Be assured my own heart will never change towards you."

"Even if I tell you that our firstborn is not yours by blood?" Thora choked out as she searched his eyes for sudden pain, and the king's eyes did brim but not for the reason Thora feared.

"I have always known it," Mitracedes gasped as the queen's fingers tightened on his.

"No…" Thora whispered to his affirmation.

Mitracedes brought her fingers again to his lips and he thought again of the son he loved without reserve.

"I suspected it shortly after the sorcerer saved you; when we were completely alone," the king continued quietly as his eyes glazed in memory, "You were entranced, and you believed I was Izhar; you had no reason to hide anything from me. And when you took my hand that night and placed it over your belly, I knew…"

Now Queen Thora wept openly, and her husband lowered his head to kiss her forehead and tightly closed lids.

"He was Izhar restored to me," Mitracedes whispered painfully, "A brother I could love without pain. I could give him what I could not give his father, his own life. I wanted him to have his father's throne…"

For some moments, the couple wept together, then Thora tried to catch her breath.

"The sorcerer…" the queen said in agony, but her husband softly caressed her face as he continued.

"I learned that as well, beloved," the king confessed as Thora gripped his robes in renewed despair, "Once the madness lifted a moment after his death and you came home one night and sobbed like you never had when Kalos died. You finally slept; then I dressed myself and went down to my son's place of rest."

Mitracedes paused again to relive the moment he dared to see his son again and found the Master Sorcerer waiting for him as though Iroh was certain the king would come. Indeed, the sorcerer smiled at the shadowed silhouette of the king as he stood at the entrance to the prince's inner rooms and drew his sword.

"Give him back to me, sorcerer," said the king with quiet menace.

The dim light between them looked eerie on Iroh's face as he answered the king.

"He was never yours to demand, King Mitracedes," said Iroh calmly.

Mitracedes stepped closer to the sorcerer and pointed his weapon at him.

"Kalos is the rightful heir to his father's throne," responded the king and Iroh raised an eyebrow in amazement.

"So you know?" Iroh said and then scoffed, "It is rare I find myself in a position where I have *overestimated* my abilities, my lord. How did you see through my artifice?"

"It doesn't matter, Iroh," growled the king, "He's yet of my blood through my father, and I want him back!"

"Now I see both king and general in you, Mitracedes," stated the sorcerer in admiration, "A pity I've already gained permission from his mother, who only agreed to it in order to protect you from the truth."

Mitracedes felt the wind leave his lungs.

"Thora...she gave Kalos to you?" he choked, "No..."

"I'm certain the queen wished to protect both her son and you from a rather difficult decision regarding his life should you see him as a threat to the throne."

"But I love him," said the king in despair, "and I never wanted his father's throne!"

The sorcerer sighed.

"I now retract my previous statement, my lord, in the face of such untruth; if you wanted Thora, you wanted the throne; it was the only way to have her, magic or no."

"And I have no doubt you love him," continued Iroh as the king drew closer to his son's unconscious form, "But Kalos cannot remain in your kingdom while you rule. I have agreed to one day return his seed to his father's throne, but by that time you and everyone you know will be long gone."

"Kalos was my only chance to know his father," sighed Mitracedes, "The only thing unsullied by my works; I wanted him to prosper."

"He will, my lord," conceded Iroh, "but far from here."

"You will allow me to see him," stated the king firmly and Iroh shrugged.

"He will not know you," said Iroh bluntly and the king drew his breath in sharply.

"You will allow it," Mitracedes repeated and Iroh appraised the king before responding.

"Very well, I will allow it," replied the sorcerer, "But you may not reveal this to Thora, unless of course you wish to increase her pain since she has agreed to never see her son again while she lives."

Silence filled the small room where the prince lay as one dead.

"Do we have an agreement, King Mitracedes?"

"What do you gain by this, sorcerer," asked the king as he gazed in despair at his son, "What treasure can be had by such pain?"

"Secrets, my lord," answered the sorcerer with a slight smile, "Secrets are the key to separation, and the guilt within the soul. An unwillingness to experience the truth is all I require to achieve all my aims. Now...do you want to see your son or not?"

"I will confess it to her on my deathbed," said the king resolutely and watched as Iroh shrugged again.

"Of course," he said wryly, "Nothing like a little word of truth before the veil, my lord. I'll give you a moment before I take my leave of your fascinating kingdom."

Mitracedes gazed with sadness on his last visit with his son before he lost Kalos forever; he pressed the fingers of the prince with his own, then stroked his face and hair. Impulsively, the king leaned over and whispered in his son's ear, then kissed his cheek. Then he took a deep breath and turned his back on both son and sorcerer.

As soon as Mitracedes left the chamber Iroh and the captured prince faded from sight.

The voice of the king's wife brought him back to the present moment.

"So you've seen him?" Thora asked in joy, "Our son is well?"

"Yes, a prince in another country; one we may never visit but for the King's Summit."

"We wasted so much time on lies and secrets, husband," said Thora weakly, "Had I but trusted your love for him, Kalos would be with us now."

"You gave him up for me," Mitracedes choked, "I still don't deserve you."

"But it was I who didn't deserve you," she whispered, "Who could have loved me more?"

Her husband had no answer for this; he leaned in to kiss her cooling forehead.

"Join me, my husband, my love, I need to feel your warmth," Thora asked as she shivered and Mitracedes quickly raised the covers over them both and held her. He rocked her slowly as she weakened then whispered in her ear.

"Let go, Thora, my love, my queen; let your spirit go where it wills to be; find my brother and your first love. Tell Izhar all is well, and I will be with you soon. Let go..."

When the queen completely relaxed against him, Mitracedes began to weep.

DESPITE HIS VOW TO follow the only woman he loved to the shade realms, King Mitracedes lived on another seven years. The remainder of his reign was uneventful, with only an occasional border war to contend with. The king was strangely unafraid as a slow weariness came into his bones and body; Mitracedes knew his long and troubled time on earth was nearing its end. His only regret was not feeling well enough to attend his last King's Summit, where surely he could see his lost and treasured offspring once more. His former prince was now a king of his own nation; not as large as the Kingdom of the Sky Vault, yet of a respectable size that his once father did not judge his life as a deprived one.

Mitracedes assigned more and more duties to his heir Crown

Prince Cullen as he found it increasingly difficult each passing day to rise and attend the morning court.

Unaware that Cullen had already drafted the letters that would seal the doom of his father's siblings, the king continued to sign ordinances into law, most of which would be repealed by his son as soon as Mitracedes drew his last breath.

With the special blindness of a parent's love, Mitracedes failed to realize Prince Cullen's jealousy of his older brother Kalos; the natural attention lavished on an expected heir to the throne. The future king felt guilt when his brother died, a guilt that increased when it dawned on Cullen that he would now be Heir Elect to his father's throne. The focus on his eventual ascension should have quieted his heart, but the lens of the past still held for Prince Cullen a comparison of affection, one that dimmed in contrast to the golden light that surrounded his deceased sibling.

On attainment of manhood, the rumors that clung to both the marriage of his parents and the demise of former King Izhar brought a crashing realization that his father was a usurper and his mother a prize of war. One day during a morning court these separate thoughts came together as the prince watched his father before his illness and Prince Cullen realized the possibility of his older sibling's true heritage. He felt his body blaze with heat as he recalled the love and affection showered on Prince Kalos:

Had his father actually intended to allow a child not of his seed to take the throne from away his true blood? Was Mitracedes blind or a complete fool?

But the thought he would not allow himself to see slowly ate away at his secret heart:

Who did his father love more? And his mother Queen Thora, who had clearly died of grief...

The prince watched with narrowed eyes as Mitracedes weakened. Despite these assumptions Cullen could not bring himself to challenge his king while he was strong enough to intercept his intent.

Yet it would not be until his father's last day on earth that the pieces fell together for the prince and he learned that Mitracedes and

Izhar were brothers. It was a day of mixed emotions for the coming king; his wife the Princess Elect was in labor with his first child, a somber reminder of life and death as his father faded.

Deathbed confessions were common in the kingdoms, and the prince felt certain that his father would tell him the truth before leaving for the shaded realms. But his spiteful heart planned to give his father a confession of his own, his shallow vengeance on his father's remaining kin.

A careless regent had sprouted the old gossip within earshot of the prince; that Izhar's father had sired Mitracedes with his First Concubine. Said foolish regent then turned pale as death when he saw the shocked visage of Cullen, who demanded his guard retain both the gossip and the unfortunate regent who had listened to it.

"Take them both to the blade," the prince commanded callously. Assured by the king's healers that his father may not last another day; Prince Cullen turned away from their cries for mercy. Emboldened, Cullen marched towards his father's chambers, ready to deliver whatever pain he could before the king could speak or hear no more.

But his servant intercepted Prince Cullen with news as he approached his father's bedside; his future queen had brought forth his offspring and according to custom no one dared to determine the sex of the child without the presence of the prince.

As Cullen hesitated, his father spoke as strongly as he could from his bed.

"You must go, my son," Mitracedes said with quiet joy, "She will be your queen and you have an heir to recognize; do not delay for me. Return with news of my grandchild; a daughter or son."

"Only if you promise to wait for me, father," said the prince sincerely, "It cannot be that we separate without our final words to each other. Surely you must tell mother of the fate of her favorite son."

Cullen watched carefully as his father's eyes shadowed at this comment; his heart now convicted of its own personal truth.

"I will wait for you," promised Mitracedes somberly, and the prince turned away to hurry to the side of his wife and heir.

The king's eyes misted as he watched his firstborn vanish from his rooms. As the veil between this world and the one to come began to thin, Mitracedes realized the pain of his eldest son and how in his efforts to make up for Izhar's absence from his wife's firstborn he had neglected his own child in some way unforeseen.

"Mistakes," the king whispered, "I've made so many..."

Mitracedes resolved to spend what time he had left to console the heir he would leave behind. He watched as the healers rushed to his side to offer balms and herbs to drink; he thought with sorrow how many lives he had taken in his grief; he could only hope his son in either rage sorrow or fear would not do as he had.

The king blinked rapidly, was he imagining things, or did his healers halt in their movements; had time ended for him without pain or awareness of it?

Mitracedes turned his head to his left in resignation as he discerned a bright light. It was time to go and leave all earthly things and tasks behind; the king but hoped for a final glance of Thora before all awareness faded.

There was indeed a figure next to the king's bed, but it was not Thora; Mitracedes gaze widened in both joy and dismay as he beheld his lost son, King Kalos, glowing with a light distilled from the sun.

"Fear not, father," said Kalos as he reached out to touch Mitracedes and the king felt the warmth of his fingers, "I have not preceded you to the shaded realms; I am here in obedience to your request."

Mitracedes could not keep his eyes from brimming with emotion at his son's words.

"You know me, King Kalos?" he breathed, "You know who I am?"

"Yes, father," responded Kalos as his own gaze misted, "I have remembered you and my former life with you and my mother, Queen Thora."

King Mitracedes shook his head as old guilt reared its eager head.

"Your father, Kalos," Mitracedes said with tears, "Your true father—"

"*You* are my true father," declared Kalos firmly as Mitracedes clung to his hand in agony of the spirit, "I am not blind to this; had Izhar lived I have no doubt he would have loved me. But it was you who held me and raised me, loving me without reservation, and it is you that I love, father," and Kalos brought his step-father's fingers to his lips in sorrow as Mitracedes took his free hand and stroked Kalos's hair, an act he'd been barred from doing for decades.

His breath rumbled in his chest.

"But you must not remain, Kalos," said Mitracedes anxiously, "Even as a king, it is not safe for you. My son Prince Cullen…"

"Cannot see me, father," responded Kalos with a smile, "No one can," and the king from another country indicated the servants and healers frozen in place. King Kalos gently pressed his hand to his father's long hair, greyed and coarse on his pillows, then met again his father's eyes, who gasped at Kalos's next words.

"You said, 'Remember me, Kalos, and if you remember me, know that I love you always, and bid you find me before I seek my final rest.' Do you recall saying these words to me father?"

"How?" his father choked, "How could you hear me, Kalos; the sorcerer Iroh had all but squeezed the life from you, and he swore you would never know me again."

"Though the sorcerer had indeed bound my memories," answered King Kalos, "faint and troubling dreams of you and mother have haunted me all of my life. A man and a woman I could not clearly see, fighting for me; trying to save my life, and a cruel man who would not release me."

Kalos sighed as he recalled the first time he saw Mitracedes at the King's Summit and how although he did not know who his father was, his face had both troubled him and comforted him in times of trouble.

"I would think of you at the strangest times; at least I thought so then," and King Kalos gave his once father a rueful smile. "When I was going through a difficult time with my own children, I heard a voice saying, 'A man feels pain, my son; You're not less to admit it, you're a strong man if you do.'"

As Mitracedes began to weep in remembrance of his words to his son before losing him to Iroh forever, King Kalos held his father's hand and recalled the event that had changed everything for him. It was during the last King's Summit that Mitracedes attended, and Kalos found himself looking for the man who had always affected him, the King Mitracedes of the Sky Vault. Kalos was accompanied by his daughter, the Princess Elect of his kingdom. When he found Mitracedes during between the endless sessions of government, Kalos approached him, noting how as always Mitracedes was cautiously happy to see him. King Kalos had long ago decided that the king's reticence was due to some obscure proclamation between their nations; he decided to respect whatever boundaries King Mitracedes had set forth. The evident joy in the king's eyes puzzled Kalos, but he was attracted to the man's company and now he wished to share an important milestone with Mitracedes.

"Greetings, King Mitracedes," said Kalos warmly, "Is all well with you, my lord?"

"Yes, and good morrow to you, King Kalos," said Mitracedes with his usual caution; his eyes fell on the young lady with Kalos, and the young king noticed how his pupils widened, "And who pray tell, is this lovely young lady in your company?"

Kalos beamed with pride as his daughter made a perfect curtsey; then reached again for her father's hand.

"I'm happy to share with you that this is her first King's Summit, my lord," stated Kalos with joy, "This is my daughter, Princess Elect Thora."

King Mitracedes froze, for a moment unable to respond as he attempted to control his breath. He blinked rapidly as he nodded numbly, and finally met Kalos's puzzled gaze with a tremulous smile.

"She...she's beautiful, my lord," stammered Mitracedes, "You must forgive my reaction; she has the same name as my late queen."

"Forgive me," responded Kalos breathlessly, "It was not my intention to offend you," but as an embarrassed Kalos attempted to turn his child away from the king, Mitracedes recovered and prevented him.

"No, please, I beg you, my lord, there is no offense," pleaded the anguished Mitracedes, "Please; may I?" and to Kalos amazement, the King of the Sky Vault asked to hold young Thora's hand, who flushed as the king of a greater nation knelt to take her hand and raise it to his lips.

"My lord," little Thora said as she should to such an honor and tried to curtsey again.

In her nervousness, the future king wobbled, causing both kings to move forward to steady young Thora, and their hands touched.

To Mitracedes, the brief touch, though welcome, was as nothing uncommon to mankind; but to Kalos, the contact sent a surge of power through his body; a quickening that jolted him; the young king barely heard Mitracedes next words.

"Do not fear me, Princess Elect," Mitracedes said deeply, "You have reminded me of something infinitely precious and I thank you both for it..." he hesitated as though he wished to say more, then thought better of it.

"Remember me kindly, I beg you," Mitracedes said finally, and his words exploded in Kalos's ears. "Forgive me now as I take my leave of you and wish you well."

The young king stood rooted to the tiles beneath him until his daughter's small voice brought him crashing back to the present.

"Father?" asked young Princess Thora cautiously, "Are you well?"

"That voice," Kalos finally said as his daughter squeezed his hand, "Those words...I know it..."

Over the course of the next year, the bits and pieces of King Kalos's dreams began to return to him, and one day, the words his once father had whispered in his ear as Kalos lay in his tomb came rushing back to him.

"Know, my Kalos, that I will always love you. Remember me, my son, and when you remember me, find me before I seek my final rest."

The king came to his feet with a cry of psychic pain.

"Father!"

The words of Mitracedes seemed to speak themselves aloud.

"When you remember me, find me..."

In a flash of light, King Kalos disappeared.

IN THE PRESENT MOMENT, Kalos felt his father squeeze his fingers and he looked at the man he had always loved.

"I'm so regretful, father," said Kalos, "So regretful to only learn my heritage now; to find you so late in life; to never see mother again or even remember her..."

"This had to be, Kalos," said Mitracedes firmly, "Your mother and I swore everything to save you. I wanted you home with us, but I see now this was folly," as his mind turned to his eldest son. "Promise me you will not tarry here."

"I won't leave while you breathe, father; please don't deny me this last moment with you."

"He mustn't see you," Mitracedes rasped as his strength began to fade.

"He won't," Kalos promised as he kissed his father's hand and reluctantly stepped back from him; the king's servants and healers moved forward as Kalos took his place to the side; invisible to all who might see him. The healers looked on the king in dismay and cried out for the pages to find the Prince Elect, who came running into the chamber.

"Father!" cried Prince Cullen in despair of his intent, "No!"

"I love you, my son," said Mitracedes in grief, but his gaze was not on the son of his blood, but on the son of his heart, his half-brother's child, who wept openly.

"I love you, father," responded Kalos in misery as the strongest man he had ever known breathed his last.

The Blood King

The reign of King Cullen, the son of King Mitracedes was one of the bloodiest in the history of the Kingdom of the Sky Vault and would be remembered long after the memory of the king's name itself was forgotten. In the centuries to come King Cullen would only be known as The Blood King. Following his father's death, the thwarted young king slew every member of his father's court not wise enough to flee the kingdom; regents, nobles, officials and staff, the hapless healers for his father among the first to taste the huge blade in his courtyard. Mitracedes's High Regent Zayn fled rather than die an ignoble death; he was a mage of considerable strength. He did not dare to strike down his former king's son; such an act would bar him forever from the kingdoms as a potential High Regent; it would be viewed as a treacherous offense.

The new king, now determined to learn if his brother really died or was saved by the former High Regent, attended the King's Summit. It was there that King Cullen learned two things of note: that his power did not extend beyond his borders and that he would have to answer for his actions within his own kingdom once High Regent Zayn sought asylum and reported Cullen's seemingly insane actions.

King Kalos, the brother King Cullen was so eager to determine the fate of, was wise enough not to attend the King's Summit on the first year of King Cullen's ascension. His memory now intact, Kalos was certain his once brother Cullen would recognize Kalos, as Kalos did him. And the young king wished to grieve the father he could not publicly acknowledge in private. Kalos suffered pain enough that he could not come in person to openly pay his respects. The burden of his secret weighed on Kalos as he spent time with his loved ones. As he watched his daughter Princess Thora interact with her mother, the king felt his chest tighten in sorrow.

"How bittersweet that in my ignorance and love I have introduced you to your grandfather Mitracedes, King of the Sky Vault, my darling Thora," Kalos mused under his breath, "...and now I cannot share with you why I loved him and why you should love him as well."

The Tents of Iroh

Lord Enith asks Master Iroh of his Intrigues with King Kalos. The Starchild is mentioned, Queen Thora, King Mitracedes and Iroh's plans for King Cullen. Also, the end of the age, and Iroh's preference for tents.

Lord Iroh was a Master Sorcerer who had lived more than seventy thousand years at the time of the reign of King Mitracedes and as such had obtained many dwelling places, most of them easily the envy of earthly kings and noblemen. Some he had built for him, others had human foundations that were augmented by means of magic. All were different; reflecting the times in which they were created; some of them even abandoned by a previous age and then returned to their former glory by Iroh's whim. However, one of the places where his former mentor could not fail to find Iroh was in a huge and ornate dwelling that consisted of a series of interconnected tents for lack of a better word.

Were you to measure these tents by modern standards they would be at the smallest ten or twelve thousand square feet, the largest of them over twenty thousand. Sometimes Iroh would create fire pits outside these tents; the inside were lit by magical means, because despite the immensity of them, Iroh was often alone. This preference of solitude puzzled his former mentor Enith, who preferred servants to tend to his every need; in imitation of the kings he both admired and/or controlled.

Iroh himself could not explain his preference for these marvelous places; he might comment on the sound of the wind on the fabrics or the pleasure he felt when he stood afar off admiring his handiwork. He filled them with artifacts and beautiful things that glimmered at night; his favorite time to inhabit it. Sometimes Iroh would simply stand on a hill above his tents or sit on a grassy knoll and stare off into the heavens above him; feeling a peace uncommon to his normal life.

The sorcerer did not remember that most of his life with his once mentor Rannea was spent in tents on the plains before what now known as Lorith Before the Sea. Iroh only knew he was happier there than in palaces of tile, marble, and stone.

As always, Lord Iroh felt the presence of Lord Enith before he spoke.

"May I join you, Lord Iroh?" asked the Ancient, and his once student smiled.

"You have little appreciation for this type of dwelling, my lord," responded the sorcerer as he greeted Enith, "so I confess myself surprised that you would visit me here. All is well, I trust?"

"All of your creations are finely made, Iroh, so I have great appreciation for your works. To answer your question, most of my intrigues are in a state of waiting so I sought your company. But where are your servants; I am in need of wine in this moment."

Lord Enith eyes sparkled in amusement as his former student opened his hand and produced a stoppered wineskin and an elegant fired glass in the other.

"This flask comes from a marketplace I visited today, and the glass from my house by the sea. I will serve you, my lord; I need no servants."

"My regents informed me of the death of King Mitracedes, Lord Iroh," said Enith respectfully, "I know you were fond of him."

The Master Sorcerer sighed deeply.

"He was a good general and a better king than I expected, Enith," said Iroh heavily, "...and you have repeatedly warned me not to become attached to their lives; it was difficult to stay away from his deathbed."

"Then you don't know what's happened," replied Lord Enith as Iroh's eyes widened, "His son Cullen has ascended his father's throne on a river of blood; the siblings of Mitracedes were lured to their deaths in their brother's kingdom."

The Ancient held up his hand in a gesture of forbearance at the sorcerer's display of power.

"Forbear, Iroh," said Enith urgently, "I learned of it too late to save but one of them; Mitracedes sister. I spun an illusion, so the new king thinks her dead. I knew you wanted to continue your intrigue with the old king's bloodline—"

"Not Mitracedes, Enith, but Thora's," responded Iroh as he caught his breath, "I thought it amusing to restore Izhar's seed to the Sky Vault throne in a few centuries or so, but I never dreamed of Cullen's discontent. Why would he slay his aunt and uncle?"

"Thora's seed?" echoed Lord Enith, "How? Prince Kalos is dead —" then the eyes of the Ancient cleared as he appraised his once student. "You saved him? Why, this is a marvel; far better than I imagined. Well done, Master Iroh!"

But the sorcerer was too astonished to accept this compliment as his mind turned to the new King of the Sky Vault.

"Cullen cannot possibly know that Kalos lives," said Iroh as his mind whirled, "Only Mitracedes and Thora knew of it—"

"Where is the prince now, Master Iroh?"

"Before I gave him to the barren king and queen of a much smaller nation, I erased Kalos memories that he might live his life out in peace." Iroh sighed again as he placed his hands on his hips and met Enith's gaze. "He's regained his memories and shook off my bonds somehow." The sorcerer nodded as Enith's eyes widened. "Yes," Iroh acknowledged ruefully, "It seems my lost prince has some abilities of his own. I've just learned that he slipped to the deathbed of Mitracedes unseen. I was in the midst of deciding just what to do about it; thankfully, you arrived before I left."

Lord Enith sipped his wine thoughtfully before he spoke again.

"Perhaps Thora and Mitracedes grieved the absence of Prince Kalos too much, Iroh," offered the Ancient, "Cullen would feel somehow he did not measure up to the memory of such perfection; this could poison his heart to anything of his father's."

"No," replied Iroh firmly, "Something is afoot—"

"This may be true," agreed Enith, "they're already calling Cullen the Blood King; he's executed hundreds unable to flee from his madness. Even High Regent Zayn has fled rather than face down the king's remaining mages."

"What?!?" Iroh cried out in disbelief, "King Cullen tried to kill

Zayn?!?"

"Is the regent important to you, Iroh?"

"He's under my protection," answered Iroh as his jaw tightened, "King Mitracedes nearly begged my vows; he must have suspected an outcome such as this!"

"A father knows his son, Master Iroh, even if King Cullen has no proof, if a rumor reached him of his own true origins, he may call all things into question."

The sorcerer's face suddenly changed as a thought occurred to him.

"Should Kalos learn of the deaths of his aunt and uncle—"

"He may be tempted to attend the King's Summit," responded Enith with a nod.

Iroh's face darkened.

"Would I had known that the son of Mitracedes was capable of such sublime evil," rumbled Iroh, "He might have been useful to me in the future; but now? One more mis-step on his part and I may have to place his aunt on the Sky Vault throne."

Before the King's Summit, the firstborn of Queen Thora received an unexpected visit from the Master Sorcerer, Lord Iroh. King Kalos granted his audience, unaware that it was Iroh who had captured him as a Prince of the Sky Vault. Lord Iroh could not suppress a smile at the young king's precautions of mages, regents, and soldiers; not a one of whom could prevent the Master Sorcerer from harming their king should he wish to.

Yet harming King Kalos was the last thing Lord Iroh wished to do.

Iroh graciously bowed to King Kalos, inwardly amused that the subjects of the king were unaware of Kalos's true heritage as the heir to a far greater nation.

"Lord Iroh," began Kalos," I'm told that you wished urgently to speak with me before the King's Summit some months away. Is it your intention that I should attend for some reason other than the usual, that my eldest daughter, my Princess Elect, should be approached for some tedious alliance?"

The Master Sorcerer's eyes twinkled in genuine amusement as he shook his head.

"No, King Kalos, as it happens, I am here on a completely different matter of succession; one concerning your father, or perhaps I should say, both of your fathers, King Izhar and King Mitracedes."

Iroh noted with some small satisfaction the shock that overtook King Kalos's body, the paling of his face and the tightening of his knuckles on the arms of his throne.

"Who are you?" Kalos whispered as his eyes scanned the face of Lord Iroh.

"So," Iroh continued quietly, "I was correct in my assumption that you have regained your memory."

The Master Sorcerer smiled slightly as the young king looked about him in dismay for the reactions of his subjects to this revelation, but everyone in the chamber appeared serenely unaware; in fact, they seemed not to notice anything at all.

"What have you done to them?" asked King Kalos.

"No more than you yourself did when you visited King Mitracedes on his deathbed, my lord," replied Iroh wryly, "A moment your once brother would have given dearly to see. As you know, your subjects will neither see nor hear what we say to one another."

Lord Iroh watched calmly as King Kalos came to his feet, blazing with light.

"And thus I know of your newfound abilities, King Kalos. Yet I am not here to test your strength. I possess thousands of years, eons, even, to your what? One turn of the seasons? No, I am here to help you keep your secrets; secrets that both Izhar and Mitracedes wanted kept."

"Then it was you who separated me from my parents; and a mother I would never see again? Do not pretend yourself a friend to me, Lord Iroh," King Kalos responded tightly.

"As the legitimate heir to her throne, Queen Thora gave you to me to save your life, my lord," replied Iroh dryly, "As your father King Izhar gave your mother to Mitracedes to save both her life and yours."

The Master Sorcerer noted how Kalos tensed his jaw and rapidly blinked to these confirmations of everything he had recently feared.

"What are you saying, Lord Iroh? My father Izhar gave my mother...I don't understand," the young king stammered, "I was always told King Izhar died at war..."

The Master Sorcerer did not respond directly to this statement from Kalos, instead the mage turned and displayed on the walls the sad fate of King Izhar and Mitracedes. The orphaned king gripped his robes over his chest as he beheld the man he loved as a father lowering his true father to the ground and heard Izhar's last words. Lord Iroh then spoke into the deafening silence.

"And now you know that despite all these complex precautions, the half-brother you once loved, who dined and played with you now seeks your life, in payment for the love you usurped from him, as the man you loved as a father usurped Izhar's life, love and kingdom from him."

It took a moment for Kalos to find his breath. His restored memory brought Prince Cullen's face before him, brotherly love and a younger sibling's adoration shining in his eyes.

"Truly, Iroh?" said King Kalos in pained wonder, "My brother Cullen seeks to slay me when I have done him no harm?"

"You have been first in love all of your life, Kalos, whose very name means, 'Light'," offered Lord Iroh. "King Izhar loved you before you were born; enough to beg his unknown brother for your life. Thora, your mother, loved you for both yourself and what you represented to her, the last part of Izhar, her first love. The father who raised you, King Mitracedes loved you for the same reason; as the brother he would never know. Even the parents I gave you to, this king and queen who loved you as their own, both barren of other children. Don't you see it, my lord, what else could Cullen do but hate you, who was never first in anything, not even as his own father's first-born son."

King Kalos covered his face then, undone by remembered separation from all he loved.

"Now you see the wisdom of all around you, King Kalos," continued the Master Sorcerer, "Do you truly believe that if you had remained in your kingdom and ascended your throne; that there would be no danger if your brother Cullen learned you were only his half-brother? A full-blooded sibling might have slain you for less provocation than this."

The Lost Prince of the Sky Vault rose from his throne and restlessly paced the tiles of his throne room, seeing nothing. Kalos finally spoke to keep his heart from breaking.

"So your audience today was to ensure that I would not change my mind and attend the King's Summit, where my brother would surely recognize me, and all your plans, and the plans of my parents, would be undone," said Kalos hoarsely.

"Surely you have heard the rumors of his already bloody reign, my lord," stated Iroh dispassionately, "Perhaps you were too humble or blind to see that you were the reason for his seemingly deranged actions. He will never give the true meaning behind it; such will warn you before Cullen learns if you live or not. Should King Cullen find out that you rule a nation he could easily conquer; be assured that he will wage war against you and take your head under any pretense he can think of."

The young king could not suppress a gasp at the implication. His legs would no longer support him, Kalos sat down heavily on the nearest bench, cushioned with tapestry and pillows. He stared at the floor as he rested his forearms on his thighs.

"My family," Kalos whispered as his thoughts went to his wife, his heir, and her siblings, "My heir, Princess Elect Thora..."

"How ironic that you unknowingly named her after your mother, Queen Thora," mused the sorcerer, "However, I sincerely doubt that will be enough to spare her life should King Cullen find her; she's a direct descendant of Izhar."

Iroh paused a moment then sighed before continuing.

"You should know that King Cullen has assassinated the siblings of Mitracedes," the sorcerer offered quietly.

"No!" King Kalos came to his feet with a shout; he had only known them as his aunt and two uncles; he knew his once father had adored them. Their faces as he had remembered them came to mind; both younger than Mitracedes; children his mother had smuggled to other women whose own young died in childbirth. And once Izhar took the throne, they no longer mattered.

"No," the young king cried again in despair, "He dare not!"

"His aim is you," said Iroh firmly, "Their deaths only served to abate his anxious appetite in the event he cannot find you. You have no power to challenge him, Kalos; your reaction is what Cullen yearns for; to drive you out from the shadows to the edge of his sword. Allow me time to anticipate him, my lord; I assure you; I am the one weapon King Cullen has no answer for," and the young king watched as Iroh's eyes darkened at this statement.

"My eyes have been opened by you, Master Sorcerer," stated King Kalos quietly, "Never again will I see the aims of mages from the surface only, from now on I will plumb the depths to see what lurks below. I am not deceived that your visit and warnings are for professional courtesy alone."

"Quite so, my lord," agreed Lord Iroh, "In this moment you and I have the same goal, the continuation of your bloodline. It is merely the reasons for such that differ between us, love versus the forbearance of evil. I have made promises to those who have gone before you to the shaded realms and I intend to keep them."

The Master Sorcerer made a perfunctory bow to the young king.

"My lord."

Lord Iroh paused at the entrance to the hall at a word from King Kalos.

"Will you speak of these promises to me, Lord Iroh?" asked the king, and the sorcerer suppressed a smile as he turned back to face Kalos.

"With your permission, King Kalos, I will reveal them all to you; it is my hope that you and I will have many conversations in the years to come."

His own face a mask, Lord Iroh did not miss the brief look of longing that crossed the king's face, a longing for knowledge of those loved ones he left behind as a child of barely sixteen summers.

"You have my permission," replied the young king hoarsely and the sorcerer nodded slightly.

"As you say it, King Kalos."

The hall sprang to life as the sorcerer faded from view and no one saw the strange gleam in Iroh's eyes as the mage contemplated his next move.

The Answer of An Enemy

King Cullen stormed back to his suites at the King's Summit, frustrated and angry. His father's former High Regent was beyond his reach, having obtained asylum from Khamis, the High King of the Western Hemisphere. The High King would not listen to King Cullen's smooth promises to do Zayn no harm; reports had already leaked out that Cullen had tried and slain his own kin, his uncle and aunt from his father's side of the family.

The King's Summit served the purpose of a governing body for the civilized kingdoms and a way to keep chaos in check. Even openly hostile nations attend and concede to as many ordinances possible within their own designs; to be barred from the King's Summit for excessive atrocities could lead to an offending kingdom being ostracized or worse, absorbed by a neighboring kingdom protecting itself from invasion. The new king learned to his dismay that his wanton destruction of his government had made both the Nine Kingdoms and the Kingdoms of the Unnamed Lands quite nervous; his terrified regents carried rumors of nations openly mobilizing and assembling armies against the Sky Vault Kingdom.

The High King of the Unnamed Lands was disinterested in King Cullen's concerns; he informed Cullen quite bluntly that he would not intercede for him to the Western High King.

"Your father King Mitracedes was fond of High Regent Zayn," stated the High King as Cullen's jaw clenched, "...and Zayn conducted himself with honor by merely fleeing when he could have slain you for executing his staff without reason. What is his offense to you?"

The High King watched with interest as King Cullen turned various shades of skin tone as he struggled to reply. The king, who was no stranger to nefarious doings, knew quite well that Cullen's next words would be a lie.

"As you say it, my lord," answered King Cullen tightly, "Zayn is a mage of some skill; that my father should die on the same day as the birth of my child is unseemly; I merely wish to question him—"

"Then Zayn has done nothing to require an answer to you without witnesses, Cullen," responded the High King bluntly. "I know not what you are about with him, nor do I care. He has wisely sought asylum among the Nine Kingdoms, where his soul cannot be purchased by you without trial or war. Therefore, you stand alone in this endeavor."

For a moment, King Cullen stood in disbelief as the realization sunk in that he was being dismissed. As he turned to go, he heard the voice of his High King behind him.

"The most important thing for any prince to learn before his ascension to his father's throne is not the domination of his subjects but the politics of the world around him, King Cullen," stated the Eastern High King soberly, "The aim of your focus thus far may cost you more than you know; your secret intent will leave you without allies and no kingdom can survive without them."

Remembering his manners, King Cullen offered a bow.

"Thank you, my lord," he said in a more respectful tone, "I will heed your words."

Cullen's mind whirled at the correctness of the king's advice; he could not bring himself to share his true intent with anyone; his shame prevented it. Therefore, who could trust him?

HIGH KING KHAMIS, who normally facilitates the councils of government during the Summit, along with a hosting kingdom, was not pleased to learn of the events surrounding King Cullen's ascension to his father's throne. An answer was required to these accusations and a good one.

King Cullen felt his heart pound as he faced a council of twelve stern kings and all their regents and generals. Even the High King of the Eastern hemisphere stood in alignment with the Western High King; a sign that what occurred in the Sky Vault was a grave offense indeed. Cullen had been wise enough not to execute his High General who stood at his side as a buffer to events that clearly marked the new king as a threat to world order.

To these accusations King Cullen had prepared an answer for his inexplicable behavior: grief.

Remembering his own father's reaction to Prince Kalos's death at the age of sixteen, the new King of the Sky Vault had pleaded temporary insanity following his father's demise.

"My father King Mitracedes was not dying of any illness my healers could detect or prevent, my king," offered King Cullen in a sincere tone before the High King, "Mitracedes died on the day my heir was born; I was devastated and overwhelmed by grief. I've recovered since then and find myself appalled at my own actions in the face of such pain. My new regents sought out the finest healers that could be found and they have helped me tremendously."

The High King nodded cautiously to this; he and his fellow kings and advisors did not miss the stiff and terrified faces of the regents and staff who had accompanied King Cullen to the summit. Khamis sighed; he anticipated that more clandestine pleas for asylum would be submitted to him before the end of the summit, and from this he would know the true weight of King Cullen's words.

"And your father's family, King Cullen," the High King asked, "Who were not present for your father's death; it is said that you accused them of treason; had them tried and slain. Can you explain your reasons for this?"

Khamis's gaze narrowed at the flush on King Cullen's face; clearly he thought himself above questioning, and the King of the Western Hemisphere made a mental note to keep an eye on such clear resentment. King Khamis remembered King Mitracedes and Queen Thora as wise rulers; how could a child so filled with poison have been born from them?

"They..." the young king stammered then spoke quickly, "I do not recall what I accused them of, my lord. Again, I ascertain it was a temporary madness that caused me to lash out at all those unwise enough to stay away. I promise recompense to whatever family remains."

The High King was no stranger to intrigue and he did not miss the sharpening of King Cullen's gaze as he spoke. It would be foolish indeed for anyone to step forth and claim bloodline of Mitracedes in Cullen's present state of mind. Whatever had happened in Cullen's kingdom he held some wrath for some offense of his father's side of the family. High King Khamis felt the slight stiffening of his own High Regent Nanos beside him and knew said regent would plead with Khamis behind closed doors for his fellow regent's life.

The High King sighed again.

"Very well, King Cullen of the Sky Vault," replied the High King Khamis, "I will accept your words of recovery. Still, your once High Regent Zayn will remain here with me for a few more months until the clamor surrounding your ascension dies out."

The brief flash of fire in King Cullen's eyes that accompanied this determination from the High King made all the kings react, however imperceptible to the incensed King Cullen. It gave the lie to all his previous words.

"Let it be as you say, my king," responded King Cullen with a careful veneer of respect, and Khamis nodded to his unspoken request to depart the hall. Once the heavy doors closed behind the Sky Vault's new king, the hall burst into loud murmuring and excited whispers. Khamis came to his feet and turned respectfully to the Eastern High King and his regents as they approached.

"The Sky Vault Kingdom is under your command, my lord," offered King Khamis, "and this hearing is reserved for the Kings Summit. Have you any thoughts on the matter?"

The Eastern High King crossed his arms and spoke quietly. "Cullen asked for my help to acquire High Regent Zayn," he said to the astonishment of Khamis, "But he would not reveal to me why he wants him so badly. All here know that Mitracedes was the usurper of the Sky Vault, but all of his family is dead; King Cullen himself has seen to it. Yet, fear nothing of me, King Khamis, King Cullen has no allies among the Unnamed Lands."

The two High Kings conferred quietly for a moment more, then the Eastern High King took his leave. He would not say however, to the Western High King what no one else besides himself and Lord Enith knew, that it was the Eastern High King who allowed the mage to overturn the bloodline of King Izhar for his own gain. The king hoped King Cullen would truly heed his warning; for if the Blood King learned of his secret intrigue, the King of the Unnamed Lands would be forced to end the bloodline of Mitracedes himself.

"Watch King Cullen's staff closely," commanded King Khamis quietly to his regents, "Keep an eye for regents wandering aimlessly between meetings; I've a feeling more will come forth in fear of their lives."

As his own High Regent leaned in, High King Khamis spoke sharply under his breath.

"You're certain his High Regent has no inkling of the reasoning behind such wanton slaughter? There has to be a purpose to it!"

High Regent Nanos shook his head helplessly.

"It seems to support King Cullen's claim of madness, my lord," said Nanos, "All High Regent Zayn knows is that two regents were executed only hours before King Mitracedes died and Zayn doesn't know why."

Khamis thoughtfully stroked his beard.

"If they were killed before Mitracedes died then it was not madness, my regent, but some thwarted purpose. Find out if the men who carried out the execution are yet alive and if they heard any confessions of the regents."

"And if all are dead, my king?" asked Nanos quietly.

"Then something evil indeed is afoot, my regent," responded the High King, "Perhaps King Mitracedes did not die a normal death after all."

. . .

BEFORE KING CULLEN retired for bed he summoned one of his mages, Titus by name to his inner chambers. The mage was stunned by the king's offer of wine. Titus was being treated as an equal, and the mage couldn't help the bright flash of hope that sprang into his eyes, a hope of recognition or promotion within the ranks of mages under the king. Titus knew that his king had been faintly disappointed by Titus's failure to ensnare Zayn, yet Cullen realized that Zayn was too powerful for Titus and his fellows to capture. Not without assistance...

"My king," said the mage as he hurried to refill the king's cup.

"Titus," responded King Cullen, "I have an assignment of grave importance for you that now requires me to bring you into my confidence. I was unable to fully disclose at the onset why I wished for you to attend High Regent Zayn rather than summon him into my presence myself--"

The king paused at these words to allow the weight of them to sink in and watched as his regent stiffened at the phrase 'into my confidence'. Cullen surmised correctly that Titus was a man of ambition and to have the ear of his king was of utmost importance to him. Pride filled the regent's eyes and King Cullen continued, sure that his next communication would be accepted by Titus without prejudice or caution.

"IT HAS COME to my attention that the death of my older brother, the former Crown Prince Kalos was not due to the whims of fate, Regent Titus, but an intrigue among magicians."

"No, my lord," cried out Titus in dismay, "Not the prince!"

Though Regent Titus had been appointed to the Kingdom of the Sky Vault after the death and burial of Crown Prince Kalos, he remembered well how the people loved him, carrying out their national mourning for months afterward. His mind reeled at the memory of how calm Zayn appeared beneath his cover of grief; could it be possible he was behind it; who could not be moved by the devastated king and queen?

"As you know, High Regent Zayn fled rather than answer this revealed information and I will not rest until the ones responsible for my brother's demise are found and punished."

"Speak, my king," said Regent Titus darkly, "Make known to me your will that I might fulfill it to the letter."

HIGH REGENT ZAYN sighed deeply as he prepared for his rest; he doubted that he would be able to sleep. He was required by law to face the king he had requested asylum from and speak of what little he knew as to why Zayn felt compelled to flee for his life from the prince who had succeeded to Mitracedes's throne.

The High Regent recalled being forced to stand by helplessly as the new king ordered the deaths of the healers and practically everyone in the room where King Mitracedes breathed his last. Zayn had resolved to speak with the grieving king in private; he remembered sadly how Mitracedes himself had reacted to the death of Crown Prince Kalos. It was Zayn who helped Queen Thora save her favorite healer from certain death and then issued a warning to all others to leave the courts of the king immediately. Yet even Mitracedes had been willing to listen to Zayn; the once High Regent of the Sky Vault remembered well the look in King Cullen's eyes as he gripped his father's robes; it was not the gaze of a man grieving his father's death. Instead it seemed to Zayn that Cullen felt cheated of something; Zayn couldn't shake the idea that it was desperation, not sorrow that caused the new king to roar at his father's corpse.

Still, High Regent Zayn was stunned when his loyal regent burst into his rooms at the palace late at night to warn him that she had overheard the new king asking Regent Titus if he was strong enough to overpower Zayn.

The High Regent immediately encircled himself and the regent in a nimbus of light; once the regent realized what was happening she cried out.

"We cannot leave, my lord, King Cullen has imprisoned his aunt and uncle without cause; we must assist them!"

The regent shook his head grimly.

"We but linger to die, regent. If the king seeks my life, he has already gathered magical aid to oppose us; we cannot save them alone."

Less than moments after their departure, Regent Titus entered his suites accompanied by fellow mages and soldiers. Titus had expected Zayn to stand his ground as High Regent and insist on speaking with the new king; he knew Zayn was not afraid of him. Titus did not have the strength to contain his superior; he had no idea until that very second that Zayn had been warned of his intent.

Zayn knew he was able to defeat any of the mages under King Cullen, it was one of the reasons he had risen to the position of High Regent of the Sky Vault. The reason Zayn fled rather than face down a group of ambitious mages was because of who they might in turn summon to assist them. There exists organizations of mages behind every throne that most kings are ignorant of; at times there can be many mages and sorcerers who answer to more than one hierarchy of magicians. And at the top of most organizations worth mentioning there was usually an Ancient.

Although it was true that Ancients rarely stooped to meddle in the squabbles of lower and mid-level sorcerers, there was always the chance that some intrigue Zayn was not aware of could be at work. Zayn was under the protection of Master Idalia, a sorcerer more powerful than himself. Still, Idalia was not an Ancient, and the former High Regent felt it wise to retreat and give himself time to learn the reasons behind King Cullen's sudden bloodlust. Time Zayn would have lost forever if he battled his once subservient mages only to face an Ancient, undoubtably irritated to be disturbed from more important matters of personal intrigue.

The balance of power between kings and mages was a delicate one, upheld by each one's need for the other. Despite what one would think, men follow kings, men like themselves and not sorcerers, men who wield forces a normal man cannot fathom or understand. This is why for the most part, a kingdom would never accept a Magician King as a ruler, no matter what the obvious advantage would seem to be. And men of magic, who rely on intrigue for survival through the ages would be hard pressed to focus on one kingdom alone as the source of all their efforts.

Thus it came about that Zayn was unsettled for many reasons as he finally drew the covers over his shoulders and closed his eyes. Master Idalia had assured Zayn that temporary asylum with High King Khamis was the best option. Out of respect for the High King alone most mages would pause before attacking Lord Zayn and the King's Summit itself was a place of cease fire for both men and mages. Idalia would thus have time to uncover the possible intrigue surrounding King Cullen and secure Zayn's safe passage through the kingdoms.

Most of all, Master Idalia reminded Zayn of the greatest law between mages: No unprovoked attack on a mage under another mage's tutelage or protection.

Ironically, despite the pit in his stomach, Zayn fell into a deep sleep almost as soon as his eyes closed. And by doing so, High Regent Zayn missed the most important battle of his existence. Barely one turn of an hour after falling into misted dreams the Master Sorcerer Iroh appeared in Zayn's bedchamber. Lord Iroh was highly annoyed to be interrupted by the instantaneous summons of a disrupted field of energy surrounding the hapless and unaware Zayn. Iroh took a deep breath as he gazed around the room at the 'insects' caught in his magical spider's web, a group of terrified mages who erroneously thought themselves on a simple errand of assassination. He briefly studied the energy signatures around each one as he rendered them to dust, sending a blast of light through the bloodlines to their masters, who died ignorant of their pupil's folly.

Iroh only paused as he gazed at the last one, the leader of them, Titus, who cried out in terror.

"Mercy, master," Titus pleaded with widened eyes, "I was unaware of your intrigue!"

"That's not the reason you're still breathing," responded Iroh dryly, and crossed his arms as Idalia appeared in dismay at Zayn's bedside, clearly an instant too slow to protect her charge.

"Master Iroh," Idalia declared breathlessly to his nod; her tone of voice sounded thankful and apologetic at the same time.

"Master Idalia," Iroh responded and watched as her eyes darkened as she gazed on Titus.

"My lord," Idalia said respectfully, "Mage Titus has attacked a mage under my protection; may I ask why he still breathes?"

"Consider his bloodline, Master Idalia," replied Lord Iroh calmly, "Even Titus does not know the root of it."

Bemused, Master Idalia gazed at the bloodline of Titus and first saw Lord Gryffin, a mage of passing skill, but no real match for her. Still, she saw a unique aura surrounding both mages so Idalia allowed her search to speed through the bloodline of Titus. Seconds later, Idalia gasped, just as the Ancient known as Arioch came into view, followed by Titus's master, Lord Gryffin. Mage Titus's silent cry for help brought Lord Gryffin, who instantly sent his own call for assistance as Gryffin sensed the depths of Lord Iroh's power. Arioch was obliged to respond, an imposition he did not take lightly; his displeasure could result in instantaneous death.

The look of irritation on Arioch's face faded as his eyes fell on first Idalia and then Iroh, a look which turned into astonishment as Arioch gazed on High Regent Zayn, who was clearly the source of this intrigue of magicians. Idalia blinked rapidly to contain her fear; she knew she could not protect Zayn, nor even herself from Arioch; an unfamiliar taste of bile filled her throat.

Master Iroh, however gazed at Arioch calmly as he nodded his respect, as did Idalia.

"May I speak, my lord?" Idalia asked bravely, but the powerful Ancient shook his head.

"Unnecessary, Master Idalia," answered Arioch gravely, "The presence of Master Iroh is all the information I require. Iroh is the direct bloodline of Lord Enith, an Ancient like me and we do not inquire into another Ancient's intrigues and affairs."

The Ancient turned a withering eye on his mage Lord Gryffin, who spoke the only words he knew he was allowed to say.

"Mercy, my lord, King Cullen has deceived us—"

"It is Titus who has deceived you, Lord Gryffin," interrupted Arioch, "This may be the last lesson you learn from me; use caution in the defense of a student..."

Lord Arioch turned to Master Iroh.

"Is it your wish, Lord Iroh," asked Arioch slowly, "That this meeting remain a secret?"

"With the exception of Master Idalia, my lord," responded Iroh earnestly, and watched Lord Gryffin and his terrified pupil Regent Titus pale as this death sentence was quietly rendered on their lives. Iroh knew that if he had not included Idalia, the Ancient known as Arioch would have vaporized her in seconds.

"As you say it, my lord," replied Arioch, "Do give Lord Enith my regards."

"It shall be done. My sincere thanks, Lord Arioch," the Master Sorcerer said as he bowed his head respectfully and Master Idalia quickly followed suit.

The Ancient known as Arioch was alone as he returned to more pressing matters than the fatal mistakes of lower level mages in his organization.

"I am in your debt, Lord Iroh," said Idalia quietly as she gazed on the small piles of grey ash that used to be human beings.

"Yes, you are," acknowledged Iroh soberly, "But your death would have been a waste, and little comfort to Lord Zayn, who no doubt would follow you to the shaded realms."

Iroh paused thoughtfully before speaking again.

"Does Zayn know anything?" Iroh asked and watched Idalia shake her head at how close she and Zayn had both come to dying for an intrigue they knew nothing of.

"It seems random and insane, quite frankly," a mystified Idalia responded. "Zayn only knew that King Cullen had two regents slain for no reason just before his father King Mitracedes passed away; it was enough to alert him to look after his own life. The old king died just after the future queen gave birth to a daughter; Cullen rushed to his father's side; too late, we were told. Following this, Zayn said the new king just started executing everybody. It was not meet in that moment to destroy King Cullen; I needed Lord Zayn to remain eligible as a High Regent for my own intrigues. Thus it was I who advised Zayn to seek out the High King; I thought Cullen was mad from grief."

Iroh sighed deeply as he turned to gaze on the soundly sleeping former High Regent.

"King Cullen has forced my hand, Idalia," mused Iroh, "We are both in agreement that Zayn must live; King Mitracedes wisely asked me to protect his High Regent in the advent of his death; he must have sensed something..."

Master Sorcerer Idalia stood respectfully silent as Lord Iroh gathered his thoughts; when he spoke again she noted the timbre of his voice as lightning crackled outside the windows, splitting the evening sky.

"I have underestimated Cullen's thirst for blood," commented Iroh as his gaze darkened. "One would believe that executing nearly a third of his regents and most of his family would be enough for any power hungry man new to a throne, but no...No, I fear there may be no end to the death our little king is capable of dealing out."

When their eyes met again Idalia noticed a change in Iroh; she was surprised by his next words.

"Idalia," Lord Iroh said before he faded away, "You would do well to consider joining my organization. As strong as you are, it is not meet for you to lack the power of an Ancient should an intrigue go awry. For your powers I would consider you an equal and train you to increase your ranks. As you can see, it would be of great advantage for you to be in my bloodline; an error of this magnitude can be made but once."

It was a generous offer and the Master Sorcerer Idalia did not hesitate.

"As you say it, my lord," agreed Idalia quickly, "Send a servant at your leisure when you have time to converse with me."

Master Iroh was pleased with her response; Idalia detected a faint smile as the sorcerer faded from sight. Then she released a great breath of relief at her continued existence; Idalia shook her head again in disbelief as she watched her pupil rest serenely through his almost demise.

"I have done my duty to ensure your survival, Lord Zayn", she mused aloud, "Little did I realize that my own life was on the line." Idalia's mind turned briefly to King Cullen and the Master Sorcerer inclined her head ruefully.

"My only hope is that King Cullen was wise enough to commend his own soul before seeking his rest."

Seconds later Master Idalia vanished from Lord Zayn's rooms.

BRINGING the Past into the Present

The new King of the Sky Vault was snoring peacefully in his rooms when his rest was disturbed by a blaze of light. Groggy, King Cullen slowly raised his hand to his face to shade his eyes, blinking rapidly and rising to a sitting position as he took in the sight of a man in silhouette in front of a light like the sun. The king turned to search for his queen, then remembered she slept in another room of their suites, nursing their child back to dreams. Cullen tried to keep the irritation from his voice; he knew his mages would only disturb his sleep for matters of utmost urgency. Surely, his mage Titus has returned to relate the success or failure of the king's assassination attempt on his former High Regent.

"Titus?" King Cullen asked in a gravelly voice, "Why have you disturbed my rest?"

But the man before him did not answer this question.

"King Cullen," said the strange man deeply with a trace of anger in his voice, "Once ruler of the Sky Vault, son of great King Mitracedes and Queen Thora. How sad you were incapable of accepting your lot in life; that of a king of a large and respected nation, with years ahead of you full of conquest and expansion, of possible glory. How sad you could not be content with riches, fine wine, and food; a future full of hounds, boar hunts and breeding horses, to have men who bowed to you and served in your armies, and women to satisfy every possible lust. How sad you traded your future children and your years with them for a sordid past you had nothing to do with!"

Lightning crackled behind the stranger and the new king brought his covers to his chest in dismay.

"Who are you?" Cullen demanded breathlessly.

"Ah," responded the stranger as his irritation peaked, "The knowledge of that question might have saved your life."

The light behind the man faded as he fully came into view and King Cullen took in the sight of his robes.

"You're a sorcerer," said the king and the man scoffed.

"I am a mere sorcerer as you are a mere servant, King Cullen," replied the stranger, "I am Iroh, who walked this earth before your kingdom existed, and will no doubt walk it long after you are gone and forgotten."

"Whoever you are," the young king blustered, "How dare you enter my chambers unannounced with vague threats to my person and lineage. As you have just noted, I am a king, anointed to the throne of the Sky Vault, and ruler over millions of lives!"

King Cullen began to regret his confidence as the storm outside his windows blew past the heavy curtains and into his suites. Lightning surged behind Lord Iroh then crackled up and down his robes, the deadly charges caressing and then sinking into his hands as the king watched with a suddenly tight throat.

"How have I wronged you?" The new king asked in a more measured tone and watched as Iroh barely withheld a sneer.

"If I had not promised your parents and myself that I would prolong your bloodline, it would end today for your stupidity. Fortunately, you have produced an heir. How sad you will never live to see your firstborn sit the throne; how sad your young wife must now seek another to warm her bed!"

"Guards!" King Cullen roared at this clear threat and watched in growing dismay as Iroh calmly crossed his arms.

"They cannot hear you." Iroh responded quietly.

"Titus! To me!" The new king cried in desperation; Iroh scoffed again.

"Dead, King Cullen," The sorcerer claimed dryly, "Your skilled mage Titus has preceded you into the shaded realms, obedient to the last breath. Yet, by all means, do summon whatever magical defense you have left."

"Mir! Eustace! Diem!" The king hastily roared every name he could think of, "Bring all your might; your king needs you!"

His irritation barely in check, Master Iroh waited patiently for every mage foolish enough to respond to King Cullen's call to enter the king's chamber where Iroh instantly froze them in place. The Master Sorcerer scanned the hapless mages only long enough to see that most of them had no bloodlines established and those that did, felt their masters hastily sever connections between them so they would not suffer the same fate as their foolish students.

King Cullen watched in growing horror as his mages twisted in agony, pleading for mercy from the Master Sorcerer who smiled slightly.

"It is an honor and privilege to proceed your king in death, mages," Iroh stated grimly without turning to look at them, "I suggest you spend your final moments saying farewell to him."

A brief flash of light heralded the end of the mages and King Cullen saw piles of grey ash littered throughout his chambers. His voice was far more respectful as he returned his gaze to Iroh.

"How have I offended you, my lord?" Cullen whispered and Iroh nodded slightly to this wisdom.

"You're a bloodthirsty little creature, King Cullen," stated Iroh tightly, "Under normal circumstances, such a willfulness for destruction might have endeared you to me; you would have been useful in many of my intrigues and I would have filled your coffers with gold. But your jealousy of your deceased sibling has unhinged your faculties; attempting to assassinate Lord Zayn has resulted in the unnecessary deaths of hundreds of able mages, the least of them worth the whole of you!"

"Spare me!" cried the young king, "Can't you see that the shame of it hung like a cloud over my head for most of my life? People whispering behind my back: How my father deceived me into believing Kalos was my brother, how my own mother didn't want me to ascend a throne that belonged to me!"

In spite of his simmering rage, the Master Sorcerer felt some compassion for Cullen's bitterness. Not enough to change his decision but still he felt it.

"Your dealings required wisdom, not brute force, King of the Sky Vault," replied Iroh. firmly "Lord Zayn knew nothing of the truth of your brother's lineage, and if he were not a man of honor, he would have slain you himself for this open threat to his life. Unknown to you both, High Regent Zayn was under my protection; a favor I owed Mitracedes, to keep him safe. You have blundered into the intrigues of sorcerers, little king, not men who live and die within a hundred to three hundred years, but eons. Five hundred years from now, I will bring King Izhar's bloodline back to this throne, just as it was I who took it from him!"

Despite himself, Cullen gasped.

"It was a mage who placed my father on the throne; Mitracedes did not slay King Izhar?"

Iroh made a dismissive gesture with his hand at this question.

"Magic brought down King Izhar. Unlike you, Mitracedes did not yearn for his half-brother's death; by sorcery we forced him to it. Mitracedes was a general in the Kingdom of the Rim of the World, King Cullen, his dreams no greater than High General when he learned of his own royal blood. It was his unrequited love for a young Queen Thora that turned him from that path to this one, a journey paved with sorcery, war and blood."

"Then it was true, what those regents said," marveled Cullen, "Mitracedes the Usurper, they called him. His mother was the kingdom's First Concubine; his survival an accident of timing."

"Why did you slay your father's siblings, your own uncle and aunt?" asked Iroh in curiosity, watching in amazement as Cullen's face distorted in hatred.

"Their mother was a whore," King Cullen said with venom, "A woman kept for pleasure, her offspring a disgrace."

"That 'whore' was your grandmother," replied Iroh with a raised eyebrow, "...and you are her offspring. Despite how you felt about your uncle and aunt's beginnings, their father, who also sired Mitracedes was a king. The only so-called pure blood you have is through your mother Queen Thora, whom if your father Mitracedes had not saved, you would never have existed."

"She should never have married him," stated Cullen resentfully, "He was weak."

"I see," said Iroh thoughtfully as he inclined his head, "Thus you hate your brother for his blood, a blood you feel is free of taint, as yours is not. You thought by eradicating your father's kin, it would somehow make you Thora's only son."

"He's alive, isn't he?" insisted Cullen with a gleam in his eyes, "My brother Kalos? Despite his death and burial, you found a way to save him. It's true; I've always known it."

Master Iroh stared at Cullen a moment then sighed.

"How sad for you, King Cullen, that belief was not enough. Without this bloodbath, this desperate search for a fruitless truth, you might have had a remarkable reign; now the only thing remarkable about your time on earth is how short it will be; the only King of the Sky Vault who reigned less than a year."

King Cullen began to sweat; he finally realized his obsession with his brother Kalos would cost him his life. Cullen had thought himself above all consequence once he ascended the throne; had felt himself clever enough to escape the snares of his fellow kings. Now he realized he knew too little of magic and had lacked the respect for it that might have made him wiser as he sought his aims. The man who stood before him was far stronger than any practitioner of sorcery the young king had ever seen. Too late, King Cullen saw everything he had traded his days for, a task that never would have brought him joy. Like his father Mitracedes and King Izhar, the uncle he never knew, the death of Kalos would have brought King Cullen only guilt and remorse. Panic came into his eyes as Cullen thought of his wife he would widow and a daughter he should have cherished while he had the time.

His tone of voice abruptly turned from arrogant to contrite and cajoling.

"Lord Iroh, you said that as High Regent, Zayn is a man of honor, that he would not raise his hand against me as king…" Cullen began to stammer. "Are not you yourself a man of honor?"

The Master Sorcerer smiled thinly at this clever attempt by the young king to save his skin. Indeed, under other circumstances Iroh might have forgiven Cullen his ignorance and foolishness and found a less lethal way to punish his audacity. Unfortunately, the doomed king had demonstrated beyond a shadow of a doubt his inability to control his emotions, his feelings about Kalos bordered on true insanity. Over time Iroh reasoned, King Cullen would likely prove more trouble than he was worth.

"High Regent Zayn swore an oath to King Mitracedes to uphold his bloodline and as a matter of honor, he kept his word," responded Lord Iroh with a gleam in his eyes, "By doing so, Zayn is now eligible to become High Regent again in another kingdom. I, however, do not answer to mages or kingdoms, therefore I go where I will and do as I please. Queen Thora made the agreement with me regarding her bloodline, and as I have already stated, you have produced an heir, King Cullen."

"You don't have to kill me," The new king bargained desperately, "You said yourself I could be of use to you. I've learned my lesson; I can keep your secrets."

"You'll keep them anyway," said Master Iroh with a deadly calm, "No matter whom you tell. You've overplayed your hand, little king. Who will believe the ravings of a madman, and a dying one at that?"

At these words of imminent doom, the young king suddenly drew a dagger from under his covers and hurled it with pinpoint accuracy at a stunned Iroh, who laughed out loud as the blade passed harmlessly through his body and struck the column behind him.

The Master Sorcerer flared with energy; his eyes backlit with distant fire.

"I shall truly miss you, you precious monster," Iroh said with a fierce grin, "…and recall this moment fondly!"

"Wait!"

King Cullen grunted as the sorcerer sent a bolt of radiation into the king's body, causing him to fall back against his pillows.

Iroh stepped closer to the king's bed as Cullen groaned.

"The only reason I won't slay you outright is my respect for High King Khamis; he'll have enough scandal to deal with investigating all the dead mages at this summit."

"Please..." The king begged as he felt the deadly radiation surging through his body, eating away at his healthy cells and blood. Unable to rise, Cullen gripped his sheets and tried to pull himself across his huge bed towards the mage who viewed these movements dispassionately.

"Comfort yourself with this, King Cullen," said Iroh with narrowed eyes, "At last you do have a link to King Izhar; his child never got the chance to know him either."

Coldly ignoring Cullen's pleas for mercy, Iroh faded away as the king's servants flooded into his rooms at his cries of distress.

THERE ARE days even kings cannot sleep. War may be on the horizon or pestilence, or as was the case for King Mitracedes and Queen Thora so long ago, the death of a treasured son. Thus it came about that King Kalos could find no refuge in dreams; though his queen knew it not, Kalos worried many days and nights about his own treasure, Princess Elect Thora.

Kalos often sought her rooms late at night to watch his princess rest. It comforted him to know she slumbered, and her nurses knew well, if she did not that the king expected them to know if little Thora was safe through the night.

When Princess Elect Thora was very young, King Kalos did this unconsciously, but now that the king remembered his own illness and separation from the ones he loved Kalos felt driven to it. Once the king saw for himself that Thora was safe in her bed, Kalos returned to his rooms with his queen, now able to sleep and seek his own rest.

One such night as Kalos moved silently through the corridors leading back to his suites, he saw a man standing in a shaft of moonlight waiting for him.

King Kalos could not keep his heart from thudding in his chest.

"Lord Iroh," Kalos said as he approached, "What tidings require such a meeting at night?"

"Greetings, King Kalos," answered the sorcerer, "Forgive me for this informal intrusion, but I would not have you taken by surprise by the news tomorrow that after a long illness, your brother King Cullen has gone on to the shaded realms."

The sorcerer watched with interest as Kalos gripped the robes over his heart.

"Grief, Kalos?" asked Iroh, "What beauty lies within your soul that you could bear pity for a man who thirsted for your death and the blood of all you love?"

But Kalos could not respond; he turned away and covered his face with his other hand, his mind filled with images of the love that he and Cullen once shared. He could still feel his younger brother's arms playfully about his waist, trying in vain to topple him as Kalos laughed and lifted Cullen high in the air.

"I will grieve him," Kalos finally choked out, "Even as I feel relief for those I love and cherish. My father was right to warn me away from Cullen, as were you. Can I help the heart that remembers a time of light before the darkness?"

The Master Sorcerer studied King Kalos for a moment as though he wished to carefully choose his next words. Then Iroh sighed.

"You have been awakened, King Kalos," said Iroh soberly, "The abilities you have displayed I believe have been passed down to you through Mitracedes and not Izhar. You regained your memories when the king touched you at the King's Summit; I felt the burst of energy as the bond I placed you under faded away."

"I feel different," Kalos agreed, "I'm not sure what to make of it..."

"Allow me to train you, my lord," urged Lord Iroh, "There are so many things you do not yet know, things I am most willing to teach you."

"A king cannot be both ruler and mage, Lord Iroh," mused the king, who missed the sharp glance of the sorcerer; Kalos did not refuse the notion outright. "These 'abilities', as you have called them, I feel only had value when I used them to reclaim my father, and now that Mitracedes is gone and my brother Cullen lost to me forever, what need have I for them? Surely the use of such power will only bring me more pain."

"Perhaps," agreed Lord Iroh, "However, you may wish to weight this against the rest you will gain knowing that your heirs are safe at night."

"Why do you care what becomes of me and my family, sorcerer?" asked the king as he appraised Iroh, "Despite my heritage, my nation is a small one and as you have pointed out before, a stronger kingdom could easily defeat me and absorb my lands. What is it that compels you to champion my cause, to care if I live or die?"

The Master Sorcerer paused a moment before answering the young king, Iroh's eyes glazed in memory.

"Your mother, Queen Thora, made quite an impression on me, young king," replied Iroh thoughtfully. "When Thora so boldly stepped before the general's archers, ready to take you both to the shaded realms rather than live without Izhar, I confess to admiration of her. Queen Thora never begged or pleaded for her life. Here was a woman who knew the cost of conquest, and if the queen was afraid she did not show it. And when she later took me to task for saving her life, Queen Thora gained my respect. It seemed a shame to allow such strength of character to end on the tiles of her throne room, so when Mitracedes cried out, I instantly halted the arrows before Thora's hope of a life with you died with her."

For a moment, King Kalos couldn't breathe as the Master Sorcerer casually shared information with him Kalos had never known. No one had dared speak of the events that preceded his step-father's reign. History, especially in the kingdoms, is written by and for the victorious. Mitracedes was king and that was the end of it; with the exception of the two foolish regents, if anyone knew differently, they were wise enough to remain silent.

"This is so?" the young king finally choked out, "My mother was to die as a casualty of war?"

Lord Iroh filled the halls around the two men with light as he indicated the lands beyond the palace walls.

"Never forget, young king," said Iroh quietly, "Although two kings decided the fate of the Sky Vault, it was the nation's queen who saved your bloodline. Thora was the key to all of it. I am indebted to her for her bravery and courage and I fear I may never see her like again..." the sorcerer's voice trailed away in the hush of moonlight.

A movement caught Lord Iroh's eye and he watched as King Kalos unconsciously reached up and drew his fingers across a fine gold chain that hung from his neck. The sorcerer studied the hammered metal a moment and then his features cleared as he recognized it.

"Your necklace is one of uncommon beauty, King Kalos, worthy of a prince—"

The young king smiled ruefully.

"Yes," he agreed, "The workmanship is quite youthful in design; almost feminine; my mother gave it to me, and I have never quite convinced myself to set it aside..."

"It was not the mother you came to, but the mother you came from, who gave it to you, my lord," revealed Iroh as the king's fingers tightened on the chain in sudden grief, "The last time Queen Thora touched you she placed that chain around your neck as a remembrance; a final symbol of her love for you."

Silence filled the lonely hall as Kalos searched his restored memory for the moment he lay bound in his tomb, his birth mother bending over him to adorn Kalos with her own jewelry. A plain gold chain to symbolize both sorrow for her loss and hope for his future. Now Kalos could feel Queen Thora's soft hands stroking his hair and face as her mother's heart broke between them.

"Twenty-seven years..." the voice of the king trailed off in the quiet.

"Love is not bound by time," said the sorcerer softly, as his own mind turned to his mentor Rannea, who died over seventy thousand years ago.

"Queen Thora swore an oath to never see you again, that you might live, King Kalos," mused Lord Iroh, "But Mitracedes loved you beyond all possibility of harm; it was why I allowed him to see you from a distance; and he kept faith with me."

"All those years and I never knew I was drawn to him…"

"Mitracedes is your father, Kalos," Iroh marveled, "Unless both brothers shared the same heart. It was the same tender heart that drove Mitracedes to love you more than his own blood."

"I am his blood," insisted the king, which Iroh conceded to with a nod.

"You are," agreed Iroh, "…and now the secret remains with you. King Cullen's daughter will grow up in peace; I have found all his foolish attempts to confound my aims. In so doing I have something for you, a way to offset the pain of missed opportunity."

"I don't understand…" began the king and stopped as Lord Iroh extended his hand and offered Kalos a bound parchment wrapped with woven cords.

"The king who loved your mother more than he should have placed this in her burial chambers. When you were sixteen and bound by my sorcery, King Mitracedes believed that he would die before his queen. He promised me that he would tell Queen Thora everything on his deathbed, but apparently he prepared in advance of either war or illness…"

The bundle was heavy in Kalos's hands; his face cleared as he realized what he held; he gazed up at Iroh in wonder.

"Letters, Iroh?" Kalos whispered, "These are letters to my mother, written in my father's own hand?"

"Consider it a gift, my lord," answered the sorcerer, "A peace offering, perhaps, for all the pain I've inadvertently caused you."

Iroh steeled himself against the raw unguarded emotion that quickly crossed the face of Kalos as the king's fingers gently pressed the edges of the bundle, causing the fabric to rustle slightly in his palms.

"I…" Kalos hesitated. "I am indebted to you…"

"You owe me nothing, King Kalos," replied the sorcerer firmly,

"Think of it as a legacy for your daughter when she ascends the throne. Perhaps you can add your own letters to it; I'm certain young Thora will find it a comfort one day."

When it seemed the young king could not find the words to respond, Iroh took this as a sign of his departure. The sorcerer faded away from the king's sight but remained where he could watch the devastated ruler make his way again through the halls.

Iroh felt some regret as Kalos moved away and barely withheld a sigh. His once mentor Lord Enith had warned Iroh many times over the centuries not to become attached to the subjects of his intrigues but sometimes the sorcerer found it difficult to heed Lord Enith's cautions.

The idea of playing with Thora's and Mitracedes bloodlines had seemed novel at the time. The brave and beautiful queen who gave away her son to save him captured Iroh's imagination; he knew he was spending far too much time with them. His anger at King Cullen's audacity was only marginally contained; it was one thing to punish a king's arrogance, it was another thing altogether to make it personal. The sorcerer sighed again as he thought of what his friend Enith would say of it. Lord Enith had promised Iroh that as the eons progressed Iroh would feel less and less compassion for the people and situations he manipulated, and the time would come where Iroh would forget any event older than a thousand years.

But this was not the case.

The Master Sorcerer remembered every single intrigue he'd been involved in and all the pain and suffering that followed in his wake. Every twenty-five thousand years Lord Iroh experienced an agony in his body so intense that it drove him into the deepest reaches of the earth in an attempt to escape it; he would linger and find himself unable to function for exactly one thousand years. Iroh thought it was penance for his guilt; he'd never heard of any other mage or sorcerer suffering in such a manner.

Lord Iroh knew that during his next cycle of anguish he would think of Kalos often; Iroh had made the mistake of growing fond of the child that so many had loved. He knew that Thora, Mitracedes and the faces of both bloodlines would haunt him. There could be no other outcome; the bundle of letters from Mitracedes outlining his whole sordid history would outlast the ages and exactly five hundred years from now would be the catalyst for yet another bloody war of siblings that would place Izhar and Thora's offspring back on the rightful throne of the Sky Vault.

HESTA: A FORESHADOWED PATH

"Service to the throne has guided the entire path of my life. Now, it is all I have left."

Lord High General Aton

Some would say that because Hesta's older brother Onan held a coveted position in the military her path into the army of the Kingdom of the Far Isles had been an easy one. Some soldiers and people of the nobility might even believe Hesta's own station of birth afforded her a modicum of special treatment.

Hesta herself might laugh if someone expressed these thoughts to her.

No doubt after knocking out cold anyone impertinent enough to say such things to her face.

YET GENERAL HESTA remembered well the day of her initiation into the ranks of one of the most feared armies in the western hemisphere; she was so nervous she had spent most of the morning unable to hold down the contents of her stomach. Her father, although he wasn't completely in favor of her decision, had tried to comfort her.

"A soldier should go into battle hungry, Hesta," he assured her, "A full belly will slow you down."

"Thank you, father," Hesta replied sincerely, and her father knew she was thanking him for more than his advice in this moment. Without his permission, Hesta could not meet with General Aton at all; could not experience this opportunity to see the realization of her dreams. When she was younger, her parents believed her aspirations were more a result of Hesta's adoration of her older brother Onan and a desire to imitate whatever his interests than an actual hope for her life.

One day her brother had playfully given a wooden sword to Hesta and directed her to engage in mock battle; he'd been amazed at her natural if clumsy ability to follow his movements. As Onan moved to Hesta's left side to throw off her balance, little Hesta instinctively switched her tiny sword to her left hand and swung with astonishing accuracy and balance at her brother, who stepped back in amazement.

In curiosity, he moved back to her right and Hesta again switched hands and lunged at her sibling, who barely evaded her enthusiastic response. Laughing in pleasure at her unconscious skill, Onan brought their father to watch as he repeated his swordplay with his younger sister; her father was stunned at her earnest talents.

"Onan," her father said sharply, "you're certain you've never given Hesta a sword before?"

But Hesta could answer for herself; she amazed them both as she raised her child's toy with a chubby fist.

"I can do it Fa-fa," she insisted in a squeaky voice, using a child's name for the word 'Father', "I can do it!"

However, if they expected Hesta's mother to share their enthusiasm for her daughter's newfound skill they were disappointed. Upon viewing her eldest son vigorously swinging a wooden sword in his sister's direction, she cried out:

"Have you all taken leave of your senses? Take care not to strike her arms and face, lest you disfigure her forever!"

Onan's father berated him in front of his mother, but his eyes twinkled where his wife could not see it, and soon the siblings continued their activity under their father's watchful eye. Hesta only remembered how much she enjoyed it and even when no one was around she took up her tiny toy and practiced whatever she could recall.

Her father spent most of her childhood telling her stories of his own battles before Hesta's bedtime, taking great care of course to phrase his tales in words to inspire and not frighten her. With a mind filled with images of great battles and heroics, Hesta soon lost all interest in the things her mother hoped she would enjoy. She could engage her tutors for hours in conversations and even philosophy, but dresses and long dinners usually bored her.

In the present moment, Hesta found she could barely look at her mother whom she knew did not approval of her actions. How ironic that in this moment both women were disappointed in each other. Hesta longed for her mother to support her choice; would it not be wonderful for a woman of her rank to take so bold a step? It would only bring honor to her family if she rose in the ranks of the military to general; but Hesta could not help her mother to see this.

Her mother, who had hoped to have given Hesta away in marriage in a few years, stood silent; her face a mask. She was angry with both her husband and her son for encouraging what she could only see as her daughter's foolishness. Hesta had the potential to become a princess, why did she wish to waste her life roaming the countryside with a group of unwashed, sweaty men, most of them uneducated and of a lower station than she could achieve?

I have been assured that she will outgrow this madness, she thought as Hesta braced herself for the day, *The idea of her dying childless on a filthy battlefield will lengthen the gray in my hair.*

Young Hesta knew better than to expect comfort from her mother; the stern look frozen on her face was enough to burn a hole in her heart. Her father's gaze, however held only approval as Hesta offered them both a swift bow of respect before turning and walking quickly from the spacious courtyard and towards the outer gates where she would wait for her brother's escort.

The silence in the courtyard following Hesta's departure was deafening.

"You know this has been Hesta's dream from birth, my wife," offered Hesta's father finally as their servants found other tasks to do.

"Then she should have born a boy," replied her mother tersely as she turned away and then paused to place a withering eye on her husband.

"If one hair on her head is disturbed from this profound foolishness, you will have no words to comfort me."

He sighed heavily as she walked away. He would never tell his wife that he, too, hoped Hesta would change her mind eventually once exposed to the realities of war. It was one thing to dream of being a soldier; it was another thing altogether to stand on a bloodied field with your arms trembling from fatigue, facing another man who was just as afraid to die as you are.

His hand unconsciously smoothed over his tunic where a scar remained to remind him of that bitter victory. He smiled to himself as he recalled his wife's constant fear that Hesta would be scarred in battle. *A scar was a soldier's friend,* mused Hesta's father, *It was a reminder of life more than anything else and a reminder to cherish it. One scar will not deter marriage,* he thought hotly, *If a man does not respect the scars of a woman he doesn't deserve her.*

He sighed again as he contemplated Hesta's desire to become a soldier for King Valtus. The reality was that Hesta could receive far more than a mere flesh wound as she pursued her goals; her dreams could end forever on a muddy field miles and worlds away from home. Yet despite his misgivings, he could not deny his daughter her chance to see if this dream were true.

The Highest Position

As the servants of her father's house pulled back the gates, Hesta could see her beloved brother Onan and her closest friend Marcus waiting for her outside, standing by their horses. Hesta broke into the biggest grin then just as quickly suppressed it; she knew her brother would expect her to act like a soldier on this day. Hesta marched silently to meet them; she did not miss the sparkle in her brother's eye though he did not smile at her in front of his men. She swiftly mounted her horse and waited; a slight smile from Marcus as he swung his leg over his horse gave her comfort; not everyone was opposed to her intent. Marcus had always been there for her and always would be. She watched as Onan signaled to his men to hold position until the three friends rode up to the front; they all then fell beside and behind them as they rode from her father's lands to the main portion of the inner kingdom where High General Aton and all Hesta's hopes awaited.

ONAN WAS a Forde General in the ranks of the Far Isles, a position just below the rank of High General. The High General was Aton, a man who was both feared and respected, not only in his kingdom but beyond it; many nations with whom the Far Isles held alliances were encouraged in battle by the sound of his name and just as many enemies were struck numb with fear at the same sound.

There were numerous women in the army of the Far Isles, thousands, in fact, so Aton was not surprised when Onan approached him a few years ago with a request to review a candidate but his eyebrows flew upwards when his second in command identified who it was. Not because Hesta was a female, but because he knew both her family and station in life.

Most women came into the military for the same reasons that some men did; to feed their families. A young woman who had lost father, husband and brothers to war might find herself in the army; it was among the few honorable things a female could do to put bread on the table. Aton's eyes had narrowed at the time because it was not Hesta's father who had approached him; he sensed and rightly so that this was not a completely approved life path for young Hesta. Still, because Onan was a trusted and respected general, Aton took him seriously; he had gruffly advised Onan to bring Hesta to him when she was older and more trained; he would test her resolve to see if she meant her words.

So it came about that the knot in Hesta's stomach this morning had been three years in the making; but it was only today that she could feel it. It wasn't difficult for her to remain silent as she rode beside her brother and friend; all Hesta could focus on was the great honor ahead and the equally great trial; surely becoming a soldier in the Far Isles would not be easy.

Hesta did not know it, but the same knot had formed in the belly of both Onan and Marcus and for the same reason. Neither had any doubt in Hesta's skill or ability; it was simply that both men knew how Aton trained his soldiers; it was enough to make their collective hearts beat faster. General Aton was not a man who gave special treatment to nobility in his ranks; the general knew that a noble who thought more of himself than the people around him could inadvertently cause the deaths of thousands. Onan in particular was grateful that his commanding officer had merely requested to see if Hesta could fight at all.

"You may face one soldier today, or many," Onan said gruffly as they rode together, "Use every skill you've ever been taught and listen closely to anything General Aton asks of you; don't hesitate to obey his commands."

"Yes, brother," Hesta replied as her hands tightened on the reins of her mount, "I will do it."

She looked briefly to Marcus, who was waiting for her gaze; he nodded encouragement.

"Don't hold back," he said seriously, and watched as Hesta's lips tightened and her eyes blinked rapidly as she agreed.

Marcus was only a little older than Hesta. He had shone great promise in the military arts and had no interest in becoming a regent, a position he could have easily taken on as an educated son of the gentry, who were only a station or two below the higher nobility like Onan and Hesta. Marcus dreamed of being a general one day like Onan, who had taken the younger man under his wing. He was experienced with a few battles under his belt and Marcus knew Hesta always wished to be a soldier; he only hoped that she would be placed in the same regiment as he so the best friends could fight together and watch each other's backs.

A Soldier's Worth

The trio entered the main gates and Hesta noticed how the other soldiers deferred to her brother; she also noticed that the soldiers she knew met her gaze briefly and looked away, not because she was now beneath their approval but because they were on duty. Hesta steeled herself as she dismounted and followed her brother into a separate courtyard where she could hear the ringing of metal on metal and the grunts of men sparring with each other. Moments later her eyes rested on the man she was searching for: High General Aton.

Aton was that rare combination of a man that was both tall and full-bodied; he looked like the legendary beasts who rumbled the earth when they ran the herd, breaking trees against the leathery armor of their huge torsos. He was faster than many men who were smaller; size yielded extraordinarily little advantage against Aton in battle; yet another reason to be wary of facing him if you wanted to live.

He stood with his arms crossed as he sharply watched the movements of every soldier in the courtyard; from time to time he shouted instructions; corrections on the stance, swing and recovery of the men and women sparring; Hesta's eyes widened as she saw blood; these soldiers were not using wooden swords for practice.

As though Marcus heard her thoughts he spoke in an undertone:

"It's not like this every day, Hesta," he nearly whispered, "But there have been rumors of the Lourdes Clan nearby the protected rivers—"

His voice trailed off, but Hesta heard the concern in his tone. The Lourdes Clan was one of the most feared and brutal of the tribes of nomadic people who roamed outside the kingdoms; the High General took very seriously any report of them that came back with the scouts.

"Those scouts are fortunate to be alive," replied Hesta quietly to her friend's nod.

As the trio came to the attention of General Aton, he made a silent gesture to his middle general who was standing nearby. This man shouted once, and every soldier in the courtyard immediately ceased their sparring and swiftly came into formation. They bowed to the High General and smartly marched away, followed by the same middle general who had shouted the command.

The three faced Aton and bowed to him in the custom of the military; short, swift and without distraction. Even when showing respect a soldier kept an eye out for attack from anywhere. When Hesta returned to attention, she noticed how Aton's eyes glinted as he appraised her show of respect for his station; Onan had trained her well.

"So," Aton said gruffly, "This is Hesta, who longs to be a member of the military."

It was not a question, yet still Onan answered in the affirmative.

"Yes, my lord."

"How long have you wished to be among us, Hesta?" the general asked her directly.

"Since I first learned what a soldier was, my lord," said Hesta earnestly, inwardly wincing as her voice cracked, but the general seemed not to notice.

"And what is a soldier to you, Hesta?" Aton continued quietly.

She swallowed before replying.

"A man or woman whose sole purpose is to protect the life of her king, my lord," she answered firmly, unable to restrain her chest from tightening and her eyes from blinking rapidly as she kept her gaze on General Aton, whose own eyes narrowed at her words.

Then Aton nodded.

"You have answered me correctly, Hesta," the general said gravely, "Yet it remains to be seen if you mean those words or merely repeated what your brother Onan has no doubt told you."

Aton's gaze fell on Onan, who flushed as he bowed sharply and stepped back from Hesta, along with Marcus who also moved back as though he and Onan were one person. The middle general had returned with four soldiers and Hesta unconsciously gripped her sword; did the general intend for her to fight them all at the same time?

She brought her eyes quickly back to Aton who slightly smiled at this, then turned serious.

"Show me the stances and positions of a soldier," he barked, and Hesta quickly and expertly drew her sword and went through her paces, displaying basic defensive and offensive postures as Aton circled her, analyzing her every move. Finally the general made a small gesture towards his middle general who responded by indicating that one of his men should engage Hesta, who without breaking her postures turned and disarmed the young man before he could plant his feet properly in defense.

Marcus did not dare to show openly his pleasure at Hesta's prowess and audacity; he knew she was skilled with a sword. He felt sorry for the soldier who had underestimated her; Marcus also knew his High General would punish any soldier who let his guard down for any reason; this was life and death to his craft.

The middle general immediately sent the next soldier forward, who lasted only a little longer than the first one had. He then indicated that the last two engage Hesta together; and now it was Onan who tightened his jaw in pride as he watched his little sister conduct herself with bravery. Both he and his father, then Marcus had shown Hesta how to defend herself against a two man attack; one soldier nearly leaped back as he lost his sword; Hesta lunged expertly forward but not too much as she both disarmed him and drew blood from the other soldier who had leaned in when he should have moved from the arc of her backswing.

The Decision

The middle general nodded at General Aton's almost imperceptible shake of his head; he did not want the middle general to engage Hesta next. It was clear that Aton was impressed with the young girl's skills and discipline; it was equally obvious that Hesta had applied herself diligently to the martial arts. Aton crossed his arms and Marcus knew that the general was making a decision; it was all he could do to remain still. Hesta was all nerves; yet she kept her place; she knew the honor and status of her family was at stake; she would not be seen bouncing back and forth on her feet.

They all stood obediently awaiting the general's next instruction; all that could be heard was Hesta's and the other young men's labored breathing.

Onan expected that the audience had ended; instead to the shock of all present, Aton held out his hand for the middle general's sword as he left his own in its scabbard; Hesta's eyes widened as Aton took a defensive stance.

"Come, Hesta," said Aton with a slight smile, "You're clearly trained enough for them, let us see if you are trained enough for *me*."

Hesta breathed deeply as she swiftly sized up the general; she knew she couldn't hesitate. She leaped forward and met the general's parry and jumped back from his backswing. But he gave her no rest; General Aton wanted to see what Hesta was made of; he rained blows down on her that Hesta parried as swiftly as she could; her jaw set in a thin line as she tried to gain advantage over his superior skills.

Even though he was looking Marcus could barely see. He knew the general did not use his own sword for a reason; his blade was meant for battle. Aton was merely showing Marcus and Onan, his anxious second in command that he was truly testing this potential soldier.

Hesta was fast and lightning quick; against the general she did as

Marcus bade her and did not hold back. Yet she could see that even with his age, height and weight, Aton was faster; his sword became a living thing in his hands and for a moment, Hesta could not distinguish the metal from his arm.

He's going to parry, she thought, *from his backswing; I should—*

Whiteness enveloped Hesta; the general and everything around her vanished; even sound; she could not for a moment hear her own breathing.

What had happened?

High General Aton calmly stepped back from Hesta and returned to his middle general his sword, who accepted it without a word and then marched away. His other men quietly followed the middle general; they all knew better than to say anything. Onan and Marcus stood in stunned shock at the sight of Hesta on the ground. The general had seen an opening in Hesta's defense; without hesitation Aton had moved into this gap and punched the young girl directly in the face, bringing her to the earth without a sound.

THE AFTERMATH of a battle between men belongs to the scavengers; crows, predator birds, wild dogs and wolves. As it happened, the kingdom of the Rim of the World was attacked by the Broken Meriden, and the kingdom of the Ardant Road came to their defense with disastrous results. An arial view of the attack revealed a desolation of dead men, horses and war dogs that spread for miles, with puddles of blood and piles of gore filled with intestinal matter, feces and split brains. Despite the trenches dug by weary soldiers and surviving regents and pages, scattered hungry animals rushed into these gaps, driven mad by the smell of blood plasma and iron.

One of the fallen, partially covered by a mound of dead and dying warriors, stirred slightly as he regained consciousness. Pain blinded him for a moment: blood seeped from a deep wound in his side; a spear from an unseen enemy had ceased all movement; he had sunk to his knees as the men who helped defend him cried out in despair.

The ones who remained lay atop him now; only a few were as he was; wounded and dying. Their lifeblood slowly drained out onto him; a trickle that filled his armor, warming his skin as he tried not to weep. Then his awareness sharpened; a sound of deep sniffing and soft growling filled his ears: wolves.

The ones that were hungry searched the mounds of the dead for the living, with a preference for blood still pumping through the veins of the near dead. He knew his armor would protect him; for a while at least, until the clever ones found a spot they could breach. The man atop him had just been discovered; he listened helplessly as a few of them banded together and began to tear at the cloth and leather straps that held his armor together; the growling intensified into snarls as they broke through. His own pain forgotten, the soldier clenched his jaw as the man covering him shrieked briefly as the fangs of the wolves found him; he knew then that they would not stop until they found him as well.

Unable to prevent it, his thoughts turned to the reason he had fought so hard to win the battle in the first place; the reason he still clung to life and dared to hope. He felt his muscles relax as her name and face hovered in memory; if he could only reach her, he knew all would be well.

Sora...

A now familiar sound brought him back to the present moment; another of the beasts had sniffed him out and a low growl warned him that the focus was now on him. A pair of wolves tried to drag him out of the pile then redirected their efforts to his exposed leg; he felt the teeth of one of them slide across his ankle as the wolf caught a strap in his mouth and began to move his jaws back and forth in a twisting motion; the man braced himself to be torn apart piece by piece when he heard another sound; the voices of men.

"Over there, Glovis," cried the soldier, "That's a general's armor, surrounded by a pack of wolves. Call the archers; we've found him!"

Sora moved silently into the huge hall of the prince, surrounded by a retinue of soldiers, regents, and servants; she focused on the light clicking sounds of the guard's boots as they struck the tiles beneath the group; it was either that or the pounding of her heart in her ears. Her mother had told Sora that this might well be the best day of her life but the young woman doubted this. How could the day when she lost everything dear to her be her best one?

Her feet, covered with padded silk and embroidered with precious stones were all she could truly see; she was veiled from crown to toe and felt smothered and ridiculous. The voice of the High Regent of her nation brought Sora crashing to the present moment.

"Most esteemed Prince," began the regent, "it is our distinct honor to present to you the finest jewel of our kingdom, the princess—"

Sora started in confusion as she heard muffled sounds of fabric rustling and feet shuffling; suddenly the cords of her veil lifted and she found herself staring into the eyes of something she had never seen close up before in her short life: a man.

Their pupils mutually widened together as they stared at each other; he looked so different from a woman that at first Sora thought he was something from all the tales of fantasy she was read to as a child. She blinked rapidly as she tried to make sense of what she was looking at; she had expected an older man; something else she had never seen. It can't be my father, she reasoned; he's not supposed to be here and his hair should be grey, like my mother's, at least that is what I was told to expect. Then she stared at his lips as he began to speak.

"Yes..." he said as though he spoke to himself, "she is quite beautiful..."

He stepped back from Sora respectfully, not taking his eyes from hers until the High Regent moved between them with his back to her, allowing Sora to take a breath before quickly replacing her veil.

"My lord, I must protest," sputtered Sora's High Regent, "It is our custom for your potential bride to be veiled until you have made a decision—"

"And how can I decide if I have not seen her, nor spoken with her, regent?" Countered the prince blandly as the regent quickly moved away. "Am I to decide based on the fineness of her robes, or the number of precious stones on her feet? Am I a man or a merchant?"

She could hear the direction of his voice turning back to her.

"Can you speak, then?" Asked the prince, "are you silent because you cannot speak, or you will not?"

"Of course I can speak, my lord," responded Sora as her High Regent turned to her in horror, "my silence comes from the respect I bear for the customs of my people; as I see you yourself bear little respect for your own."

This time Sora knew that the rustling of fabric beneath the shocked gasps of the room came from the prince, and just before he could reach out for her veil, Sora gently lifted it herself and brought the prince to a complete halt; he stared at her proud gaze and rapidly blinking eyes for a moment then he unexpectedly grinned before he could stop himself.

"Beautiful...and quite spirited..." he whispered, then turned to gaze back and to his left at his own High Regent, whose face was a controlled mask.

"I like her..."

But as the prince turned to her again his eyes narrowed.

"Princess Sora of the Kingdom of the Rim of the World," intoned the prince as he used her royal title, unknowingly causing her heart to pound. Had she said too much? Was he about to dismiss her and send her home in shame?

"You have spoken of customs as one well versed in them," he continued, "so tell me what do you think of this custom, of being given away in marriage to a man you have never met?"

Her High Regent took a deep breath and bravely again registered his protest after briefly glancing helplessly in the direction of the prince's High Regent who stiffened at the prince's question and clenched his jaw to withhold his words. His silent response to the other regent's unspoken plea was unmistakable:

Tread carefully.

"My Lord Prince," began the regent, "I must implore you to reconsider the question you are asking of the princess; surely you are aware that she has never been in the company of men and has not been exposed to such levels of higher thinking..." he began to stammer, "She...I mean...she's—"

"Only a woman?" Came a voice from beneath the layers of fabric.

Her statement both galvanized and froze the room; anyone who had ever attended the normally boring and long process of displaying and questioning a potential bride was delightfully horrified. The interview was usually filled with insincere flattery on the part of the future bride and bravado on the part of the future groom; most marriage alliances were made on the strength of the political connections and potential assistance during times of war, not compatibility and congeniality of the future couple.

The prince's hands clenched on the arms of his chair as his eyes sparkled.

"You will answer me without your veil, princess Sora," commanded the prince deeply, and watched with a small thrill of anticipation as the princess complied, lifting her veil slowly and meeting his gaze. Then his hands again tightened on the arms of his ornate chair as the princess boldly moved closer to him; from his peripheral vision the prince noted with some amusement her High Regent gripping the front of his robes with subdued shock.

"What do I think of it?" She replied softly. "When I was four years old I was separated from my younger brothers; I have never met my older brothers, and I do not remember what my father looks like. Men, in fact, are never mentioned in my world, except in context of my future service to the man I will marry. Today, I have lost my mother, my aunts, cousins and sisters and all of my friends. I am here for a stranger to declare my worth, to accept or reject me. No one has ever asked me what I thought of all this," and the prince's pupils widened as he detected a hint of emotion in her voice. "I should think..." she paused. "I should think that in this moment all I might have asked was for a voice, to speak of my life and what it has cost me and you, prince, have granted it...thank you..."

The room was silent.

The prince brought his hand to his chin as he studied her; covering his face to hide his reaction to her words. He made a dismissive gesture as Sora began to lower her veil and in obedience to his wishes she released it. He was struck by her beauty the moment their eyes met and though he had already seen many lovely princesses during this tedious process, hers had marked him differently. There were many things about her that moved him profoundly, most notably Sora's heartfelt story of her life. Her intelligence was refreshing and her spirit...

A hidden smile began to grow inside of him that widened into a grin.

My mother will be furious...

The prince stood up from his chair and the princess remembered herself and stepped back. But the prince continued his advance until the princess was forced to stop and unconsciously raise her hands up between them.

"You have thanked me for giving you a voice today, princess, and now I grant you a choice; where you may accept or reject *me...*" he said with emphasis and watched as her eyes locked on his, blinking rapidly.

"Will you marry me willingly, Princess Sora," he said breathlessly to the shock of the court, "Not for the honor of your kingdom or even your family, nor for mine, but for the sake of a man who truly values you for you, and not merely his possession?"

He watched in wonder all of the emotions crossing her face along with her efforts to hold back tears.

Her answer was whispered but strong.

"Yes..."

As the hall erupted into loud murmurs from the regents of both nations, the prince took advantage of the chaos to gently reach for the hand of the stunned princess and bring it to his lips.

"You are a prize beyond measure, Sora," the prince offered, then gently tightened his grip on her fingers as he continued.

"Ah...how I regret the custom of giving inexperienced women in marriage," he whispered as her face burned, "else we could consummate our union tonight. But do not fear, my beauty," he continued in a lowered tone, "I will follow all the protocols and use all patience until I can finally make you mine..." he respectfully moved away as her female servants approached. Sora's heart pounded recklessly as she watched the prince place his hand over his chest; he gave her a final slight smile and a bow as the women discreetly covered her face.

"Until we meet again, my princess, my wife..."

Sora felt her legs were made of wood as her retinue again surrounded her. She had just met a man for the first time in her life and married him in an evening. She wasn't quite sure what had happened but the intensity of his gaze and the shape of his lips would haunt her innocence and keep her from sleep. She closed her eyes as the women expertly guided her from the presence of the prince.

What have I done?

The prince crossed his arms as his High Regent approached.

"My lord," he began, "there is yet time to reconsider this course of action; you have not finished interviewing the other princesses—"

"Dismiss them," the prince replied firmly.

"My prince," he pleaded, "such an action will give insult to the families..." the regent's voice trailed off as the prince gave a wave of dismissal. "Surely you can imagine the outrage—"

"The outrage will be much greater if they learn that I have married princess Sora while continuing to interview women I can no longer offer an honorable alliance," said the prince dryly, then turned a discerning eye on his servant. "Earn your keep, regent; this is not an unprecedented occurrence. Do what you're trained to do while I prepare for my wedding."

The prince walked away and his High Regent steadied himself as the other High Regent made his way to his side.

"Were you able to reason with him?" And the regent shrugged, completely at a loss.

"He offered her a marriage alliance in front of witnesses, and princess Sora verbally accepted it, regent. Like it or no, it is binding by law; they are married."

The High Regent sighed.

"By our custom, they were legally bonded the moment he looked at her; this is a disaster..."

"You're not the one who has to inform the prince's mother," retorted the regent. "Thank the Great One the prince is not her eldest; I might have lost both my position and more importantly, my head."

~

A FULL MOMENT passed before Hesta noticed her arms were beneath her; one elbow was painfully wedged under her stinging cheek. A dull roaring hammered at her eardrums and white streaks blinded Hesta when she tried to move her head. She was barely fifteen years old; she'd never been struck that hard in her whole life.

From a faraway place she heard her brother's voice tense with menace:

"What are you about, Aton? That was a coward's blow...!"

Hesta could not see General Aton draw his sword on her older brother Onan, but she heard it ringing as it left Aton's scabbard; heard the heavy sound of Aton's boots as he stepped over her prone body and challenged his second in command, who drew his own sword in response.

"Desist, my brother..." Hesta moaned in painful alarm as she realized her brother had just done the unthinkable.

Onan's temper was legendary once it was set off, and in this crucial moment he'd forgotten he'd just drawn his sword on his commander, High General Aton of the Far Isles, a man just under the position of High Regent and two steps from the status of the king himself.

"Do you defend her honor, Onan?" asked the general in a stern voice and Onan paused because he realized his superior asked a question unspoken from this surface one. Marcus, Hesta's closest friend and her staunchest advocate for a position in the military, stood frozen in misery and dismay. His vision had whitened with Hesta's, his hand a tightened fist over his own sheathed sword. The sight of her on the ground instinctively brought out his protectiveness, a feeling uncommon to Marcus before this moment.

But the words of General Aton stopped both men where they stood.

"Do you defend her?" Aton asked Onan and Marcus again as he pointed his sword at Hesta's prone body. General Aton's eyes flashed like fire as he moved towards Onan with the flat of his blade pointed at Onan's chest.

The general's tone was deceptively soft.

"Is she a soldier or your sister?" he said tightly as her brother's eyes widened.

Onan stepped back from Aton's advance, his jaw clenched and rigid. No one had ever dared strike Hesta in front of him without hope of a deadly response and now Onan saw this test from the High General was for all three of them.

Aton's face darkened as he now demanded a response.

"Answer me! Is she a soldier or your sister!?!"

Hesta's older brother quieted his breathing with difficulty. Onan knew full well if he claimed that Hesta was a female that required protection, Aton would bar her forever from her dream to serve King Valtus and send Hesta home in shame. From the corner of his eye, he noticed his younger sister struggle to her feet unaided. He was proud of her, even as he realized his own need to shield Hesta from harm had endangered them both.

Onan answered his general.

"She's a soldier," he responded through gritted teeth. Onan threw his sword to the ground and bowed his head.

"With your permission, High General, I'll confine myself to the jails for my impertinence."

Aton grinned fiercely at this statement as he lowered his own sword.

"A wise decision," the general agreed aloud, and then stepping closer to his second in command, he added in an undertone, "If you ever again draw a sword on me in anger, be prepared to use it, Onan, for I will gut you where you stand."

"Yes, my lord," replied Onan respectfully, then stepping back from the general, he finally turned and marched away without looking again to Hesta, who stood bravely biting her numb and swollen lip to keep from weeping at the pain in her face.

General Aton turned to look at Marcus, who placed his feet together sharply and bowed to his superior and turned to follow Onan to the jails.

"I did not dismiss you, Marcus," said Aton sharply, "Why do you follow Onan?"

Marcus took a deep breath and responded, "I reacted without thinking, my lord; this is inexcusable..."

But the general interrupted him.

"You touched the hilt of your sword, but you did not draw it, Marcus. This is the response of a soldier, not one overcome by emotions..."

Aton now turned to Hesta, who was beginning to feel her flesh swelling over her brow. She turned to face the general who narrowed his eyes in approval at her bravery.

"Who trained you, Hesta?" asked Aton, who knew the answer.

"Onan, my lord," she answered through stiffening lips, "Mostly Onan; my father trained me a bit at the start a few years ago, but Onan took me seriously---"

"He did well, Hesta," said Aton heavily, "You are a fine swordsman, with superior skills for one so young. I have little doubt that in a fair fight, you could best any soldier in your weight class or perhaps higher, due to your abilities."

Now the general pointed with his blade at Hesta's fallen sword.

"Yet," he continued, "As I have just demonstrated, all the men you have faced in your short life know you, love you, and respect your skills. This is not so on the battlefield. The men and women you will face care not a whit for skills or bravery. The objective of a soldier in battle is to slay everything around him until there is nothing left to kill. He will use sword, whip, axe or even his fist if he sees an opening, and step over your body to rip apart whatever else is in his way. If he notices that you are a woman and there is time, he will callously and viciously slash your clothes and rape you atop bleeding and dying men, and then cut your throat or stab you through the heart, all without regard for your humanity or the ones who love you..."

Marcus felt his heart thud and his body flush at the thought of his dear friend ravaged and slain. He tasted salt in his mouth and restrained the protest of his stomach; he nearly missed the whole of what the general had said.

Marcus started as he felt Aton's sharp gaze on him and tightened his jaw.

"What say you, Marcus?" asked Aton, "Can Hesta stay the course, or will she falter?"

Hesta's best friend did not hesitate.

"I trust her, general," said the young soldier quietly, "What Hesta sets her mind to, she will learn with all heart."

Marcus kept his gaze strong on the general, who nodded once before speaking again to the young woman he had floored with one blow.

"This," stated Aton, "Is what your father and your brother failed to teach you, Hesta; how to survive in a windstorm of flailing and struggling bodies. How to guard yourself and slay anything that moves. Other than his back, a soldier does not need protection; his king does. Now--"

Aton pinned Hesta's eyes to his, though she noticed how quickly the vision in her right eye was fading.

"Do you still want to learn how to protect your king?"

Her single eye was fierce and unwavering; a precious dream within her grasp.

"More than anything," she answered in a strong voice.

With these words, the general made up his mind. Hesta had responded with discipline to the unexpected; something many soldiers had to be taught, and character when faced with humiliation; something that cannot be given; it must already reside within. Even without advanced skills, Hesta was better than some of the men who had fought beside the High General for years, and in this moment it meant more to Aton than numerous battles. With proper training,

Hesta would be a great asset, and if she could control her emotions better than her brother, one day she could even reach the rank of general.

"Good..." General Aton said grimly, "...pick up your sword, Hesta."

At the incredulous look on her bruised face, General Aton laughed in true merriment. Then he crouched with his blade.

"Do you think an attacker will wait for your face to heal? This is the best way to learn how to fight with impaired vision. Prepare yourself...soldier!"

Though her heart nearly burst with joy at the general's use of the word, 'soldier', it wasn't hard for Hesta to control the urge to smile, she could barely move her facial muscles. She mirrored the general's stance and kept her good eye sharp for Aton's free hand; she wouldn't be caught off guard like that again.

Marcus watched intently as the talented young girl fought her new mentor with renewed vigor and will.

A Hole That Only Light Can Fill

One might imagine the furor in the court of King Valtus once a rumor began to spread that his High General had knocked out cold a prospective soldier during a training session. And not just any trainee, but a member of his upper echelon of society, and a woman at that. High Regent Galen kept his face a mask as he gave his report, but inside his own mind was in turmoil as he considered how he might react had Aton struck his own daughter. Onan's father was a fool, he seethed, to even allow Hesta to apply for the military. Hesta was a potential princess; her lineage worthy of kings. What was he thinking?

King Valtus sighed deeply at this latest diplomatic breach of his nation's greatest warrior. Yet everyone of his court would be shocked to know the king's true thoughts; that he agreed with what Aton had done. Being a member of an army is vastly different from almost any other function of the kingdom; with life and death decisions made everyday. No one could be coddled or treated as special; hundreds, even thousands of men could die for a lapse in judgment.

Valtus mind wandered as his High Regent spoke; to the last time his High General made a decision during wartime that impacted his court directly; the death of a highborn noble of one of the nation's most prominent families. Against his own better judgment King Valtus had allowed this young man to join his military and persuaded his general to give him a chance.

General Aton of course, had protested the man's appointment.

"My lord," Aton had said, "we have an agreement—"

"Yes, Aton," Valtus acknowledged heavily, "we do; I run our nation and you run our military—"

"With full discretion as to who attains a position in it!"

The two were alone, so Valtus was inclined to forgive his general's outburst; but Valtus felt pressured to allow this appointment.

"Place him in a regiment far away from your line of sight, Aton," the king cajoled, "perhaps under one of your firmer generals to keep him in line--"

Valtus sighed and his voice trailed away at the expression on his High General's face; he knew the general felt his authority was being compromised and he was trying to soften this obvious blow.

"He'll have to prove himself like everyone else, my lord," conceded Aton gruffly, "and no promotions without my approval."

Valtus walked over to his favorite warrior and gratefully pressed his hand to Aton's shoulder, and felt his general visibly relax his tenseness at this honor.

"I will not promote him, Aton, you will," offered Valtus with confidence, "I'm certain he will eventually prove himself to your usual exacting standards."

In the coming years, the young noble had shown wisdom and applied himself; also showing caution to avoid any direct contact with the High General. But despite all these things, General Onan would have nothing to do with him. He spoke about him only with Marcus, who he knew would never repeat his words.

"Yes, he's done well, but there's something about him; Marcus,"

Onan shared one day, "something that tells me he's not really aware of what he's in for..." he watched as Marcus nodded agreement.

"His eyes are full of future glory," added Marcus quietly as they observed the young man walking past piles of the dead, nudging his fellow soldiers and telling jests that no one gave mirth to.

Then came the day every soldier dreads, and often, many kings...

There are battles where every single man of the infantry is needed on the field and more where they are not. The middle general of the fifth regiment of The Far Isles lay wounded and the lower generals were in a heated debate regarding the deployment of the remaining men while waiting for reinforcements.

"...we don't have enough men to hold the ground without a calvary, my lord, we should wait for the agreed signal," began the leader of the lower generals, but his suggestion was overridden as the man before him stared him down.

"I outrank you, general," replied the man with contempt, "by both position and intellect; you will follow my orders or I'll see you hanged!"

The lower general stepped back from his superior breathing heavily and turned away from him, knowing that if he said another word that he would likely have to fight him to the death. As much as he might long to, he knew this would be a dishonorable act that might disrupt morale even further. The lower general was not deceived by the orders of Lord Argus; clearly the noble wanted to divide the regiment in order to save his own skin; the only outcome from such a foolhardy decision. His second in command, who was standing nearby, blinked rapidly as his leader confirmed the order.

"You heard the man; divide the regiment and meet the enemy on the field."

"Sir?" His second in command whispered fearfully; he turned to gaze on the rows and rows of the enemy infantry waiting below them on the fields; they needed at least two more regiments to even have a fighting chance, and now their leader wanted them to divide their forces and attack?

Before long, the general turned toward his soldiers who had

drawn lots for the privilege of dying first for their king; he spoke quietly to their stiff and frightened faces.

"I won't give you false hope; without calvary, our only aim is to sell our souls at the highest price possible; a price so high they'll wish they'd never come against us."

The lower general grimly drew his sword, and the eyes of his men widened as they realized that he would lead them. Then he shouted,

"Remember today who you are; we are the men of The Far Isles, and we bow to what?"

"No one!" The men roared.

"To what?!?" He bellowed.

"NO ONE!"

The enemy generals moved out of their tent at the faraway sounds above them and looked to their scouts in puzzlement.

"What is going on?" Asked one of the generals as his lieutenant approached.

"It appears my lord, that the remnant troops of The Far Isles are going to attack us before nightfall...sir."

"Is this some sort of ruse?" Questioned the general as his scout shrugged. "Could it be a trap?"

"According to our latest reports, the closest reinforcements are miles away..."

The scout's voice muted as his commanding officer stood thinking.

"Charge the hill," he finally said with deadly calm, "slay them all to the last man."

LATER IN THE BEGINNING TWILIGHT, High General Aton stood up from his chair in astonishment as the young lord entered his tent, his armor shredded; his face and body bloodied.

"What are you doing here?" Asked the general in surprise, "where are my scouts?"

"Ambushed, my lord," replied the man breathlessly, "the enemy came from nowhere; I barely escaped with my life; there's no one left..."

The general made a hurried gesture and a page handed the young lord a ladle filled with water; he drained it in huge gulps and wiped his mouth. Then Aton's eyes narrowed; he stared at Onan, whose face was unreadable.

"Did you see our reinforcements on the way back?" Asked Onan and watched as the man's gazed shifted back and forth as though searching his memory. Then he shook his head.

"I saw no one, not even a horse..."

His eyes lit on a skein of wine on a table near the maps; he looked to his commanding officer; Aton nodded and without another word he drained that as well. All the men then looked to the opening of the tent as two men entered; Marcus, who was holding up another man who limped and hopped slightly as he walked; the second in command of the leadership that was left of the fifth regiment. The young lord's eyes widened as he pointed in shock.

"You! You betrayed us all!"

He swiftly drew his sword in one motion to gut the hapless soldier, but Onan was faster; his blade fell with a clatter to the ground.

"He's earned the right to speak," growled Onan, "as a survivor of the conflict, just as you did."

"Forgive me, my lord," said the young lord contritely, as he continued to glare at the soldier, who could barely stand, much less defend himself from attack. Still, his fear of eminent death quickly turned to resolve as he looked his High General.

"What say you, soldier," asked Aton.

"My lord, our middle general fell in battle and Lord Argus assumed command over all of us; he threatened to hang general Spandil if he did not split our regiment and attack the enemy..." the soldier paused to restrain his emotions as he continued speaking. "General Spandil led us into battle; he followed orders to the end, my lord..." and Spandil's second in command reached into his tattered armor and withdrew a pouch he then handed to Aton. The young lord looked puzzled until he saw the High General's face drained of blood as he gazed on the contents; wordlessly Aton opened his palm and everyone else in the tent reacted to the sight of Spandil's sigil and hammered coins with his likeness; proof that the wounded soldier before them had stood next to his commanding general as he died.

"He's lying, High General," said the young lord desperately, "Why would I give such orders; the enemy attacked us from nowhere!"

"Why, indeed…" responded the general almost to himself.

Then the tent flaps parted again and a middle general bowed to his high commander.

"My lord, we've found another survivor of the conflict…"

At the general's swift gesture to escort the soldier in, the middle general shook his head.

"He's dying, my lord," the man nearly whispered.

"Bring them both," said Aton as he exited the tent, and Onan and Marcus complied with the entire company of men within the tent.

It is an honor for a dying soldier to see his high commander before death, and though he could not rise to properly greet Aton, the poor soldier attempted to; his fellow soldiers gently restrained him at a nod from the High General. Aton reached out for his hand, a gesture that brought tears to the man's eyes.

"My lord…" said the soldier and coughed roughly; his healer wiped the man's face and shook his head slightly at the general's questioning glance.

"Where are your men, soldier?"

"Half of us charged the bottom of the hill with General Spandil at Lord Argus command, general," the man responded weakly, "the rest of us held our position when the enemy moved to crush them and then charged the hill. Then Lord Argus turned his horse and left us to our fate…" the soldier's voice trailed away in a soft gurgling; his jaw went slack and he moved no more.

"I sought reinforcements, general!"

High General Aton asked this next question quietly, and those of his men who knew him, including Onan and Marcus began to move back.

"Which way did you go, Argus; north, or northwest?"

The young lord began to stammer. "I - I don't understand; what -"

Aton stood with his back to Argus; he was still looking at the dead man before him when he roared.

"WHICH WAY DID YOU GO?!?"

His confidence fully shaken, Argus almost shrugged as he blinked rapidly and tried to respond. He noticed the men around him stepping away and he tried to gather his wits about him.

"North..." he stammered, "I believe it was towards the north; what difference would it make...?"

"You assumed command without my authority; you sent over five thousand men to their deaths without reason..." and now Aton turned to gaze on a paling Lord Argus. "Then you tell me you sought reinforcements and yet saw no one, not even a horse where I placed over thirty regiments...and you ask what difference it would make?!?"

Lord Argus dropped his veneer of compliance and lifted his nose and almost sneered at the general.

"Of course I assumed command," he blustered, "I was born a noble; it is my right to rule over these men; over all of you! My father has the ear of the king-"

Without another word, High General Aton drew his sword.

"You're a deserter, Argus, and a coward. Because you're a noble, I'm going to give you a choice; you can face execution or you can fight me to the death; either way, you're going to answer for the blood of those men with your own."

The soldier closest to Argus handed him his sword as he stared at Aton incredulously.

"Why this is preposterous," he began, "I'm not going to fight you..."

Aton grimly stepped forward and Argus began to swing wildly.

"No! No!"

In seconds, the general disarmed Argus, who turned blindly to run; Aton grabbed his cloak, swung the young lord around and without a second's hesitation ran him through. Argus gasped and stared at Aton in shock; blood ran from his mouth as his hand closed painfully on the general's cloak; he sank to the ground and died. Aton sharply flicked his blade to spin the blood of Argus from it; he pointed to the body.

"Wrap him carefully and place him on the cart of nobles so we can return him to his mother..." he turned to glance at the fallen soldier and sighed. "Record his name for the king; then bury him with the others..." then the High General of The Far Isles walked heavily away.

The pages, scouts and soldiers hurried to fulfill the general's will; Onan and Marcus looked to each other but said nothing; what, indeed, could be said?

King Valtus sighed deeply again at this memory as related to him by his High General and reported by his High Regent Galen from the surviving second in command of General Spandil. Again, Aton had been right, but his execution of the young noble had cost the king a crucial alliance, and now years later, the family of Hesta might threaten the same.

Yet as difficult as the king's task was, that of his middle general Marcus of his first regiment was greater. With Forde General Onan in jail and Hesta confined to her new barracks while her face healed, it was left to Marcus to explain to Hesta's family all the changes that had come to pass since the day began. Marcus swallowed hard to get past the lump in his throat; he would rather face his own commanding officer than Hesta's mother.

Yet the young general used wisdom in his tale; merely conveying that Lord Onan was held up by his duties and that Hesta had been accepted into the military and would start her training immediately. If Hesta's father suspected anything amiss he gave no sign of it; he offered Marcus food and drink which he respectfully declined; he must return to the High General at once. Hesta's father was distracted by a servant; as both he and Marcus turned away from each other, Hesta's mother chanced to speak.

"Young Marcus..."

"Yes, my lady," responded Marcus with a slight bow, "how may I be of service to you?"

She lifted her chin as she continued.

"I realize that you and Hesta have been friends for a long time and have no doubt become quite attached to each other. But Hesta is swiftly becoming more a woman and less a child; her acceptance into the military, though against my will, still bears proof of such. I know that I can trust you, Marcus, to look out for her and ensure that her... innocence...will not be taken advantage of while in the company of such men."

She narrowed her gaze as she took his measure; Marcus didn't yet realize that he was holding his breath in shock at her words; she stepped closer to him and watched as Marcus stepped back.

"Now, her brother Onan is quite protective of her; I know this. Yet... he may turn a blind eye to...others...who have already gained his trust. Our family is highly ranked in King Valtus court, Marcus; it would not do for someone...beneath...Hesta's station in life to take advantage of her unfiltered...affection. She...has always been unduly affected by war stories and the like. So...may I rely on your discernment, young Marcus?"

Marcus blinked rapidly, trying to keep the heat from his face and failing to. He could not mistake her words.

"I would do nothing to bring dishonor to Hesta or her family," he whispered. "Onan is like a brother to me; I would die for either one of them."

She held his gaze unwavering for a moment, then nodded.

"I believe we understand each other. Good evening to you, young Marcus..."

He could not move for some time; once Marcus had his wits about him he noticed that he was alone in the hall.

HESTA COULD NOT TELL you the moment she realized that she was in love with her best friend; there wasn't a particular day or moment that completely stood out from the rest. It was simply a rather painful growing awareness that began as a thought in the back of her mind that she constantly scoffed at and pushed away. Of course she loved Marcus, she told this wayward and persistent thought, he'd always been there, and he'd supported her less than girlish dreams from the beginning. Marcus never made fun of her, as some of the other boys and even girls Hesta grew up with did; he would leave his friends and practice with her whenever Onan or her father was unavailable.

So it just made sense that she would be fond of him.

Still, it was around Hesta's sixteenth summer that she began to notice how her thoughts and her eyes began to follow Marcus's movements as he made his way through the army compound. He made it a ritual to discreetly check on Hesta before he made the rounds with his men. Marcus was already in a leadership position; Hesta had stood proudly at attention when Onan decorated him before Aton and his men. She was possibly the only person who detected a slight tensing in his jaw; an indication that Marcus was concealing his emotions at this great honor. She knew him like no one else did; the thought brought an unaccustomed flush to her face as Marcus quickly gazed in her direction; Hesta saw the grin in his eyes that his lips expertly concealed.

She was too young to attend his unofficial celebration; her older brother had crossed his arms and shook his head sternly at her unbridled request.

"No, Hesta," Onan said firmly, "You're too young, you know this. A tavern is no place for you; must I remind you of the trouble I'm likely to suffer if our parents find out?"

"But, brother," Hesta reasoned, "The safest place for me is next to you, correct?"

Her brother smiled and scoffed at her efforts.

"Your flattery has overreached your intent, sister," replied Onan with a smirk, "You've just reminded me that I myself will have little to celebrate if I spend the evening watching you."

"Onan, wait!" cried Hesta as her sibling turned away, "I'll be quiet as a mouse—"

"Don't make me repeat myself, Hesta," Onan said over his shoulder, "You're a soldier, remember? Marcus will be recognized at the next General's Dinner, where you'll be in attendance in unofficial capacity because of your station."

Hesta felt her face change from despair to happiness.

"I will?" she said as Onan paused at the door to look back at her.

"Remember to keep that look of joy on your face, sister," continued Onan sardonically, "Since 'unofficial capacity' means that you'll have to wear a dress."

Hesta felt her jaw drop in disbelief as her beloved brother turned the corner and walked from her sight with a laugh.

As it turned out, the General's Dinner was an amazing event that Hesta enjoyed more than she thought she would. A highlight of the evening was being introduced to King Valtus, the man Hesta had pledged life and limb to; a rare honor most soldiers never experience. It was the one time in her life Hesta was glad of her vaulted station and that of her brother Onan. Hesta was in awe of King Valtus; he seemed to be robed in light and his eyes were kind as he accepted her bow of respect. And Queen Inka—it took every ounce of Hesta's training not to stare at her; Hesta was convinced the queen was the most beautiful woman she'd ever seen.

But as gracious as the king and queen were, Hesta had to stifle a laugh when she spied Prince Sumter and Prince Rasdeter trying hard not to fidget as the soldiers passed. Hesta caught Sumter slyly pinching his cousin as she walked by. Rasdeter gasped, drawing a stern glance from a stunning woman who Hesta later learned was Lady Irisella, once of the Kingdom of the Western Hills. Hesta grinned inwardly; it was nice to be reminded that people were people no matter their station in life; she imagined now those two cousins playing like she and her own siblings. But she did not miss how Prince Sumter gazed with delight on Marcus, who was very respectful as he bowed to the two princes. Marcus was closer in age to the prince of course than either the High General or her brother and held in high esteem for both his devotion and his prowess; naturally, Sumter looked forward to seeing him. Yet the young prince also smiled at Hesta and she could not help but marvel at his interest and knowledge of the people in his father's military.

He will make a wise king one day, Hesta mused, may I live to see it.

Her thoughts turned to her mother reluctantly; despite the terrible separation Hesta endured from her mother, she was quite civil towards her military daughter, no doubt in part due to her shock at seeing her child in an evening gown befitting her standing in palace society. Hesta realized in that moment that Onan had somehow arranged to keep the knowledge of Hesta's attendance from her parents; no doubt to lessen any possibility of strife between them because of her. The emotions that unexpectedly crossed her mother's face when she saw Hesta brought both pain and insight:

She doesn't hate me so much as I believed, she thought ruefully.

Yet she will never accept my decision, Hesta noted as her mother took great pains to avoid contact or interaction with High General Aton.

I suppose it's quite possible she will never forgive either one of us.

"You are well?" her mother had asked rather stiffly, and Hesta nodded.

"Yes, my lady," she answered respectfully, and blinked rapidly as her mother turned a sharp discerning eye on Hesta's gown and hair.

"You look—" her mother paused to catch her breath, "You look as you should," she continued finally, "You've brought honor to your house."

Her mother turned away but not before Hesta detected the emotion behind her barely polite comments; she didn't realize that she was holding her own breath until she felt a slight touch on her arm.

She turned expecting to see her brother Onan, but it was Marcus, his face flushed with pleasure.

"Hesta," Marcus exclaimed in unabashed admiration, "You look amazing!"

"Oh, Marcus," replied Hesta in exasperation, "Not you, too."

She felt inordinately pleased at his compliment and embarrassed.

Marcus tried to compose himself and restrain his emotions, but it was too late; he grinned from ear to ear.

"I'm a traitor, I know," he confessed, "But you must forgive me this once, Hesta; you're quite lovely; may I?" and he reached for her hand and brought it to his lips as politely as he could; then both friends dissolved into laughter at his mock chivalry.

Hesta curtsied awkwardly to return his sport.

"Oh, my lord, I should die from your admiration!" she cried in a mocking tone and Marcus stifled his urge to laugh louder.

"Hush, now, they'll think we've been drinking," he lightly cautioned, and Hesta restrained herself with difficulty.

"Well, we can't have that," Hesta pretended to whisper, "My reputation is at stake!"

Hesta watched as her playful words brought a slight shadow to the face of Marcus, and she felt him pull back from her emotionally. He had held her hand a little longer than he intended to; Marcus brought it back to his lips more seriously this time and Hesta's fingers tightened on his as he turned to go.

"Thank you, Marcus," Hesta said softly, and he gave her a slightly puzzled look.

"For what, Hesta?"

"A little levity was needed just now," Hesta replied, "My mother was here."

"I know," he said kindly, "I saw her walk away."

He squeezed her fingers and released them.

"Perhaps we'll dance later?" she said cheekily to draw another smile from the sudden somberness of his face and succeeded.

Then Marcus shook his head.

"It's one of the few things I'm certain I'm no good at, Hesta," he answered with a half-smile, "Best I stay in the places I'm familiar with."

He held her eyes a moment and then winked before turning away and Hesta knew she'd lost more than a dance with him; an invisible hole in her chest had suddenly opened wide, and she knew she could never close it again without him.

❧

A YOUNG MAN waited silently in the trees covering the main plains of the lands of The Far Isles; from time to time he wiped his face on his sleeve. In his hands rested a lone spear, the handle of it reinforced to accommodate a longer, thicker blade. He'd been shadowing a herd of great beasts that would one day be called a variation of the modern rhino, one of the most dangerous animals on the western plains, the exception being a few of the carnivorous Great Lizards.

He did not reveal his hunt to his mother and family who were already occupied with the burial of a loved one. By the time they missed him, the boy grimly reasoned, he should be either home or being prepared for his own funeral.

Coated with the scent glands of a rhino he'd purchased from a town merchant, the young man endured long hours battling gnats and flies attracted to the aroma, and a few puzzled glances from the dim sighted males who seemed to detect a rival above them in the trees.

It was the rutting season, and one of the few ways a hunter could find a rhino separated from the herd. The one he was looking for had finally persuaded a female in heat to mate with him; the boy listened to the sounds of their courtship while he awaited his chance. He knew he had found the right one; a tell tale band of pink white flesh on his left hind leg disturbed the perfect deep grey of its body. The boy wanted to be sure that he'd located him; it would be dishonorable to slay the wrong beast.

Reflecting on his training inevitably brought thoughts of his father to mind; the boy quickly wiped his face against his sleeve again and set his jaw. He knew he only had one slim chance to complete his mission; he must land atop the beast and bury his blade in the only vulnerable area: the part where neck, shoulder and torso meet in the small radius as the head turned. His blade must be long enough to sever the connection before either reflex or instinct gave the creature time to swivel and crush him.

His reverie was shattered by the sound of the female moving away and the boy's heart pounded; if the male followed her, it would not move under the tree where he waited, and he would have to risk running over the connected tree branches in a desperate attempt to catch it. But the male snorted and came towards him as it finally detected the odorous scent glands; instinctively protective of its potential legacy.

As other males before it, the beast stopped below the tree in confusion; it slightly lifted his head and the boy dropped without a sound, his mind ablaze with one thought:

In the name of my father...

The blade went true to its target, and the creature made the expected popping noise of a severed spine and windpipe; still it ran a distance before crashing to earth and the boy released a war cry as he slid to the ground, his limbs trembling from adrenaline and exhaustion. He quickly sawed and hacked to remove the lower leg streaked with white skin and tossed it aside to the trees for his trophy and proof of the hunt; then turned to the arduous task of separating the horned head from its body. He was thus engaged when he felt the ground beneath him shaking; the boy looked up to see the herd he'd been stalking charging towards him in an avalanche of horn, muscle and bone.

Desperately he glanced at the trees and knew he'd never make it. He curled up and tucked in his head as the herd came crashing around him, the huge carcass of his prize the only thing between him and crushing death. Normally the short, squat legs of the rhino would render it almost impossible to climb over the dead body of a full grown male, but a panicked female slammed into it and pushed forward by the press of the others, found her thrashing bulk halfway across the flank; the boy looked up in time to see her teetering towards him; the sharp horn over her nose poised to gouge him. But he saw an opening; as he crouched to launch himself away from her the whole world turned white as a Great Lizard, the cause of the stampede, scooped up the female as though she weighed nothing; her death shriek echoed through the forest.

The boy rested nearby his trophy, panting and trying to catch his breath. Adrenaline fading, a sharp pain went through him as he tried to come to his feet; the horn of the doomed rhino had ripped his foot as she was lifted from the earth. Falling back to the ground he swiftly tore his clothes to make a binding for the wound and halt the flow of blood. Finally he searched the killing area for his spear, which was miraculously intact; it served as a makeshift staff to help him limp in the direction of home; he only made it a few miles before falling again to the earth and passing out.

The Mastery of Aton

The year Hesta turned sixteen, her older brother Onan married, to the great relief of their parents. Though on the surface the marriage appeared to be arranged to please his mother, General Onan worked diligently behind the scenes to influence the family of the young woman he most desired to be bonded with, whose parents most fervent hope was to find a suitable match for their daughter. Onan, as a Forde General, appeared to be next in line to be High General of the Far Isles; only a Crown Prince or High Regent was of higher station; an unlikely match for the middle daughter of a landed lord.

The young lady in question was more than pleased to bond with Onan, having met him a few years ago at a similar state dinner and exchanged secret letters that tied her heart to him with cords of steel. A few close calls where she had almost been married off to another lord caused Onan to step up his timetable and reveal his intentions to her astonished and thrilled parents.

Hesta was overjoyed for Onan, though she did not see anything extraordinary about the woman who was betrothed to her brother. She was pretty enough and well educated; but what Hesta liked most about her was the look of adoration the girl reserved for her future husband; that, for Hesta, was all she required to approve of her.

Onan and Hesta's mother was beside herself with happiness; her grandchildren would be suitable alliances for princes and princesses upon birth; she spent the days leading up to the nuptials pouring over the noble bloodlines of neighboring kingdoms and preparing alliance proposals with her regents. Their father, inordinately grateful for peace in his home, ordered caskets of fine vintage and his best veal; hired hunters to bring back several does and a stag to be dressed and smoked for his guests; sent servants to harvest the fields and bring the bounty to their tables.

Hesta could not help herself from jesting her sibling:

"My deepest thanks, brother," said Hesta in an undertone, "For giving our mother something else to battle with our father about other than me."

The corner of Onan's mouth lifted.

"You're not out of the woods yet, my sister," said Onan, "Pray that my soon to be wife conceives before you're promoted to an entry leadership position, which is likely to happen in the next few months, unless of course, you're willing to fail at something."

Onan crossed his arms and grinned at the darkening of his sibling's eyes; Hesta would willingly fail at breathing before her craft. Yet she doubted that even her promotion in the ranks of the military could dampen the good spirits of her mother during this time of promise and bright futures ahead.

From the beginning Aton worked with Hesta almost every week and tested her skills constantly. He wanted Hesta to excel at her ability to work both hands equally; it was the best defense against a left handed soldier, like the general was. Aton reminded Hesta more than once that it was because she was focused on defense of right handed men that he was able to easily penetrate her formidable skills.

"In battle, thinking will get you killed, Hesta," cautioned the general, "If you rely on twin swords, you will have no shield to protect your body from blows; therefore your objective must be to slay anything before it can touch you. You must create a wall of air that nothing can penetrate; an invisible defense that moves without error."

Hesta learned from General Aton to use a shield as well as any other soldier, but still the general focused on her prowess without one.

"Suppose you lose your shield in a fight," stated Aton, "What will you do then? Stand there and allow your enemy to run you through? If your shield is shattered, you must fight without it; using anything at hand, unless and until you gain another one. A soldier truly only needs a shield for protection from arrows, and if your archers are doing their job, you won't need it; a dead body is better protection anyway."

Hesta had nodded at this wisdom; her father had recently shared tales of being forced to use the body of a soldier; friend or foe as cover from arrows and even catapults.

Despite her determination, there were days and even nights when Hesta questioned her own resolve, as any sane human would do when faced with a lifestyle that could end any given day in the demise of the practitioner. She hadn't experienced her first battle yet, though there wasn't a day she didn't practice every single strategy she learned.

Hesta fought left handed, right handed and ambidextrous warriors as she was; Aton literally tied one arm at a time to her side and made her fight until she could no longer stand.

"You've still too much pride in your skills, Hesta," the general barked at her, "What will you do if an arm is damaged or maimed; how will you make it to the end of the day?"

"I'll fight until I fall!" she cried out and Aton roared:

"A soldier stands from the rising of the sun until it sets! Stand up, damn you! You fall when you die!"

He grabbed her arm roughly and set Hesta back on her feet; she stifled her sobs and swung her sword until she fell senseless to the ground where her general left her, refusing to allow anyone to assist her. When Hesta came to herself, Aton stood over her with his arms crossed and she felt fear in her heart.

"Go home, Hesta," Aton said gravely, and Hesta raised herself up.

"Please, general," Hesta pleaded as she tried to struggle to her feet, "I'm ready, I swear it—"

"You've not failed me, Hesta," continued the general dispassionately, "I asked you for everything and you've given it to me. Go home and rest; be back in formation at dawn and we will begin again."

She looked up at him in disbelief and Aton's eyes narrowed.

"I never repeat commands to a soldier, Hesta, when speaking to one," General Aton said quietly, "Am I speaking to one now?"

Though her limbs were on fire, they obeyed her; Hesta came to her feet and forced a bow to her commander before turning to march as well as she could away from him.

The next day brought new trials; General Aton placed Hesta in a field and commanded mounted soldiers to run towards her repeatedly; she learned to wield a shield and sword from a disadvantaged position.

All day long Hesta was thrown to the ground as the mounted soldiers passed her; sometimes she was able to strike either sword or shield to bring the soldier either off his horse or close to it; her fellow warriors suffered bruised ribs and arms as much as she did. More than once she was dragged, and her mentor said nothing as Hesta learned to cut whatever reins had bound her. Her legs, arms and even her cheeks were skinned and bruised; Aton remained silent as she returned from the fields bloodied and trembling. He did not need to tell her what might happen if she fought on hard ground instead of grass that merely whipped her skin as opposed to ripping chunks of it on unyielding rock.

He never once told Hesta exactly what he wanted, but by the third grueling day General Aton had what he was looking for; the first soldier who passed Hesta found himself sharing a saddle with her, at least, for a few seconds before she kicked him to the ground and took off on his horse.

Aton roared again, this time with approval:

"Yes!"

His middle general grinned.

"It seems our Hesta has stopped trying to think things through, my lord," he said as he watched the dismounted soldier come to his feet and limp from the field; Aton placed his hands on his hips and nodded.

"Her training now begins in earnest," agreed Aton, "She's finally given me something to work with."

General Aton was a master of his craft, both the training of men and women and the ability to pass on his mastery. A soldier that was worthy of his best efforts were not easy to uncover, and when Aton found such a gem, he placed that person, male or female into his forge of artistry and would not pull them out until he either broke them or made them into something that could never be broken. Onan, who was perfect except for his temper, took Aton ten years to find and well worth the occasional conflict. Marcus, however, was General Aton's hidden jewel, with all of Onan's strength and a far better temperament; Aton felt himself blessed indeed to have two such men in his army. And though he would never say any of these things aloud, the High General was most impressed with Hesta; not because she was a woman but because it didn't matter.

She had not been afraid when she first faced Aton; nervous, yes, but not afraid. That she was equally skilled with both hands caused him to test her as though she were more adept than she was, and he was quite impressed that she lasted as long as she did. Yet he knew that without training Hesta would die in seconds in a real fight, so he fought her like a man to teach her how to fight like a master.

His eyes narrowed as he watched her ride across the fields towards him.

Even among thousands of men, mused the general, *A good soldier is hard to find, and a warrior, that perfect blend of discipline and controlled chaos, is even more difficult. Now I have three, out of more than a million; I count myself rich indeed.*

Hesta, who was too far away to hear her mentor's shout of enthusiasm was astonished to notice the change in her mentor as she rode back to where Aton stood and dismounted. General Aton did not smile but she saw the glint in his eyes that she knew meant that he approved of her actions.

"My lord?" she asked tentatively and watched as General Aton crossed his arms; ever a signal of what was to come.

"Get back on that horse, Hesta," Aton commanded, "Now that you know how to get on a horse from a disadvantaged position, I need to see if you can defend an advantaged position. Go!"

Hesta grinned and swiftly complied; determined that it would not take her three days to complete this next assignment.

Aton's middle general commented again:

"She's unstoppable, general--" the middle general began but Aton interrupted him.

"Not yet, she isn't," he growled, "She's still waiting for me to tell her she is, and I'm still waiting for her to show me."

Aton turned a piercing eye on his middle general.

"On the day, those two objectives come together, middle general," he rumbled, "Then you'll see something. Hesta will no longer be a soldier or even a warrior; she'll be a force of nature itself."

PRINCESS SORA soon learned her prince was true to his word; despite the protests and general furor over their unforeseen engagement, she married him months later in a lavish ceremony at his palace, where she eventually and briefly met her new family. It seemed her new husband relished her nation's custom of secluding their noble women; immediately following the marriage banquet, Sora was hidden away from almost everyone, the exception, of course being her mother in law. All males were forbidden to be in her presence, even servant boys, to the high amusement of his brothers, including the Crown Prince.

"Once I am king, brother, be sure I will demand that you both attend my feasts," related the Crown Prince gravely with a twinkling eye, "else my own wife might feel somehow in the presence of her betters."

To this his younger brother replied with a sly wink, "Or you might well turn this custom into law once you endure the benefits of it..."

Since the princess was accustomed to this lifestyle she did not protest her lack of outside male company and found herself eager to engage with the ladies of the court; the older women a source of comfort while she mourned the loss of her relationship with her own mother, a relationship replaced with letters instead of physical proximity. Her new husband granted her a long courtship and her eventual initiation into womanhood was tender, gentle and soon, quite passionate. By the time her prince relented and allowed Sora's official presentation to the court, it was nearly time for a seclusion of a totally different kind; that of a happily married woman about to bear a child.

The announcement of Sora's pregnancy, however, caused an explosion in the King's court; the wife of the Crown Prince had not yet produced an heir. Unconsciously following his younger brother's seeming jest, the Crown Prince had her placed in seclusion immediately; whispered rumors of her possible barrenness flooded the curtained suites of the palace. Sora's husband was wise enough to say nothing and quickly returned his wife to her previous refuge away from all gossip. Alone in their rooms, the couple celebrated the coming fruit of their deep love for each other.

The only other thing casting a shadow on this future event was the news of war on the horizon; from a nation large enough to require the attendance of every able bodied male; from king to the youngest noble, Sora's husband, the prince.

Naturally, the princess protested her husband's absence.

"Must you go, my lord?" She whispered late one evening. "Surely, there are enough princes to go in your place."

At first the prince chuckled softly.

"Where is the trembling girl I held in my arms but a year ago; the one who had never even seen a man? Will you miss me so much?"

"But...but I've never been separated from you since that night—" she began, then stopped as her husband placed his fingers beneath her chin.

"I do this to protect you, Sora, and our child," he continued gently. "You must remember your training in politics; to remain home would be a clear indication that I desire the throne. My brother has no heir; he could have me executed for treason, with the option of taking my child for himself."

"No..." she breathed at his somber nod. Then the prince took her hand.

"You must say nothing of these things we have discussed, my beauty, not even to the servants who tend to your needs…" he placed his other hand over her swelling belly. "All of our lives are at stake here; familial bonds mean little when it comes to the needs of the throne."

The prince drew Sora into his arms for comfort.

"Then I shall pray that the Crown Princess conceives before you head out to war," Sora said as she rested her head against his chest and listened to her husband sigh.

***

In the beginning, Hesta would practice with Marcus when she wasn't with her commander, but as the days progressed, often Hesta could do no more than go home to her barracks and fall on her bed, asleep instantly. She bathed when she awoke, whatever the hour, dressed herself and ate a few bites of food before falling back to sleep, rising just in time to reach her post and stand in formation as the first rays of the sun touched the nearby mountains.

General Aton ran Hesta for weeks at a time, then gave her two, perhaps three days to rest before her grueling regimen started again. Her soft edges vanished, and Hesta turned lean and stronger than she'd ever been before. She thought she knew what it was like to depend on her weapon but that was before Aton; soon her sword became a part of Hesta; she no longer felt dressed without it.

Her own brother's marriage celebration was almost a blur; Marcus sat next to Hesta so he could discreetly prop her up; at one point she slumped against him and Marcus was forced to slip his arm around Hesta to keep her from tumbling to the tiles. Her best friend felt compassion for her; Marcus had trained under the same stern and unforgiving task master.

"Hesta," Marcus whispered desperately, "you must try to rouse yourself; everyone will think you've been drinking; including your mother!"

These words pierced the haze and fog surrounding Hesta's brain; she shook her head and tried to appear alert; the pounding of her heart kept her awake for half an hour, long enough for Onan and her parents to toast both guests and the bride's family. Then the needs of the body overrode all others; even the fear of her mother's distain was not enough to keep Hesta's eyes open and she succumbed.

But when she opened her eyes again, Hesta was not at her brother's wedding; she wasn't even in her simple bed in the army camp. She turned groggily on soft sheets and bedding; a full minute passed before she recognized her old bedroom in her parent's house.

A TRIBE of healers found the boy and after diligently making inquiries, they located his home and delivered him to his family. Fever set in, and the young man remained unconscious for several days. Still, his family was shocked by the tales of his rescue.

"What are you saying, man," asked one tribe member incredulously, "that Artan's boy went off to hunt a horned beast, all by himself, and slew it?!?"

The healer the tribe member was speaking to crossed his arms.

"He told the tale himself," responded the man resolutely. "Yes, delirium was beginning to take hold, but his directions made sense, and we found the carcass and the severed leg just the boy described it…"

Another healer pointed at the partially severed head of the rhino, the meat of which and the body were already deep in the process of being preserved and divided up for storage to sustain the tribe families in the coming days.

"Look, there, you can still see the wound from the death blow, and here's the spear—"

"No one helped him," stated the first healer who spoke, "believe it or no, the child's done something nearly impossible, and he did it alone; how he survived a rhino stampede…" the man shook his head and shrugged in wonder at his own words.

They all turned in silence to gaze towards the house where they knew the boy rested with his mother attending to him, wiping his fevered brow quietly as he slept and drawing covers over his shivering form. She said nothing, even when the healers first brought his limp, unconscious body on a cart to his home. Nor did she weep, and others marveled at her composure.

Had she not just buried her husband?

But her thoughts were her own, and she kept them to herself; they would never know how fiercely proud she was of him. Those unwise enough to advise her to upbraid her son for going off on a hunt while his father lay cold in the ground met a daunting eye.

"You will say nothing to him of what he's done, none of you," she'd said sharply on the first day of his return, "whether he recovers or not—" and then she'd turned away from them all, to maintain both composure and self defense.

But the child clung to life, and some days after these events, he opened his eyes to find his mother beside him. Remorse crept into his face as he looked at her.

"Mother..." he croaked hoarsely, but she shook her head firmly.

"No...don't you dare apologize for something you made up your mind to do; I won't hear of it..."

She turned pointedly to stare at her servants and the healers, who swiftly departed the room. Then she came to her feet and stared down at him.

"You invoked an ancient law of our people; one that is yet binding today. It is the law of the Avenger of Blood; against man or beast," she said quietly as he looked up at her in amazement. "You had every right to hunt the beast down and slay it before it left our lands. Your father..." and here she paused to regain her emotions, "Your father would be proud of you; as am I."

His mother held herself tightly as she left his room; she'd had neither rest nor sleep during his fever and her body was trembling from exhaustion. A page met her in the hall with news.

"My lady, an envoy from the king himself waits outside to speak with you..." and she took his arm for the length of the hall to the front doors and then released him. Another page stood mute with an outer robe on his arm; she allowed him to cover her so that she appeared her station as a lady of the king's court; not a mother giving everything she had to save her son.

She listened carefully as the envoy gave the reason for his visit; the king wished an audience with the son of a lord both brave and skilled enough to hunt and kill a rhino on the plains alone.

"...and thus it is by the graciousness of the king's request that young Lord Artan should attend his master's court—"

"Do cease your prattling, page," interrupted his mother tersely, "Before you unduly embarrass our king. It's quite clear your message was drafted by a scribe completely unfamiliar with our family line. Lord Artan was my husband, and now he's dead, which the king surely knows. You speak of our son— his name is Aton."

GENERAL ATON never again struck Hesta as hard as he had the first time, but her face, arms and ribs endured many bruises before she learned to close any gap he could take advantage of. And although he never said it aloud, Hesta knew he would not allow her to go into battle until she could maintain her invisible defense.

Many times General Aton would have Hesta stand on a hill with him as he gave orders and devised strategy on the movements of his regiments. Hesta realized this was not favoritism; Aton had many inexperienced potential soldiers listening in as he talked with his middle and lower generals.

To Die for A King

Soon it came about that the Far Isles answered a call for aid against a common enemy; the Kingdom of the Golden Round was ambushed by the Kingdom of the Broken Meriden. The Broken Meriden was a constant thorn in the side of the Nine Kingdoms, taking any opportunity to raid and pillage the borders and lands of any nation they marched through.

One hundred and seventy regents, scouts and messengers set out to obtain assistance; only thirty made it to the roads between the kingdoms, and of that number, two made it to the borders of a neighboring kingdom; a scout and a regent. The scout died before the outer gates of the Kingdom of the Rim of the World; the regent died at the feet of the nation's king after delivering his precious parchment; collapsing from a fatal loss of blood from his many wounds.

King Valtus was enraged by the attack; both the Golden Round and the Rim of the World kingdoms were important to him for personal reasons. The Golden Round had a long history of alliance with the Far Isles and thousands of years ago was among the first government to advocate the appointment of the Far Isles as the seat of the High King of the western nations. The Rim of the World was the birthplace of King Valtus mother, the Queen Eminent, and the guardians of the actual Rim of the World, a vast land with a wall of ice that held the Great Lizards during a continuous hibernation that cycles every twenty-five thousand years.

The march to the battlefield had taken four months; the Rim of the World was nearly as far away as the Unnamed Lands; and at the request of High General Aton, King Valtus remained behind.

It was the third day of engagement; the Far Isles had arrived in time to prevent an ambush on an unprotected flank of the Golden Round, which had been lured into a strategic feint: the clever High General of the Broken Meriden had appeared to retreat into an ancient canal that the High General of the Golden Round knew was supposedly blocked on three sides with a bottleneck impossible to safely pass through. But the Broken Meriden General had sent men months in advance to dig out the gorge and the unsuspecting men of the Golden Round pursued the retreating army into what might have been a fatal mistake. Forde General Onan, spurred by High General Aton, rode his men at the break of dawn into the opposite valley and into the midst of the surprised Broken Meriden infantry, breaking their line of fire into the bottleneck, trampling their archers from a higher position and wreaking havoc on their now vulnerable lower generals.

The High General of the Broken Meriden cursed softly under his breath; the unmistakable signature of High General Aton meant that this time, the retreat of his forces would be real.

Late morning sunlight spilled on the battlefield; Aton, Onan,

Marcus, and an untested Hesta stood on a hilltop far above the conflict. Swarms of men looked like dark birds moving through the trampled grass below; a scout from the Golden Round was escorted to the generals tent where he gave both thanks to General Aton and tidings of his lower generals movements. The retreat of the Broken Meriden was temporary; Aton was not deceived by the defeat of their northern flank; he knew reinforcements were only miles away. He formed a wedge between the lesser ranks of the Golden Round and the enemy to give them pause while all three nations regrouped for the main battle of the swiftly coming afternoon.

"You have saved us, General Aton," said the Golden Round scout in gratitude, "If not for your assist, the Broken Meriden may have crushed us beyond recovery."

The High General snorted.

"We're not out of the woods yet," rumbled Aton, "If I know King Bokmal, and I do; there is an objective to this attack well past simple aggression of your borders. He wants something—"

"I have reports on the way," interjected Forde General Onan, "My trained hawks have gotten past their arrows; they'll be word of their movements to the east soon."

Hesta waited respectfully until the generals finished their discourse, then she approached and bowed smartly to her High General.

"Permission to speak, my lord."

"What say you, Hesta?"

"I'm ready to engage, General," said Hesta firmly, and Aton turned sharply to stare into her unflinching eyes.

"What do you see, Hesta?" asked the general quietly, and both Onan and Marcus turned to look at her. Aton did not ask Hesta to confirm her readiness; he asked a field question designed to ascertain what if anything she saw on the battlefield that would indicate an action on her part, and her brother hid his shock at her reply.

Hesta turned without hesitation and pointed to the far most western part of the battlefield where she could detect a garrison of the Broken Meriden that seemed to hang back further than the rest of the troops.

"There, my lord," responded Hesta, "Their movements are inconsistent with the usual precision of the Broken Meriden infantry; I suspect that during the main engagement that this portion will be missing; perhaps to set a trap or guide reinforcements to an area our scouts may be unaware of."

The general's eyes narrowed in admiration; Hesta could not possibly know that her upper level generals were aware of such machinations during a battle, and it was something he never taught his pupils until they had at least several battles worth of experience. That Hesta had detected such a maneuver before he taught her showed Aton that she was already thinking like a leader, not just a soldier.

Aton crossed his arms and Hesta held her breath.

"You will wait until the main forces are engaged, Hesta," said the general quietly, "When the enemy forces are focused on where I have them; then you will take a remnant and retreat to the southwest. I'll have forces in reserve to cover you; circle back to the east and take them down; slay everyone who tries to escape you. If even one soldier evades you, they will bring reinforcements into the area behind us and thousands of your brethren will die. Can you do this?"

The general watched as the pupils of Hesta's eyes widened; she nodded firmly.

"I will not fail you." She said this breathlessly, and Aton gave a wave of dismissal. When he turned away from her, the sharp glance he gave Forde General Onan was clear:

Do not follow her.

Onan breathed deeply and nodded to this unspoken command; he turned away so his sister would not see his reaction to her exchange with her superior. So it came about that Onan missed the equally silent order given to Marcus:

You will be her reinforcement.

Marcus touched the hilt of his sword so that his High General would see his agreement.

The opposing forces met at the very top of the afternoon, where all shadows had vanished; the sun and wind hammered without mercy on the armies that merged at first and then slammed each other back.

Bokmal, confident that his remnant had slipped away to the west, focused his archers and infantry on distraction; his mounted men came forward from the north, naturally drawing the attention of the men of the Golden Round, whose advancing horses had formed a gap between themselves and the Far Isles.

An hour into the main conflict, a strange thing happened; another gap formed between the rear of the Far Isles infantry and the Golden Round to the northwest, and as the Broken Meriden swarmed into the opening, forming a damaging wedge between the forces, three regiments under the guidance of a middle general by the name of Kiran, noticed the surge of Hesta's remnant being cut off by the Broken Meriden as she pursued the nearly hidden flank of retreating enemy soldiers that began to melt away into the hills.

General Kiran shouted to his forces to redirect the lower generals:

"There's an opening to the western flank, general," barked Kiran, "Close it!"

Hesta boldly rode straight to the hills where she could see the hidden soldiers beginning to scatter; her comrades pushed hard to maintain their wall of defense. Her heart pounded as a stray arrow took down the man riding next to her; a soldier on her other side seamlessly pulled his bow from his back and returned fire in the direction he detected it. Hesta pressed on, her eye on the last group of fleeing soldiers who realized that their ploy was uncovered; she mentally calculated the distance between them and her tiring mount.

"Estan!" she cried to the soldier who kept pace with her, "We must overtake them!"

The soldier named Estan set his lips in a thin line, spurring his horse forward as they passed the line of trees between them and the desperately running men.

Using the skills she so diligently gained from General Aton, Hesta ran down the hapless foot soldiers who strove with all their might to reach the crest of the hill; Estan placed an arrow in the back of the last one, who fell as their horses sped past his sprawling form. Hesta gazed behind her at the comrades who were catching up to them, so she initially missed the gasp of Estan:

At the very bottom of the hill stood a regiment of warriors from the Broken Meriden, quietly waiting for the soldiers who had just died to warn them of the enemy's approach. They were outnumbered by thousands; Hesta could see no end to them. Her heart pounded in fear and she tasted salt in her mouth; she would die in her first battle before the conflict ended. She could see the face of her father contorted in grief; her mind would not turn to her mother. It seemed time halted as she took in how the horses in the front row raised their heads and shook their manes:

She knew that they were dead men, every one of them.

"We have to flee," said Estan hopelessly, but Hesta shook her head.

"We'll never make it," she replied hoarsely, then her eyes narrowed; she dared a glance at Estan.

"You do as you see fit, Estan, but I'll be damned if my brother finds me with an arrow in my back," she whispered as she blinked back tears.

Hesta pressed her knees against her mount, who surged forward at her command; Estan and the rest of her men followed, roaring as they charged the waiting men of the Broken Meriden, who smiled grimly at their bravery.

As a people, the Kingdom of the Broken Meriden had no regard for those they considered weak. The middle general felt a small thrill of respect at this display; he barely heard his subordinate speaking.

"What is your will, my lord?"

"No arrows," replied the general quietly as he waited for the small group to come closer, "They deserve better for such courage."

Princess Sora waited tensely on the main balcony of the palace, her eyes on the horizon where she hoped to see a scout coming with news of the battle, or even better, the banners of her husband returning home with him alive.

One of her prayers had already been answered; the Crown Princess had indeed conceived before her husband the Crown Prince rode off to war; all the brothers were jovial as they confidently marched through the kingdom's gates.

Months later, however, a carrier hawk landed with a parchment tied to its leg that was smeared with blood; the last battle had ended in disaster; three princes were dead, and both the Crown Prince and her husband could not be found.

The news traumatized Sora and she went into labor; delivering her child under the watchful care of the queen and her healers, whom days later reported to the king the birth of a son, which pleased him greatly under the current circumstances. Sora wept that the man she loved could not be present for the birth of his child and in fact may never come home at all.

Her son was three months old when the Crown Prince was finally located; his body alone on the cart of nobles; drawn in silence through the yawning gates as the whole kingdom wailed in grief. The king aged overnight; his dark hair greyed from temples to the back of his head. Undone at last, the queen threw herself over her son's prone body, heedless of the blood and spices packed around to preserve him on the road home.

Sora could barely keep herself from visibly quaking as she watched this horrid change of events; surely the enemy was searching as diligently for her husband as the kingdom was. Killed or captured, he was the last of the king's direct bloodline; all eyes were now on the Crown Princess; if she birthed a son, all would be well. But if she did not...

Though she said nothing, Sora could feel the eyes of the queen watching her. If Sora's husband returned alive, he was the next king; yet even that was predicated on the Crown Princess; if she birthed a daughter, the debate was over. The king wanted an heir; although he had loved his firstborn, he would be content with a grandson on his throne because the bloodline would be intact. Still, Sora knew the queen's favorite had been her eldest son and she felt sure that no matter what happened, she and her child were in grave danger.

GENERAL KIRAN of the Far Isles gaped in amazement at the charge of the small group ahead of him; he'd never seen such fortitude by soldiers so young; he and his army strained to give their aid before it was too late.

But as Kiran and his soldiers came into view, the middle general of the Broken Meriden felt the ground shaking beneath his troops; from the eastern hills the forces of General Marcus descended on the enemy's flank, and the enemy general released a war cry:

Any day for a Broken Meriden soldier was a good day to die.

Hesta and her men plowed into the front lines, followed closely behind by the armies of the Far Isles dispatched to render assistance; she remembered little except to do as her mentor had bid her:

Slay anything that moved, and do not stop while she breathed.

Marcus was an unrelenting engine of destruction as he annihilated every obstacle between himself and Hesta; his heart stopped as her horse went down screaming and she vanished into a horde of struggling men and women. Seconds later, she resurfaced; swinging her double swords with wild and deadly accuracy; her eyes vacant as she cleared a path before and around her; mindlessly keeping a field of impenetrable air about her at all times.

Hesta heard Estan cry out; she whirled and beheaded a man standing over him; kicked his body out of the way and looked down at Estan.

"Get up!" she roared, and he obeyed her, stabbing an enemy warrior with his short sword until he could bring his long blade back to his defense. They backed into each other and fought madly until the fighting moved away from them; Hesta saw Marcus and began to run towards him, her legs like wings beneath her. Estan was beside her until he staggered and fell; when she turned back, she saw a Far Isles middle general urging her to continue running.

"Estan!" Hesta cried out, but the general waved her off.

"Regroup your men, soldier," said Kiran firmly, "I've got him."

She hesitated; Hesta knew she should not leave a soldier behind, but General Kiran was adamant; he pointed to one of his own men.

"Tie him up," Kiran barked, and one of his men lifted Estan to his horse.

"It's alright, Hesta," gasped Estan, "They won't leave me."

She turned to Kiran, whose name she did not know.

"Thank you, general," she said sincerely, and raced to rejoin her regiment under Marcus, who swiftly lifted her to his horse and thundered across the plains back to the tents of High General Aton and Forde Onan, whom he knew would not breathe until he saw his sister alive or dead.

Hesta was surprised to find Aton's tents miles away from where she left him; Marcus answered her unspoken question:

"A wave of mounted horses changed direction and charged our position; General Aton held the high ground until Onan could return and crush them."

Hesta could not keep the alarm from her voice.

"Is the general alright?" she asked and watched as Marcus chuckled.

"Aton slew the middle general who led the attack and stood fighting atop a mound of slain soldiers until Onan reached him; he's barely scratched."

Marcus felt Hesta relax against his armor and smiled against her wind bound hair. General Aton had that effect on his soldiers; on one hand they thought him immortal, on the other, they all feared the day Aton could no longer lead them.

Hesta wisely kept her gaze on General Aton as she and Marcus approached his tent; his arms were crossed, and she wasn't sure if this was a good thing or not. She dismounted without assistance and followed by the soldiers Aton had sent with her, Hesta marched into the open tent and waited until the general acknowledged her. She did not expect her brother to give note to her presence and he did not disappoint; but Hesta knew her brother well enough to realize that he was relieved to see her alive.

General Aton turned to study Hesta dispassionately as he spoke.

"Where is your shield, Hesta?" asked the general and watched as her face cleared. Not only did she not know where her shield was, Hesta did not recall how she had been separated from it; her focus had been where Aton had advised it should be; on fighting, not thinking about weapons and how to defend herself.

"Forgive me, my lord—" began Hesta as her voice trailed away; and Aton almost smiled.

"I've been advised that you didn't need it," he answered his own question with narrowed eyes, "That you fulfilled the assignment I gave you to the letter, and that you showed uncommon bravery against a foe that out-numbered you and your men."

"As you say it, my lord," said Hesta faintly as she felt her skin burn; she did not dare to glance in Onan's direction.

"Assemble your men, Hesta," ordered General Aton, "I'm going to add five hundred to their number. You'll assign scouts, give field assignments and outline to them how you want them to organize battle reports in the days ahead. For now, you'll report directly to Marcus; when we return, I'll give you the names of the lower and middle generals you'll report to from then on." Aton tilted his head as he appraised her.

"Do you understand these instructions?" he asked a stunned Hesta.

"Yes, my lord," she stammered, "As you say it."

She bowed quickly and left the general's tent; Aton gave a brief gaze to Marcus, who turned to follow her.

After a moment of unbearable silence, Aton finally addressed his second in command.

"What say you, Forde General Onan?" asked the general quietly.

Onan breathed deeply.

"Permission to speak freely, my lord?" he asked, and Aton turned to gaze at him.

"She should be dead," said Onan with a catch in his throat, and blinked rapidly as his commanding officer nodded once and turned away.

. . .

LATER THAT SAME EVENING, Onan searched for Hesta and found her dry retching in her shared tent; her fellow soldiers quickly left after less than a glance from Onan. The day had ended with her still breathing and as she watched the setting sun Hesta felt the adrenalin rolling off her in waves; the sheer need to survive abated and suddenly her eyes had widened as images rushed into view; the faces and limbs of men and women running towards her. Their faces— Hesta looked down at her hands which began to tremble uncontrollably. What did she do? She could see them; some young, some older than her, and some younger still, and then she—what? Hesta clenched her fingers to keep them still; but it wasn't working. She was supposed to do it; her mind was trying to form the words; she was supposed to take her sword and—and stop them; but—why were they still looking at her? Even after she stopped them, when the surprise and fear and every other emotion drained from their eyes; they kept on staring at her.

An experienced soldier, only a few years older than Hesta noted the color of her skin and the vacant emptiness in her eyes; she walked over and helped Hesta bend over in time to keep the contents of her stomach from splattering her armor. Wordlessly she had guided Hesta into her tent and covered her suddenly cold limbs. She left when Hesta's tentmates silently entered to offer a soldier's best comfort; a quiet companionship. They too, departed when General Onan entered; any warrior worth their salt could see that it was Hesta's first battle.

Her brother sat down heavily on the edge of her soldier's bed and patted her shuddering back in sympathy.

"I won't offer you false hope, Hesta," said her brother soberly, "And say that one day you'll forget their faces, or not remember what you've done. You're a true soldier now, and you've slain people. You may not sleep tonight, or even tomorrow; but you've done your duty, and kept your oath to your king. Children will rest in the Nine Kingdoms this night who will never experience a time of dread because of your deeds today."

Onan sighed deeply as his sister began to sob aloud in earnest; he gently stroked her hair as Hesta pressed her face into her covers in horrified despair.

THE FOLLOWING morning a weary Hesta rose early and met with her newly formed company of men and organized them according to her mentor Aton's will. She then sought out the welfare of Estan by way of the general who cared for him, whose name she learned was Kiran.

General Kiran was the same age and build as her friend Marcus; his hair dark and curly where Marcus's hair tended to be unruly and slightly straighter. He looked younger to Hesta until his eyes crinkled; she wondered unconsciously why she even took note of it.

"He's with the healers, Basic General Hesta," related Kiran with a grin, and she flushed down to her feet. Almost everyone had heard of her brave deeds the previous day and how she had refused to run from the fearsome Broken Meriden.

"Does everyone know who I am, General Kiran?" she asked in embarrassment and Kiran's grin broadened.

"Count yourself fortunate to have lived to tell it, Basic General Hesta," offered Kiran with a raised eyebrow, "Many a brave soldier from last day's battle is recounting their deeds in the shaded realms. Indeed, I count myself in awe to have witnessed it; you acquitted yourself well for your first blood."

Hesta saw the compassion behind his jest and found it oddly comforting.

"Do you recall your first battle, Lord Kiran?" asked Hesta in curiosity and watched as Kiran shook his head in a self-depreciating manner.

"No soldier ever forgets his first blood," offered Kiran soberly and gestured for Hesta to accompany him to the healer's tent where Estan rested. "The experience makes or breaks you; there are no other outcomes."

They walked in silence until they reached the healer's tent where General Kiran insisted on holding the flap of the tent open for Hesta, who gave in and entered.

Her gaze fell on an ashen looking Estan laying on a cot like one dead; she rushed to his side in concern. At her touch on his arm; Estan slowly opened his eyes and stared upwards at the fabric of the tent above him; he turned his head painfully at the sound of Hesta's voice.

"Estan; are you alright?" she asked, and he tried to smile and failed.

"General Hesta," he whispered, and she flushed at his words.

"I'm not a general, Estan," Hesta protested in clear embarrassment; Estan tried to shake his head and grimaced instead.

"You should be," he rasped, "What you did—" Estan broke into fevered coughing and Hesta gently pressed his arm again.

"Don't try to talk, Estan; get some rest, I'm just checking on you…" her voice trailed away as she looked up at Kiran, whose face was unreadable. He turned to look for Estan's healer, who came quickly at a glance from him. The healer brought herbs and warm broth; Estan struggled to take a few sips then lowered his head, exhausted. When the healer's soft hands reached to change the strips of cloth around his torso, Hesta noticed a seeping wound at his side and gasped.

"He's bleeding," she said in despair and Kiran nodded.

"You killed the man who stabbed him," Kiran confirmed, "Only strength of will kept him standing afterwards. His exertions however, ripped his stomach muscle."

The healer agreed.

"We're doing all we can for him," she said softly, "It's up to him now."

Hesta leaned over Estan and stroked his face; his eyes opened again and focused on the tent ceiling before he met her eyes.

"Don't you die on me, Estan," said Hesta strongly, "Don't you dare."

He blinked rapidly and she watched his pupils widen.

"I'm trying, Hesta," Estan said weakly as he tried to keep his eyes on her face, "I'm trying—"

Hesta felt the warm fingers of Kiran tighten on her shoulder; she responded as she continued to look at Estan.

"I can't leave him," she began, but Kiran shook his head above them both.

"You must," he said gravely, "Over five hundred soldiers are counting on your guidance; Estan will be fine."

Hesta swallowed with difficulty; she knew the general was correct.

"I'll return to you, Estan," Hesta vowed, and finally Estan managed a faint smile.

"I know you will," he rasped, and Hesta came reluctantly to her feet; the healer offered her a comforting smile.

"Come back tonight," she said kindly, "I'll stay with him, Estan won't be alone."

Impulsively, Hesta leaned again over Estan and planted a kiss on his forehead; the coolness of his skin frightened her.

"Please..." she whispered as Estan stared at her, then slowly closed his eyes again.

Unable to bear anymore, Hesta left the healer's tent, and General Kiran followed her. There was a knot in her throat that wouldn't dislodge itself; she heard the general's voice behind her.

"Your men are waiting for you, Basic General Hesta," he said softly, and she turned to stare at Kiran with wide eyes.

"Is he going to make it?" she asked breathlessly, and Kiran said nothing for a moment.

"Does it matter?"

Blinded, Hesta turned and marched away from the middle general, afraid that if she stayed one more moment, she would dissolve into tears.

Presently the healer joined Middle General Kiran outside the tent.

"He's in a lot of pain, healer," stated the general in a matter of fact tone and the healer tightened her lips.

"Please forgive us, general," stammered the healer, "But for Basic General Hesta's sake we've already given Estan more than his allotment, and we've many other soldiers to care for—"

Kiran sighed and fished a gold coin from his purse, which he then handed to the flustered healer.

"Keep him comfortable," he said quietly, and the healer gratefully promised, disappearing back into the tent to fulfill his will. Kiran crossed his arms and watched as the small figure of the broken hearted young soldier eventually faded from his sight.

PRINCE OF THE FAR ISLES: AN AUDIENCE WITH THE MAGICIAN

"Our entire biological system, the brain and the earth itself work on
the same frequencies."
~~~Nikola Tesla

Long ago, less than a millennium after his decisive victory over the hated creators, the being known as The Magician removed himself from the world scene. You might think that after such a life-altering success at the very dawn of mankind's memory, that he would set up his throne and build a city around it. From there he would rule over men, and every child born on earth from that moment to now would grow up knowing his name.

But his mind didn't work that way.

The one who had learned the secret to confound the once invincible creators was not given to overconfidence. The Magician's vision was a long one; he wanted the earth and its inhabitants for all time, not just a million years or so. He had broken the trust and faith that man had in the creators; they no longer flocked in droves to learn the universal laws and science that governed all of creation. Instead, man
~~~

feared them, leaving their halls of learning abandoned and desolate . Fewer and fewer creators were born or developed; most men doubted they ever existed; the stories of them were relegated to myth and speculation.

It appeared to be a glorious victory on the surface.

When The Magician faced Lord Master Theron and the remaining creators on that faraway day in the distant past, he revealed to Lord Theron that he, The Magician had learned far more than just how to destroy them. He had discovered the creators most cherished secret, that one day a child of prophecy would be born that would be greater than all of them. One that would break The Magician's stronghold on the thoughts and hearts of men. Mankind would once more embrace the inheritance of creation; they would understand quantum physics and the elements on levels unheard of. They wouldn't need his magic; man would create their own universes without the need to unnaturally change the chemical properties of the earth and elements around them.

It was a brave dream, one that The Magician was determined to destroy.

Mankind had always loved and been influenced by legends. Stories of adversity and bringing forth the best in man's own spirit were the things that inspired and drove mankind to greatness. So, the one who first showed man the dark side of his nature decided to become a story himself, to all but those of his inner circle, those who loved power and corruption as much as he did. To those he granted his own dominion over the earth, by use of magic and illusion, a way to separate men and women from their own innate power. The Magician wanted man to rely on the tools he made more than the Invisible Intelligence that inspired man to create them.

A brilliant strategy, that once The Magician set it in motion, he need do nothing else. It ran smoothly on its own, enticing man to greater and greater inventions, while his most marvelous tool, his mind, shrunk more and more from disuse, until only ten percent of its potential was available to advance the progress of mankind.

There was only one threat to this strategy; a fully aware creator with the ability to reawaken man.

The mage and Ancient known as Enith did not know the whole story of the battle between The Magician and the creators, nor did he care about it. What mattered for him was his own dreams of power and control; it was the only thing that kept Enith engaged and alive. Without this need to meddle in and subvert the dreams of others, Enith himself would fall prey to the bane of every ancient sorcerer: Madness. He refused to see, as did all others like him, that the longer he lived, separated from the call of creation, the more he would become like the source of his power, The Magician, who was completely insane.

For all Enith's great power, he was like any other man who needed stimulus and growth to develop. If he wished, he could stand on a hilltop, and watch the centuries fly by him like a breeze. He would watch cities and kingdoms rise and fall, men scurrying by like ants, building, fighting, dying, until just the sight of it would entrance him.

The mage shuddered at this thought; he'd seen it before. An Ancient would stand on a high place, like a hill or a mountain, and after a while, he or she would grow still and unmoving, seduced by the tapestry of life unfolding. The earth and trees would grow up around them and fall again as the land masses shifted, and still they would stand there, watching everything and now seeing nothing.

Edith had approached such mages, and gently wave his hand before their faces; few responded. Some had actually shifted their gaze to look at him briefly. One had shed a tear, and Enith knew then that there was no offer he could make that would cause them to move and rejoin him in the flow of natural time. Enith had walked away from these encounters with sadness. He knew that eventually, he would return one day to find them gone. They would finally close their eyes and just let go; the particles of the body no longer held together by sheer will, and they would fade away to dark grey ash.

It was either that, or unrelenting battle with any and all who crossed their path. Enith's mind turned to his former pupil and now partner in his schemes, Iroh. The mage had saved Iroh from a maddened Ancient who had broken the one cardinal rule among magicians: Never attack a student who was under the protection of a mage or sorcerer. The insane Ancient had lashed out and destroyed Iroh's mentor, Rannea, who was not an Ancient or as powerful, for the sole purpose of slaying Iroh, a fledgling of much promise.

Edith had watched the battle with interest and stepped in at the last moment to save Iroh, who should have died immediately with his hapless mentor.

Lord Enith's deep reverie was interrupted by his arrival at The Magician's retreat. Edith had made a request for audience with his master and was gratified that it had been accepted. The Ancient had wisely also included a request for protection from The Magician's bound servant, The Rook. This was also granted by his master's word, which was the only reason Enith resolved to come.

The Rook was a former creator, now bound by a blood oath after The Magician's discovery of a creator's only weakness, the knowledge of their True Name. The Rook, who once went by the name Michael, was a prize from the war near the beginning of time. Although The Rook was no longer connected directly to the source of creation, he cannot be killed by magic, and his power seems to yet be without limit. He takes out his pain on any follower of The Magician, who in turn is unaffected by either The Rook's rage or the decimation of his mages.

Yet, none can deny The Rook's value to his master: any task The Magician sends him on is fulfilled, typically in the most destructive way possible. Hence, it behooved Enith to ask for protection as he sought his audience; he had no counter to The Rook's massive power.

The Magician also had a High Regent named Alaric; it amused the creature to mimic the ways of men. This High Regent met Enith at the entrance to his master's retreat. It was a courtesy and an indication of The Magician's favor; this move made Enith breathe easier as he followed the other mage through the torchlit halls that led to his audience.

The throne room of The Magician dwarfed any room that Enith had ever seen, including his own. Filled with light, it was difficult not to admire this tribute to the ages. Enith saw some reference to every civilization ever known, and some that were not yet known. The mage watched the comings and goings of thousands of mages, running errands for their master. There were some humans who dared to serve this great company, their minds sealed against any memory of whatever tasks they performed.

Yet the closer Enith came to The Magician's ornate throne, the more he marveled at the raw power emanating from the man who stood to the right of his master, the former creator known now as The Rook.

Enith was millions of years old, and secure in his power. He had even faced down and destroyed other Ancients; the one who attacked Iroh came to mind. Before this moment, the mage had been sure that no one other than The Magician could separate him from his body before he could strike back. But now that his eyes met those of The Rook, who returned his gaze without emotion or interest, Enith was certain he was in the presence of one who could summon force without end. The mage breathed deeply to contain his alarm. Surely, without the bonds of The Magician surrounding him, this man could level this entire mountain, and the plains beyond it, blackening the hemisphere.

The voice of his master brought Enith back to the present moment.

"Well met, Enith," said The Magician, "it has been long since we spoke last, eons, even."

"Yes, my lord," replied Enith with a deep bow.

"As you know, I am intrigued that such a powerful sorcerer as yourself would need anything from me, as evidenced by said lack of contact," continued his master, "Yet, here you are. Speak to me, then..."

And Enith gave his tale, well aware that his master now scanned his mind as Enith did Keoni. It was a lesson in humility, one that Enith had lived millions of years without. He noticed the creature on the throne above him reacted in the same places Enith himself had done, and he worried that perhaps he would lose this enterprise that meant so much to him to another, even The Rook.

He worried needlessly. The Magician was fascinated by the story, that was all. But he had questions for his servant Enith.

"Is the child a creator?" He asked the mage, and Enith blanched; such a thought had never crossed his mind. He could not help but glance again at The Rook, who almost smiled at this...almost.

The Magician sat silent a while, thinking.

"If the child lives, Enith, what do you plan to do with him?"

The mage considered his answer for less than a moment. It was best to speak plainly of his desires; The Magician was very good at discerning a lie.

"It is my hope to place him on the throne of the Kingdom of The Far Isles," Enith responded softly.

After a moment, The Magician did something rare; he laughed aloud. The mages in his retreat paused at this unusual sound. The creature's eyes twinkled as he appraised the Ancient.

"It would be well if the Nine Kingdoms fell before the great battle at the end of the age, mage Enith," said his master, "Providing of course that the first cousin of King Sumter lives..."

Silence again took over the hall as The Magician searched his mind, sifting through the images he gleaned from Lord Enith. Then he spoke aloud to the Ancient.

"You have stumbled across someone protected by a creator, Enith..."

The Magician nodded as the mage both flushed and blanched from his head to his feet. His master thoughtfully stroked his chin as he considered his words.

"Nothing can be seen that they do not want seen," he continued, "Such is their power. Whoever it is, I cannot learn the identity of such...without the aid of another."

Enith couldn't help himself, he gazed at The Rook, but his master shook his head. Then lifting his gaze slightly, the creature gave a meaningful glance to his High Regent, who immediately vanished. The Magician came to his feet, and all turned to him.

"I will help you, Enith," he said simply, and the Ancient blinked rapidly before he nodded quickly.

"I owe you great thanks, my lord—" he began, but his master stopped him.

"You will owe me far more than that, mage," The Magician said with a slight smile. "For now I seek the company of one who has shunned my presence far longer than you yourself have been living. In order to learn the truth of the prince, Enith, my hand cannot be seen. My schemes for this world lie in the beginning of it, and there are many things I do not wish for those now living to know…"

The Ancient felt the subtle shift in energy, and he looked in alarm at The Rook, whose black hair and robes began to move as he stood still. Enith could see certain elements become visible around his master's servant, and the atoms enlarged themselves and spun rapidly.

Millions of years in the future, scientists would 'discover' plutonium, a transuranic element derived from uranium and create isotopes from it suitable for use in nuclear reactors. It is said that when a uranium-235 atom absorbs a neutron and fissions into two new atoms, it releases three new neutrons and some binding energy in what is known as a chain reaction, that can cause a massive explosion. The Rook did not create the plutonium and uranium elements that danced before his eyes. He summoned them, from deep within the earth and from comets hurtling by in outer space, along with radium, mercury and phosphorus. The only true joy he could now know The Rook experienced as the deadly particles paused at his mental command.

Many of those in the hall stopped their pace and looked to their master, suddenly uncertain. The mage turned back to lock eyes with The Magician, who watched Enith with an unfocused gaze.

"I will find her, of course," the creature seemed for a moment to be speaking to himself. "I have always found her, no matter where she roams this planet. From time to time, she leaves Earth to be free of me, but it calls to her as I do…"

"Enith..." The Magician now said to regain his attention, "stand still..."

The mage felt the power of his master enfold him. Seconds later, Enith was blinded by a bright light; it took everything in him to remain unmoving. But he did so, and when the Ancient could see again, he gasped:

Every living thing in the building, other than himself, his master and The Rook had been vaporized. At his feet were piles of dark grey ash and above him, a mushroom cloud blossomed and crackled with the energy of split atoms and nuclear dust. All else was unharmed; the fronds of palm trees waved in the transformed air; gold twinkled from the painted artwork in the vaulted ceiling, an uncaring witness to the devastation.

From what seemed a faraway place, Enith heard his master's voice.

"Have you ever watched the sun descend into the ocean, Enith? No doubt you've seen that lovely final flash of green light as the very top of that great ball of fire appears to vanish beneath the waves. It is a reminder of creation, what the Egyptians will one day call the crackling of the goose that brought forth creation at the speed of light, and future generations of scientists will refer to as the 'Big Bang' that started it all..."

The Magician pointed to his servant, The Rook.

"This is but a taste of what these people we call creators can do. In the future, man will build machines to do what The Rook can do with his mind; call forth the elements in the combinations necessary to reduce the cells of the body to the state before the zygote, to the flash of light that signals the possibility of life..."

"This..." the creature continued passionately, is among the skills and powers that the creators want to place in the hands of farmers, wanderers and...sheepherders, Enith! Do you not see that the only possibility, the only way the world can be safe is for these creators to be either controlled or destroyed!"

The Rook added nothing to this discussion. His eyes became blank again after fulfilling The Magician's will, focused inward to the agony of the distant past. The Rook cared not one whit for his master's plans or his forced execution of those same schemes. His thoughts were his own and they boiled with only one thing: Revenge.

The Rook's mind turned briefly to the mage Enith who supplicated his master for the domination of men with this thought:

It matters not your plans and schemes; I will see you all dead along with him. The Magician will die if I have to crack the Earth in half to accomplish it.

His hair and robes returned to their former state as the winds of radioactive destruction dissipated at The Rook's command.

"Go your way, mage," said his master to Enith, "I will send word of what can be learned of your precious prince..."

Lord Enith turned swiftly to go, unnerved by this display of raw power. Willfully destroying a cavern full of hundreds of people to both keep a secret and make a point was more than enough for the Ancient. The High Regent of The Magician reappeared at Enith's side as promptly as he left, and the mage breathed deeply at this reminder of his master's protection.

He heard again the creature's voice as he reached the hall doors, still sparking and tinged with smoke.

"Do give my regards to your former pupil Iroh, for me, Enith," said The Magician smoothly, "I look forward to meeting him."

"As you say, my lord," replied Enith more courteously than he felt.

The Ancient turned back to offer his master a final bow, then vanished as he crossed the threshold.

MOMENTS LATER AND LEAGUES AWAY, Enith stood atop his own mountain, trying with difficulty to control his emotions.

His audience with his master merely confirmed Enith's wisdom: it was right to keep away from the direct source of all magic in the world, The Magician. And not just because of his exceedingly powerful servant, The Rook. Even though the creature was not human, the laws of the universe still applied: separation from creation eventually leads to madness and more separation until the will to dominate and control others is all that is left.

Enith's thoughts went without fail to Iroh, whom he warned early on to stay away from The Magician, for just such an event as Enith had witnessed; the wanton annihilation of hundreds of able and talented sorcerers to prove a point about the creators. More than once The Magician had boasted that he could raise up mages and followers from the mud and dust of the ground, so eager was mankind to embrace his illusions. Little wonder the creature cared not how many died as he pursued his plans to dominate the Earth for all time. Enith, in his stead had his own schemes and had decided to have Iroh spearhead their conquest of another kingdom, The Kingdom of the Circle of the Earth. It had a direct bearing on Iroh's life and Enith's future plans, so it was an assignment important to them both. In this moment, the Ancient was glad his friend Iroh was distracted, and did not ask to accompany Enith to offer support.

For all the good it did.

The price for my request has been set, the mage thought sadly. Of course, The Magician would ask of me the only thing I cherish other than the destruction of the Nine Kingdoms, my prized former student and present ally, Iroh. I have dared much for this enterprise and now everything that matters to me is at stake.

The mage gazed down at his hands which now burst into flames.

If the prince is alive, Enith thought grimly, and I learn the name of the one who cloaked him from me these seven long years, that same one will feel my pain, to their extreme detriment.

The flames followed the lines of the Ancient's body and the mountainside erupted in fire.

THE DEATH *of Starlight*

The sorcerer Paza had always trusted her dreams. They had guided her from her very first days on the earth, back when time was not measured by days, or even years, but ages. From the very beginning she had a dream that her life on earth would end in a blaze of light and fire. Paza didn't fear the dream when she young; she watched it with peace and wonder. It felt like creation, like how the stars are born and burn out. She thought of herself as a living sun. Everything has a cycle of transformation; what was there to fear?

But that was before she met the one who would change her life forever. Once he taught her how to see death she feared it; she would never again awaken peacefully from her dreams.

SHE RECALLED the day when she came to realize that her body was separate from those she knew as parents or progenitors. Before this time, Paza knew she was a part of everything she saw, the people, creatures of the earth, even the stars and planets. Because Paza saw both the microcosm and the macrocosm she recognized no distance between herself and the star bodies; if their light could touch her, well then, she could touch them. She danced dimensions and wove stardust molecules into things she could use. Paza watched as the earth impregnated itself and brought forth life. She loved to sit on the shores at night and watch creatures crawl out of the seas and send images to her mind that she translated into thoughts of beauty and wonder.

Her dreams had told her that soon she would see a phenomenon outside of eternity.

It happened that she was among those precious few now living who witnessed two beings who looked like men step away from a massive burst of light. They were huge and beyond comprehension. One stood still as the other moved quickly across the planet. Paza sensed one was waiting for the other to return so they could both go back into the light. She waited also but the one who moved away did not return. Finally, Paza turned again to her favorite pastime; watching the birth of stars and planets. She loved draping herself with starlight. One evening she was thus engaged when the being who first moved away from the light approached her. Smiling, she held out her hands to him, offering a robe of starlight to adorn himself.

He returned her smile as he accepted the garment.

"Paza," he said, and her hands flew up to her ears in astonishment.

Human communication was mostly telepathic back then; human sound was used only for creation. Didn't he know this?

She gazed at him in confusion. Why did he call her Paza?

He answered her question aloud.

"One day, millions of years from now, Paza will mean 'golden' in a language that will be spoken by the tongue and not the mind. I prefer to speak to you, Paza, I like the power that it gives me."

She had no place for the concepts he was offering her, so she mentally asked him something else.

The one you came with; he is waiting for you at the light that never dims. Are you going back?

The being smiled again at her.

"No," he answered, "I like it here. The contrast is...interesting."

He looked around at all the people and creatures moving around the land. Then, he pointed at the ones that began to approach them.

"So..." he said in curiosity, "You see yourself as everything around you? Nothing is separate?" He now raised his head and looked up at the same stars and planets she danced with. "The idea seemed so much easier to me when light surrounded everything," he mused, "When there was no contrast. Now...I want to see, touch and learn..."

Paza's brow furrowed.

.   .   .

Learn? Separate? You say very strange things. Is it because you are using sound to communicate? If you use your mind it will be easier for me to understand you.

There was a strange look in his eyes as he gazed at her; almost as though he could see something hidden inside of her that she was unaware of. The thought of this made Paza step back; how could something be in her that no one knew of?

"I like you, Paza," the being said as he appraised her, "But your eyes need to be opened like mine. I now see things that you cannot, things that I am willing to teach you."

He looked down at the robe she had offered him, and with a thought, he shrunk down his body from its great height to seven feet and placed her robe around him. It morphed to fit him as her mouth gaped. The people gathered around them silently, drawn to him by his deeds and the vibrations coming from his lips.

Sound without creation; how was it possible?

What they failed to see was although it was not creation, he was making something; a world apart from what they now lived and moved in. A world that, if they entered it, would exchange knowledge for learning and creation for tools, causing them to forget everything they once knew.

He closed his eyes and listened for the last time to their collective thoughts.

"You think of me as the First Brother," he mused aloud to their astonishment, "Very well, let it be as you say."

He looked around at the people.

"Say it," he commanded firmly.

.   .   .

AFTER A MOMENT, to Paza's amazement, the people began to repeat his words aloud. They began to laugh and chatter words they were thinking. It became a canopy of noise she could make no sense of. It was so strange. When people thought telepathically it didn't matter how many thoughts were streaming it all flowed perfectly because the mind was infinite. Paza again covered her ears as order faded into chaos. As he began to walk away, they followed him. Then he stopped and looked back at Paza.

"Paza," the being now known as the First Brother said gently, "Follow me and I will teach you the right way to see this world."

He stretched out his hand to her. "Come."

IT SEEMED the cells of her body exploded with light as Paza looked at him, but the truth was her cells were dying. She was about to enter the world of time where everything bound by it eventually dies. She took one last look at the stars raining light for her to gather and make garments, music, and other things with. Stay, they begged her, but the sound of his words rang in her ears. She was beginning to question whether sound should only be used for creation; perhaps there were things beyond it. Lifting the hem of her gleaming robes Paza turned her back on the stars and ran to join the one who would teach her the meaning of separation.

NOW IN THE present day of the Nine Kingdoms, the sorcerer Paza could feel the press of time on her life. When she was alone, she sometimes wept for what she had so eagerly turned her back on. Now when she stood among the stars they were silent. If perhaps they spoke to her, she could no longer understand their music. Paza could sense creation but she could not interact with it. Each age she depended more and more on the power wielded by the mysterious being she had once been enchanted with.

. . .

WITH OVERPOWERING DREAD, Paza saw the slow but steady transformation of the First Brother into The Magician, how he began to go mad under the heavy burden of separation. He was angry that he could no longer hear the thoughts of others; that the power of creation he had discarded with arrogance would not now return to him. The Magician was convinced he could force his brother to give back what he must have somehow taken from him. Paza remembered how he demanded that his followers help him find the one now known as the Second Brother.

AT FIRST, The Magician said he needed his brother to return to the light. Then he decided that his brother was keeping him from the light, and finally he determined that he was the light, and once his brother was dead, all power would belong to him.

Paza's dreams warned her to flee while the First Brother was occupied with the initial search. When she beheld him use his now twisted powers to slay the followers who failed him, Paza experienced something never felt before in all her eons on the earth: fear.

THOSE WHO COULD SEE TRIED to tell The Magician where his brother was, but he did not believe them. And this was but the beginning of his fall into madness. When Paza witnessed The Magician slay his most trusted advisor for telling him the truth, it was at last too much for Paza. She fled to the Rim of the World, and from there, she vaulted herself among the stars. Perhaps now was the time of her death, perhaps now she would find the peace denied her. But Paza only floated in the emptiness alone.

IT SOMETIMES TOOK centuries to find her, but The Magician always did; he was connected by darkness to everyone who used his power.

The older Paza grew the more powerful she became; eventually Paza shone like a dark star no matter where on the planet she stood. She spent eons on other planets and solar systems where The Magician could not go. Like the humans he longed to control, The Magician was bound to the planet earth until he found his brother. Yet, Paza too, felt a pull irresistible to the magnetic force of her home. Sirius and Orion's belt did not look the same from other galaxies and she loved the way earth's moon pulled at the iron particles in her blood.

THE MAGICIAN eventually found her walking the edges of the sea at night. Paza had gone as far back in time as she could yet it was impossible for her to return to a time where she did not know The First Brother. Once on the path away from the light, one must walk the full journey back to it; she could not return to union without fully realizing what had first separated her from it. Paza was weeping because the creatures now crawling from the waters in the darkness didn't speak to her. She found no images in their minds of beauty, only blind survival. But Paza didn't try to run from her former mentor, instead she wiped her face and waited for him.

THE MAGICIAN WAS UNCHARACTERISTICALLY gentle with Paza. Not because he felt compassion; he was incapable of loving emotions. It was because she was one of the few living who remembered him and one of the first to follow him that he was lenient with her madness.

LIKE THE ROOK, Paza was his plaything; it amused him to indulge her.

"First Brother," Paza whispered faintly, "I want to go back…"

"YOU CANNOT GO BACK, PAZA," replied The Magician, "if you mean before you joined me in time, you can only go forward."

The creature stepped closer to her.

"I NEED you to stand with me, Paza, like you did before. If you'll see this through with me to the end, and help me defeat my brother, then I'll be free of this planet, and I can take you anywhere you wish to go."

PAZA TILTED her head a bit as she gazed at him. Why was it so hard to understand him at times?

"You know that I'm going to die here, my lord," she answered, "you know I've told you my dream."

"BUT YOU DON'T KNOW when, Paza," said The Magician with a shrug, "and neither do I. Perhaps I'll bring you back here when the planet dies, if that's what you want. Just say you'll stand with me, that's all I ask."

His words brought a smile to her lips.

"That's not all you want," Paza said wryly, "you always say you want one thing, and then it turns out to be everything."

He held out his hand to her, and suddenly Paza felt like they were standing on the earth when it was new.

He's so good with illusions, she thought.

"THAT SOUNDS LIKE A 'YES'," he offered.

SHE PLACED her hand in his and gasped as she felt herself again bound to him. The darkness in The Magician roared through Paza and temporarily dispelled the madness running her mind. The look of satisfaction in his eyes confirmed her thoughts.

Such a fool to return where he could find me, Paza thought, I should have died in space between the moons of Saturn.

Paza looked up at The Magician sadly.

"You're going to make me kill someone, aren't you? Why do you enjoy causing death so much?"

"I wouldn't call it enjoyment," The Magician replied in a nonchalant manner, "everything here has a cycle of birth, growth and decay. The earlier they start, the sooner they can return; it's all one to me."

They walked together along the shore quietly for some time before Paza spoke again.

"You didn't answer my question."

"I'm uncertain you'll have to kill anyone for me, Paza," mused The Magician, "but I do want you to help my people find someone, or at least determine for sure if he's dead. He's a prince of the Nine King-doms...his name is Rasdeter."

The Sacrifice of the Fawn

Paza walked the earth several times before she came to the Kingdom of the Far Isles. She walked through time and dimensions, long before Saramis and Rasdeter were born. She did not need to meet with the mage who faced the power of Saramis in the tavern; as soon as The Magician thought of Keoni, Paza saw him. Through the mind of Keoni, she saw everything that transpired. When she beheld the mage hurled against the wall, Paza knew it was not Saramis who defeated his enhanced might.

Her breath quickened, but she said nothing of it to the First Brother.

"I see the one who cloaks her abilities and confounded the mage who serves Enith," Paza had stated, "A woman of the woods, the

Wanderers of the Plains People. A child really...and yes, these emotions are connected to a memory of Sumter, High King of the Far Isles."

THE MAGICIAN already knew of Saramis, he'd learned it from The Rook, so Paza's confirmation merely allayed his constant suspicion of his bound servant's motives. But the failure of his Legion made The Magician cautious; his hand must remain unseen to those who could confront him before he was ready. The light of a creator can pierce any darkness; for now, he needed to remain unknown and unsuspected in the doings of the world.

YET HE WAS INTRIGUED by the Quest of Enith; anything that might affect the outcome of the final battle must be controlled by The Magician and he alone. There was only question uppermost in the mind of the First Brother, and he voiced his concern to Paza.

"If you find the prince alive, Paza," asked The Magician quietly, "and he is under the protection of this child of power, will they be able to escape you?"

The woman who dreamed of Starlight met The Magician's gaze and shook her head sadly.

"No, First Brother," she replied, "they will not."

PAZA STOOD CLOAKED in the dimensions as she watched time roll before her from her perch on the mountains facing the Far Isles. People swarmed in ribbons below her; the pageantry of ancient kings ebbed and flowed before her eyes. Paza stopped the river of years as she beheld the destruction of the Hall of Mages. A lonely figure stood at its epicenter, a girl of nine years. That this child was the cause of the massive detonation, Paza knew; she watched the grieving child fall to her knees, stunned by her loss. The daughter of Lord Brayten, unknown until this moment. With a wave of her hand, Paza quickly rewound time and watched Lord Altus riding up to the palace gates, on his fateful, tragic errand. The Ancient from the Time of Starlight did not gaze into the palace to witness the death of King Valtus; this was not her focus. It was the aftermath and the events that unfolded.

THIS WAS why The Magician sent her, Paza was the only one who could approach and not be detected. Yet still the ancient Starchild took precaution to cloak the dimensions. Had the daughter of Lord Brayten not been so distraught with grief, she would have detected Paza's power, and the story would have a different end.

Soon enough, High General Aton gathered his men and left his new king for the estates of the nation's traitor, Lord Altus. Paza calmly watched the general's men round up and slay the innocent, named as conspirators by Lord Altus guards under torture. Though it disturbed her, these were events she could do nothing about, and she knew The Magician cared nothing for such lives. He cared only for what threads of fate might affect the outcome of his future battle with the so-called child of prophecy; nothing else concerned him. When young Prince Rasdeter came to the courtyard under escort, her eyes brightened. The boy threw his arms around the general's waist and Paza's heart finally constricted; the light of the child's innocence burned brightly, and the ancient was reminded of the stars she long ago turned her back on.

PAZA FOLLOWED the general and the prince, the horses they rode could not leave her behind. She listened intently to the words they exchanged, and when the boy dismounted, her own heart began to beat as hard as his. Could she watch the general slay the child? Should she change these events? The Magician only asked her to find out what happened to the prince, not save him. Paza saw the stars again in memory, pleading with her to take their light and make music with it; the dimensions around her shimmered with her indecision.

. . .

PAZA'S EYES widened as Saramis appeared from nowhere; the general and the prince could not see her. Paza gasped as power flared from the young girl; she watched it arc and stop the flow of time.

The girl is powerful, thought Paza, such promise...

Events, as before, unfolded quickly and soon Paza watched the deceived general ride away.

CLEVER GIRL, thought the ancient, Lord Brayten will only see what the general saw, and he will not have opportunity to verify it, for his own time has run out...

She watched the fallen prince and his protector walk quickly away, the power of Saramis causing the miles to vanish under their feet.

Paza sighed.

Poor, gifted Saramis, thought the ancient, you have meddled in the affairs of great monsters, and you will not escape their wrath.

She wiped tears from her face.

The prince will not thank you for the fate you lead him to, child of power. Hard as it was, Paza grieved, you should have let that beautiful sweet child perish.

QUEEN OF THE DISTANT CHANT: A SIMULTANEOUS LIFE

"In some sense, man is a microcosm of the universe; therefore what man is, is a clue to the universe. We are enfolded in the universe."
David Bohm

A Tale from a Tribe Called Human

Lady Emmia was on the road to her future life with Regent Mautin, of the Kingdom of the Western Hills, an alliance kingdom of her former lover, King Sumter of the Far Isles. She made a brave effort in her looming separation from Sumter; they both knew one day, if she remained barren, they would part. The kingdom required an heir, and as much as he loved her, he would have to let her go. The combination of a visit from a neighboring kingdom with eligible daughters and the accidental revelation from Irisella of his father's affair during his marriage to Sumter's mother, Queen Inka, led Sumter to do the honorable thing and release her.

Irisella embraced Emmia tightly before she left; Sumter told her he would not watch her leave him they said their goodbyes the night before. The king sent his soldiers with her; he wanted to be sure she was safe; regent Mautin would meet her at the halfway point between their two kingdoms; he had his own escort from King Roe. Lady Emmia gave her tears to Irisella; they hugged like sisters; she could not know the true level of the pain Irisella felt; Sumter never mentioned how he came by his revelation. Still, Lady Irisella felt a tremor of premonition; and shivered as she watched Emmia on the road, safely surrounded by the king's men.

You know the story by now, that Emmia never made it to the halfway point, and that is still true. The thief showed up at the appointed time, and he cowardly shot down her escort, and her cowl slipped as before; and he hesitated, and then rode up beside her, to reach and pull her down from Oriscinder. What happened differently is that the creative force, drifted back to that point of pain in Sumter's life; following the thought of love from Sophia; touched the already weakened heart of the thief, and he felt that muscle spasm. The thief grasped at nothing; his fingers slid lightly across Emmia's shoulder; he fell from his horse to the ground. Emmia felt a touch; she lifted her head and turned in dismay; surrounded by dead men. She leaped from her horse and went to the thief, still shuddering his life out on the cold ground.

The thief's last thought was not repentance; he did not regret the murderous greed that led him to slay innocent men unaware. He regretted thwarted rape; the halt of his last desire; he reached for Emmia's chest and died as his hand closed painfully on her robe. Unaware of his intended fate for her, Emmia tried to help him; she did not yet realize he was the author of her near destruction.

Shadows fell across her in the swiftly fading afternoon light; but it was not Marcus and his men, but total strangers; men in draped clothing, and battle weary horses. Marcus would not reach her in time; his own premonition delayed for this moment. Emmia stood up but waited to draw her sword; the men who surrounded her held higher ground. They were silent as they gazed at her, and she detected no air of menace, but curiosity. The men seemed to be like the Lourdes clan, but they were not.

They deferred to a man who must be their leader; he spoke in a language she almost recognized, but had some trouble following.

When it became clear to her they were speaking of the man at her feet, and that he was the assailant of her escort; she looked down at the thief in dismay, and they discerned she understood them. The leader spoke to her; a tall and handsome man with dark lustrous hair and sharp defined features.

Who are you? He asked; and pointed to her, so she would not mistake his meaning.

"Lady Emmia," she replied, her heart thudding loudly in her chest.

The men about her began to murmur in soft voices, and the leader signaled for silence. Emmia looked about her; she wasn't sure if what she said was a good thing or not, to identify herself as a lady of a nearby kingdom. His next words confirmed her fears.

What kingdom? He indicated his words with a sweep of his arm.

"The Far Isles," she answered; she was not yet a citizen of the Western Hills, and she began to doubt she ever would be; her heart increased its thudding beat.

'Sumter', the leader said, and the men began to chuckle amongst themselves. Emmia looked about her in confusion; what cause for humor was the mention of the High King's name?

What king would allow such a great beauty to leave his lands, the leader said to her; and with a small lump in her throat she discerned the main portion of his words by the way he was looking at her.

"Great leader," she said respectfully, "I was on my way to the kingdom of the Western Hills to meet my husband, if it please you." Emmia hoped the word 'husband' would translate to something these men might respect or heed.

The leader of these men shook his head.

"No longer," he said in her language, and she stepped back unconsciously.

Two men were already behind her; they grasped her arms, and one of them held a blade to her neck as they swiftly disarmed her; Emmia wisely stood still. One man admired her bow and arrows; the leader indicated he was to keep them, for now. Oriscinder snorted nervously; she made soothing noises to him, her main fear that they would kill him if he defended her. The leader nodded in admiration to her actions; she was a warrior, he could see by her weapons, and the way she related to her horse. All the horses of the dead men, including the thief's, were roped, and bound.

I claim her, he told his men; bind her horse and bring him.

He looked down at her, and for a moment, his desire for her was clear in his eyes. The King of the Far Isles must be weak, to release such beauty where it can be claimed; I will show you, how a man treats a woman warrior such as you, he said to Emmia, and what she understood made her clench her hands to keep from shuddering.

Then he offered his hand to her.

"Come with me willingly, Lady Emmia," he said in her language, "you will not be harmed."

What choice did she have; she knew his offer was not open ended; she took his hand, and he pulled her up in front of him, forcing her to place her hands on his thighs, so she would not be thrown from his horse. He placed his arms underneath and around her, and gently slapped the reins on his steed; they took off, swift and silent. From time to time, he held the reins in one hand, the other he placed across her stomach, to steady her on his horse; and of course, to touch her with his fingers splayed; he enjoyed how she trembled when he did so. She drew her breath sharply and tried to stave off despair. Perhaps she could later escape, or even be allowed to leave, once he learned what any man who claimed her would eventually know; she was barren.

The leader rode off with his prize, and his men followed with the bound Oriscinder; their powerful horses were like ghost; as quickly as they appeared, they were gone.

And Marcus came an hour later; to find Sumter's men full of arrows, on the ground, a dead thief, and no sign of Lady Emmia. His men searched for hours; he had others split up, only to find the regent still waiting at the halfway point; devastated at the news she was missing. He sent men back to the Far Isles to alert the king.

Sumter was inconsolable; over time, he had various parties of his men looking for months; she could not be found.

Lady Emmia could find no words for her despair. At least if she remained with the regent, there was hope she might see the king again, if only from a distance; now she faced an uncertain future, and Sumter would surely consider her death the only possibility.

As she rode on the leader's horse, he spoke softly to her in her ear, his words a mixture of poetry and conversation in his language; she mostly noted how leanly muscled he was; his chest was rock hard as the motion of his horse repeatedly thrust her against him; this was not a man who could be easily defeated. Emmia could discern parts of his whispers; he repeated over and over not to fear him; that he would be gently with her; that she would be his.

You are strong, and worthy he said in her ear, you will be my warrior queen, you will bear me sons and daughters, and they will rule our people.

Emmia closed her eyes and tried not to weep; she understood the word for 'offspring' and would give her whole future for the ability to bear a child. I can but hope he will not slay me when he learns the truth, she thought, I know not what kind of people they are; though their words and ways, are like my father's. She did not notice the warmth in her body; in her hip and groin area, the creative force gave her back not only her life but healed the damage from her first husband's cruel hands. To what purpose or agenda, she may never know, but her days as a barren woman were at an end.

THE DWELLING PLACE of the men who kept Lady Emmia captive was leagues away, among the people of the Unnamed Lands; and if that were not cause enough for despair, when she saw how they lived off the land, moving from place to place, she watched her hopes for escape dwindle to nearly nothing.

Mizrah, was the name of the man who claimed her; Emmia learned this from the shouts of his people as he rode into camp. She noticed a young woman in the gathered crowd staring at her with open dislike as their eyes met; the hostile stare softened, as her gaze moved to Mizrah, and Emmia sighed. Although it was fortunate to learn quickly who your enemies are, she would have to find out the circumstances with haste so she could properly watch her back. Perhaps these people allowed the men multiple wives; Emmia nearly groaned at the thought of sharing living quarters with jealous females.

She felt Mizrah's arms tighten unconsciously around her as the people took notice of her; the people were many shades and complexions, including her own; but she was still a stranger, excited whispers and murmurings surrounded the group as they began to dismount. Another group of warriors approached, led by a man who resembled Mizrah; they might be brothers. He greeted Mizrah warmly and made note of Emmia and Oriscinder; a brief explanation from Mizrah brought a smile to his brother's face, and Emmia felt her own grow hot; clearly, he was boasting.

A nudge at her shoulder; Oriscinder had been allowed to close the space between them, and he sought comfort, among so many unknown humans and beasts. Emmia also needed him; she returned his request by stroking his nose and making soothing soft clicking sounds; he shook his mane and pawed one hoof on the ground. She saw Mizrah watching her, she took the reins of her horse and walked towards him; he turned and strode away; she knew to follow.

His dwelling place was a huge tent, made of a combination of thick woven fabric and animal skins; when she finished securing Oriscinder, he held open a flap for her, and she entered. Inside, it was full of what looked to be animal trophies and small functional hand-made furniture; the bed was ample, multi layered and soft looking; her stomach churned in fear. To her surprise, Mizrah directed her to a small seat; when she took it, he turned from her and stirred the coals in a tiny fire pit meant to give light to the interior. Emmia could not help but notice how strong Mizrah looked; how his muscles flexed in the dim lighting and swallowed hard; he could do a lot of damage to her if she fought him; she weighed the chances that he might even kill her, in order to subdue her. Sumter's face loomed before her, and she wondered with a heavy heart if she would ever see him again; if she fought Mizrah for her virtue, the chances were slim.

With hand gestures, he inquired if she was hungry; and Emmia shook her head; afraid she would be too nervous to keep anything down. Then Mizrah took a seat across from her and tried to communicate with her; she could make out he was speaking of their laws and beliefs, but there were nuances she couldn't completely follow.

Finally, shaking his head, he pointed at himself, and then her.

"No rape." He said in her language, and nodded when her eyes widened, and then she covered her face, overcome.

Because we live simply, does not mean we are not people of honor, Mizrah continued, though he knew she did not understand all his words. A man does not force a woman if he wants her heart; you will not be strong or love my children, if I force you to bear my seed.

Mizrah waited in silence, while Emmia controlled her emotions; when she raised her head again and looked at him, he gestured again if she was hungry, and when she nodded shyly, he grinned broadly; he knew why she was afraid at first to eat.

I gave my word I would not hurt you, when I claimed you, he said to her puzzled face; you will learn to trust me, and he pointed to his heart, and watched her smile.

Then Mizrah picked up a bowl and taught her the word for it; after the meal, he spent a great deal of the evening pointing to various objects in his tent and teaching her the words for them. When he saw, her eyes grow heavy, he asked her to stand; when she did so he wrapped a blanket skin around her and directed her to sleep on one side of the bed; he wrapped himself and took the other.

Lady Emmia was exhausted from her ordeal; she tried to keep her eyes open; her body had other ideas, and she succumbed. Mizrah turned over presently to watch her rest; he knew what she did not, if he had not claimed her before returning home, either his brother or another leader in the group would have. He told the truth; no one would force her, but he also knew he alone would take the time necessary to fully bring Emmia into the group; he felt something he'd never felt before when he looked in her eyes.

The words of their wise woman came back to him; she told him he would save a woman not of their people, who would then save him; a warrior queen on a red brown horse. His mind went to Oriscinder, and he shivered. She was the one foretold for him; he would treat her well. Behind him sat a covered bowl with beaded bracelets in it; saved for him by his father. He never believed he would ever use them; never believed what happened for others would be true for him.

Mizrah turned away from Emmia and sighed deeply; he would chant the laws and beliefs of his people in his mind until hopefully, he fell asleep.

In a matter of weeks, Emmia was allowed by Mizrah to wander freely around the campgrounds; it didn't take long for her to find the source of his confidence. The campgrounds were surrounded by sentries and dogs; even if she found a way to get past them, she would have to leave Oriscinder, something Mizrah knew she would never do.

Emmia sighed in frustration; she was his willing captive for now.

Nondra, was the name of the young woman who hated her for existing; Emmia tried to ask Mizrah about her and was mystified by his response. He shook his head and refused to speak about her. One day she spied Nondra in the open areas with the man Emmia learned was Mizrah's brother; he was speaking to her when she looked up and saw Emmia. This time, she did not glare at her; she gazed at the ground in front of her, and Emmia noticed for the first time several bands of white beads on her arm, the brother was stroking them gently as he spoke to her. Emmia did not have a name for the expression on Nondra's face, but it bothered her; it was clear Nondra belonged to this man and did not want to; and it had something to do with Mizrah.

Not long after this, the group gathered their things to move to another land. Emmia watched in amazement as they worked quickly and silent; everyone knew what to do, even how to help each other without making a sound. There was no pattern to it; they moved early in the day, or late at night, the only constant was the silence. This is how they move as ghosts, thought Emmia, and no kingdoms nearby could track their movements. Once everything was gathered, a small group of men moved about the area, obliterating obvious signs of the camp site; their feet stamped the ground to make the dirt even, scattered leaves over the open areas and brushed the grass with their hands so it stood up as before. Emmia marveled, then she saw an older woman stand at the edge of the transformed camp and raise her arms in a silent blessing; everyone stood still as though they gave respect to her unspoken words.

They all walked away to their horses, and Emmia looked back; she knew even if Sumter had sent trackers this far, they would return to him and claim no one had passed that way. She turned around and found Mizrah watching her; he held out his hand to her, and she pressed her knees against Oriscinder, to spur him forward. It didn't take a mind reader to know what she was thinking. But when she reached his side, she found no anger in his demeanor towards her, instead his eyes held compassion, and he lightly found her hand and squeezed it; when she looked at him in surprise, he held her gaze until she looked away.

How strange my life has been, Emmia thought, first a man who tortured me like a wild animal, then a man who loved me, but could not keep me by his side, and now a man who won't hurt me, but will not let me go. What am I running to, she asked herself, if you manage to flee this man, and the regent is yet waiting, you still won't be with Sumter.

I tell myself I just want him to know I'm alive, but the truth is, I want the knowledge to change something, and it won't.

When Emmia looked again at Mizrah, he was still watching her; she then surprised him by squeezing his hand in return. He nodded, as though a question he posed to her had been answered; he released her hand and used hand signals to urge her to keep up with him, and she did so; the group would travel for several weeks before they stopped again.

Early on in her captivity, Mizrah showed Emmia how to make her own clothing; she had several garments to change into. At the camp, she was expected to do her own laundry; she smiled inwardly at this; it recalled the Hall of Women, in the Kingdom of the Far Isles, and some of the duties she both performed and supervised. Deep in thought, Emmia made her way to the stream where clothes were washed and rinsed; she felt the hairs go up on her neck, she turned to find a young girl, barely six, following her. The girl closed the space between them and reached for some of the clothes Emmia was carrying; she then kept pace with her as she continued walking. Along the way; Emmia pointed to her, to ask her name.

"I am Mari," she answered in Emmia's language, to her surprise.

"You know my language?" said Emmia in astonishment.

"Of course," Mari said with a shrug, "it is not an unknown language, or even a difficult one."

"Then why does no one speak it to me?" Emmia said as she looked at the people around her, going about their duties.

"Because if we do, you will not learn *our* words, and there are times when the words don't match, and what then?" replied Mari in a matter of fact tone of voice.

Emmia made a combined sound of amusement and frustration as she recalled Mizrah's patient lessons; her mind raced as she tried to remember if she'd ever said anything out loud in front of him that she thought he wouldn't understand.

She groaned.

"Well", she said as she turned to gaze at Mari, "you seem very advanced for your age."

Mari shook her head.

"Not so," she replied, "as children, we are considered the first elders of our people, being so close to the source of all things." Mari nodded to Emmia's unasked question, "and the oldest of us are called the second elders, because they are closest to the return to source."

Emmia's brow furrowed.

"Do you not play, as children do?"

"Of course," Mari smiled, "and we vote in the council once we demonstrate higher reasoning. In fact," she continued, "I'm very interested in you..."

Before Mari could finish her sentence, Nondra came into view, alone, and walking in a quick and determined pace towards Emmia; who did not like the expression on Nondra's face; she set down her laundry.

Mari moved in front of Emmia and spoke harshly to Nondra.

Nondra, she said excitedly in their language, you do not yet have permission to approach Emmia!

She has no bands, first elder, replied Nondra, I may say what I will.

You are immature and inhospitable; I will report this breach...

Nondra turned to look at Mari.

You will not...

Mari looked from Nondra to Emmia; she could see the wheels turning in her head, while they did, Nondra turned to stare at Emmia.

If she expected to find a cowering newcomer, Nondra was in for a surprise; Emmia spent the seconds of conversation well, sizing up Nondra's stance and clothing. She did not come to make peace but confrontation; Emmia already took her own battle ready stance, her feet apart and rocking lightly on the balls of them; she expected Nondra to be fast and brutal.

I don't like you, stranger, said Nondra as she stepped into Emmia's personal space.

"Well, I'm not fond of you, either," replied Emmia in her own words, and watched as Nondra's eyes widened; she thought Emmia completely ignorant of her language and betrayed her own knowledge of Emmia's.

You think Mizrah favors you? Nondra's lip curled, He only seeks solace from his loss of me.

You wear his bands, then? Asked Emmia in Nondra's language, and watched her words hit home.

Nondra's jaw dropped, and her pupils darkened to blackness.

In that instant, she struck, fast as Emmia anticipated, her hands were waiting as she caught the first swing, and then the second, and when she had both of Nondra's arms bound, she used her momentum to flip the young woman over and onto the ground, landing on top of her. Nondra's breath came out in a whoosh sound.

But Nondra wasn't finished; she grunted and then spun over to break Emmia's grip, and Emmia barely missed being kicked in the face as she rolled away. Both women came to their feet, circling each other in a crouch. Before they could engage again, a warrior stepped between them and two other warriors grabbed them from behind; Emmia allowed herself to be pulled back, but Nondra flailed wildly and broke free.

Nondra.

Her transformation was fascinating to watch; Nondra's face changed from a snarl to placid calm; she dropped her arms and stood away from the warrior between her and Emmia; the only evidence of their conflict, her labored breathing. Emmia's eyes narrowed; this was something she would not soon forget; they both turned to gaze on the source of the voice, Mizrah's brother.

She fully expected him to be staring at Nondra, but he was looking at *her*; it made her notice now the swelling of the side of her mouth; she touched it unconsciously. Emmia looked to his left, and Mizrah approached, followed by his men; he held out his hand to her, she walked over and stood by him. His eyes held a question; she was learning his silent language; she knew he wanted to know if she was hurt; she shook her head. He nodded, his eyes never left hers until he looked at the ground and turned from her; she knew to follow. He did not acknowledge Nondra; he nodded to his brother, who returned it, and they left.

Once in their tent, Mizrah prepared a salve for Emmia's bruised lip; she sat still while he ministered to her, the mixture stung as it met her split skin. Mizrah focused on her lip; when he sat back to look at it; she spoke.

What is the meaning of the white beads Nondra wears in bands around her left wrist and ankle, asked Emmia in his language, pointing to her own skin so that Mizrah would understand; his eyes widened at her question, and he shook his head.

This is sacred, he said softly in response, and paused, then shook his head again; he would say no more about it.

"You dishonor me, Mizrah," Emmia said quietly.

His eyes flickered, then he answered with a stare; Never.

"Yes," she continued, "you kept me ignorant of Nondra's feelings for you..."

She did not have permission to approach you, Mizrah said, in the grip of some repressed emotion. She behaved shamefully.

He couldn't look at Emmia.

Mizrah, Emmia said in his language, you must tell everything; why bring me here if you love someone else, she insisted.

It is not love that binds Nondra to me, answered Mizrah, but disappointment.

He was still for some moments, and Emmia knew he was gathering his thoughts, finding a way to share this tale.

"Nondra has always...wanted to be with me," Mizrah said finally in Emmia's language. "I did...care for her, but I did not encourage her emotions; I knew there would be many years before that decision had to be made. She wanted me to...claim her," he struggled with the words, "before her maturity; I refused her, it was...dishonorable."

He shrugged his shoulders, his arms embracing his knees.

"My father had not appointed which of us brothers would be over all things; that one would have first choice of everything; animals, horses, tents, skins, and...life mates. Nondra knew if I...claimed her, no one else could; and she was willing to do anything to ensure this; but I was not."

Mizrah looked at Emmia, and she could see his dilemma; how could he, as a future leader, do something so against what his people stood for?

"So, your brother was chosen."

Mizrah nodded, then shrugged, remembering.

"I tried to tell her, that such excess of emotion and turmoil would only draw attention to her, and perhaps bring about what she feared, but she would not listen...and when my brother completed his ceremony of leadership, he chose Nondra as his life mate. Every brother has his group of men, but this brother is over us all; it is a great honor for her."

"Mizrah...do you love her?"

He held her eyes unwavering.

"No...but I would have claimed her at the appropriate time...to make her happy."

Emmia did not delve into Mizrah's answer, it drew uncomfortable comparisons to her situation with King Sumter; honor in relationships became a two-edged sword she found herself on the opposite end of where he was concerned. As much as she wanted to remain with Sumter; the prospect of staying with him, while he married another, offered heartbreak equal to the pain she felt to leave him.

It was easy to see how such attraction, from Nondra for Mizrah, would make her more desirable to his brother; for a man, one could see how he might wish to see if such excessive passion could transfer once he became the people's leader. How sad that Nondra could not, even now, control her emotions; Emmia began to wonder just how deep Nondra's unhappiness ran, and if it had no bottom.

"Nondra said...you chose me to console yourself for her loss."

Mizrah shrugged his shoulders and scoffed.

"Do you believe this?" he asked as he held her gaze.

Emmia looked down at the floor of the tent they shared.

"No... but I cannot believe, you couldn't have found someone among your own people, Mizrah."

He touched her, then, lifting his hand to her chin, holding it as his warm eyes held hers.

"I wasn't looking for *anyone*, Emmia...yet here you are."

"I'm your captive, Mizrah," countered Emmia softly.

"Yes...and if you love the man you were on your way to meet with, the one you say is your husband, I will let you go," said Mizrah to Emmia's stunned face.

It would be so simple to say she loved the regent, to obtain her freedom, but they both would know she lied. Emmia's personal code of ethics prevented such a breach; even to reach that fervent desire.

She shook her head at his words.

"He...was not yet my husband," said Emmia in a small voice, "but my intended; it was a word I used, that I hoped your people would respect."

"We do respect it; but I knew you were not in love with him, by the look on your face. And you now see; if I did not claim you, someone of my people would. But..."

Mizrah continued with a smile, "...as you say, you did not answer my question; did you love this man?"

Emmia pulled her face away from his touch; it disturbed her for reasons she could not fathom; she looked to the ground.

"No...I do not love him..."

"No," said Mizrah, "you loved the one you left behind."

And Emmia's head snapped up, and for a moment, her pain was undisguised on her face. He was a little too good at reading her.

"And you still love him."

She nodded, and Mizrah smiled sadly at her.

"Then you have more in common with Nondra than you think."

Emmia could take no more; she stood abruptly, and Mizrah took a blanket and wrapped it around her; he cupped her face in his hands.

"We must forgive each the other tonight for speaking the truth," he whispered.

Emmia nodded, and for no reason she could put a name to, she reached up on her toes and pressed her lips to Mizrah's cheek; he stiffened in surprise, and moved back, his pupils dark and warm as he looked at her. He then pointed to her place on the bed, and she lay down without another word, mystified at her own actions. Mizrah stood a moment more looking at Emmia, as she curled up into a ball underneath her blanket and lay still. Instead of wrapping himself in his own blanket and lying across from her, he walked to the opening of their shared tent and stepped outside.

The Labyrinth

The next day Mizrah changed their routine; he took her to visit a second elder, the one who gave him the prophecy. Her name was Affi-Tosla; he held open the flap to her tent, and Emmia stepped in, and paused. The interior of the tent was larger than the outside of it indicated; she was tempted to step back out and compare the dimensions. When she turned back to look at Mizrah, she noticed a very slight smile on his usual taciturn features; then she knew she didn't need to check.

Affi-Tosla sat in the center of the space, surrounded by beads, pottery, talismans, and dried herbs. In front of her was a large bowl filled with heated coals; in it she tossed seeds, dried flowers, and herbs; Emmia smelled white sage and bitter citrus. The second elder gestured for Emmia to approach; Mizrah gently held her shoulders and whispered to her not to step on anything as she made her way. It was then Emmia noticed, that the woman sat on the opposite end of a labyrinth; as she began to carefully walk through it, Affi-Tosla started a low chant that increased in volume and timbre with her progress. Emmia stopped in places as she walked, looking for space to move; it seemed some objects moved out of her way, others rolled onto her path, forcing her to go a different way.

She thought of her father, and her heart grew warm and sad at the same time. Thoughts of other family members brought forth different emotions, a sense of betrayal, anger, fear; the faces of her small helpless cousins, painted despair, and forgiveness on her mind. A dark stone rolled in front of her feet, and King Sumter rose before her; his eyes full of pain and self-reproach; Emmia almost reached out to him and felt herself falter. She looked to the second elder, who held out her hand and beckoned to her; eyes shining and warm. Emmia moved to her left on the path, and Oriscinder reared up, calling to her; as she came closer, Mizrah stepped between them, and her beloved horse nudged his shoulder, causing him to smile, but when their eyes met, he crossed his arms and watched her, his face unreadable.

Just before she reached the end, a white stone rolled on her path, and Emmia saw her mother smiling at her; she was holding a child resting on her hip; it was Emmia. She watched as her younger self kissed her mother's face and climbed down from her hip to approach her; she took Emmia's trembling hand and pulled her down so she could whisper in her ear, words of her father's language. Emmia shook her head, she didn't understand what it meant; her younger self just smiled and transformed into the second elder, who waited patiently for Emmia to place her hand in hers.

When Emmia complied, the woman took her right arm and gripped it firmly; Emmia cried out in pain and came to her knees. Mizrah moved from the entrance of the tent to the elder's side at the edge of the labyrinth, but Affi-Tosla continued to chant and hold her in place. Emmia felt the woman use her other hand to touch her head; she guided Emmia's forehead to her knee; she rested there, gritting her teeth at the pain in her arm. Before she lost consciousness, the woman released her, and Emmia remained where she was, crouched and trembling. Affi-Tosla completed her chant; both hands on Emmia's head.

She spoke tersely to Mizrah.

This is a human being, Mizrah, Affi-Tosla said in their language, Give her back her arrows, and her sword; she will hurt no one here; I have seen it.

Emmia could not make out most of the woman's words, but she felt a change in Mizrah; whatever she said answered yet another of his silent questions. She did not look up; her head remained on Affi-Tosla's knee, but she heard him take and release a deep breath.

The woman patted Emmia's head, and she looked up and met her eyes.

"Let go of your pain, little queen," said Affi-Tosla in Emmia's language, "It nurses only darkness...starve it."

Emmia took a startled breath; she nodded at the second elder, her eyes brimming. She choked out the words 'Thank you', in the people's language, and saw the woman smile in return. Mizrah took Emmia's left forearm and raised her up; helping her step away from

Affi-Tosla and the labyrinth; he stopped at the entrance to steady her still shaky feet. He made a sound when she started to look back at Affi-Tosla; when she met his eyes, he shook his head. As Emmia stepped outside, Mizrah felt a tug on his consciousness; he turned to see Affi-Tosla gesturing for him to come back in; when he did, she spoke softly to him in the language of the people.

I know of your feelings for her, Mizrah, said Affi-Tosla, But she is not yet awake. A woman does not know the difference between forcing her body and her mind, to her it is the same.

The mistake your brother made with Nondra has hurt us all; do not repeat it.

Mizrah nodded in respect to the second elder, his throat tight. Later he would bring her tribute for her words of wisdom; for now, he must see to Emmia; he did not turn his back to Affi-Tosla as he exited her tent.

When they returned to his tent, Emmia had questions for Mizrah.

Why did you take me to see her, asked Emmia.

She asked for you, he answered with a shrug.

Mizrah began to move things around the tent; it appeared he was cleaning it, but Emmia was beginning to understand certain things about him; she knew he was troubled about her walk through the labyrinth. After a time, he stopped moving and sat on a covered seat; his eyes as he looked at her were sad and distant.

Emmia was troubled as well by the things she saw in the labyrinth; it seemed her life had only been happy when her father and mother were alive, and those three short years with Sumter. She was especially troubled by the way Mizrah looked at her in the labyrinth as he stood next to Oriscinder; Emmia could not fathom what it meant.

Did you see me fall, she asked in his language, her mind turning to the moment she saw King Sumter on her path; it hurt her to think he only saw pain when he thought of her.

Mizrah smiled at this and shook his head.

"You walked without hesitation," he replied, "Eyes on your feet; looking neither right nor left until you knelt and took her hand."

Mizrah then placed his hands together before continuing; his distress was evident.

"When you cried out, I came as close as I could; it would be wrong to interfere with your journey, but your pain sounded real."

Emmia was astonished; she could not tell what was in her mind, or physical.

I was sure I faltered, Emmia replied, using hand gestures to convey meaning for the words she wasn't sure of. Affi-Tosla looked up and held out her hand to me, Emmia continued, so I could go on; I saw you standing in front of me before I reached her; none of this was real?

Mizrah's eyes were now warm and compassionate as he gazed at her.

"The labyrinth walks the walker, Emmia," he said gently in her language, "...and you do not use the eyes for seeing, but the heart. You but learn yourself, and what you believe."

Lady Emmia had no answer for this; it implied more than she could understand, and the thought that she gave the emotions to the people she envisioned, and not what they may have felt, disturbed her profoundly.

Mizrah then signaled for her to come to him, and she did what had become their routine; Emmia would sit with her back to him, on the floor of the tent, as he sat on a covered seat above her; he would show her things using his hands over hers. Today, he showed her how to knit the baskets; Emmia did not know this was something the women could show her; Mizrah wanted this. He did not press his body to hers, but it gave him an opportunity to touch her hands; something he enjoyed without her knowing; at least he hoped.

From time to time he would whisper the poetry of his people in her ear; this Emmia did know was a sign of his affection for her, but it did not bother her; instead it brought her comfort; some of the words sounded like her father's people, and this Mizrah did not know.

So, they both derived something from this quiet time together; and if any of the people knew of it, they said nothing.

Later that same day, he gave Emmia her sword, bow, daggers, and arrows; she looked at him in amazement; she never dreamed he would return her things to her. This act of trust warmed her heart towards Mizrah and made her want to embrace him. She didn't; Emmia could see this was somehow inappropriate, she merely did as he, and let her intention show in her eyes; and Mizrah smiled broadly; he understood.

Emmia did not see Nondra for a long time after she attacked her, and then only from a distance; whatever was said or done to her, it worked; she left Emmia alone; not even looking at her. However, Emmia would never let down her guard around the subject of Nondra; though she never broached the topic with Mizrah again.

But the bands she saw on Nondra and the other women disturbed her; she wanted to know the significance of it but dared not ask; perhaps it was only for the people, and she was not one of them.

Months had passed and Mizrah still did not attempt intimacy with Emmia.

He had proven his intention of not forcing her, so she began to relax around him and focus on learning the ways of his people. Yet she recalled his words of having children with her, so a part of her remained uncertain of his future actions. Did he wait for her, to release her desire to return to the Kingdom of the Western Hills; she did not know. The people had moved many times since she walked the labyrinth, and Mizrah kept her on one side of the bed they shared, and himself on the other. Sometimes even Mari came and slept between them; Emmia enjoyed the opportunity to play with Mari's long thick, shining hair, and listen to her stories; the sound of laughter was introduced to the space they shared.

One day Mari was present, when Emmia remembered part of her journey on the labyrinth; she asked Mizrah with words and hand signs if she could share with Mari, and Mizrah answered, yes, of course. Emmia was curious; some of the words her younger self said, sounded like what her father said to her before he died; and she wondered if Mari could translate. But when Emmia said the little she remembered from her father, and the words from the labyrinth, Mari started and looked sharply at Mizrah, who paled somehow under sun brown skin.

Without another word, he came to his feet, and left the tent; he did not return before sundown. Mari remained with Emmia, but would not respond directly to her questions, as she had before; only to tell her not to fear, Mizrah must meet with the elders and decide what to do. This, of course, increased Emmia's concerns; what did she say and what did it mean, that the two of them reacted so?

Things became strange, when Mizrah returned, and appeared to be moving out. Emmia found herself distressed at this, for reasons she could not bring to the surface of her thoughts; when she tried to engage him, he kept his eyes cast downward, reluctant to look at her. Mari and another female named Asai, spent the night in the tent with Emmia for a week. When Emmia would search for Mizrah, she was told he was gone with his men, and would return soon; she was completely undone.

"Mari," said Emmia in despair, "Why won't anyone tell me what's going on?"

"We will tell you, Emmia," answered Mari, "...as soon as we know; you must be patient; and trust Mizrah; he has always acted in your best interests."

This information warmed Emmia's heart and frightened her at the same time; that Mizrah was concerned about her well-being, and that something needed to be done about that well-being, that she was totally unaware of.

But when Mizrah finally returned, things got even stranger.

Emmia happened to be standing near the common area when she saw him approach, walking with his horse trailing behind him; weary as though from a long journey. Mizrah's eyes met hers; he paused but did not hold out his hand for her to come to him, so she watched him, unable to keep the questions from her gaze. She could tell he wanted to be with her; his stance and stare betrayed it; then he turned and continued walking through the common area; the people parted like a sea of faces; no one stopped him.

He sat with the elders all day, and then alone with Affi-Tosla; that evening, he entered the tent after Mari brought in a bowl like the second elder's and prepared it the same way; with heated coals and fragrant herbs, dried fruit, and seeds. Mari began to chant, and Emmia's heart began to thud in her chest; Mizrah had her sit on one of the covered seats, while he opened a basket with hands he frequently clenched, to keep them from shaking.

Emmia knew to remain silent; she watched as Mizrah removed white beads from the basket, and her eyes grew huge; she almost couldn't hear Mari chanting for the loud beating of her own heart. Mizrah measured a string around her ankle, when he had the right length, he began to bead it. Mari's chant seemed to require response, yet Emmia still started when she heard Mizrah's low voice chant in answer to Mari's. He wouldn't look at her until he finished; then he paused and made a silent request for permission to place the white beaded string around her ankle. Emmia didn't know why, but she nodded as she looked in his eyes; she didn't know what any of it meant; but she wanted him to, and his gaze was his heart offered to her; she nodded again and felt tears on her face.

He beaded her ankle then, his fingers warm, as the knots were tied. He made another for her wrist; she couldn't help but notice that Mizrah made only one beaded string for her left wrist and one for her left ankle; she wanted to know why Nondra had more, but she hoped he would explain later, or that she could ask. It meant some bond between them, but she didn't know if she just became a member of the people, or if she married him; she couldn't be sure, but she did know when he looked at her, she wanted to say yes, so she did.

As the ritual ended, Mizrah's left hand closed over first her wrist, then her ankle; his hand seemed to linger; he stared for a moment at the beads; then he took a deep breath and sat back from her. Emmia could still feel the warmth from his hand, as though it pierced her body; inexplicably, she wanted him to press his hand against the beads again. Mari completed her chant, and they both looked at Emmia; Mari's eyes held such hope and joy in them that Emmia was sure, whatever just happened, had to be good. Mizrah's gaze was of such longing that Emmia shyly looked away; he hadn't looked at her in that manner for a long time. When she dared look again, he was smiling a small smile at her; she returned it.

When Mari made to leave; Mizrah shook his head; and she began to clear the things of the ritual away; he waited until Mari came back before he wrapped Emmia's blanket around her. The message was clear; it was not his intention to be intimate with her; she was puzzled but strangely relieved; so, it was not a marriage ritual. She at least wanted to know that, before anything else happened, she smiled to herself.

What was now unreal to Emmia, was the thought of intimacy with Mizrah, was no longer something she feared. He was not the frightening jailer she feared so many months ago; though she was still his captive; she wondered what the day would bring; hopefully, answers.

When Emmia awoke in the morning, Mizrah was gone; Mari stayed with her as she dressed for the day; she noticed her things were missing. She asked Mari about it, and she directed Emmia to follow; she would take her to her things. They walked past everyone going about their tasks and duties in the camp, past the outskirts of any common areas; Emmia snapped to attention when they began to walk past the sentries and dogs. She was just about to take Mari's arm and question her, when she looked up and saw Mizrah standing on a hill some distance away, with Oriscinder beside him, the reins in his hand. She looked again to Mari, who was gazing up at her; eyes full. She touched Emmia's face, then hugged her tightly. Emmia returned it; but when she tried to ask why, Mari shook her head and pointed to Mizrah.

"May you always have everything you need, including my love," said Mari, as a blessing. She then turned from Emmia and began walking back to the camp.

Lady Emmia approached Mizrah on the hill; Oriscinder shook his mane and neighed a proper greeting; she stroked his nose and face. She looked at Mizrah, and shrugged, as he was wont to do.

Will you tell me anything, she asked him in his language, Or just send me away?

I'm not sending you away, he answered as he looked at her in a way he'd never done before, but I am setting you free.

He turned and pointed northward to the distance behind them.

"We've returned to a place only miles from where we first found you," Mizrah said in her language to her stunned face. "Just over that range, you will find the same road where you met the thief who killed your escort; you can continue on your way to the kingdom where your future husband awaits you."

"So, you've decided you don't want me?" Emmia asked, unable to stop herself.

Mizrah's brow furrowed, and he scoffed at her.

"Now you ask me foolish questions, Lady Emmia; I release you *because* I want you."

He pointed to the beaded bands on her ankle and wrist.

"While you wear those, you are under my protection. Though you ride alone, any man who approaches you on the road, will die; you have my word on that."

He pointed again to the land around them and beyond. "My people encompass all kingdoms; you need fear no arrows before you reach the safety of the civilization you crave."

Emmia felt only shock; she could not process what Mizrah was saying; he would protect her, and let her go? She held up her left wrist, and the small white beads made musical sounds in the breeze.

Mizrah could not prevent himself from staring at it; his face still and controlled.

Will you at least tell me what the beads mean, she asked in his language.

Mizrah stepped closer to her and placed the reins of Oriscinder in her right hand. Almost as though he couldn't help it, he then took her left wrist in his hand, and caressed the beads; the controlled look on his face slipped, and she saw his longing.

"As I said, it is sacred," he responded in her language, "Meant to represent the love and respect between two human beings. The rest is a mystery; and I cannot share that with you." He looked in her eyes as he continued, "You have shown me great respect while amongst...my people," he said with effort, "But the love is not shared; therefore, I must return your respect, and release you."

"Where did you go, Mizrah," Emmia asked plaintively, "When you left me; why did my words from the labyrinth bring about these events so swiftly?"

Emmia was beginning to realize that she had felt a pull towards Mizrah the whole time; but it was only when he left her, that she noticed the absence of that pull, and missed it.

"When my men and I first found you," Mizrah replied sadly, "we thought that you might be partially human, simply tarnished by living in 'civilized' kingdoms; your name is human; we were surprised that you understood us."

Emmia made a puzzled face.

"Isn't everyone human?" she asked, "what is the distinction?"

"True humans do not make kingdoms, and so-called civilizations, where people are treated like animals, and killed without reason, Emmia," Mizrah answered patiently.

Emmia looked at the ground; she could not argue with this, her own family had treated her badly, and sold her, for no other cause, than they didn't want to be responsible for her well-being; even King Sumter's uncle had slain his brother for a throne, and left Sumter fatherless; Mari's words came back to her, and it suddenly felt odd that she wanted to return to any kingdom.

"My father named me..." Emmia pondered, "does that make me human?"

"Your human name gave us pause; it was also the way you interacted with your horse, and you named him Oriscinder; in our language, it means, 'made from sunlight'," continued Mizrah, watching as Emmia's hand flew to her mouth, the horse's name was a memory from her father's lands.

"You think I'm one of you?" she asked incredulously.

It was not beyond the realm of possibility; her father came from the Unnamed Lands; it was her mother who was of the kingdoms.

"We weren't sure, but it was enough to claim you, and try to restore your lost humanity," Mizrah said quietly. "When you did not wake up, after spending time with us, Affi-Tosla asked for you; the labyrinth revealed you had a soul worth saving. But...when you told Mari your father asked you to find your people, we realized you were fully human, even if you are not awake, and must be accorded the full rights of a human being, which is freedom."

Emmia's body went rigid with shock; her father's final words were a plea to find his people? Then who were the people whom she called uncle and aunt, and cousins? Mizrah answered her unspoken question.

"If a human is dying, surrounded by people who are not awake," said Mizrah, "the final request is always to find the people who will bury them properly; treat the offspring well, and bring them back to life. You did not understand his words, because you were asleep, and the people around you were not human."

Lady Emmia could not dispute this, simply based on how they treated her; selling her as a child to the first man who could buy her, before her father's body was fully cold. Her chest tightened as she realized the truth of what she suspected, when they laughed at her; they had no intention of giving him a proper burial; hopefully, they at least put his body in the ground, deep enough so that wild animals wouldn't dig it up and tear him apart.

Her hands covered her face at Mizrah's inescapable logic; not all people can claim the title of human; at least in terms of how they are with each other.

Oh, father, she thought in misery, how have I honored you; I may never know your final resting place.

When she recovered some control of her emotions, she asked him a question.

"The words of my younger self, from the labyrinth," she asked cautiously, "were they a variation of my father's?"

Emmia was beginning to wonder, why she was trying to leave.

Mizrah was looking at her with the strangest look on his face; his voice sounded unlike him.

"How I have longed for your awakening," he whispered, his gaze soft with anguish.

Emmia could not hold this gaze; it was too intimate, and it stirred her; she looked down at the beads again, breathing deeply.

"Are you bound to me, if I keep them?" She asked softly. She looked up again as he made a self-depreciating sound.

"I am bound to you, if you do not," he answered, "But if you take them off, I am free."

"How will you know?" Emmia asked, her voice inexplicably small.

Mizrah laughed softly, almost a whisper.

"I will know..."

Emmia then turned fully towards Mizrah, and he saw her intent in her eyes, and stepped back. Using his silent language, she held his eyes and would not let him look away; after a moment, she saw his surrender, and she closed the space between them, and placed her arms around his neck. Mizrah shuddered at her touch; they'd not been this close since he found her and placed her on his horse; after a moment, he crushed her to him; and she tightened her arms, as his poetry found her ears for the last time.

His breath quickened, and his hands caressed her back as he gave Emmia final instructions.

"Do not remove the beads before you reach the city, and the house you seek within it; the beads are a dual sign, you are protected by the people, and cherished by them..."

And you? She asked in his language.

He sighed deeply and whispered the answer in her ear.

And me, Lady Emmia; and me...

Mizrah gently drew down her arms from his neck, his fingers lightly touching her beads as he did so. He stepped back from her then, and crossed his arms on his chest, watching her calmly; her heart skipped a beat, as she remembered what she saw in the labyrinth, but never told him. Oriscinder walked over to Mizrah and nudged his shoulder; he turned his cheek to her horse and smiled, then looked back at her, his face unreadable, and she almost wept.

Emmia mounted Oriscinder and looked back to Mizrah.

May you always have everything you need, she said in his language, and his eyes flickered, his body tensed.

She had given him the farewell blessing of his people; he could take no more, Mizrah turned and walked quickly down the hill and away from her.

Emmia could not explain what was happening to her; now that Mizrah released her, she didn't want to leave. She saw Mari's face, and the stern, but kind eyes of Affi-Tosla; these people loved her, and the one Emmia thought she wanted, she could not return to. She lightly tapped the reins of her horse and rode towards the Kingdom of the Western Hills.

For two days and nights Emmia traveled, and slept under the stars, Oriscinder by her side. As Mizrah promised, she saw no one on the road; from time to time she sat perfectly still, imaging she could feel the silent presence of the people looking out for her; it was of great comfort. Each night the light from the stars caught the brightness of the white beads she wore; one such night Emmia thought of Mizrah; she lifted her wrist and brought the beads to her lips; she saw his eyes, dark and warm, as he tied the string around her ankle.

In the morning, though she drew nearer and nearer to the Kingdom of the Western Hills, the world of the gentle regent who may yet wait for her, seemed farther and farther away. Emmia didn't know why her father had taken her from the Unnamed Lands, or even if she grew up there. Perhaps he met her mother on his travels and fell in love with her; and decided to stay where she felt safe. Emmia was young when her mother died, she thought, why did her father not return; did he want to stay where the memories of the woman he loved were strongest? There were too many questions.

On the third night, she began to dream of the thief who died after killing the king's men; this time, he did more than reach for her; she woke troubled. The light on her blade as she defended herself, looked too bright, too real.

By the following night, she woke from her dreams shaking; the thief hovered over her, ripping her clothes; she didn't know why her arms lay still by her sides, as sweat dripped down on her from the thief's face; he was trying to kiss her, and she couldn't move to stop him.

Oriscinder neighed gently from the ground next to her; Emmia lay across him and wept.

In the morning, Lady Emmia could see the roads growing wider; a clear indication she was nearing the kingdom of the Western Hills. Emmia knew she should feel happy, to be so close to the world she'd been absent from for so long; instead, her heart thudded with dread and sadness. She stood on a high hill, under a huge tree with majestic drooping branches; she sat down with her back to it, legs crossed, eyes closed. After a time, Oriscinder joined her; she felt herself going into a trance, lulled by the peaceful atmosphere and gentle breezes.

Father, she said to herself in her mind, Help me; do I belong in my mother's lands, or yours?

Emmia felt her heart call out to Affi-Tosla, who responded instantly, as her image came before her eyes. The wise woman stood before the labyrinth in her tent, which expanded to fill the hills and plains around Emmia.

Affi-Tosla pointed to the labyrinth; she told Emmia, in the language of the people: Unravel it.

Emmia heard a chant in the distance as she began to walk; she saw her mother and father, holding her as a child between them. As she reached them, they let her go; as the smaller Emmia moved away, she heard her mother say, You must decide, Emmia; and her father said, Don't worry; somehow, some day, I will save you.

Little Emmia began to run the path, she saw the man who would be her first husband; the child stumbled in fear, but the man only stood there, holding her wedding gown. He said to her, Sometimes, we forget we made the choice to be here, and we suffer for it.

He handed the gown to her, his eyes full of compassion; Emmia took it from him, when she saw the blood smeared on it, she began to weep. She felt his hand on her arm; when she looked at him in confusion, he said:

I'm sorry I hurt you; I didn't know I was asleep.

Emmia's little self, tugged at her; when she looked up, the child self, pointed, and King Sumter stood there, his arms open to her. She ran to him, and he embraced her with tears.

Thank you, he said, For showing me my fears, even while you refused to look at your own.

An arrow landed at his feet, and Emmia looked up to find the thief waiting for her, and Sumter was gone. She picked up the arrow, meaning to defend herself with it, but when she reached the thief, she merely handed it to him, and watched as he cocked his bow with it, and aimed at the men surrounding her in the distance.

When she screamed at him to stop, he looked back at her calmly and said:

This is where you decide, Emmia, me; or Life.

He looked sad for a moment, then continued; I always die here, or later; because of you. If I ever change my mind before I see you...he raised his arm, and released the arrow; Emmia followed it, and found herself on the ground, broken, and dying, with Marcus holding her, weeping.

Her younger self knelt and touched Marcus; he became Mizrah, and Emmia paused. He was holding her body, and whispering to her:

One day I will find you in time, and you will choose life. Until then... and Mizrah lifted her up and kissed the ruined half of her face.

EMMIA'S EYES OPENED: The sun was setting on the hills, bathing her in glorious light. She shaded her face, as she gazed past the tree branches, her soul at peace. Whatever messages the labyrinth held, she unraveled it, as Affi-Tosla said to do; it would haunt her no more, and she knew she would not dream of the thief again. In this moment, Emmia wasn't sure if anything was real; her life now, or this life she beheld in the Shadow of the Labyrinth, with its sad and touching end. Her right palm felt the softness of the grass against her skin; a tiny ant scrambled quickly across her fingers.

What was life, she thought, but a great whirling mystery? The only constant between it, and everyone on her path; was love. Her horse grazed in the distance; Emmia clicked her tongue, and presently, he trotted to her, and nudged her face, to make her smile.

"Time to go, Oriscinder," she told him softly. She mounted him and rode swiftly down the hill towards the sun.

MIZRAH WAS FORCED by his people, to return to his tent; Emmia had been gone five days. Mari and her younger brother, Drini, stayed with him, while he worked through his grief at her absence. Everything in the tent now called him to remembrance of her; he wanted to go hunt with his men, but Affi-Tosla said the signs were not good, and to remain with the people.

Mizrah brooded, as he recalled the various meetings he had with his people, and the scattered groups of human beings he sought out for over a week; as he tried to find old stories that would lead him to the people of Emmia's father. His heart had wretched, as he knew Mari's did, when Emmia unconsciously said the words that marked her as a lost soul, separated from her people. Whatever dreams he had of being with her, of re-uniting this lifetime, as the prophecy foretold; was secondary to this.

Lost souls were the heartbreak of the people; asleep or not, he must help her.

His journey led him to a people who had never left the high hills; the second elders had an old story of a young male, who saved a non-human female from wolves; her family came from a kingdom called the Far Isles; most of them died in the attack. The young warrior tried to save the female, but she was too afraid to live with him in the hills, because of the wolves. The humans tried to convince him, but his heart was now in her body, and hers in his; they could not be parted.

He was the first of their people to leave; a ceremony of remembrance was held; the young warrior promised one day to return with his children, so they would be saved, but he was never heard from again. When the Second Elder said, the female had thick blond hair and dark blue eyes, Mizrah turned his face away and nearly wept; it must be Emmia's mother.

Mizrah never told Emmia the exact meaning of the words she

gave to Mari; he did not want her to think they tried to influence her, but the translation was clear:

Emmia's father said to her on his deathbed, *'Find my people; they will forgive me, and save you.'*

But Emmia's vision self, said to her in the labyrinth, *'It is safe to wake up, you are home.'*

Pain enveloped Mizrah's heart at these words; he felt Emmia was torn between her longing for her mother's, and her father's world. Yet the council was clear; she was fully human. Awake or not, she was free to decide if she wanted to live as a human or return to the familiar world of the so-called civilized kingdoms.

His mind wandered a moment, and Mizrah smiled, as he saw her again in his tent; listening with her soul as he gave her the love and life words of his people in her ear. Mizrah knew Emmia did not know what he was doing; pleading with the part of the human that never sleeps; always hungering for the truth; that being human is more than dust and salt; ever struggling for what the body needs to flourish; that the heart is the only real part worth fighting for.

How he watched for signs that she heard him; that silent moment when her heart spoke from within and said to him; I know.

Mizrah sighed as he thought of Nondra; how her invitation to be afraid, undid his work with Emmia. She could not forgive Nondra, he saw it every time Emmia walked through the camp, she looked for her; on guard for attack. The people worked with Nondra and gave her time to reclaim her own lost humanity; he healed with her and his brother their youthful foolishness; all they could do now was allow those seeds of forgiveness to bloom.

The white beads Mizrah strung on Emmia's wrist and ankle hovered before his mind's eye; there was a moment, during the ceremony of a free human, where he thought he saw her soul looking at him; tears were on her face. The 'Yes' came from there, he told himself, as a comfort; she would have said 'No' otherwise.

His gaze fell on the basket his father gave him years ago, when he completed the ritual that marked Mizrah as no longer a First Elder, but a normal human of the people. His father told Mizrah he would find the one he left behind; and he would know her, if he was willing to look deeply.

He never found the look in Nondra's eyes, he found it in Emmia's; a person he thought at the time only partially human.

I will never have a chance to share with you, the mystery of the beads this lifetime, Lady Emmia, Mizrah mourned; May our fathers forgive us; I know not, how many times I have failed.

At the end of the week, he began to gather herbs, for the ritual of separation from her. Emmia should be in the Kingdom of the Western Hills by now; Mizrah was waiting for confirmation from the men who protected her progress. In the morning, he would sweep the tent empty and begin; tonight, he refused food and welcomed sleep; he was told the men would return to camp by dawn.

As expected, the flap of his tent opened before dawn; Mizrah turned in his blanket for the silent communication, but he did not recognize the shadow that fell across him. He sat up quickly and rubbed his eyes; then started, when he heard beads jingling around Emmia's ankle as she entered the tent and sat down on the floor near his bed. Mizrah was now fully awake, his heart beating wildly; and moved to join her on the floor. They both sat across from the other; and gazed into each other's eyes.

Mizrah was cautiously hopeful, and completely confused at her presence until Emmia extended her arm and pointed at the beads on her wrist; then touched her arm several times, in an upward line to indicate she wanted more.

He nodded at this, his throat tight; Mizrah reached for her blanket, to wrap it around her; but Emmia shook her head. When he paused in confusion, she pointed at his blanket, then him, then herself. He stared at her then, his heart in his eyes, and found her heart in the same place. She'd embraced the language of his silence; without prompting, Emmia rose and sat in the middle of the bed, her legs tucked under her, looking at him; his heart full, he joined her.

As the two nestled in the pre-dawn light, Mizrah quietly wrapped his blanket around them both; sighing as he felt her head rest against his chest. Then he gently took her arm and brought the beads on her wrist to his lips.

Mizrah went hunting with his men the same day; before he left, he began the preparations for his marriage to Emmia, to the joy of his people. He was adamant to hold his passion for her, until the ceremony was completed; and Emmia was also insistent that he know her secret before he made plans for her to become his wife. She could almost laugh at herself; now that Emmia wanted to be with Mizrah, she felt compelled to give him information that may ensure he send her away forever.

The morning had been difficult for them both; when Mizrah first pressed his lips to her beads in the pre-dawn light, Emmia drowsily in turn pressed her lips to his chest where she cradled her head. In response, he tightened his arms around her, his breath quickening; but when she moved her lips to his chin, he cupped her face, and she saw in his eyes a silent plea, not to tempt him further. Emmia then nestled closer to him and drifted to sleep, comforted by the thrum of his heartbeat and his gentle stroking of her hair.

When later they both stirred from resting, Mizrah explained to Emmia his intention to be honorably bound to her, and she began to gesture excitedly, trying to hold back the tightening in her chest.

There's something you should know of me, before you tell your people I'm to be your wife, she said to him with her heart and hands.

He looked at her with a bemused expression, then shook his head.

Lady Emmia, he replied with his own words and gestures, I know that you have been barren.

She could not keep the shock from her face; how could he possibly know?

Mizrah smiled sadly at her and spoke in her language.

"Lady Emmia, you are in your maturity as a woman. For years, you have had both a lover and a man to be your husband, yet when we claimed you, you did not plead for your children, or beg to be united with them, as any mother would do. Nor did you mention the loss of a child, in any of the stories you shared with me. How is this possible unless you could not conceive?"

Emmia was undone; she could not take a breath, or speak; or course, anyone with eyes could see her shame. She covered her face, and silently wept.

Mizrah watched her pain, and his hands ached. He wanted to comfort her, but he knew to wait until she sought it; now Emmia needed to harvest her agony, she couldn't let it go before then. When she looked up at him, Mizrah was waiting; he held out his hand to her, but she shook her head.

"Why do you want me, Mizrah," she asked, inconsolable, "Why do you want me?"

"The reason is as clear as your pain," said Mizrah quietly, "My heart is in your body now; is yours in mine?"

"Yes," Emmia cried softly, and came to him; he pulled her into his lap, embracing her tightly.

"Then either we will heal this pain together, or we will love the children born to us among the people; what more can we ask of the Spirit that holds all things together?" he whispered against her hair, and she embraced him fiercely.

They held each other a moment too long, and when she gazed at him again, her heart in her eyes, he touched his lips to hers tentatively, and groaned at her response. Before all Mizrah's plans of honorable restraint were completely undone, they both heard a respectful cough; Mari was holding the flap to the tent, her brother Drini behind her, the two of them grinning from ear to ear.

"I knew you two could not be trusted alone for long," Mari said with a playful smile, "Your men are waiting for you, Mizrah; the hunt you requested has been organized," and Mizrah groaned again, for an entirely different reason. He and Emmia stood and disentangled themselves from the other, and then he quietly held her face in his hands.

I will notify our people of our intentions, he said to her, and Emmia did not need an interpreter to understand what he meant.

Let it be as you say, she responded, and her heart warmed again at the silent joy on his face.

He nodded, and dared to press his lips to her forehead, drawing a delighted gasp from Mari and Drini; their assigned chaperones until the ceremony was completed. Technically, it was not a public gesture; they were in the privacy of their shared tent; Emmia's eyes were shining as Mizrah followed Mari and Drini outside, after one last look at her. As soon as he was out of earshot, she made a soft sound of delight as she covered her face; she knew his gentlemanly conduct towards her was nearing its end.

She felt a feeling of bitter sweetness overtake her; for so long she determined her worth by her inability to bear children. It was still hard for her to accept that Mizrah would love and cherish her though barren. Emmia hugged herself; she would see this through, and if sometime in the future, Mizrah changed his mind about her, she would do as before, and go her way. We're both young still, she thought, Can it be a leader of men does not desire his own children; we shall see.

She saw him again in her vision on the hill, holding her cooling body and kissing her face; Is such love possible, she pondered, feeling a familiar tightening in her chest, as Emmia willed herself not to think of the king.

The hill of her trance came back to her, as she sat contemplating her motivations for returning to the kingdoms; the only ties she had, she could not go back to; and would not the presence of the regent be a constant reminder of what she lost? Would she be able to watch King Sumter marry another, and hear news of their happiness from a distance? Here, among these warm and loving people, she felt cherished; felt the joy of her father as they embraced her and gave her the choice to follow their ways. Mizrah's arms held no shadow of future separation; and despite Sumter's attempts to treat her as his equal, she was not. Although Mizrah's people clearly had leadership, no one seemed to her to be different or lower in stature than another; it was simply that someone had to make decisions for the group, and even this appeared to be a consensus.

Emmia remembered thinking that perhaps her disappearance was a good thing, for the time being, and if the future did not include her remaining with Mizrah; it was very possible that the next part of her life's journey may be for her to find at last her father's people and live out her life with them. The thought comforted her; it was better than musing on the disappointment of Mizrah when her womb bore no fruit.

She thought again of herself on the hill, thinking of Mizrah with his arms crossed against her; Emmia longed for him to open those arms again to embrace her, and hold her tightly, and never let her go. The image went before her as she raced back on Oriscinder to his tent, the dogs, and sentries silent, as though hoping she would come home to them; and Mizrah. When she lifted the flap of his dwelling and saw him lying there asleep, she only wanted to join him, in his blanket, apart from him no more.

THE DARK ONE: THE MEASUREMENT

"Because you were created in the image and likeness of God, your thoughts have absolute power. This very important fact carries with it both good and bad news. The good news is that what you think has to manifest. The bad news is that what you think has to manifest."

    Dr. Carolyne Fuqua

Over Two Million Years Ago

Before the days when people living on the earth felt that the passage of time needed to be recorded, eons passed as it should, without interruption. In those days, there was a place difficult to find called the Rim of the World. The Rim of the World has a basin with a wall of ice. Miles high, it spans a continent, easily holding tons of frozen water and glistening snow. Nothing living appears on the surface; no plants, animals...except for one thing, visible several thousand miles of the interior.

A man is standing there, looking at the frozen wall in front of him. He's not dressed for the weather; because it doesn't affect him. If you were close enough to see, you'd notice the cape he is wearing isn't thick or lined with animal fur; though his cape is cowled and draping his head.

The wind is blowing, but he doesn't feel it. He's surrounded by light; a barrier of power unyielding to the elements. The power is not his; not directly; he's not the source of it; but he is the channel for it; and the focus of it. He's looking at the wall of ice in front of him; and he is weeping.

He never needed the recording of time, to know the passage of it; he instinctively knows that exactly 180,000 years have passed because the creative force within him knows it; knows the exact moment he should be here.

He weeps because of the price he paid; the cost of his service to this task.

It takes a special kind of person, to embrace the turning of the earth and the planets for millions of years; to watch the rising and setting of the sun and moon, the turn of the seasons, the rotation of the stars from the same position on a particular planet.

Not many can achieve it; and certainly, not alone.

He last spoke her name aloud 50,000 years ago; she was his mate. She had the ability but not the will to go on; and he swore an oath to her, he would stay, and say the words required; be the channel needed for the servants of the planet, to come forth again and hold all things in place.

"Lemaquey," he whispered, and invoked her spirit into the moment, "because I promised you..." and he lifted his head and began to chant and sing the words that bound the bowels of the earth and sky. The creative force within him, burst forth in waves of joy. Lit up like the aurora borealis in crystal form, it struck the ice wall with a particular vibration, and the rim began to shudder, and release the ice and snow in a gorgeous avalanche of powder, it feathered out in waves that raced towards him like a pounding surf of wind and water.

It seemed to cover him; and he stood calmly in it, knowing he was protected, and nothing could harm him. From the thickest part of this curtain of powder and ice came the outline of huge shapes moving towards him; miles away and fast moving from a human standpoint; finally, the closest ones came into view.

One day, in the far and distant future, they would be called dinosaurs; this day they are called friends of mankind, and servants of the earth. He could see the brontosaurus, the tyrannosaurus, all the ones who would one day be broken up into classifications as to which ones came first and which ones would be found last, in mud, tar, snow, ice, and thermal layers. Their future, carbon dated bones secured; while tectonic plates shift and ancient continents divide, elevations and seabed move from lush deltas to barren wastelands and thinner air.

One day their bones will be found everywhere, as predicted from the beginning; but today, they move together, shaking off the blankets of millions of sleeping years. The velociraptors reached him first; still dripping icicles from their trembling legs as they found their bearings. The largest was a male; his mate at his side; he greeted the man, not with a roar, but with respectful images mind to mind, that translated into words he understood.

Lord Theron, the velociraptor said, I am Borca, and this is my mate Marta. I offer thanks, and the hope, that the cost of your service was not too great; for I see you are alone and mourn your soul's companion.

Lord Theron reached up and stroked the face of the raptor and pressed his own against his flank. Borca snorted his appreciation for this gesture, after so long a sleep.

Any task rendered in love, pays its own way, friend Borca; he replied, and this I do for the benefit of all. It makes my needs selfish in comparison.

I see her name and image in your mind, Lord Theron, said Marta, we owe her a great debt.

As do I, he said, fighting back tears. Are you ready then; is everyone free from the wall?

The brontosaurus lowered her head to his level and spoke into his mind.

All are free, Lord Theron, we await your will.

So, the man, who would be one day known as Lord Master Theron, turned, and released once again his creative force, and the ice cracked and blew away in some swath miles wide and deep, revealing the green life trapped underneath. He grew a bridge of good land to walk upon, that would take them across the frozen tundra, to a gentler clime. Borca walked with him a while; speaking of their life before; he sensed it would comfort Theron, and it did. When they reached the borders between their former resting place, and the world beyond the rim, Theron stopped, and Borca turned back to say farewell.

May I ask, Lord Theron, how much longer will you stay?

Borca knew that even a strong channel like Theron, who made the decision to live past the timeline of his mate, may not choose to live much longer than his task required.

The question brought tears again to Theron's eyes.

I promised her too much, he answered.

Lord Brayten's Daughter

The five-year-old version of herself sighed in the night, her eyes opening on cotton satin sheets. S'ateegra spread her fingers across the fabric and gave in to the temptation to view the atoms between the gaps of the fibers; how she loved to see the universe in microcosm, everything invisible mirrored the stars and galaxies.

In the midst of the battle, her older self, pushed her out of the way again. S'ateegra would leave her alone for the time being, they agreed; it was for the best. She sat up then, and looked through the walls, gazing at various dimensions; she could not sleep.

After a moment, she smiled to herself, as she felt the energy of her mother rising; she loved how intuitive the feminine was. How she wished she could share more with her, but her mother was easily frightened, even as she came to comfort her. The child knew, she could only say so much; her mother would never understand what she had to do.

Methara, her mother, paused at the door after opening it. She started to speak, and then caught herself, as she often did; she could not say her daughter's name aloud, and it saddened her at moments like this one. What mother cannot speak aloud her child's name, when she can't sleep at night?

"Why are you sitting here in the dark, sweetie?"

S'ateegra turned at the sound of her voice and smiled patiently at her.

"Mom," she said, "you know it's never dark to me; I could see through the floor to the other side of the earth, if I wanted."

"Okay, smarty-pants," her mother responded, and her daughter grinned; she loved the language of her mother's world, sometimes, the awkwardness of it suited the moment. "Why are you awake?"

S'ateegra's face changed then, and she looked at her mother wistfully.

"Mom," she asked softly, "Can you tell me again, what it's like to be human?"

Methara sat on the edge of the bed, gathered her daughter into her lap, and held her tight, as she kissed her rumpled hair. She could always tell, when her child was walking dimensions, and playing with time; she always felt warmer, and tachyons streamed light around her body. Her mother breathed deeply to control her heartbeat, and maternal concern.

"You're still human, baby," she whispered, "it's just that, without guidance and training, we can't see what you see, and do what you do."

S'ateegra sighed and snuggled closer. Although she could walk into volcanos unharmed, she still needed to experience human touch, and bask in her mother's emotional love for her.

"I just don't get it sometimes; most people spend their whole lives remembering things that happened before, and I spend most of my time forgetting things, and choices I haven't made yet, so I can experience it in real time, so to speak; seeing that, actually, there's no such thing as 'real time'..."

"Hey, hey, hey," Methara gently tightened her arms around her daughter, "earth to baby, earth to baby, come in, please."

S'ateegra looked up at her mother.

"But I have to forget all the possible timelines, mom, or it'll make me sad…"

"Stop now, sweetie," her mother responded, and S'ateegra saw the hidden fear behind her eyes; she didn't want to know the future, she just wanted to feel safe. Her daughter reached up, and pulled her mother's hair around her shoulders, to where she could play, with her wayward strands; Methara's smile returned.

"Everything's going to be fine, mom, like Shakespeare said, 'all is well'…"

"…'that ends well'," said her mother, as she finished her sentence. Her daughter could feel Methara's heartbeat increase, as she rested her cheek against her chest.

"He's coming back," she said softly, referring to her father, "he doesn't like for me to look for him, in case my energies can be traced, but I can still feel him, mom; it won't be long."

As S'ateegra felt the tenseness leave her mother's body, she consciously erased, from her own memory, every possible timeline regarding her father, and his eventual fate. She decided not to revisit her future self again, lest she harden the thought choices, around all the decisions she would make, effectively destroying other possible outcomes.

It was the man who was holding her so tightly in the future, she thought, as she dozed off in her mother's arms; he seemed to be a good person, and she liked his face. That memory also faded; it appeared this future man, was too instrumental in her father's life, and its coming end.

Her mind went back to the last time she saw him, and some of the things he taught her.

THEY WERE SITTING in a field of high grasses, after a training session. Lord Brayten did not wish his daughter to feel as though all her time with him, would be spent on hard work. But this morning, she was full of questions.

"Dad…" often S'ateegra loved to use her mother's words for the term 'father'.

"If all power has only one source, what is the real difference, between a creator and a magician?"

Lord Brayten smiled at this; his child could not know, this was a question every student of the mysteries must ask, and one day answer for themselves. Yet, it was an opportunity to explain the difference between Metaphor and Myth; Truth, and Illusion; he would not pass it by. He pointed to the high grasses, and the blue sky, and everything surrounded by those two things.

"The answer is all around you, my daughter," he replied, "constantly trying to get your attention."

At that moment, a nearby butterfly drifted over to Lord Brayten, and carefully latched on to his outstretched finger. S'ateegra laughed, as it flapped its wings, and clung to him, when he tried to gently dislodge it.

"You know that the word 'desire,' means 'of the Father'," Brayten continued, and his daughter nodded. He went on.

"Creation desires to *see* itself, through you, and *be* itself, through you. When a creator recognizes this, he or she opens herself, and gives permission, for creation to express its power directly, with you, as a willing channel. And according to your willingness, you are limited, or limitless, in abundance, manifestation, and power."

Another thought, and question, came up for Brayten's daughter.

"Dad, did you know that people have *cloned* butterflies?" at her father's nod, she asked, "Why would someone want to clone a butterfly?"

"Competition," replied Lord Brayten. He lightly traced the wing of the butterfly with his other finger; the insect trembled slightly but held on.

"Sometimes, it is the most fervent need of the created, through the ego, to attempt to upstage the Creator; to say in effect, to All That Is, 'I can do more than You, and better.' In other words, 'I will take your power, and make it my own', instead of, 'I allow your power to flow, and express through me.'"

Lord Brayten's daughter eagerly shared her understanding of his words.

"So, it is the same power; one is undiluted, and channeled, the other is filtered, and changed."

He nodded.

"Exactly. If you reject the invisible behind the visible, you cannot create, or bring forth, a butterfly from the Infinite; all you can do, is take the cells, or the smallest components of a butterfly that already exists and make another; a semblance of misdirected life. A magician, only wants to see him, or herself, as the Author, and Source of Creation, as a direct wielder, of power and might. This nuance, of intention, misdirects creation; it is why a clone is a copy, of life manipulated, and not life itself."

Lord Brayten's daughter nudged him with her elbow.

"Hey, that's pretty good, daddy; good explanation."

"Thank you," he replied indulgently, "it is also why, you can easily turn a magician's power back on them; it is already separated from its true source."

S'ateegra was quiet for a moment, thinking. Then she spoke.

"Is that also, why a magician can destroy a creator, if they learn their true name?"

It was Lord Brayten's turn to be quiet; after a moment, he soberly answered her.

"Yes..." he said slowly, "your true name, is directly connected to your source, and creation itself. It is the only way, a magician can turn your channeled force against you, and destroy your physical body."

When he turned to look at his daughter, and his heart, he saw tears brimming in her eyes.

"Does this mean, that for my whole life, no one, will ever be able to say my name aloud?"

Her voice tremored, and instinctively, he placed his arm around her, and drew her close. A moment passed, and he spoke again.

"One day, when you are safe, when everyone's true name is safe," her father said soberly, "I will tell you, your true name's meaning; until then, you must trust me, and the plans I have for you; as your mother, would say, for good, and not harm."

The tiny butterfly moved, then, as he wrapped his other arm around her, in comfort; she watched as it hovered over her father's shoulder, as though looking at her. But her tears dimmed the sight of it, and finally, it drifted away.

FINIS

ABOUT THE AUTHOR

"One day She tied the Universe around her finger, and made a Knot..."
~~~T.M. Elzy

T. M. Elzy, also known as a Person in Love with the Cosmos, is a writer, poet, screenwriter and now author of her own vision of the Universe called the Hidden World Book Series, inspired by studies of Metaphor, Quantum Physics, Science, Philosophy and Universal Law with Dr. Carolyne Fuqua. The author presents her viewpoint in an entertaining way using storytelling and life lessons for her characters (and perhaps the reader's) personal growth.

A staunch proponent of Speculative Fiction, (Which is an exploration of science that may yet be possible and not pure fantasy) T. M. Elzy is passionate about human potential and taking us far beyond the present reach of our abilities using science, quantum physics and the future Invisible Things we have yet to know. If she's not at home writing or driving through the Angeles mountains, you may find her in India, Egypt, Peru, London, Athens and maybe Bolivia if she missed her train.

∞

SIMPLE TALES OF POWER
A HIDDEN WORLD SHORT STORY COLLECTION

By T. M. ELZY

Hope you enjoyed these collected tales of the Hidden World! For more information about my upcoming books, please visit my Author page: https://www.amazon.com/author/t.m.elzy and click on 'Follow' for the latest updates.

Also, feedback in the form of a review of this title or my debut novel, 'Prince of the Far Isles' would be lovely. You can visit my website: https://www.hiddenworldbookseries.com for summaries of The Dark One Trilogy; 'The Dark One: A Hidden History of A Previous Earth' (Book One), 'The Destroyer: Battle for the Heart' (Book Two), and the conclusion, 'LightBringer: The End of All Shadows'.

At the back of this book you will find a list of Companion Books exploring the themes of Creation, Science, Magic, Relationships and Human Potential using Metaphor and universal storytelling elements.

Thank You!

ACKNOWLEDGMENTS

First and foremost, this book, and those that follow would not exist if not for the teachings and presence of Dr. Carolyne Fuqua, Ph.D., who gently, patiently, and lovingly assisted me in freeing my true voice. These characters and concepts would yet be pleading with me for their freedom if Life had not placed my feet unerringly on the path that led to her. Yes, and Thank You!

Many thanks are due to those who continue to support me as I dedicate time and effort to this mighty task: My sister and fellow author Denise L. White, my brother Willie D. Elzy, and my brother Kevin Spencer, all of whom sent a new desk to replace the stacked ottomans; on my birthday, of all things. I love you all so much.

My sister Lisa Elzy Watson, who kept a much needed roof over my head in the midst of a global pandemic, for which mere thanks is not enough. She is also my partner in creativity. Her long awaited book is next, then Willie's; we are after all, a literary family.

Special thanks to ladies and sisters Deonae McMillan and Chanel Brown, for love and brilliance. Thank you for your questions, reviews and discussions; I think of you often as I write the next installment of the series. And marketing maven Shirley Muhammad Robinson for her support and her book club, Elegant Sisterhood.

Love and thanks to Vionela Maria Vaughn-Austin, for her unwavering encouragement and support. To Dr. Maisha Hazzard, who was an honor and privilege to know. I will always cherish your email review; thank you for loving my work.

And my sons, Paul, Shawn, Turhan and Josiah, who came to me if not through me.

Just because.

BIBLIOGRAPHY

Bibliography and Resources
A partial list of books and sources that inspire, support or compliment my work:

Dr. Carolyne Fuqua, Ph.D. The Keys to the Kingdom, A New Paradigm for Humanity vol I, vol II, Circles of Light Publishing, Beverly Hills, CA.

Three Initiates, The Kybalion: Hermetic Philosophy, Yogi Publication Society, 1908; reprint Devorss, 1999.

Albert Einstein's 1912 Manuscript on the Special Theory of Relativity
Albert Einstein, The World As I See It, 1949.
Albert Einstein, Cosmic Religion: With Other Opinions and Aphorisms

Theodore Gray, The Elements: A Visual Exploration of Every Known Atom in the Universe. Black Dog and Leventhal Publishers New York, 2009.

Nikola Tesla, The Eternal Source of Energy of the Universe, Origin and Intensity of Cosmic Rays, New York, October 13, 1932.
Nikola Tesla, How Cosmic Forces Shape Our Destinies, New York American, June 5, 1915.
Nikola Tesla, On Light and Other High Frequency Phenomena, Franklin Institute, Philadelphia, February 1893, and National Electric Light Association, St. Louis, March 1893.

David Bohm, Quantum Theory, 1951, 1979, 1989. New York, University of London.

MEANINGS AND PRONUNCIATIONS OF NAMES
MAJOR CHARACTERS ACROSS THE SERIES

Adidas (Uh-dye-us) The Father King of the Southern Arc

Altus, Prince and brother to High King Valtus

Amara, (Uh-mar-uh) Queen of the Eastern Crest

Andron, (Ann-dron) King of the Southern Arc

Arbu (R-boo) Crown Prince of the Unnamed Lands

Arioch, (R-ree-ock), an Ancient Sorcerer

Ashlan, sorcerer and cousin to the Ancient Eridon

Aton, (A-taun) High General of The Far Isles

Bokmal, King of the Broken Meriden

Cassum, King of the Sealed Gates Kingdom

Cullen, King of the Sky Vault Kingdom

Driken, soldier refugee from the Far Isles

Enith, (Inn-ith) A powerful Ancient Sorcerer

Eridon, (Irr-ri-don) an Ancient whose fate is tied to the Kingdom
of the Far Isles

Estan, a soldier of The Far Isles under General Hesta

Falquin, (Faul-quin) (sounds like falcon) father to Quin, a Hound
of The Kingdom of The Circle of the Earth

Gara, Queen of the Western Hills Kingdom

Gervaise, former nurse to Prince Rasdeter of The Far Isles

Hesta, a Forde General in the army of The Far Isles

Iroh, (Eye-rock) a Master Sorcerer

Izar, (Eye-zar) the Twin Star in the constellation Izar

Izhar, King of the Sky Vault Kingdom

Jadu, High Regent of Worm's Hollow Kingdom

Kalos, (meaning 'light') a prince of the Sky Vault Kingdom

Kerion, sorcerer and High Regent to King Cassum

Kiran, a middle general in the army of The Far Isles

Loan, (La-own) a prince and youngest son of High King N'Goth

Marcus, a Forde General of The Far Isles

Mora, (More-ah) sister to King Ruan

Naboth, prince and second born of King N'Goth

Onan, Forde General under High General Aton

Osolum, High King, father of High King N'Goth

Rasdeter, (Raz-dee-ter) meaning "to rule with determination", prince of The Far Isles and first cousin to Prince Sumter

Roe, King of the Western Hills

Ruan, (Rue-ahn) King of the Circle of the Earth

Saramis, (Sara-miss) meaning 'female minister', a Wanderer of the Plains

Sirk, High Regent of the Kingdom of Lorith

Sumter, (Sum-ter) High King of The Far Isles Kingdom

The Rook, Bound Servant of The Magician

Thora, Queen of the Sky Vault Kingdom

Tyant, (Tee-aunt) an ancient hunter from the beginning of recorded time

Valgus, High Regent to The Magician

Valtus, (Vault-tus) High King and father of High King Sumter

Rusch, (rusk) another name for The Rook